A DEEP BLUE ABYSS

The First Mill Meacham Story

By

Carson A. Pierce

Copyright © 2011 James A. Caplan

The characters in this novel are entirely fictitious and bear no resemblance to anyone living or dead. Character names were checked to make sure none used in the book represent actual people working for the agencies mentioned. Certain living and deceased historical figures may be included to give the novel verisimilitude.

Library of Congress Cataloging-in-Publication Data is available from the Library of Congress

ISBN 978-0-9827537-3-6

Acknowledgements

A Deep Blue Abyss would never have been completed without the invaluable support of friends and family. Blending Alaskan adventure, characters' personal growth, and environmental strife was a real challenge for me--one that I would not have met without significant help from others.

My wife, Cheryl, is my constant source of insight and encouragement. She served ably as idea checker, proof reader, and editor.

Forest Service Law Enforcement Officers Ted Rainville and Javier Masiel gave me useful insights into the equipment used by Forest Service law enforcement, martial arts, and how they and their colleagues conduct operations.

Several people read the book in draft and provided me useful edits and comments. These caring critics include: Allen Gibbs, Ted and Christine Rainville, Jim Van Loan, Meg Mitchell, and Javier Masiel.

My profound thanks to everyone.

Message from the Author

Is *A Deep Blue Abyss* an adventure in wild Alaska? A future reality show? A love story? Is it about a young woman painfully coming of age? About agencies and their cultures? About environmental politics and conflicts? Is it a narrative? A commentary on good and evil? On conflict and dispute resolution?

Maybe it's all of these things, a spicy cocktail blended for readers who want their literature to shake and shock them, to inform and intrigue them and, if they choose, to educate and uplift them. Read! Enjoy!

Cap, 2011

Dedication

To
the
people
of Alaska,
living close
to the land and
among wild creatures,
in places of remote beauty.
I pray you the best in all ways,
always. *You readers there*! Lift your
glasses! Here's to wild places and to the
wild things that live in them! And here's to the
people who care for those wild places and things!
The wildest ever!
Now
drink!

Table of Contents

Chapter 1 – Alaska, Elephant Country, 2000

Alsek River, Southeast Alaska.

Raw day.

Raw place.

A small, red-faced miner sits by the Alsek and fumes. He's here for nickel, that precious, little-thought-of mineral vital to the defense of nations. But he's more truly here for the money that mining nickel will bring.

No, not just money…riches.

After twenty-five years of empty holes and dreams, Hard Rock Gruber has just enough cash left for one more prospect, a big one…this one. If this nickel strike proved up, the payday would get him even for years of losses.

But he's screwed before he starts.

Hard Rock knows a good screwing. He started treasure-hunting at fourteen, stealing artifacts from Tsimshian burial sites.

Got caught. Took a beating that put him a week in bed.

He had made and lost a fortune or two since then. Some had gone to bad prospects, more to fines for illegal mining on Canada's Crown lands. And then there were the two years he did in the Ottawa pen. Yes, Hard Rock knows a good screwing.

And here he sits.

Screwed again.

The richest nickel deposit in North America sits just over there, less than a kilometer south, across the broken white plain of Blue Glacier. Sits an up-thrust, ice-bound mountain. Not in Canada where he could concession it or steal it, and then get unspeakably rich off it. But in a Goddamned American National Park, off-limits to any kind of mining.

Gruber glares at the fog-shrouded mountain, "I will mine this bitch or I'll die trying."

He squares his strong shoulders, clenches his jaw, and turns his gaze back to the Alsek, staring into it as if inspiration could rise from its grey-dark, roiled waters.

Gruber draws back his arm and throws a rock. It cuts the river's surface and dives, invisible, to the bottom. He throws another.

Splash.

As he watches the wavelets disappear, an idea creeps into his mind. He throws another rock, considers its fall, its splash...its disappearance. He turns and stares at Blue Glacier.

Yes, that could work.

Hard Rock smiles for the first time in a week. He stands and walks back to the white, two-seater helicopter he uses for mineral surveys.

Minutes later, the little aircraft spools up, lifts off, and thumps its way to the east, back into Canada where an elite, well-paid group of mining engineers and miners waits for him. From among them, he knows just the right crew for this operation—the brightest ones, and most importantly, the greediest ones.

The rest can go.

Hard Rock will bet everything he has on this mine, the best prospect of his lifetime, of any lifetime.

Screw 'em.

Screw 'em all.

This time, Hard Rock Gruber gets his payday.

Chapter 2 - Goat Floatin', 2002

North of Cordova, Southcentral Alaska.

Cold day.

Cold country.

Millicent "Mill" Meacham struggles slowly up a steep, ice-crusted snow bank above Kushtake Lake. She moves a few feet at a time, eyes the ground, pokes snow with her walking stick, and peers at the holes she makes. Her meandering steps take her gradually closer to an anxious mountain goat kid who paces where the snow bank she is climbing meets a rock ledge.

Her behavior calms the yearling because her movements mimic how goats graze on the sparse food available here. The little critter looks away and down a hundred feet below to where his mother lies tranquilized, tied, and masked. A red and white Bell 427 helicopter squats near her motionless body. The sight of his mother lying unmoving, maybe dead, makes the little goat anxious. He stares intently, looking for signs of life in his mother.

"Keep watching mama, baby boy," Mill orders the little goat silently. She edges forward to within ten feet of him, darting quick glances at him from under the brim of her hat.

Glancing at her, the kid steps to the edge of the ledge. A rock drops away under his hoof and he almost falls into a fifty-foot tumbling drop onto cobbles and boulders. He hops back and, terrified, eyes first the abyss and then Mill.

Mill looks away from him and studies the snow. The billy once again calms. He paces back to the edge of the ledge and stares down at mom again, momentarily ignoring Mill.

Now!

Mill takes three running steps forward. She tackles the kid around the flanks. Rolling them both away from the precipice, she bulldogs him to the ground. The little goat begins a violent struggle. Snow and soil fly from his wind-milling front feet. He hurls his body back and forth. He arches and flips his head and neck to butt her with his little nubs of horns. The billy lowers his head and drives it back at her again and again.

Timing his horn-thrusts, Mill waits until his head swings away. Then she hurls herself forward and tries to throw weight on top of the frantic little animal. But his gyrations are too violent. She can't get on top of him and avoid his horns at the same time. Ducking back, she holds on tightly around his lower body.

His thick oily smell fills her nostrils.

Whew!

"You bastards better get up here," she yells.

Grinning, three of Mill's teammates rush forward from behind the helicopter. They slip and curse their way up the icy bank carrying a tranquilizer syringe, cords, blindfold, and short pieces of garden hose to put over the little horns. In a few moments, two of them fall gently onto the frightened little animal and pin him down.

A thankful Mill lets him go and gets up. She shakes dirt and snow from her clothes and snorts to clear his musky odor from her nose.

The men keep weight on the billy until the tranquilizer takes hold. Then they quickly bind and mask him.

Although he is tranquilized, he is still aware of his surroundings. Without the mask, he would see his captors and might die from sheer terror.

They had darted the billy's mother from the Bell 427 an hour or so before. After they landed and secured her, the little goat appeared from under a rocky overhang.

Once he showed up, they knew they probably should free the mother. Yet they were unwilling to let her go. They usually relocated only adult mountain goats in a ratio of five or six nannies to each billy. The transplant of even twenty or thirty animals could create or reestablish a herd in a new location. With this nanny, the team had met their goal.

But when it came to the little ones, the stress of capture and transplant could be too much. They often died from shock.

Still, to leave the little billy alone at the capture site made no sense. He would certainly die after being abandoned. So, they had agreed to try and relocate him too.

The smallest person on the relocation team, Mill, reluctantly agreed to stalk, grab, and wrestle the goat.

"I thought he was going to kick your ass, Mill," says a smiling Carrie Muir. Carrie is the wildlife biologist on the Cordova Ranger District, a part of the Chugach National Forest.

She had asked Mill along on this "goat rope" because, as the new fisheries biologist on the district, Mill needed to get to know the other biologists working in the area. That and the capture team needed more hands.

4

Mill smiles broadly back at Carrie, her three dimples—chin and both cheeks—deepen. Mill's laugh bursts out into the clear Alaska air, a series of four joyous upward notes.

The sound causes the whole team to smile, "Carrie, he almost did. For a forty pounder, that little guy can fight! If he coulda punched a couple of holes in me with those horns, he woulda done it.

Shaking her head ruefully, she laughs with grudging admiration, "They sure build 'em tough around here."

Mill gestures down the u-shaped "hanging" valley that surrounds them in Alaska's Chugach Mountain Range, a place carved by glacial grinding over thousands of years. Mill's pointing finger traces the edge of the Bering Glacier at the valley's north end, a jumble of rocks, soil, and ice at least a mile away.

"Yes, they do," Carrie replies.

Her eyes follow the direction of Mill's arm, "This Bering River area is about as tough a climate as you'll see mountain goats living in. So many of these little guys don't make it. They drop down cliffs after one misstep and wind up food for bears and wolves or lost in the rocks. It's amazing they survive at all."

Pointing to two cup-shaped valleys on a nearby mountain and the mountain's sharp pyramid of a peak, she asks, "See those two circ basins and the big glacial horn up there? I've seen goats in that area and it's got to be one of the coldest and windiest places in the world. Mountain goats…tough critters indeed."

Carrie takes her eyes away from the wild scene. She shakes the numbing beauty of it out of her head and turns her gaze back to the team.

She gives a "thumbs up" to the team leader, "Okay, Chick, we're ready to go when you are."

Chick Sorensen looks at Carrie from under his bushy eyebrows and nods. He makes lifting gestures to the waiting team, "Okay guys, let's get this little guy out of here, fast and easy."

They gently lift the little trussed-up goat and start carefully moving him towards the waiting helicopter and his mother.

Born to an Eyak mother and Norwegian father, Chick's an Alaskan through and through. His native ancestors lived around Prince William Sound for thousands of years…been there long enough to have stories about glaciers coming and going over the landscape. He personally knows every acre and island within a hundred miles and knows them well.

As they slide and lurch downhill, Mill asks Chick, "How'd you get the name 'Chick'?"

He blushes a little, "Well, I got the name when I was seven. I found and saved five Dusky Canada goslings. They'd been orphaned by a wolf attack on their mother."

Duskies are a unique sub-species that summers in the Cordova and eastern Prince William Sound area, just like Chick's Eyak people.

Mill nods, "Nice. But why didn't they name you 'dusky'...or 'goose?'"

Chick laughs, "Well, I guess they could have hung either one of those on me, but I'm glad it was 'Chick' and not 'Goose.'"

He shudders a little at memories from his young life. As Chick grew older, he found out that "goose" referred to more things than just bird species. Like boys everywhere, Eyak teenagers play lots of physical jokes on each other. Chick would have spent most of his teen years looking over his shoulder to make sure his friends weren't getting ready to goose him with anything handy--fingers, toes, driftwood, boat hooks, and who knew what.

Chick had tried commercial fishing for awhile but that ended in 1990 when the effects of the Exxon Valdez oil spill ruined the Sound. Now he works as an area wildlife biologist for the Alaska Department of Game and Fish, the agency in charge of goats and their transplants.

These Kushtake Lake goats would be the genesis of a new herd northwest of here at an isolated spot along the Copper River.

He thought they had a good chance of survival. The rocky valley they were going into had plenty of forage, some good cover, climbable cliffs, and, at least for now, no predator sign. Of course, once the goats were established, the predators would come. They always did.

Chick had been glad when Carrie asked Mill to join the capture team. Although he is incredibly skilled at living in Alaska's bush, Chick finds it hard, really hard, to approach women. In fact, the prettier and more competent the woman, the more tongue-tied and mumbly he becomes.

And Mill strikes him as the prettiest and most competent woman he has seen in a long time, maybe ever. He sometimes wonders if he has ever completed an intelligible sentence while talking to her.

To make matters worse, Mill exhibits a calm, professional poise each time they meet. She doesn't give the slightest hint of interest in him.

Chick can't tell whether she even knows that he is even a guy, a real Alaskan, a real catch. Well, maybe not that good a catch....

Anyway, he is attracted to her curvy muscular build, dark hair, cool competence, and well, that wonderful smile and laugh, and well....

Chick pulls his head out of the ozone and realizes his "goat roper" team is standing by the helicopter looking at him for orders. He tries to pull it together.

For a moment, the constant cold wind off the Bering Glacier stops blowing. Chick hears the Bell 427's exhaust tick as it cools. Impatient, the pilot leans against the fuselage, kicking snow. Her flight boot makes a chunk-scratch noise.

Grimacing inside at his foolishness, Chick orders, "Okay, let's get this little guy weighed. From that, we'll figure out if he can go with his mama now or have to go later on his own."

The goat ropers weigh the little goat. As Chick had figured when he saw the billy, the two animals' combined weight is well below the 427's limits.

The pilot starts the engine and spools the helicopter up. Most of the goat ropers walk away to the north of the helicopter's westerly take-off path.

The distance is enough to keep the rotor wash from blowing snow, ice crystals, and small pebbles at them. If they stand too close, the effect is like being sandblasted.

Chick stations himself southeast of the helicopter, but closer in so he can watch the goats go airborne.

The helicopter sits for a moment rocking slightly as it approaches take-off power. The whirling blades cut the air faster and faster and the pilot tests the lift.

Finally, the pilot moves the collective and the chopper moves gently upwards. Beneath it, two large nets pull taut. Cradled one to a net, the goats leave the ground and dangle thirty feet below the chopper.

As the nets clear the ground, Chick says, "Go, go, go" into his hand-held radio. Then he ducks down to avoid the powerful blade wash.

The chopper lifts higher, blade tips curved upwards slightly under the load. It flairs to the west, gains altitude to clear nearby ridges, and thumps away towards the release site up the Copper River, a twenty-minute flight away.

The team watches the goats float out of sight.

Mill wonders how they feel--animals used to dizzying mountain heights—still earth-bound animals now flying like blind birds to a new rocky home. What a day for them. She sympathizes with the chaos and terror they must be experiencing.

As the 427 fades into the distance, she wishes mama nanny and little billy plenty of warm, fat winters.

Chapter 3 - Alsek Blue Billions, 2002

Hard Rock Gruber stands at the entrance of Alsek Blue Billions. Gruber had named the mine for the nearby river, the glacier he has overcome, and the dollars he expects to get from the ore within.

He looks proudly down into the main shaft, or adit, at the work he and his men have done. Beside him is his foreman, Casey Summerland.

He mentally dares the National Park Service to catch him mining in one of their precious national parks, "Screw the park pansies. I've made it work."

Hard Rock turns to his foreman, "Casey, looks like we'll be ready to ship in a month or so. You'll have to order up the bigger ship and all the landing craft."

Casey smiles grimly, "Yeah, okay. But, Hard Rock, aren't we trying to ship at a bad time of year? Late summer, eh? Boaters still on the river. Hunters coming in. Sunlight's still more than twelve hours a day. We could slow production a little and ship in a month when everything's gone darker and quieter."

Hard Rock has always been able to count on Casey's unshakeable greed, the lust that kept past miners delivering at top pace. Now, he looks up at the taller man and wonders if Summerland has lost his craving, gotten soft. Maybe being so far from a casino and his endless losses at blackjack has dulled Casey's edge?

Hard Rock looks intently at his foreman, "You trying to mess with me, Case? You know the production plan. Work three shifts 'round the clock. Do everything we can to max production. Fill the shipping room…ship. That's it."

"The only time we don't ship is during the two months on the sides of the summer solstice in mid-June. We can't get boats in and out in the four hours of dark then. So, I set up the whole year's production schedule to ship now and every two months after, as long as the Alsek's open enough for the boats to get through."

Gruber lightly punches the much-taller Casey on the shoulder, "So let's get this first shipment organized. We got an anxious customer waiting and boatloads of money to follow!"

Casey nods, "Okay. Right."

Beginning eighteen months ago, Gruber's elite, and well-paid team had drilled and blasted the adit, and then a system of tunnels and caves beyond. Hard Rock had chosen the entrance site carefully. It drove down through rock face well away from and out of sight of the Alsek River, and was hidden under a massive rock overhang.

No one floating by or flying over can see the entrance. Inside, the adit leads down and travels underneath the aptly named Blue Glacier. Then it climbs up into the huge nickel-bearing, tooth-like mountain sticking up out of the glacier's white-blue, cracked surface.

From the first landing in a little cove along the Alsek, Gruber and his team have maintained the highest security. Dangerous though night operations can be, they do nothing on the surface except at night.

Men and equipment come to Alsek Blue Billions from ships that stop briefly in the Gulf of Alaska off the mouth of Dry Bay. Camouflaged landing craft quickly drop into the water, drive through the bay, and travel swiftly up the Alsek loaded with equipment, supplies, and fuel. Navigating the berg-filled Alsek Lake and the shallow, channeled river with depth finders and night-vision goggles, the boat drivers follow close on one another like beads on a string.

When the landing craft reach a little cove near the mine, Hard Rock and several tracked, electric-powered cargo haulers, or "crawlers," meet them.

"Okay, boys," he'd say as the landing craft reach shore, patting the revolver on his hip, "You've got twenty minutes to get unloaded, no more. After that, I start shooting."

Looking at his grim face and remembering his reputation, no one doubts his deadly intentions. Aboard the landing craft, the crane-arm operators go to work like robots, hoisting pallet-loads rapidly into the waiting crawlers.

Over the many months, the longest the sweating crews took to unload had been eighteen minutes. Once unloaded, the boats line up and head downriver like chunky baby ducks swimming for mother.

After the boats clear the shallow cove safely, Hard Rock and his team motor silently back to Alsek Blue Billions in the crawlers. A small, tracked four-wheeler follows them, carefully smoothing away any signs of their presence. At daybreak, a two-man team walks the route and eliminates any four-wheeler tracks with gravel rakes.

Down in summer-busy Dry Bay, Hard Rock had paid off several people to spread rumors that the blacked-out night-running boats are military tests of stealth technology. His agents also report any rumors about up-river mining or strange activities. There have been none, a sign his security is working.

Like the rock Gruber had thrown in the river a year and a half ago, Alsek Blue Billions first made a tiny splash and then went invisible.

Under Blue Glacier, near the base of the nunatak, Hard Rock and his crew had built two large caves. The miners use one for living quarters and storage. The other holds sophisticated nickel-ore milling equipment, electrical generators, pumps, and ventilation machinery.

Throughout the mine, water, waste, and tailings collect in ponds for nightly pumping into the Alsek River through a hidden pipe.

Near the entrance is a third, smaller cave where Hard Rock's crew stores drums of concentrated nickel ore. It's half full now. Soon, instead of running empty, the landing craft will carry heavy loads when they return to the mother ship.

Someday, in maybe ten years, Hard Rock's crew will finish mining the nunatak, and a hollow shell will remain where a protected mountain once stood. The miners will abandon all equipment in place, worn out, serial numbers removed. The last miner out will blast the adit's ceiling down, closing the mine permanently.

Gruber figures that the National Park Service will never know about Alsek Blue Billions, unless one day, an earthquake fractures the nunatak and it collapses like a rock soap bubble. Even then, in a nowhere place like this, who would ever try to find out why a mountain crumbled or wonder about deeply buried mining gear?

After all, God alone causes mountains to crumble. And Alaska's history is filled with buried mining equipment.

Chapter 4 – Cordova

Over on the Copper River, the pilot drops the goats into the waiting hands of the two-person release team. Then the helo returns to the Kushtake Lake site to ferry the Forest Service goat ropers to a nearby Forest Service cabin on the Bering River.

The goat ropers pile into the chopper, pleased at the cabin's warmth. The helo lifts off north before turning. They first fly north over the Bering Glacier, an endless broken plain of dirty white snow, deep blue crevasses, and azure ice lakes larger than the State of Rhode Island, and then turn southeast over the Bering's bergs and terminal moraine.

Mill drinks in the magnificent view.

As they approach the cabin, Mill spots a bright yellow float plane waiting at the dock. It will fly them home to the town of Cordova at the east end of Prince William Sound.

Federal employees use helicopters for field work but not for "point-to-point" transportation. For safety reasons, the government requires them to fly in fixed-winged antiques, often Grumman Gooses and DeHavilland Beavers built in the 1950s by people now the age of Mill's grandparents.

Today's plane is a Beaver. The goat ropers board the heavy little aircraft. These "antiques" are inspected annually and certified safe and airworthy. So Mill feels fine about flying in them.

Still, she finds it odd to ride home in a plane built in 1954 when a helicopter built just last year has to drop her off to do so.

"Just part of the whole Alaska experience," she muses as she watches the roof of the Bering River cabin shrink to a tiny square, a tiny human symbol in the immense, wild Bering River Valley.

The Beaver begins to shudder and buck in the powerful west winds flowing in off the Gulf of Alaska. Low clouds scud past the plane's wing. Gulping a little at the turbulence, Mill pushes earplugs deeper in her ears to blunt the booming roar from the Beaver's unmuffled rotary engine.

She closes her eyes and pretends to sleep.

Today is Wednesday. Friday she will fly to Anchorage…to the other part of her life.

She smiles grimly. She senses that hungry, growing darkness within her; something that pulls at her even as she resists, a kind of black hole she will go through as she has done before. Mill nods off….

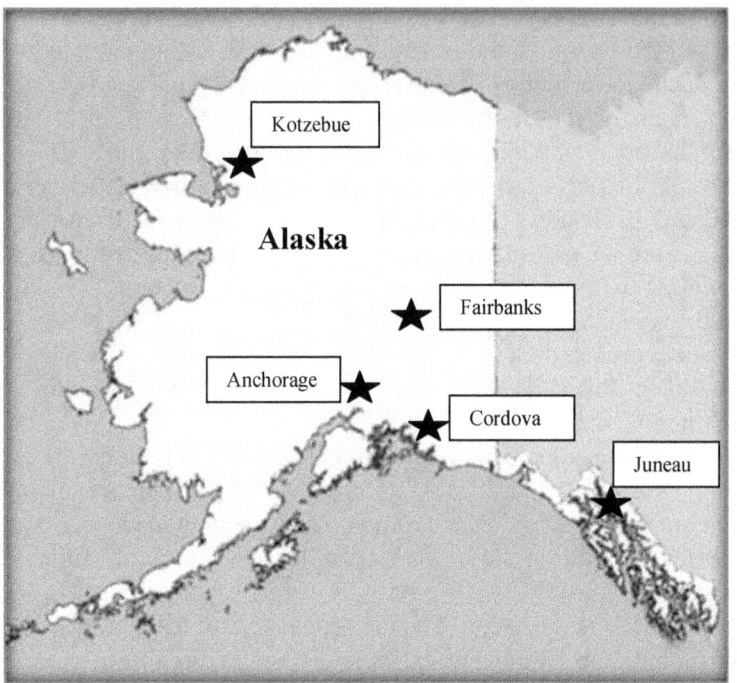

The bright-yellow Beaver circles Eyak Lake east of Cordova. At 500 feet, the pilot mutters into his headset and looks around for other aircraft.

Seeing none flying in the area or taxiing on the lake, he lines up into the west wind, lowers his flaps, and throttles back. The heavy Beaver glides steeply down towards the lake.

Mill wakes as the plane's pontoons touch the water. The aircraft begins to jump, shake, and jig across the choppy surface, trying to transform itself from bird to boat. Its pontoons grip the surface and it quickly slows to a stop.

The pilot lowers two rudders, one for each pontoon. He revs the engine, and steers the plane towards a solid little dock moored against the lake's north shore.

The Beaver motors up to the dock. Twenty feet away, the pilot cuts the engine.

A dockhand catches a rope dangling from the plane's starboard wingtip and guides the plane into its berth against rubber-tire fenders bolted to the dock. Moving quickly, the fellow jumps to the windward end of the dockside pontoon and ties it off. Then he races aft and secures the pontoon's other end.

Tired and joking, the goat ropers drop out of the Beaver, grab their gear from the cargo compartment, and step onto the dock. They walk up the dock's short gangplank.

Some rough but weather-tight, brown-grey buildings squat there. Amphibious planes sit in a disorderly row next to the buildings. Steel drums and aircraft parts too large to fit in a small warehouse scatter across the area.

Carrie goes into Glacier Air's Fixed Base Operation office. As crew chief, she has to sign the paperwork to officially end the trip.

When she emerges, the goat ropers jump in an aging Chevy Suburban. Carrie starts it after several tries.

They chug and clunk back towards the ranger district work center a couple of miles away.

The decrepit Suburban is only used to go back and forth to the float planes on Eyak Lake or down to work boats moored at the ocean docks in town. Each year, when inspectors come to inventory the district's vehicles, the old Suburban somehow vanishes, only to reappear after they leave, like skunk cabbage breaks through spring snow.

The Forest Service field organization is like a cake with four layers. At the top is a National Headquarters in Washington, DC, where agency's head, "The Chief," sits. In the next layer down lie nine regional offices, mostly in big cities, where Regional Foresters preside. The third layer contains over one hundred twenty national forest headquarters offices scattered all across America, the lairs of Forest Supervisors. Most of the Forest Service's thirty-five thousand employees work within the national forests.

There are two national forests in Alaska. Mill is stationed on the Chugach National Forest which surrounds Prince William Sound in Southcentral Alaska.

At more than five million acres, it's the second-largest national forest in America. The largest, the Tongass National Forest, is a seventeen-million-acre giant mostly made up of wooded islands, large and small, in Southeast Alaska.

The bottom cake layer is composed of over nine hundred ranger districts. On ranger districts, waders meet water, boots meet ground, and mountain goats get roped. Mill works for the Cordova Ranger District, one of the remotest sites in the Forest Service, located at the eastern end of the Sound.

Mill looks out through a rusted-away spot at the base of the Suburban's door next to her. She sees the gravel road zipping by below…a little unnerving…and wonders to herself, "Maybe it's time to let this old rattletrap die a graceful death before the frame folds up and traps a crew inside like canned salmon."

Shaking her head, Mill yells up to Carrie, "Hey, stop this bucket of bolts next to my rig, will you? It's parked right where you pull in."

Carrie lets go of the gyrating steering wheel for a moment and gives Mill a one-hand wave. The Suburban shudders into the driveway, power steering whining. Carrie brings it to a stop by Mill's Toyota Tacoma mini-pickup.

Mill jumps out, waves goodbye, and throws her gear in the little truck. The Suburban spits gravel from its back tires as Carrie guns it towards the parking area.

Beyond the cracked asphalt, warehouses and workshops fill the two-acre site. The buildings look much like the aviation buildings at Eyak Lake, weathered and stout, but carry newer-painted white walls and brown trim.

Mill opens the Tacoma's door. She slides in wearily. Goat roping is tiring business.

She had left the truck unlocked. No need to lock vehicles here. You can't drive anywhere much on the hundred miles or so of roads around Cordova.

Many local people just leave the key in the ignition. They figure that, if someone takes the vehicle, it will show up in a few days likely with a full gas tank.

But because Mill has a new truck she never leaves her key in it. And when she hits the bars downtown, she actually locks the truck.

Mill muses, "There may be no rodeo cowboys around Cordova. But there are plenty of Cordova boys looking for a wild ride…they can just do that in someone else's truck, not mine."

Mill smiles at her next thought, "And not on my belly either. Imagine that, Millicent Meacham, Cordova's new-truck-ownin', gun-totin', resident nun."

She shakes her head and starts the Tacoma.

She drives to her one-bedroom apartment. It's attached to a private home sitting above the dockside Reluctant Fisherman Hotel in downtown Cordova. She had chosen it for its great view looking west across Prince William Sound, and for its snug, warm-and-cozy construction.

Mill loves to sit in the tiny living room looking out the large picture window at the restless Sound waters. To her, they seem so much like her own soul...peaceful and sunny one moment, then, boiling grey with storm and wind the next.

———————————————//———————————————

An hour later, Mill towels off wet from a hot shower.

She looks shyly at herself in the bathroom's steamy, full-length mirror. Her black hair drips wet to her shoulders, temporarily robbed of its waves. She quickly wraps her hair in a towel, and then looks at her oval face.

She sees a little wind burn from today's field work, a few freckles, and a couple of small scars from childhood misadventures. Just missing pretty, her face wears a slight frown as it has since she was raped at fourteen.

She looks down at her strong body and turns to view it in the mirror. Good muscle tone. High waist. Tight boy butt. Breasts proportionally a little larger than her body size.

She returns to a past thought about breast-reduction surgery. It first came to her in the karate dojo as she worked her way up the ranks to black-belt, certified instructor.

In competition, her breasts had been in the way, at times painfully pummeled. But breast reduction?

Mill grimaces at the thought of surgery. "No, no needles, no surgery on 'the girls' please," she says to herself.

Besides, her lovers always like them...yes, they do.

Her lovers! She looks quickly into her brown-flecked-with-green eyes and finds them suddenly dark with desire and rage.

Without willing it, she takes her breasts in her hands and gently rubs the nipples. They harden quickly. She feels the answer of a warm thickening and throb between her legs.

She sighs at her weakness and drops her hands, wills them to stay down, dismayed at what they had done.

When she had moved to Cordova, she pledged that she would have no sex, no lovers here.

No, those things were for Anchorage, or other bigger places, where she could be anonymous or nearly so, places where she could let herself go. Not for little Cordova and gossips' wagging tongues.

She knows she should stop now before her lust rises and takes over.

She whispers, "Not here. Not *here*."

But the thought of her upcoming Anchorage weekend blooms, rushes her feelings…her self-control.

Her mind goes blank. She moves, agitated, knees close together, to the side of her bed.

Her rebellious, quick hands open a drawer in her bedside table and take out a tiny gold vibrator. They turn it on and press the buzzing cylinder between her legs.

She falls back on her bed, tightening her body around the sensation…rising…rising…orgasm…unh…orgasm…unh…orgasm. She shudders again and again.

Burning hot waves of release run through her.

Tears of self-loathing run across her face, over her nose, onto her pillow.

On…and…on. Good…so good. Weak…so weak.

A half-hour later, the vibrator's batteries run down.

Mill pulls the covers over her head and hugs knees to chest. Shamed, she cries a little more.

For God's sake, why had she even brought a vibrator to Cordova? She should have left it in Anchorage locked up in her safe haven.

Once again, she has failed to hold back the throbbing, angry beast—the one that dominates her when she gives it the slightest chance.

Filled with knowing regret, Mill falls asleep.

Chapter 5 -- Mill Floatin'

Mill dreams.

She hangs in a net below a red Bell 427, bound and masked. She hears nothing, feels no wind.

Yet, somehow she knows that she flies over an unseen abyss, a broken glacier perhaps, waiting below...deadly...implacable.

Pools of dark-blue water look up at her, frozen, knowing eyes.

Then suddenly the wind courses across her body. Her naked skin ripples under its touch...cold...cold.

She tries to move, to curl for warmth. But the net resists her...tightens, tight...tighter.

And now a conviction seizes her. She has done something horribly wrong and *they* know. Those icy, deep-blue, glacier eyes know.

Shame ripples over her like the wind. She writhes.

She *must kill them* before they tell, must destroy their power...take it into herself.

The net tightens more. She can't move, can't breathe. She panics, struggles. She screams...screams.

Mill wakes with a soft moan on her lips, body twisted into the covers of her sweat-soaked, feather-topped bed.

She recognizes this night terror. She can't predict when it will strike, just that it will.

And, as it does now, that the dream will leave her feeling empty and parched.

She had gotten some relief from rape counseling in college, but nothing had cured the dreams...or the raging desires that seem tied to them.

And it's not the dream's sex and shame that scare her. No, her terror comes from the murderous rage that drives the dreams...tangled, twisted rage.

Mill rolls wearily out of bed. She locates the vibrator under the sheets, snake-warm from her body. She drops it with a spiteful wrist-snap into the bathroom trash can.

She looks at it. Silent, spent, it still has a hold on her. As Mill turns on the shower, she is grimly certain that, in a moment of disgusting weakness, she will fish it out....

Chapter 6 - Cubie Life

Later that morning, Mill tucks herself into her cubicle on the third floor of Cordova's old Post Office building, upgraded by the Forest Service for modern use when the Postal Service left.

Like Mill's apartment, the refurbished spaces are small but much better than the old, drafty district offices now used for storage. Her "cubie" is tiny, about eight feet by eight feet, about average size for small Forest Service offices in places like Cordova.

Mill's predecessor, Samuel "Quick" Silver, had left behind piles of paper, magazines, professional journals, and books. When Mill arrived for this assignment, her first permanent one, she quickly sorted his mess and built stacks all along one cubie wall. She plans to cull and file those stacks down to nothing as soon as she catches a break on day-to-day work.

Terrific at field work but lousy with paper, the former district fish biologist could never seem to file reports either. So, a year's worth of unfinished reports also awaits Mill's bewildered attention and clumsy computer skills.

Quick or not, she is determined that she will travel successfully through the bureaucratic labyrinth and emerge uneaten.

Mill has many things going for her. Born and raised in Forest Service ranger district compounds-- little federal communities in remote places--she developed an understanding of natural-resources management from the cradle. All through her childhood, she heard her dad, W.A. Meacham, talk about day-to-day agency business. So, she has a good feel for what matters and what doesn't.

She is also a fifth-generation Forest Service employee, a "Legacy," as some people call them. In fact, her great-grandfather, Nelson Meacham, had been a "Firster," one of the men chosen by Gifford Pinchot to mark the boundaries of new national forests back in the early 1900s.

Mill can't get any closer to the heart of the agency's Legacy aristocracy than by being the direct descendant of a Firster and herself a fifth-generation employee.

In terms of rank and privilege, the Forest Service operates on a caste system. With her pedigree, Mill could draw on a far-flung network of well-informed and influential Legacies and other key employees and retirees.

They would be eager to make sure she got promoted quickly, and protected jealously, if she screwed up.

Mill largely ignores her Legacy resources, choosing to make the grade on her own.

Still, the aura surrounds her. Everyone on the Cordova District feels it and understands it, including District Ranger Percy Brodigan. The staff's reaction to Mill's status is to bestow on her an extra measure of respect and support even while they pretend to ignore her Legacy "glow."

It helps that Mill is also a smart, hard-working woman. Taking advantage of correspondence courses and summer school, she had graduated from high school at seventeen and finished college at twenty. Her Master's in Limnology and Aquatic Biology arrived just before her twenty-second birthday.

Mill spent the last two years of college summering on the Cordova Ranger District, working as Quick's assistant, enrolled in the federal Student Career Experience Program.

The program gave Mill a little money.

But more importantly, it also meant that when she graduated she could be placed in a job without competition. Open to every U.S. college student, but little known to most, many Legacy families use this program to get their children first jobs with the Forest Service.

Mill had also gotten a break when, just before she graduated with her master's, Quick got a new assignment at the Forest Service Intermountain Regional Office in Ogden, Utah. Quick said he was moving there to be closer to his family, a true statement on the surface.

But, down deeper, lurked a harsher truth. W.A. Meacham, now Utah's Deputy Regional Forester for Natural Resources, had offered Quick a promotion and, thereby, ensured Mill could have Quick's job.

Legacies follow the "Green Creed," a philosophy of serving self over nation. They take pleasure in pulling invisible strings to get the results they want.

Daughter needs a job? Give someone a promotion to get them out of the way. Ruin someone's career if need be.

Like Mafia dons, Forest Service Legacies take care of themselves and their own first.

Mill would have been outraged if she had known about W.A.'s manipulation. But she never found out.

And W.A.'s friends in the invisible Legacy Empire smiled on the whole business. Legacies were used to children who want to "make it on their own" and all that crazy crap…children whose career paths always needed some trajectory-alignment and obstacle-removal.

Mill is unaware of how she got her job. But unlike many other less-than-competent Legacy children, Mill is certainly up to the "fish squeezer" field work.

Not only well prepared culturally and academically, she is also physically tough and woods-wise. Years of martial arts have taught her self-discipline, resilience, and balance.

Growing up roaming the backcountry of Utah and Idaho, she is comfortable anywhere outdoors. From childhood play, she is good at skiing, rock climbing, and trekking. Not really a hunter or fisher, she knows her way around guns and poles, all-terrain vehicles and boats, hunting blinds and fishing tackle.

Most importantly, she loves where she works now—in the wild country of the Cordova Ranger District. With millions of acres to wander in, she looks forward to years of work along the Copper and Bering River watersheds and across the huge Copper River Delta, some of the most important fish and wildlife habitats in the world.

Mill looks longingly out her third-floor window at the harbor filled with boats, big and little, struck by a sudden desire to go walkabout. Then her eyes travel beyond the breakwater to the restless waters and wild islands of Prince William Sound. Out there, wild places sing to her spirit…wind and waves beckon and offer her rest.

Mill sighs deeply. She really does have work to do.

She reluctantly accepts the dark toil of today's work destiny. She drags her eyes away from the sparkle and rush of the water and turns to her computer screen.

Mill steels her mind to ignore Friday and…Anchorage.

The "Aqua" section of the cumbersome Natural Resource Information System opens.

Her nimble fingers dance over the keyboard, building corporate knowledge from Quick's data chaos.

Chapter 7 - Up and Down in Anchor Town

Alaska Airlines Flight 61 shakes and bounces on approach into Anchorage's Ted Stevens International Airport.

Mill looks out her port-side window over the wing. Even seated over the wing, she is actually only a few rows back from the bulkhead because the front one-third of the aircraft is taken up by cargo space.

Alaska Airlines provides unique service with Boeing 737s especially made to fly both passengers and bulky freight at the same time. Mill knows of one woman who had an Anchorage Ford dealer fly a new Bronco to Point Barrow on such a cargo-configured jet. The "dealer-destination charges" were a mere twelve thousand dollars more.

The dealer even threw in two "free" tickets from and to Point Barrow so the woman and her boyfriend could "drive" their new purchase home.

Mill shakes her head as she thinks again of the old Alaska saying, "God surely made the airplane for Alaska." To this truism, Mill mentally adds, "And Alaska for the airplane."

The plane drops below the low cloud cover. Mill can see Turnagain Arm and its treacherous, life-taking waters. The tide is boiling in--wild, choppy, grey waves ripped by swirling winds, currents, and tides.

Beyond Turnagain, she sees Cook Inlet's grey-blue waters, coldly obscured by wind-thrown mist.

The plane makes a slight turn north. Elevators whine. Below Mill, the white peaks and grey-brown valleys of Chugach State Park open up. The sight takes Mill's breath. She almost forgets the plane's violent bucking and slewing.

The plane straightens and drops more quickly. The outskirts of Anchorage appear. Far below, Mill sees a lonesome-looking bull moose plod through wetlands, making a beeline for the nearest suburb.

A friend of hers lives on Oakwood Drive right in that area. Mill wonders if the moose will come foraging into the woman's yard. She smiles as she thinks about the loud reception he might receive—dogs barking, neighbors beating pans together, firecrackers popping, police sirens wailing, and cruiser lights flashing.

She wonders if the moose will feel honored by this greeting and stay to eat the landscaping. Or will he wisely turn back to the bush? As the moose disappears under the wing, Mill wishes him common sense and bon voyage.

Coming in "hot and fast" to counter cross-winds, the plane drops lower, then without warning smacks down on the tarmac. The pilot brakes hard and engages the reverse thrusters.

The force throws Mill and the other passengers against their seat belts. They grab armrests and plant feet hard against the floor.

The 737 shakes violently. Doors bang. Frozen tires thump. An errant oxygen mask falls out of its tiny compartment.

Along with the other Alaska sourdoughs on the flight, Mill smiles grimly. The locals are almost used to this.

Newcomers, called "cheechakos" by Alaskans, panic…curse.

Everyone wonders if they about to disappear in a ball of flame and tumbling parts.

The 737 stops its violent motion. A few cheechakos applaud.

The fast-rolling plane veers suddenly onto a taxiway, throwing people and property sideways. More muttered curses.

Then the heavy aircraft straightens and rolls on, buffeted by the winds off the Gulf.

Passengers begin gathering their children and personal gear. They harden their resolve, knowing it's time to throw themselves into Anchorage's baggage- and bumper-smashing machines.

Mill grabs her small overnight bag. She is dressed now in jeans and a light cotton top, casual Friday work clothes. Her thick wool "halibut coat" rests up above in the overhead compartment with her overnight bag.

These clothes are designated "Cordova" in her mind.

In her Anchorage haven, she has what she needs for her Anchorage life—clothes, a fake ID, and cash. Her Cordova stuff will be locked up, safe, while she parties.

Thoughts of what she will do tonight suddenly make her leaden, blank.

Then her mind clears. She is focused…ready…. She stands with the other people in her row.

Time to go.

Watch out Anchor-town.

Wild Girl Hunting has arrived!

Chapter 8 - Aurora Rave Club

Two hours after Flight 61 smacked down, Mill starts her first-night hunt.

She divides her wild-girl hunts into up-scale and back-alley nights--different bars, different people--less chance of getting known.

One lover at a time, man or woman, it doesn't much matter to Mill. She knows ways to pleasure them all as long as they release her in return.

No, she looks for the right "vibe," a kind of gravitational force that tugs the weight of Mill's almost uncontrollable lust towards another person's heavy, dark core.

Drugs help find the vibe.

Mill had learned about drugs her junior year in college and tried a bunch.

Once she overdid, got crazy. Now she drugs just enough to stay clear-headed…prey focused.

A careful cocktail of drugs and alcohol, topped off with hours of exciting sex, brings pleasure so intense it pushes the bad out of Mill's life.

After she scores, she feels perfect, whole, all in control. She gets a mellow week or two.

Then the mellow ebbs. She turns restless, irritable.

She feels more and more flawed, hungry.

Rage builds within her, like inky teeth waiting to erupt.

And inevitably, Mill returns to the hunt…to get right again.

By seven this night, Mill has already hit a few of her favorite, more genteel bars like those in the big hotels. She checked out a few people at the Captain Cook Hotel. No one gave off the vibe.

She drifts on. By eight, she is jacked on a few drinks, a short, fat joint smoked quickly in a parking-garage stairway, and half a tab of Ecstasy.

Once high, Mill carries no dope. No need. Her high will last for hours.

And it's Anchorage after all. If she wants a hit, she can always find a pusher. Let them run the risk of being caught with dope.

Mill leaves the Cook. She catches a cab, "Aurora Rave Club."

Twenty minutes later, she walks slowly towards the club's huge building, once the home of a later-bankrupt "big-box" retailer. The vast cube stood vacant for a year but now rents for enough to gladden the owner's greedy heart.

The Anchorage police hold a much gloomier view of the place—too many fights, working girls, and drugs—too many call-outs altogether.

Mill wears one of her best first-night dresses--a close-fitting black sheath, thigh-length, one side slit up a few inches. A pleated strap curves over one shoulder and leaves the other shoulder bare. A narrow leather band at the level of her collar bones secures the top-front. Beneath the band, the low-cut bodice has a sewn-in shelf that lifts Mill's breasts, letting them move naturally. The thin fabric reveals their soft outlines and nipples.

Invisible beneath the dress, Mill's boy-cut black-lace panties are made so that she only needs to spread her legs for sex.

She carries a black push-dagger in a thin padded sleeve sewn into her panties behind her right hip.

Shomer-Tec makes her six-inch, plastic knife. Snug in its sleeve, the flat little dagger barely shows through her dress. Invisible to metal detectors and most x-ray machines, it's sharp enough to open an artery or stab a penis through.

She was once half-choked by a coked-out drummer--his powerful hands locked around her neck from behind--and found that expert karate wasn't enough. Mill pats her right hip, satisfying herself that her "persuader" is there.

The bouncer guarding the Aurora's entrance watches her walk slowly towards him. He mentally calculates, "Beautiful. A little stoned. Ready for anything. Wish I was off duty tonight...."

While Mill is still ten feet away, he picks up the end of the blinking rope of white lights that serves as a barrier to the club's entrance. He smiles broadly as she sways past.

Mill smiles back, "He might just do. Maybe later, mister muscles...."

At the reception area, two buff, leather-clad women welcome Mill. They stamp her right hand with a black-light-visible "A."

The tallest smiles at Mill, "Here's some drink tickets to get started, honey."

Mill returns the smile and thinks, "This one might do, too."

For pretty women like Mill who arrive alone, the Aurora owner waives his hefty cover charge. The greeters also hand them several free drink tickets. The owner knows beautiful and available women sell the club better than advertising ever could.

Everybody else pays, including working girls and their pimps. They have to pay the cover and add a hefty "tip" to the bouncers and tough-girl reception crew to get in at all.

Holding the short string of tickets, Mill walks slowly towards the inner-club's draped doorway. A poster announces that tonight's entertainment is a tribute band from New York, already amped up, doped up, and blasting Rolling Stones to a more-or-less grateful city block.

Mill feels the vibration of the band's hard-driving beat through the soles of her boots. It's almost strong enough to tickle her feet.

Pausing at the entrance, she looks into the vast, darkened interior filled with loud, thumping music. Across the high ceiling, neon tubes flicker and pulse greenish-white, blue, and red to represent the club's theme, Alaska's famous Aurora Borealis. At floor level, the light is just strong enough for Mill to recognize faces, but she sees no one she recognizes. Good.

Off to her left, the band prances on a three-tier stage. It rises from six feet off the club floor at the front to twice that at the rear. On both sides, speaker stacks reach up towards the high ceiling.

Just inside the stacks, a couple of big security men wearing ear protection stand on each side of the stage. The men watch the crowd, ready to stop flying moshers, stage-crashers, and groupies with throbbing libidos.

She looks around the club's interior. Good band. Friday evening. No limit on what might happen.

The club is half full now. But, based on past experience, Mill expects it to get crowded soon. She looks more closely at the people dancing near the stage, intent on lining up someone before the crowd got so packed in she couldn't talk or move.

No vibe…yet.

Mill turns and hands her coat to the hat-check. As she walks away, she slides the hat-check stub and all but one of her free drink tickets into a tiny zippered pocket sewn into her pleated shoulder strap.

Another pocket in the strap holds Mill's "get-out-of-jail cards," three crisp, flat-folded, one-hundred dollar bills. Between the dagger, her

29

fake ID, and this rat-hole money, Mill feels prepared for whatever comes her way.

Mill walks to one of the full-service bars and orders her favorite pick-up drink, a "TNT" or tequila and tonic. Tart, light, and effective. No stains if spilled.

She gets a short drink in a tall glass with an orange slice on the rim. Glass half-full signals that Mill is a little drunk, available… vulnerable.

Taking small sips, Mill drifts out onto the dance floor and begins dancing alone. She moves slowly, her shoulders and hips swaying at half the thudding beat.

Mill knows her moves work something like trolling for fish with cut bait and a flasher. Movement. Seductive scent. Eye-attracting flashes. Inside her, a sharp, barbed hook.

A well-dressed, twenty-something woman appears out of the crowd. She takes Mill's free hand and begins to dance, matching Mill's movement. She moves easily, controlled…sensuous. They dance, eyes locked.

The woman leans forward to brush Mill's lips with hers. Mill kisses back. The woman's lips are warm, nice…but no vibe.

Mill pulls her hand away. The woman stares blankly at Mill for a moment, doped mind trying to catch up. Disappointment registers slowly. She turns, walks away, and doesn't look back.

Mill looks out across the huge space again. The club's managers have set some cushioned chairs and love seats off on the right side so people can talk and make out away from the full force of the speakers. Carrying her TNT, Mill wanders towards the half-full seating.

She slides into an empty love seat…crosses her legs. Her dress rides up to mini length. She sips her drink.

After a few moments, her head lolls back against the cushions, eyes closed. She relaxes, enjoying her high, the music building energy within her. She cautiously touches her hunger, the darkness…the lust-anger.

It pulses hard.

She has score soon, really soon.

A man's voice intrudes, "Done so soon, beautiful lady?"

Mill opens her eyes. Unfocused for a moment, she is unsure where the voice has come from. Then looking to her right, she sees the speaker. Smiling. Dressed well. Medium height. Wiry strong. Wide shoulders. Big, scarred hands. Alaska Native, Aleut maybe.

Best of all, she feels the vibe...light, then more intensely.

Mill smiles at him, pats the cushion next to her, "Join me."

He drops into the seat.

He holds out his hand a little drunkenly, "I'm Bill. In from Seward for some fun. What's your name?"

Mill studies him. He has a great face--brown, broad, smallish eyes below wild brows, a small tattoo along his jaw line to his ear. His face is well shaved and is filled with white, slightly crooked teeth and a warm, crooked grin.

The dark vibe runs through Mill again, stronger now. She feels a chill of anticipation along her thighs.

"I'm Lucy," Mill smiles, taking his hand first to shake and then to hold briefly.

"You've got the feel of a guy who works in the woods or on the water. What do you do for a living?" she asks.

In keeping with Aleut traditions, Bill looks down modestly, "I own a fishing boat. We operate out of Seward or Homer depending on the opening. Salmon and halibut, some bottom fish."

Mill dimples, "Just the man I've been looking for. Someone to take me fishing. Long-liner? Seiner?"

Bill smiles, "Seiner, but I change gear for different openings."

He goes on to describe his boat. Mill soon realizes he owns a bigger boat than many in Cordova, a place where the smallish "bow picker" fleet does most of the fishing. Or rather the fleet had done so before the Exxon Valdez oil spill had wiped out many fisheries.

She pats his hand, "Tell me more about your boat...about fishing."

Bill launches on a longer description, proud of his boat and crew, speaking in a soft, guttural accent.

Bill describes wild times on the Gulf of Alaska taking "green water" over the wheel house while his rope-tethered crew frantically hauls in gear and fish. A good story teller, he draws Mill into his tales even while she distracts herself with rising thoughts of bedding him.

When his story finally runs out, she dimples, "Well, I'm really impressed. If I brought lunch sometime, would you take me fishing?"

Bill smiles a wide grin, "I'd take you wherever you want to go!"

He raises his eyebrows in what he hopes is a roguish expression but the gesture merely makes him seem boyish. Perfect.

Mill takes Bill's hand, "Let's get a drink…dance. Okay?"

With a big smile, he leaps to his feet. He pulls her up gently by her hand.

As she rises, Bill takes an appreciative look at her bare legs and inner thighs. He holds her hand while they walk to the bar.

They sip on new drinks, set them on a small table, and walk onto the dance floor.

Bill begins to dance to the Stones '60s sounds. His limbs follow traditional Aleut dance curves and angles—ones he had learned from his elders. Fascinated, Mill watches as he weaves the modern-now and the long-ago-then together.

A slow number follows. Bill takes her in his arms and holds her close, but not tightly. Mill snuggles in, her face on his chest.

She takes his right hand and guides it to her bottom. Soon he places both hands there, gently touching her. He doesn't seem to notice the dagger in its padded sheath or, if he does, makes no comment.

Just before the song ends, Bill moves his face down and kisses Mill on the mouth, his lips a little tentative. To encourage him, she responds with her whole body, pulling him close, pressing up and into him.

He kisses her again and she flicks her tongue over his. He laughs through their kiss. Seems like he is going to get lucky with a beautiful woman.

He asks, "Would you like to go somewhere? I mean other than here. Over to the couches?"

Mill glances over at the seating area. The chairs and couches are full of people talking, some making out. No sex for her on those very public couches.

Mill shakes her head, "No, looks like standing room only. I have an idea. Follow me."

Mill takes his hand. She leads him towards the left speaker stack. Just beyond it, a long drape hangs down, concealing what's under the stage.

She pulls Bill to her…kisses him hard on the mouth. Over the blasting sound, she yells, "Ready for an adventure?"

He yells, "Yes!"

"Okay, in a minute, when no one's watching, I'll duck behind this drape. Wait just a little while and then follow me in. As long as no one sees us go in, no one will follow. I bet no one cares what we do back there."

Bill catches on right away. He smiles, "Could you wait for me a minute? I have to hit the rest room and…well…you know buy something."

Mill nods her understanding, "Go, but get back quickly. I'm ready…for you." She pushes him towards the men's room.

Reluctant to leave her, he takes her in his arms again and kisses her strongly. Then turning, he hurries off.

Mill leans back against the speakers. The beat penetrates her skin, pulses through her bones. In her pelvis…between her legs…a tingle, a sizzle.

Mill gives in to the rising…there…there.

But not enough for release.

Suddenly she can't wait for Bill's return.

She peeks around the speakers towards the men's room. No Bill. Anger cuts through her…fills her. Where is he? She wants him *now*.

For a moment her hand grips the push-dagger through her clothes. If Bill doesn't show up soon, Wild Girl might stab him when he does.

Mill realizes she has to act before rage takes over and she does unimaginable things. She ducks behind the drape and enters the dark, slightly stuffy space beyond.

Inside the atmosphere feels dense, compressed, like being underwater inside a sunken ship. Little fingers of light poke down tiny squares here, larger triangles there. Pipes and braces web, anchored to the floor, disappearing into the dark. Music filters in--tones and words distorted, muffled…alien.

Mill touches a pipe and feels the intense sizzle…guitars…drums. Drone…drone…vibrations running in waves, first separate and diffuse, then synchronous…intense.

Mill presses her pelvis against the pipe and feels it. There. Rising…but not enough.

She looks around wildly. Twisted cables drop from above, puddle on planking, coil around pipe stanchions, and run out across the floor into darkness.

Mill moves quickly. She pulls herself up, sits down on the cables, and brings her legs around a stanchion. Holding it tightly, she presses her pelvis into the metal. It's warm from the energy coursing through the cables.

She pulls with her arms and presses her hips in harder. Buzz…buzzzzz… there…right there.

A light orgasm shakes her…there…another more intense… there…now.

Good, but not enough.

Movement in the shadows.

Bill stands before her, his face hidden in the gloom. His white teeth flash as he sees how she pleasures herself. Mill knows his grin, his hands, and his hips…and the vibe.

Impatient, she swings her legs out from around the pipe, her movements cat-like, quick…precise.

Wild Girl Hunting bares her teeth, unseen by Bill in the dark. She vows that if he denies her full pleasure now, she will bleed him.

She lies back across the warm cables, moves her hips to the edge of the planking, and opens to him.

He drops his pants. A long, thin penis… just right. Condom…just right.

In.

There…right there…now …now.

A long, blank, pleasuring time passes.

Then, as Bill did, quiet fills her.

Mill wakes up with a start, disoriented, most of her high gone. How could she have fallen asleep? She remembers Bill's touch, his deep thrusts, and her strong orgasms squeezing him.

But where is Bill now? Mill looks around desperately, a little whine in her throat, anger-pressure gone but lust remaining. Nowhere!

Mill swivels her body urgently. She wraps her legs around the buzzing pipe again and presses in. There…right there…now.

Chapter 9 - Second Day

Saturday, 8 p.m.

Second-day hunt.

Jeans low across her hips, taut girl-belly showing. Low-cut sleeveless blouse. Breasts free. Embroidered denim jacket. More makeup. Bigger jewelry.

Plastic push dagger sheathed in a roper-style cowboy boot.

A thicker stick of pot smoked. A whole tab of E swallowed. A few beers at a low-rent dive in Spenard.

Hunter rage muted, at least for the moment.

A man Mill calls "Wyoming" comes in.

Wild Girl Hunting doesn't know his real name or where he is from.

Better yet, he doesn't want to know anything about her.

She takes the barstool next to his. She puts her hand on his shoulder and rubs his arm with her breasts.

Wyoming doesn't seem to recognize her from their past two times together. Good.

She buys him a beer, then two. Finally, she pulls him toward the door. Glad to get lucky-laid without paying, he walks with her willingly to the cheap motel next door.

After a couple of dry preliminary kisses, he screws her with the same motion as those oil-production pumps you see all over that wide-open western state.

Gaunt and metal-solid...always moving, up and down...up and down...his stroke never varies. He moves as if Mill isn't there.

She imagines his dusty skin, motor's whir, drive rod in a steady push-pull, oil flowing thickly into her.

Yes, the man screws like a Wyoming pump jack.

Wild Girl rests her imagination and lets sensation take over. Lying under him, she takes him in fully. Her calves and heels rest on his hips. Her hips follow his movement. Up and down, up and down....

From past sex with him, she knows she can look forward to an hour or so of this. Because he is so consistent, Mill places and moves her hips so that each stroke rubs her perfectly. Up and down, up and down.

There...right there...now.

A pleasuring hour passes.

Wyoming shudder-grunts his finish. He presses himself deeply into Wild Girl and lowers himself gently onto her body, warm from exertion.

She feels his breath lightly in her ear. It's the closest they've been all night. She waits for a kiss.

Then, without kiss or comment, he leaves her body and goes into the bathroom. She hears the shower run.

A few minutes later, he emerges, toweling his hair. Sitting on the edge of the bed, he puts on his clothes and stands. He walks around the bed to where she lies, kisses her right nipple, and musses her hair…his only signs of affection.

Then, he tosses her a smile and walks out the door without a word.

Wild Girl's perfect second-night man.

After the door closes, Mill pulls the little golden vibrator from the watch pocket in her jeans. Fresh batteries.

She presses it home.

There…right there…now.

Chapter 10 - Anchorage Sunday

Sunday, 7 a.m.

Mill wakes in the cheap motel room, Wyoming's pumping a strong memory.

Using the vibrator, Mill finds two more good orgasms.

Shower. Scrub the face until the makeup's gone. Change into Cordova clothes.

Leave and grab a cab to Hogg Brothers for a big greasy breakfast. Breakfast over.

Suddenly tired, running on coffee nerves, Mill takes her Anchorage clothes to a dry cleaner on Third. She will pick them up in a month or so when she returns for her next hunt.

Mill grabs a cab over to her haven, a heated storage compartment in a multi-storied warehouse near the airport. Inside the dusty compartment, she carefully puts her hunting gear away.

Money, dope, and dagger go in a small lockbox, which she hides at the back of a tall, cedar wardrobe.

After her first Anchorage trips, wanting to keep her things better organized and neat, she had bought the wide wardrobe at a second-hand shop. It just fits under the low ceiling, an ideal place to store her dozen nice first-night outfits and at least as many scruffier second-night ones.

Mill lights the storage space with two floor lamps, one on each side of a full-length mirror, and with two small table lamps that sit at the edges of her small, mirrored vanity. The lamps plug into an extension cord she connects to the room's single overhead light socket.

Mill sits down on the vanity's little bench and tidies up the glass surface. While she puts her Wild Girl makeup back into the table's small drawers and uses a tissue to clean the mirrored top, she avoids looking into her eyes.

Finally, she looks up. The woman's eyes in the mirror are frighteningly strange. Brown-dark eyes dark with hurt.

Mill looks away, then back. Now the dark eyes are clearly hers, Mill Meacham's, once baby Milly to her Mom and Dad.

Her Mom, Rebecca, gone forever when Mill was seven…gone… into darkness. Gone out of Milly's life, when Milly needed her most…as she grew up, after the rape.

Mill sits and stares into her own eyes for a long time, back stiff. Tears run down her frowning, beautiful, natural face. She stares down her darkness.

Suddenly resolute, eyes locked to eyes in the mirror, Mill slides the golden vibrator out of her Cordova jeans. Without looking away, she sets it down firmly on the vanity's top.

The vibrator's edge catches the glass and makes a harsh rasping sound. Using both hands, Mill stands it straight up at the center of the table, a bent golden bullet she will leave here to fire on her next visit.

Mill walks to the door. She opens it, turns off the light, and steps outside. Alaska Airlines Flight 66 will soon take her back to Cordova.

Mill's haven now holds Wild Girl.

Tame Mill leaves.

Chapter 11 - Squeezing Copper Fish

Springtime along Alaska's Copper River--one of the few untouched rivers in the world.

Mill and her fisheries technician, Dill Dillard, work their way along the Copper's west bank. Around and above them, bright sunshine lights up white-blue glaciers. Cold wind sweeps down from grey-blue mountain heights and cuts the river waters. Small bergs from calving glaciers drift by. Pushing-up patches of green grass, willow, and alder brush fill rocky side hills and creep onto cobbled beaches.

Above, gulls and eagles wheel, rising on the wind…dropping in the hunt.

The two Forest Service employees surge upriver in their aluminum work boat and then turn sharply into a stream mouth. The boat grates on a pebble beach.

Mill jumps out, hauls the boat higher, and ties it off to a large rock. Dill jumps out, too, and reaches back to pull out their gear.

They drop their warm Mustang float coats in heap. For the work ahead, the heavy garments are too bulky.

As they do at each stop, they will keep a wary watch for hungry, grumpy bears fresh from winter dens. It's hard to have eyes in the back of your head doing field work but you have to do it to survive along the Copper.

Each biologist carries a holstered can of bear spray that shoots a stream hotter than a thousand jalapeno peppers. Sometimes bear spray shoos an approaching bear away. Sometimes it doesn't, particularly when a wicked wind blows the spray back in a human face.

Because spraying a bear can be tricky, the two keep a .375 H&H Magnum rifle propped within easy reach.

Both Mill and Dill hope never to use either spray or gun. They fancy a quick retreat into the boat and fast trip out into the Copper instead.

The two fish biologists have come here to check smolt traps. Smolts are little fish grown big enough in fresh water to be ready to head out to salt. Once there, if they survive predators and disease, they will grow huge before returning here to spawn.

Days earlier, the biologists had set the traps in streams known to produce these anadromous, or sea-going, fish. Now, they enter the rushing stream, open the traps, and stare down at the wiggling, wavy schools inside.

Dill uses a small net to lift fish from a trap. Mill measures each fish. Weighing a couple of ounces in the trap, they may weigh fifty or even a hundred pounds when they return.

Mill records species, size, sex, and any signs of disease. She types what she finds into a small, rugged field data recorder. As the data go in, Mill thinks about how tasty the five kinds of native Alaska salmon and two kinds of trout, steelhead and cutthroat, will be many years from now.

After awhile, trap empty, Mill tallies the results. She reports to Dill, "Not so many *Oncorhynchus tshawytscha* in this bunch."

Dill knows the tongue-twisting Latin refers to Alaska King Salmon. The two biologists like to use scientific names for fish, insect, and aquatic plant species.

Like code words in a club, it drives their non-biologist colleagues nuts and serves to tighten bonds with other fish biologists. Mill knows that the few fish biologists in the area have to be tight.

Within the twenty-four thousand square miles drained by the Copper River, Alaska Game and Fish biologists manage the fish. Forest Service and Park Service biologists manage most of the gravels and waters where the fish are born and develop.

So, as it was with the goat roping, agency people must cooperate to get their jobs done.

Dill thinks for a moment about the low King salmon count, then replies, "Yeah, numbers have always been low on this creek. Not much rearing habitat, I think."

Even though Dill has been around the district a long time, she wonders how he can remember such stuff about the 300-mile-long Copper. Mill nods, "Yeah, okay. Let's plow through the historic data when we get back. Okay, time to pack up."

Dressed again in their float coats, they throw the gear back in the boat.

Dill jumps to the stern. He starts the still-warm outboard and the motor purrs in neutral. Mill gives the bow a huge shove off the beach, jumps in, and settles low on the forward bench seat.

The boat spins out into the hasty current, which twists the hull and thrusts it downstream.

At the steering station towards the middle of the boat, Dill quickly engages the drive. He pulls the throttle-control back hard and gains control of the spinning boat. In moments, the boat slams and swoops upriver again.

As they go back by the stream containing the traps they just surveyed, Mill looks hastily upstream to see if she can identify any *O-tshawytscha* rearing habitat. But she can only see up the tumbling waters for a hundred feet or so before the stream twists out of sight into the tangle of alder brush.

"No way to tell from here," she thinks to herself, "We'll have to run a stream survey if none's been done."

Dill drives the boat to their next stream. This landing is easier here because the river pushes out and around a small gravel bar at the entrance. He motors inside and cuts the engine. The boat touches muddy bottom.

Mill leaps easily off the bow. She grabs the small anchor and its line, pulls the boat up on the bank, and drops the anchor behind a large boulder.

The two follow the same process they used at the last stream. Dill nets. Mill measures, counts, and records.

As an undergrad, Mill read Ralph Waldo Emerson's comment that, "Foolish consistency is the hobgoblin of little minds...."

She talks about Emerson's complaint with Dill as they bend to their tedious, exacting jobs.

"What a pain in the ass way to make a living...or at least a pain in the lower back," she says with a grimace, "But wouldn't Ralph Waldo like to be with us here and now!" Mill lifts her head up for a moment to stretch out a crick. She takes in the incredible, wild landscape all around her and says, "Boy, like nothing else on Earth."

Dill looks, too, "You better believe it!

The way they gather their information is a pain in the ass but it's also essential for managing fish scientifically. This season's smolt counts are just as important as making sure enough salmon escape hungry nets and hooks and come home to the Copper to spawn. And they're just as important as salvaging eggs from returning females or squeezing the semen from returning males for the fish hatcheries.

In the past, Mill helped hatchery biologists combine these genetic materials and then gently tend the fertilized eggs in incubators. When the eggs hatch, they are fed and raised in hatcheries or placed back in wild stream gravels. Eventually, those tiny fish eggs become smolt to go back out to sea. In all this, the biologists help sustain the fish in their ancient lifecycle.

Mill slits her eyes against a puff of fine glacial silt caught up by the keening wind. She smiles up at the mountains and rubs her neck.

She lets go of the magnificent view, bends down, and gets back to her wonderful, hobgoblin job.

Chapter 12 - Ursus Arctos Horribilis

Alaska. May.

Short summer.

Long days.

The Copper basks in eighteen hours of daylight.

Days will get even longer. By mid-June, the sun will barely dip below the horizon before rising again to dominate the sky.

To make the most of the summer season, Mill and Dill push their schedule to the extreme. They work three twelve-hour field days, followed by one four-hour office day. In the field, they keep moving, camp out if work is too distant from home, eat on the fly, and get stuff done.

Mill looks at her watch. 7 p.m.

"Damn," she says to Dill, "where did the day go?"

Dill glances at his watch, "Yeah, this time of year, it's so hard to tell. But, hey, we have enough time to get this last bit done and then get back. We don't want anybody worrying about us."

Each field crew files a trip plan with district dispatch that notes destinations and likely times in and out. The dispatch office would be checking on them soon if they didn't hear from Dill first. Dill picks up his hand-held radio.

"Cordova…Dillard," he calls, using Forest Service radio protocol. He repeats, "Cordova…Dillard."

A moment later the crackly voice of Cordova dispatch calls back, "Dill, this is Cordova…what can we do for you."

"Meacham party ready to head back," he reports, "ETA one hour fifteen minutes."

"Cordova copies," the dispatcher confirms, "Arrival time about twenty thirty."

"Roger," says Dill, "Dillard clear…"

"Cordova clear…."

Mill finishes her records. The two quickly pack their gear in waterproof bags and containers. They load the cargo in the boat and secure it under a net clipped to D-rings in the deck.

They are miles from the boat take-out on the lower part of the Copper. Their trip there will be fast because, rather than travelling against the Copper's powerful current, they will swim with it.

But it can also be rough in spots…and dangerous. The river's gravel bars, boulders, and occasional glacier-ice edges create sudden shallows, standing waves, and small white-water.

Bergs dot the water and move unpredictably, some parts of them submerged. Logs roll in the opaque current and rise unexpectedly. Both bergs and logs can flip the boat or breach its hull.

Dill starts the outboard, lets it idle, and takes the wheel.

Mill grabs the gunnel and pushes hard. But the boat is stuck in the muddy silt. Damn! The river must have dropped a little while they worked.

Dill grabs the little steering station and rocks the boat side to side, trying to break the suction of mud on the hull.

Mill shoves harder and, slowly the boat begins to slide off. Suddenly, the boat breaks free and its fast movement almost throws Mill down to her knees. Double damn! She struggles in the gooey shallows.

Just as she gets her feet back under her, Mill hears an enormous crashing in the willows behind her!

A brown bear, ears back, mouth open…headed right for her!

The huge animal hurtles forward, grass and mud flying from his paws, trying for a quick grab and kill.

Mill screams, "Yaaaaah."

Panic-thrusting her legs, she drives the boat out from the shore. Just as she readies herself to jump in, she trips on a river rock, loses her grip on the gunnel, and falls on hands and knees in muddy water.

Rallying up, Mill leaps awkwardly for the gunnel, feet slipping on cobbles and mud.

Her hands miss the gunnel by inches.

She trips and sprawls again, half under water. Just beyond her reach, the last piece of a trailing line slips away.

Equally panicked, Dill jumps forward for the rifle. Spinning in the current, the boat dips under his weight. Dill loses his footing and crashes headfirst into the pile of gear. He does not rise.

Mill watches the boat whirl out and disappear downriver.

The boat's gone and the bear is twenty feet away!

No place for Mill to go but into the Copper!

Half hopping and half running through the last few feet of shallows, Mill hurls herself into the rushing river.

Glacial water hits her abdomen below the Mustang coat and fills her hip boots, instantly cold. The icy water also fills in between the coat and her torso, but, trapped, it warms a little.

Floating like a cork, Mill quickly spins around and looks back at the bear.

"My God, she thinks, "That crazy-hungry animal has jumped in after me."

She spins back downriver and looks for Dill and the boat. There's no sign of them in the rolling waves. She is on her own.

Mill rolls face down and tries to swim with the current. The bulky float coat makes arm movement almost impossible.

She begins a powerful swimming kick but her water-filled hip boots slow her up.

She unsnaps the boot straps at her belt. Pushing and kicking, she forces the boots off. There, now she can move her legs. She starts a powerful frog-kick.

She can swim better but whatever insulation the boots provided is now gone. Mill feels her legs start to chill and weaken. She kicks hard as much to keep blood circulation going as to get away from the bear.

The bear has few of Mill's problems. The bear's fat, fur, and barrel chest insulate it well from river-water cold. Bears are slow but powerful swimmers, none more so than polar bears, which are actually classified as marine mammals because of their swimming abilities.

And Mill knows that Copper River brown bears are close relatives of polar bears!

Mill drives herself across the river even as the river current takes her swiftly down and away.

She pauses again to look back at the bear. For a second, Mill can't see him. Relief washes over her.

Then she rises on a wave. No! There he is!

Although the bear is well behind her now, he is definitely still on her trail. And as near as Mill can tell in the rolling, rushing river, he is gaining on her.

Mill yells at him, "Stupid bear. Turn back. Leave me alone!"

She waves her arms and smacks the water to make him think she is too big and too tough for dinner. She yells some more.

The bear keeps coming. Mill turns around and starts swimming and kicking again.

Minutes pass. She struggles along, tiring ever more quickly.

Now more than halfway across the mile-wide river, she tops a wave and glances back. Behind her, the bear still swims after her, a patient demon pursuing a sinner.

The river starts a long curving sweep. The current carries Mill quickly towards the far shore.

Here's a break! She might get away yet.

Mill spots a rock outcrop coming up. It's covered with boulders and extends out into the current like a curving arm.

Maybe she can land on it and haul her weary butt up its steep slopes to safety.

And, better yet, Mill can see a green fringe beyond the rocky arm. Once ashore, she might be able to hide from the bear in the tangles of brush and wetlands off in the distance.

Mill figures her chances of actually escaping the bear are slim. But those chances are way better than bobbing around the river like an egg on toast, bear breakfast.

She glances back. The animal is only a hundred or so feet behind her. So, she will have to be fast and focused when her chance comes.

Mill tries to forget about the bear and focus on getting ashore. She looks up at the high bank zipping by and readies herself for a landing.

But the Copper proves capricious. A sudden swirl carries her away from the high bank.

She misses landing by ten feet and thrashes the water to get closer…gets nowhere. Damn!

Then the Copper turns generous. Mill's feet touch gravel. She grounds abruptly in a broad shallow at the end of the rocky arm.

The rushing river urgently tugs at her, trying to pull her back.

Quickly now.

Thrashing water, she staggers up onto numb, uncooperative legs, sock-clad feet sliding in the loose gravel.

Mill takes another quick look back. Where's the bear?

There he is, fifty feet away, looking straight at her…swimming hard. She hears his huffing grunts.

Wait…her bear spray! She reaches for the fat can on her belt. Gone! Gone to the Copper's roiling, rolling current!

She runs up the gravelly slope, numb feet dragging. She sees the green fringe beyond—the fringe she had hoped would be her refuge—her green haven.

Too far! She could never make it before the bear got to her, ripped her open.

No place left to go but into the large pond behind the bar. She loathes entering the water again but she sees no other choice.

Mill plunges in and strides forward. Below her feet, a ledge of silty cobbles ends abruptly. No current to help her now, she has to swim further into the deep, opaque pool.

As she starts her kick, she hears the frenzied bear splashing behind her. He's coming fast.

Mill realizes she can't move fast enough to escape him. She has to get out of the clumsy float coat.

She uses her cold, cold fingers to rip the zipper down. Thank God, for once, it doesn't get hung up at the bottom.

Cold water rushes inside the coat. Her chest tightens. She forces herself to take a deep breath…two.

Then she slides out of the coat, rolls clumsily, and dives into the dark waters below. She holds her breath for as long as she can. Icy water steals her energy and needle-stabs her face and eyes.

When she can't stand the pain any longer, she lets herself rise. She hopes to break the surface gently, quietly, with her nose and mouth just far enough out of the water to breathe. This way, maybe the bear won't hear her or see her.

Her face touches light. Mill gets a couple of quick, shallow breaths, then a blessed deep one.

A growl.

Water thrashing.

Where is he? Unseen, the bear is clearly coming at her again.

Down! She fills her lungs and dives again…deeper…looking to touch the bottom, grab something to hold her down. Her fingers touch cobbles but, numb, can't grip to hold here there, safe.

Hovering close to the bottom, cold creeps into her brain.

Mill realizes this has to be her last dive. When she surfaces this time, she will have to deal with the bear. Or he will deal with her….

Now, chest aching…choking…Mill rises again.

She breaks the surface so carefully, not a ripple, no noise. She breathes slowly, deeply, deliciously.

She lets her head slide gently out of the water, so quietly, opens her eyes, and looks around.

Her painfully beating heart almost stops.

My God, her face is three feet from the bear's rump! The bear's back is maybe six inches above the surface. His head bobs in the water at the level of her face.

She waits for him to turn, drive his claws into her chest, and crush her skull in his teeth.

Maybe it would be easier just to let the bear take her and be done with this.

But he does not turn.

Chapter 13 - Mining for Billions

Hard Rock Gruber walks past tier after tier of palletized drums, each filled with pulverized, high-grade nickel ore. The storeroom will be full soon. There's room for another twenty pallets or so, eighteen drums to the pallet. Then, time to ship!

Hard Rock turns to Casey Summerland, "All these counted, tagged, and on the inventory?"

Casey nods, "Yeah, Hard Rock, I have the whole list here. Each drum has a radio-frequency tag inside it as well as a bar code on the outside. We'll code them all in as they leave here and watch them on the internet as they move to the broker, then on to market. Can't beat technology for this kind of thing, eh? Even if part of the load gets left on a dock for awhile, we'll be able to figure out where it is."

Hard rock smiles, "Okay. And you better believe I want to know where each and every one is…all along the way."

He looks inquiringly at Summerland, "So, when do you figure we'll get these picked up?"

Summerland looks at his clipboard, "As soon as the ship refits for the cross-Pacific trip and the daylight gets shorter here. Looks like the third week of July or thereabouts. Once the ship is ready, we'll have a firm date."

Seeing Hard Rock squint skeptically at the shrinking free space in the storeroom, Casey continues soothingly, "We'll put any pallets that can't fit in here out along the adit starting by the entrance and working back. Shouldn't be a problem as I figure it, eh?"

Gruber glowers. You can't make money with ore in the mine. But then he smiles grimly. Casey's only doing what Hard Rock's ordered him to do--stick to the production plan.

"Okay," Hard Rock says, "But this shipment goes at the earliest moment or there'll be Hell to pay." He pats the .44 at his hip, whirls, and walks back towards the milling room to "help" the operators speed up production.

Summerland winces…and finishes his count.

Chapter 14 - Bear Floatin'

The bear has Mill's Mustang coat in his mouth, chewing it, while he rests and waits for her to surface. She can hear his breath bubble in the water as he chews.

Mill bobs quietly behind him...the cold fear of imminent death creeping into her soul. Why this...for her...now?

Mill's fear turns into anger. She can't let him get her! She has to drive him off...hurt him...somehow.

But she has nothing to work with—no gun, no spray.

Frustration turns her anger into rage. What to do?

A crazy idea comes into her mind. Like the little billy goat from months before, she could bull-dog this bear...scare him...hurt him enough to drive him away!

She rests for a moment, rehearsing mentally. Then, she grabs the bear's hairy flanks and, in one smooth motion, she throws herself forward onto his back and grabs his neck fur.

Instantly, the surprised bear roars and twists in the water, almost throwing her off.

Mill knows that male bears, or boars, like this one really have no enemies in the wild besides bigger bears. And this puny thing on his back? Well, that thing is just muscle to be ripped and bone to be crunched.

Not a threat, just dinner.

For her attack to work, Mill has to make herself bigger and badder than anything he has encountered in the wild before.

Now astride him behind his hump, she clumsily punches at his head one-handed, then gouges at his eyes.

The bear twists to meet Mill's attack with his teeth. But he has nothing but water under him. So, he simply thrashes and wallows.

As he bucks, she drops low and holds on. Her weight upsets his balance and forces his head under water.

He snaps his jaws...takes water down his throat and into his lungs. Struggling back to the surface, he coughs and gasps for air.

Mill smells his foul breath. Freeing a hand, she starts to gouge at his eyes again. Then she stops. What if he sinks his teeth into her hand...pulls her off his back and into the water...grabs her in his jaws?

She decides she has to keep the initiative...strike differently each time... strike hardest.

What to do next? Bite his ears! Savage with fear and adrenaline, Mill leans forward and bites his right ear through.

Bear blood spurts. He bawls loudly.

Mill spits out the smelly chunk. She leans forward and aims a bite at the other ear. Sensing her movement, he thrashes his head and twists, almost flinging her into the water.

She tightens her hands in his neck fur and grips him tighter with her knees. Forget the other ear.

Not knowing what else to do, she tries to throw him off balance so he can't twist and bite at her legs.

Bears are heavily weighted towards the shoulders and comparatively light in the flanks. When Mill pushes her weight forward, she drives his head down.

His nose sinks below the water again. Bubbles rise. He drives hard with his powerful front legs, forces his head up…gets some air.

Mill rides him down again. More bubbles.

Will shoving his head under take the fight out of him? Maybe as long as she doesn't tip them both all the way over! If the bear rolls over or dives, he can throw her off, grab her, and rip her.

But bears don't present their bellies willingly to an attacker. Mill has proven she can inflict pain. And the young bear is panicked by having his head shoved under the water. So the boar refuses to roll over and he won't dive.

Mill dunks him again. The bear starts to swim in circles. He wants firm ground under him to deal with the horror on his back.

Mill realizes she can't let him get ground under his feet…get his confidence back…attack her.

Frantic, Mill thrusts his head down, then again…over and over…able to hold him under a little longer each time. Minutes pass, then ten.

He gradually tires.

His legs slow.

His head drops, resistance gone.

He drowns.

Mill holds his head under until she is sure he is dead. Ready to let go, she realizes that her numb fingers are locked in his fur. She painfully forces her right hand open, one finger at a time. Then she uses her right hand to uncurl the fingers of her left.

Hands free, she notices that she can't feel her legs from the knee down, numb from the water.

Exhausted, Mill looks around. She's floating fifty feet or so from the alder-topped, pebbly shore.

Peering down the shallows, Mill locates her Mustang coat. Wind and circling currents have brought it close by. The coat bobs next to the pebbled beach, an orange patch in grey water a hundred feet away. Numb with cold but filled with intent to retrieve the coat and reach shore, Mill rolls off the bear.

She panics when her head goes under. Fighting back to the surface, she finds she can't lift her arms above her shoulders to swim. She can't flex her legs enough to kick. She begins a desperate dog-paddle, struggling through the water like a little child.

After minutes of thrashing, her bicycling feet touch the bank. With the last of her energy, Mill lifts herself out of the water and staggers up the slight slope. At the top, the cold glacier wind steals what little of her strength remains.

She drops to her knees, arms around her chest, her mind blank. Minutes or hours later, Mill becomes aware of kneeling somewhere down the shore in silt and pebbles, holding her float coat.

Then her mind wanders again, sliding towards eternal sleep. Urgently, she tells her arms to put on the coat...the coat...on. Slowly, painfully, her arms obey. The soggy garment slides around her shivering body.

She tries to close the zipper with stiff hands curved like claws.

No go.

In spite of being soaked, warmth starts to build under the coat, small but welcome warmth. Mill rolls down from her knees and sits, legs crossed. She wrap-tucks the coat around her and rests, head down on her arms, her face in the coat.

Warmth builds gradually. She drifts off.

Mill wakes herself with an effort. Where's Dill, the boat? How the Hell will he find her, stuck as she is off- river and out of sight?

She peers around. Fifty or so feet downstream, the full river flows once again against the bank she rests on. To be seen, she won't have to stagger back up the length of the rocky arm, just move a little further downriver.

She doesn't want to move…so tired. But she draws on some hidden reserve of will power, climbs to her feet, and moves five feet…ten…twenty.

Strength gone again, she flops down and huddles again within the float coat.

But what about Dill? The last she had seen of him he was headfirst down in the work boat. Was he alive? Or had the Copper taken his life as it might still take hers?

She could only hope he was alive and looking for her. Only one way to find out.

Each Forest Service float coat comes with survival gear. Mill fumbles for the small sky flares in the right pocket. Dragging the waterproof package out, she sees that the bear's teeth have mangled one, leaving five intact. She rips the package open with her teeth.

Fire one into the big, empty Copper sky! The little flare soars in a long, wind-bent curve. But the downriver wind whips its tiny smoke and fire away too soon.

Fire two! Same thing…nothing…no sign of Dill.

Fire three! Again nothing.

No, wait. A gunshot, another …then another.

Fire four! Mill hears a far-off, boat-horn blast, an obvious answer to her last flare. Then another horn blast, closer this time!

The Forest Service work boat rounds the end of the rocky arm, skirting the shallows. Dill stands at the steering station, hand on the throttle, eyes searching the pond. He drives the boat powerfully, his panic for Mill's life revealed in the large bow wave the hull throws up.

Then Dill sees her. He turns the boat sharply in her direction. Barely keeping his balance, he waves his arm in a big, arcing movement over his head.

Dill straightens the boat on its course, going even faster now, closing the distance between them rapidly. Soon Mill can see his wide grin.

She lies back on the gravel and curses her violently shaking limbs…her weak tears.

Chapter 15 - Hypothermia Home

Long-shadow dusk along the Copper's banks.

In the rushing river, small icebergs crunch and boulders grind, all tumbling downstream.

Cold rolls down from the wide ice fields above Mill and Dill.

Mill is finally warm. She lies huddled in a Land Shark emergency shelter, gratefully toasted by a small, smoky campfire Dill had made.

After landing the boat, Dill had opened the cumbersome Land Shark, basically a pup tent made out of strong space-blanket material. Then, with Dill's help, Mill stripped down to her long underwear, wrapped up in Dill's float coat, and slid shivering into the Land Shark.

Once he had Mill in the belly of the Shark, Dill built a quick "Boy Scout" fire using driftwood, gasoline from the boat's tank, and waterproof matches. Dill cursed his slow fingers as threw the fire makings together.

But once he lit the fire in a vapory blast, it brought them both instant warmth and a grateful smile to Mill's blue lips.

Now Mill has stopped shuddering, turned mostly pink, and quit saying vague, weird things.

Hypothermia kills far more Alaskans than bears do. Dill had been very worried that Mill, even after she escaped the water, was going to be the cold Copper's next victim.

He also knew that, if the shelter and fire hadn't worked, the next cure he had to try would have been to strip Mill down totally, disrobe himself, and roll them both up together in the Land Shark, warming her with his body heat until she recovered.

Dill would almost rather be grabbed by that bear than trying to live down cuddling mostly naked with his beautiful girl boss.

Sure, he might have had a great couple of hours. And yes, he could have justified his hands going places they shouldn't.

But when his buddies heard about it or his *wife*…or when he next saw Mill. Just the thought of the teasing and embarrassment made him cringe.

Sitting by the successful campfire, Dill's cheeks glow bright red at the thoughts. Yes, Dill is very relieved when Mill's lips turn pink, she stops shuddering every few minutes, and her teeth chatter less and less often.

Then there is Mill's crazy bear story.

At first, Dill told her he thought it was a hallucination, something the cold creeping into her body brought on. Through chattering teeth, she defied his skepticism.

Now that she has warmed up, Dill says to her, "Mill, I'm not saying the bear didn't charge you. I saw that. But chase you down the river, across it? Just doesn't seem right. I mean that was a big bear or seemed so when he charged. As bad as it seems for me to say, I figure if he wanted you, he would've got you."

Mill teeth chatter out her words, "Damn it, D-Dill, I'm telling you wh-what I did, not what I d-dreamed. It's th-this s-simple. That son-of-a-sow wanted m-me for dinner. I d-drowned him instead."

Mill stares at Dill a little indignantly, "Okay, I know th-this sounds like a r-really w-wild story. You don't ha-have to believe me. And the b-bear m-may have sunk already-y, but at l-least we can go l-look before we l-leave."

Dill tries to sooth her, "Okay, okay, we'll go look for the bear before we go. Nothing like a dead bear to prove your story."

After another ten minutes by the fire, Mill recovers enough to go. She shrugs off the Land Shark and stands up on shaky legs.

Dill had set her coat and clothes near the fire and they're damply dry now, reeking of smoke and gasoline. Every muscle protesting, she shoves her limbs into them, setting off another round of shakes.

She climbs stiffly into the boat and flops on the bench, exhausted once more.

Dill throws a baling bucket of water on the fire and loads everything. Untying the boat, he pushes off and starts the motor.

Mill tells Dill to drive around in a slow spiral starting from the center of the pond. Using the boat's bright spotlight, they eventually find the bear's carcass floating just below the surface near the pond's upriver end. Dangling bear legs seem to have caught on the shallower rocks there.

Dill asks, "Mill, hand me that boat hook, will you? We have to secure this bear." Mill passes the hook his way.

Dipping down, Dill snags the bear's head and pulls it to the surface. He sees the bitten ear.

Dill looks thoughtfully at Mill, "So remind me never to let you near my ears. And, if I ever say, 'Don't bite my head off,' I mean that literally. Okay?"

Mill laughs a little at his craziness. His weak humor helps get her mind off the awful, nauseating feeling that had come over her when she saw the dead bear--the fear, cold, panic, the long struggle, a horror far too fresh for her to joke about. But she is glad Dill now understands some of what she had gone through, and more, that he now knows her story is true.

Alaska Game and Fish officers would want to retrieve the bear for study and evaluation. Dill ties a line around the bear's neck. Then he ties a boat fender to one end of the line to serve as a buoy-marker. He ties the other end of the line to the work-boat's spare anchor. Tugging the bear as close to the shore as he can, Dill drops the anchor down to hold the carcass in place.

Game and Fish would never find the soggy body without the fender-buoy; the anchor would make sure it didn't drift away and down the river.

Dill also takes pictures of the heavy, hairy mass. He takes close ups of the bitten ear.

Although the pictures would make Mill famous in some circles, Dill wants to document the kill while it's fresh for other reasons. Every human-caused bear death in Alaska has to be reported. Dill's report would be a doozey. No one would believe it without the photos. And, even with the photos, many people would call it bogus.

And who knew what condition the body would be in when Game and Fish got out here? Without the photos, no matter what the two of them said, they might not accept that Mill had killed the bear "in defense of life or property" as Alaska law said she could.

Dill shrugs under his Mustang coat. What the State did was nothing he could do anything about.

He releases the dead bear. The soggy body slumps under the water, dropping almost out of sight. Only the fender-buoy remains visible. Dill turns the boat away and motors towards the rushing main stem of the Copper.

Past time to head home.

Mill's teeth have begun to chatter a little again. She huddles within her damp float coat warm and tight around her.

With a quirky grin on his face, Dill says, "Oh well, all in a day's work along the Copper, boss. You know, back when, one of us used to drown a brown bear at least once a month! Sometimes, we'd grab an eagle and live-pluck it!"

Mill laughs wearily at Dill's craziness, "Yeah, a regular day on the Copper alright. I'll be ready to dunk another bear next month. I don't know about that eagle thing though…symbol of freedom and all that. Doesn't seem right."

Laughing, Dill is glad that Mill has her sense of humor back. Dill pulls back the throttle and drives the boat faster into the dusk.

As they run out into the Copper, he yells to Mill, "Point the spotlight at the water ahead."

Mill waves and picks up the spotlight. She turns its bright beam on the grey-dark river ahead. Ever so tired, she still knows she must add her eyes to his. Just a glimpse of something in the water might mean the difference between getting home safely or having a hole punched in the hull and both of them dying.

After what Mill has been through today, she doesn't want any more adventure or drama. So, she ties the hood of the Mustang coat tightly around her head and squints into the cold wind.

After a few moments, cold river spray and tears run back from her eyes. The water turns warm again when it seeps under her hood and reaches her ears.

The boat pounds the river hard.

Thankfully, the trip to the landing turns out to be uneventful and less than an hour long.

Idling back at the take-out, Dill steers the boat towards the ramp. There, a dozen vehicles sit with bright headlights pointed out over the Copper. From a hundred feet out on the water, the lights remind Mill of an airport runway…of a welcoming for weary travelers.

Mill wonders to herself, "Why the headlights? Is there some kind of party going on? Is the Copper River fishing fleet in for supplies?" She turns to question Dill, but he is busy driving the boat.

Just before they touch land, Mill realizes that Dill's radio has kept everyone informed about her loss and rescue. Of course! Those lights aren't for the fleet. The ranger district folks are here to meet the work boat.

She hadn't figured on anyone being here.

How awkward!

The keel grates on gravel. People rush forward.

Percy and Carrie take Mill's arms as she struggles clumsily to climb over the gunnel.

Carrie has tears of relief in her eyes. Mill cries, too.

After damp hugs, Mill's colleagues see she can stand alone and they let her go.

Mill starts to walk stiffly towards her Forest Service rig.

But, before she takes ten steps, a large group of employees and their family members descends on her. They welcome her with warm blankets, hugs, and pats.

Then, best of all, Carrie hands Mill a flask. Mill takes a couple of big slugs of what proves to be sweet, homemade blueberry brandy.

Warmth starts in her tummy and radiates out to her arms and legs. The cold-hiccupy feeling in her chest disappears.

Mill is suddenly happy. She smiles at Carrie, "Nice. Great reception. But what happened is no big deal...really." She raises her voice and tries to say that to the others, too. A hubbub of kindly protest washes over Mill.

Finally, motherly Molly Sanders raises her hands to shush the others, "Mill, dear, we're so glad you are home, safe. You see we've lost too many friends and family to the Copper. Please let us tally this one salvation against a long list of injuries and deaths." Molly hugs Mill against her ample chest and asks, "Please?"

Realization strikes her. They're celebrating her successful return to soften cruel, cutting memories of loss.

She whispers into Molly's ear, "Okay, thanks, for caring...for everything." Molly gives her one last squeeze and lets her go with a teary smile.

Surrounded by well-wishers, Mill begins to dread the attention that might come from other sources. However brief it might be, the notoriety will be more than she wants.

What if someone from her Anchorage life, one of people she had done drugs with or screwed, saw her...remembered her...even contacted her?

Mill shudders, this time, not from the cold.

Mill says a little wistfully, "Can we at least keep all this out of the papers? I mean...."

The assembled group laughs. Too late. Everybody in Cordova knows already. Soon the news services will track Mill down.

Mill begins to think a trifle more fondly of the bear. At least he would just have killed her before devouring her.

Not so, the media and the gossips. Well, she can always say, "No comment," and hope that works.

By now, Dill has warmed up their SUV and waits behind the wheel. He honks the horn and yells, "Hey Mill, stop partying. Let's go."

Mill jumps in, glad to be out of the spotlight.

Dill spins wheels up the hill to the highway and heads for Cordova's nice little clinic.

Any Forest Service employee with hypothermia has to be checked there before going home.

Mill doesn't care. She is asleep before they travel a mile, a slight frown on her lips.

Chapter 16 -- The Great Land Geo-Challenge

Two days after her struggle in the Copper, Mill gets back to her cubie. She edges into the crowded space.

In the middle of the muddle on her desk, sits a large, fuzzy, brown-bear toy. Her eyes widen with surprise.

The cross-eyed bruin wears a little float coat and swim fins. It also holds a sign, crafted in beautiful script, which says, "Next time, Baby!"

At first taken aback by the message, Mill goggles at the bear. Then her wonderful laugh rings out.

Mill yells, "You guys are too much. This is great."

She laughs again, stronger and louder this time. Infected by the sound, nearby employees jump up and come over to look at the not-so-kind-but-clever joke.

Mill knows this is the way Alaskans mock the things they fear. In this case, the target of their humor is the very real threat of wildlife attacks in the field--mainly bears, moose, and sea lions--but also smaller creatures like wolverines, foxes, and coyotes, too.

Mill appreciates the grim humor, "You know this is better than flowers and cards. Who made this? It's really well done."

Indeed, the finely made, puffy, orange, float coat fits the bear perfectly. The little sign in the bear's paws looks like something printed on a press.

Carrie laughs, "Well, Mill, I have to confess. I got the bear and made the float coat. Percy's wife does calligraphy. She nailed the sign. Somebody at church had the fins from years ago when their toddler was doing swim classes."

Carrie looks a little worried and lowers her voice, "Mill, you're being a good sport about this. I mean, this kind of thing might remind you too much...well...you know."

Mill hugs Carrie close. She whispers close to her ear, "You did just the right thing. Thank you. I'll look at this bear every day. It'll help get the whole thing behind me."

Mill releases Carrie. She glows with Mill's praise but a little embarrassed by it, too.

To break the tension, Carrie yells, "Okay! Bring on the donuts!" Some of the staff cheer as a big, flat box of donuts appears in Dill's hands.

He carries them to the staff's little meeting space at the center of the cubies. People grab coffee and tea. They drift in to select a donut.

Mill starts to make her donut selection but Dill stops her.

"This is for you," he says, offering her a large cupcake decorated with white frosting. Across the center is a fuzzy arch made of what appears to be brown-dyed coconut.

At first, Mill can't figure out what the coconut arch is supposed to be. Then she realizes it's a crude attempt at a bear's furry ear!

Good Lord! She grimaces and groans inside. Her stomach turns over with the memory of the grainy, smelly ear she had bitten three days before.

What could Dill be thinking?

She gets a grip on her emotions and rounds on Dill.

Mill scowls at him, "Dammit, Dill, I've talked to you about this before. I like my bear ear raw, not cooked!"

She holds the scowl as long as she can, then her laugh peals out again. Her eyes almost disappear in her grin.

Dill tries to look abashed. But he, too, can't stop his grin. Then his face gets serious.

He shakes his head, "Boy, did you ever scare me. I've been in some tough situations before, but yours tops them all."

Dill's voice begins to shake a little. "When I got up from the bottom of the boat, I couldn't see you anywhere. I thought you were a goner. I didn't know where to look...or even...if you were alive."

His voice takes on a despairing tone, "I drove the boat back to the last place I saw you. By the time I got there, you and the bear must have been pretty far down the river. It's a big river. I never saw you or the bear on the way. I checked to see if he'd...uh...dragged you off the beach, but nothing."

Dill doesn't mention that, once ashore, he looked carefully for a blood trail...Mill's blood. He expected to find her body covered with soil and branches and left until it turned ripe enough to eat.

He had walked into the dense brush scared spitless, senses cranked to the highest pitch, moving with care but with no hesitation. Foot by quiet foot.

In the end, grateful that he found nothing.

Dill lives by Alaska bush code: you don't leave people behind to be bear food...even if it cost you your own life.

Dill draws a ragged breath, "After I walked the stream, I got in the boat and ran down the Copper a couple of miles. Then I'd go back up. First I searched the west bank and then the east, hoping you'd gotten into the Copper and made it to shore. Finally I saw a couple of your flares. That was a good sight…"

Dill finishes with an understatement, typical for the quiet backwoodsman.

Mill puts down her coffee and the cupcake. She hugs Dill warmly, careful to not get too close or hold on too long. She doesn't want a whiff of scandal to contaminate their work relationship.

Letting go, she holds him at arm's length and looks him in the eye, "Dill Dillard, I owe my life to you. If you hadn't found me when you did, I would have died. I didn't have the energy to get a fire started or open up that crazy Land Shark. So, thanks for looking for me but double thanks for *finding* me."

Embarrassed, Dill blushes red under his wind-burn and tan. "All in day's work, Mill. All in a day's work…," he murmurs.

The employees laugh. After a few more questions and back pats, the group breaks up. Talking about close calls they'd had or heard of, they head back to their work.

When Mill gets back to her cubie, she looks at Dill's bear's-ear cupcake, shudders, and drops it in the trash. She takes a piece of scrap paper and carefully covers the discarded treat.

Mill doesn't want to offend the man who saved her life by leaving it visible. But, sweet-treat coconut or not, she can't stand the idea of biting another hairy, grainy bear's ear.

Ever again.

After her cubie-mates walk away, chow hounds from other parts of the building zoom in to grab the last donuts. With mouths full, most stop at Mill's cubie to mumble, "Nice to see you back safe, Mill" and things like that before they scurry back to other floors.

Mill hopes that once the food is cleaned up, people will put the whole Mill-drowns-bear incident behind them.

———————————————//———————————————

The doctor at Cordova's clinic had told her the effects of the hypothermia might last for a few days, perhaps a week.

When Percy first sees her back in the office, he comes right over, "Meacham, I talked to the clinic. I want you to work half days until you get back to normal."

Mill begins to protest, "Percy, I just have so much to do, and…."

Percy raises a hand, "You heard me. Rest now to do well later. It's an order, Mill."

"Okay, Percy," she says, "I'll knock off early."

Knowing how hard Mill drives herself, Percy gives her his "ranger warning look" and walks away, repeating, "Half days, Mill for the rest of the week at least."

But there's all this work…. Mill figures if she hides from Percy in her cubie, he will never know if she quit work at noon or not. So, she works through the morning, eats at her desk, and lays low at the start of the afternoon.

At two though Mill hits the wall, energy gone. She realizes that she is glad of Percy's support and doesn't want to lose it. She really can quit early and not feel bad about it.

About the time she starts filling her backpack to head home, her desk phone rings. She picks up the handset.

Before she can say, "Hello," her father's voice booms out of the earpiece. "Milly," he yells, "It's your Dad!"

"Who else could it be?" Mill thinks to herself. "Who'd ever start a conversation without even knowing who was on the other end?"

"Hey, Dad," she replies, "What can I do for you?"

W.A. Meacham had called and talked to her while she was in the clinic. His main point then was how her narrow escape and heroism had been a reflection of his influence on her life. About how she was spawn of another great outdoorsman.

Used to his ego and craziness, Mill dealt with him using her long-time approach, "Un-huh…yeah…sure…you're right…you bet."

Now, in answer to her question, W.A. hollers, "Milly, it's not what you can do for me. It's what I can do for you."

Instantly wary, Mill asks him, "Well, what do you have in mind?" She goes on a little insincerely, "I can always use help…."

W.A. laughs, "Yes, and you need more help than most!"

Mill winces as W.A. tries to take the sting out of his words, "You know what I mean, Milly. I know you're all grown up now, and in-de-pen-dant and all. But I can still do a favor for you now and then, can't I?"

64

Mill thinks for a moment, letting his question dangle a little. "Well," she hesitates, thinking of some social disasters he had created for her in the past, "I guess it depends on the favor...."

"Okay," W.A. replies, "Hear me out. Some guys have approached the Forest Service in Washington, DC...some of those hippy-dippy Hollywood types. Only these are guys in suits...big money TV producers. The Chief's Office asked me to work with them, to serve as Forest Service lead."

Mill realizes this fits with her Dad's work. W.A. presently serves as a Deputy Regional Forester in Ogden, Utah. Part of his job is the recreation program across that vast region.

Mill catches up with his rambling monologue, "....they want to film an adventure series on public land. Big budget. People running all over everywhere, climbing shit, rafting...whatever. Kinda like the Olympics, I guess. You with me so far, Milly?"

Slightly bewildered by her Dad's careening barrage of words, Mill says, "Yeah, I think so. They want to do a show based on outdoor sports, some kind of competition. That right?"

W.A. yells back, "Yeah, yeah, you got the picture. Anyway, first they wanted to tape the whole thing here in the lower-48. But when they found out how many jurisdictions they'd have to work with--us feds, the states, locals, and private land--they thought better of it. There's a whole buncha other shit, but my big point is that they decided to take their action to Alaska. Up there's where there're really big blocks of federal ownership. That way, they'll only have to deal with a few of us feds and they can get their whole business done a lot faster and maybe a lot cheaper, too. You still with me?"

Mill starts to feel a little worried. She doesn't want her big summer work program interrupted if possible.

"Yeah, I'm with you, Dad, they've decided to come to Alaska. But what does this have to do with me? Are they coming to the Cordova Ranger District or the Chugach National Forest?"

"No, no, Milly," he says, "Not there. They haven't picked locations or anything yet. But they *are* coming to Alaska. They've named the whole shitteree, 'The Great Land Geo-Challenge.' What do you think of that flower-fairy name?"

W.A. pauses, slightly out of breath. Then, before Mill can answer or ask a question, he starts again, "The Fish and Wildlife Service didn't want them on the refuges...doesn't support their agency mission or some crap…so the Service's stepping back. They'll let the BLM handle any details for the refuges, but they don't want people there if possible."

"The producers don't want to get separate permits for each agency one-by-one. So, the Parkies, the BLooMers, and the Forest Circus are forming a team to get the producers through one permit as fast as possible. But you don't need to worry about that paperwork crap. Your Regional Office in Juneau will handle that."

Mill breathes a sigh of relief, "No paperwork. Okay to that."

She almost misses what W.A. says next, "But the Forest Service will need a field person, somebody working in the field with the people doin' the real work…filming…whatever. And, you being a bonny-fiddle hero and bear killer, I put your name down for that job! The Chief loved the idea. So, what do you think of your old man now?"

Mill is struck temporarily speechless. Getting thrust into the media spotlight!

She starts to sputter and tell him, "I can't. Too much work!"

Instead, her Legacy Dad, convinced that this will add luster to both their careers, yells, "You don't have to thank me now. Do it later!"

With that, W.A. Meacham slams down his phone, convinced his daughter's gratitude has struck her dumb.

What a bunch of bullshit! At first Mill wants to call him and throw the whole mess back in his face.

But she is so tired and it's time for her to go home. She hasn't the energy to scrap with anyone, let alone her relentless father.

She picks up her backpack and heads out to her truck.

Mill figures she will take the hot bath the emergency room nurse recommended as good therapy for hypothermia recovery. And once floating in hot bubbled water, she will figure out how to get out of the crazy Great Land Geo-Challenge assignment.

She climbs into her pickup, heart sinking. The bother aside, what if someone does a background check on her and finds out about Wild Girl and Anchorage, about everything? This is much worse than hand-drowning a bear.

Chapter 17 - No Way...Well, Okay

Chick Sorenson stares angrily at Corporal Thaddeus "Tad" Craven of the Alaska State Police, Game and Fish Enforcement Division. Chick knows that every word oozing out of Craven's fat, red face is wrong, deceitful.

Chick fumes inside, "What a stupid fucker this clown is...! No wonder even his buddies call him 'Toad' behind his back."

Beneath the table, Chick's hands ball into fists, "What a freakin' mess. Toad's got his hooks into Mill and Dill. Nothing's more of a target for these idiots than a couple-a feds. And Toad will make the Alaska Rights Committee so happy. He is probably already talking to them about the best way to smear Mill and Dill in the press."

Craven smiles as he addresses Chick, Dill, Percy, and Mill who are seated across from him at a small conference table at ASP's Cordova office.

Mitch Mendenhall, a Forest Service attorney in Juneau, is a part of the meeting too, connected by phone.

Craven's oily voice oozes over them as he summarizes, "So, I've reached a conclusion after extensive interviews and a thorough necropsy of the bear's remains. Ms. Meacham, I can only conclude that you maliciously and illegally killed a 3-year-old Alaskan brown bear without a license. Furthermore, I conclude that you and Mr. Dillard attempted to conceal your crime by concocting a fairy tale about you drowning the animal."

Stoic on the outside, Chick winces inside. Poorly trained and poorly led, ASP's "fish cops" come as close to an Alaska-sponsored Gestapo as Chick can imagine.

But Chick can say nothing, at least in this meeting. This is because employees of the Alaska Department of Game and Fish where he works pretty much roll over for almost everything the fish cops say and do. They have to, both professionally and personally.

Chick can't write citations against violators himself. If he crosses the fish cops and later needs enforcement help on the job, the lazy jerks would stay in the office or look the other way in the field. So, there would be less enforcement of the state game and fish laws that protect the very species Chick works with and cares about.

Closer to home, Chick doesn't want the fish cops coming after him or his extended family.

Unlike urbanized lower-48 folks, most people in Alaska depend partially or even fully on wild foods to live. Chick knows that the state's game and fish laws are a mish-mash, open to interpretation by fish cops in the field. Innocent people are often cited, dragged before courts, and wrongly convicted.

And Chick knows that the fish cops have no problem filing phony charges–charges that cost bush Alaskans scarce dollars to fight. Bottom line: if you depend on wild foods to live, as Chick's extended Eyak family does, you might find your family broke or starving if you crossed the fish cops.

Making today's matters worse, Chick knows that fish cops like Toad are a part of an unofficial group of Alaska politicians and bureaucrats called the "Alaska Rights Committee."

Their high-sounding name is quite misleading. They're not about anybody's "rights." The group maneuvers to get federal land, money, and resources transferred into state ownership or, better yet, into private hands.

He knows ARC to be a pack of political thugs, out to take care of their cronies and make themselves rich. ARC members couldn't care less about average Alaskans like Chick or his family. If ARC wanted to ruin Chick's family and friends financially, ARC would have no problem doing it.

With a contemptuous flourish, Craven tosses paperwork in front of Dill and Mill, "I am citing you under Alaska Statute, Title 16, Section 5, for these violations. I warn you your crimes are punishable by fines up to $10,000, incarceration for a year in the state penitentiary, and loss of hunting privileges for life here and in all other 34 compact states. You will sign these citations today so our prosecutor may later file them with the court."

Percy, Mill, and Dill sit looking at Craven, stunned. Before any of them can move to pick up the papers, the attorney in Juneau speaks in a firm voice, "Ms. Meacham and Mr. Dillard have nothing more to say to you, Corporal Craven. Our cooperation with ASP on this matter ends today. No one will be signing any citations or other paperwork. I'll be letting your Deputy Attorney General know that the Department of Justice will likely move to quash the citations sometime in the next two weeks."

"Fat chance of that," a scowling Craven mutters just loud enough for the group to hear.

At this interruption, Mendenhall's voice changes, "Forest Service folks, you should leave now. Don't speak again about this matter with Officer Craven or any representative of the State of Alaska."

Percy, Mill, and Dill gather their materials and solemnly file out.

Chick Sorenson stays behind, madder than Hell but more cautious than ever about offending Toad Craven, "Tad, I understand that you want to cite Meacham and Dillard, but I guess I'm not clear on the necropsy. I thought the bear had been worked on by fish and otters or something to the point where cause of death wasn't clear. How do you figure Mill killed the bear illegally when you have no evidence of it?"

Craven face grows an angrier red, "What the fuck, Chick, you siding with those damn Freddies now? Are you trying to get into Meacham's pants or something?"

Chick thinks for a moment that word has somehow gotten around his interest in Mill. Who could have guessed what was on his mind when he could barely get out a full sentence in her presence?

But then he realizes that Toad's just blowing off steam, probably expressing his own fantasy. Was that what this fiasco is about? Did Toad plan to use this to force himself on Mill? Chick wouldn't put it past him.

Chick raises a placating hand, "No, no, not that, Tad. Looks like we're going to have to take on the federal government over this. So, don't we want the strongest case we can get?"

Toad glares at him contemptuously, "Look, Chick. Just the leave the police work and politics up to me."

Toad sees Chick's face cloud with anger at being patronized. He realizes he will need Chick's cooperation down the road.

Toad says grudgingly, "Okay, here's the case in a nutshell. Meacham admits to killing the bear. Dillard admits to helping her. That's in their statements. Statute says they are required to do two things: report the killing to us and secure the bear's carcass for our investigation."

"True, they reported the next day. But the remains were not secured in a way that allowed us to investigate. They submitted photos, but what does that show? Just a dead bear with a gnawed ear. Could have gotten that in a fight with another bear. Happens all the time."

Toad scowls, "Dillard's an old Alaska hand. I figure he knew that if he left the bear in the water, it would get messed with…even eaten…fast. It did. When we got out there after two days, very little soft tissue was intact. So, by leaving it in the water, he covered up Meacham's kill. They could've dragged the bear to shore and covered it with the tarp or, better, a space blanket to help keep scavengers off. Then we would've had a better idea of how the bear died."

Chick stares at Toad for a moment. Then he asks, "So, you're saying the lack of evidence means they're guilty? Or maybe, even though they secured the carcass with a buoy, it wasn't enough?"

Toad nods, "Yeah, that's right."

Chick frowns, "But wasn't Meacham hypothermic? Didn't Dillard need to get her to town as quick as possible?"

Toad waves his hand dismissively, "Shit, Chick, anybody can fake hypothermia. Besides, according to both of them, Meacham recovered before they went out to find the bear. So, where's the hypothermia now, huh? Gone! Probably never was."

"And," Toad says leaning forward conspiratorially, "I know how Meacham killed the bear! It wasn't drowning. No 125-pound woman can drown a 400-pound brown bear."

Toad spits his contempt for the idea, "That's bullshit. No, the .375 had been fired. Dillard told us that. I figure Meacham killed the bear with the rifle. Hit it in soft tissue like the throat. Sure, the necropsy showed no trauma to the bony structures. But there're lots of places you can shoot a bear without hitting bone and still kill it. Dillard told us about firing three signal shots, but he told us that just to cover up."

Toad slams the table with his fist, "We've got these two Freddie fuckers. We're gonna nail their hides to the wannagin door."

Chick covers his feelings with a grim smile, "Okay. I guess you're right, Tad. We've got a solid case alright."

Chick points at the wall clock, "Look, I've got to go. If you need any help from me, just give me a call."

Craven climbs to his feet and shakes Chick's reluctant hand across the table, "Nice having you on the team, Chick."

Chick walks nonchalantly out of the ASP office and onto the street. His casual pace masks profound inner turmoil.

Chick can see that Tad is manufacturing another ridiculous case against innocent people. What a farce! Why would Mill and Dill have even reported the bear if they had killed it illegally? Why not just let it sink to the Copper's bottom or push it out into the river and be done with it?

Toad has no case. And yet, he is going to make the two Forest Service people's lives miserable just because he can do it. Maybe destroy their careers. Or even put them in jail!

My God, what craziness. Chick clenches his fists again. He has to do something...anything.

But Chick can do nothing. The cost to him, his family, or many of his Eyak people, could easily be too high.

No, not even for Mill.

She wasn't Eyak.

Wasn't family.

_____//_____

The next morning, Mitch Mendenhall's comes tinnily out of Percy's speaker phone, "Okay, so here's what I know. The U.S. Attorney's office in Anchorage has tentatively decided to defend you against the state's charges, even though the state asserts that you acted as individuals, not federal employees. They think that the case seems to be more about anger towards the federal government than it does about evidence of a crime. All to your good."

"But, the USA's agreement to defend you comes with one stipulation. If evidence turns up that you actually did kill the bear illegally, he will drop you, and this is a quote, 'like a hot rock.'"

Good news and bad news all in one summation. Mill and Dill stare numbly at the phone.

"So, Mitch," Percy asks, "What should these guys do? I mean, the state wants to drag them in front of a judge for some reason. How can they be expected to deal with evidence the state puts together from sea foam and bullshit?"

"Well," Mitch replies, "First, I'd advise you both to get your own attorneys. Get separate attorneys because the state could decide to call you to serve as witnesses against each other. Just better to get your own."

"Second, I'm recommending that Forest Service Law Enforcement gets involved. I want someone from out of state to review the evidence at a minimum...maybe do some field work. Our Alaska Region LEOs carry Alaska State Commissions so they can enforce Alaska laws like the fish cops do. They also work closely with the fish cops on a lot of cases. They're good guys but they might not take as close a look as I'd like or be able to ignore their friendships with state employees. So, to keep everything above board, I'll ask for an investigator from the lower-48. That okay with you three?"

Mill and Dill nod.

Percy says, "Sure looks like we have agreement here, Mitch. Let's do it. Will you let us know, hopefully soon, about the LEOs getting involved? I'd like to get office space cleared for them as soon as you know they're coming. And Mill and Dill will have to schedule time to meet with them."

"Sure, Percy," Mitch answers, "Look, I have to go, but…look….keep the faith. We'll get you through this." They end the call.

All three Forest Service people in Cordova let out sighs of relief. Dill says, "Boy, I feel a little better…but only a little. I guess we have to get us each an attorney."

Mill smiles grimly, "Yeah, time to pull out the 'ol check book and start writing. I called Jerry Spencer yesterday. He wants a $5,000 retainer before anything happens." Jerry Spencer is a Cordova attorney who gets a lot of business from fish-cop citations.

Mill finishes her thought, "I guess we could also get somebody up in Anchorage…."

The three of them kick several attorney names around. Then, frustrated by their situation, the need to wait, and the high costs that face them, they agree to end the meeting now but check in again in a few days.

As Mill starts to leave, Percy asks, "Mill, how about hanging around for a minute? I have a couple of other things to discuss."

Mill stops moving towards the door and looks attentive.

Percy says, "Dill, close the door on the way out, will you? Nothing big here but nothing the office gossips need to hear about either."

Dill softly closes the door as he leaves. He is a little worried that Percy is going to dress Mill down for the nearly disastrous field trip.

Percy waves Mill back to her chair, "This will take a couple of minutes. So, please sit back down."

Now a little nervous, Mill takes her previous chair.

"Okay," Percy begins, "This is about mandatory drug testing."

Mill's heart almost stops. Had someone told Percy about what she does in Anchorage…the dope, the Ecstasy? Had someone seen her…filed a complaint or something? Called Percy?

Mill can see nothing on the ranger's face that might signal concern about her behavior. She catches up with his comments, "....You probably don't remember this from when you signed up with the SCEP program. You signed an agreement back then. It's still in force now that you're a regular employee. Because you carry a rifle in the field and drive Forest Service vehicles, you're subject to random drug testing."

Percy stops and smiles encouragingly, "I know this comes on top of the state making problems for you. That's why I'm delivering this notice in person."

He hands Mill an official form, "You've got two days to get down to the clinic and pee in a cup."

Seeing the suddenly scared look on Mill's face, Percy says, "Easy as pie. I've done it myself a couple of times."

When Mill's look doesn't change, the shrewd ranger asks, "Is there something you and I should be worried about, Mill?"

Not wanting any trouble with her boss and certainly not wanting to talk about Anchorage, Mill smiles tightly and lies, "No, no, Percy. It's just, coming on the heels of all this state crap, I flashed on the idea that this drug test is connected somehow."

"Can't see how it could be," Percy replies, looking less worried. Mill fakes a relieved look.

Percy smiles at Mill to reassure her, "Okay, can we move on?" Mill nods. She is trying to keep her expressions confident and focused on him.

Inside, her mind whirls with anxiety. How the Hell will she deal with this *drug* test? She knows traces of dope and E can stay in her body for several weeks. Damn, another big problem to worry about.

And what would shitheel Corporal Craven do if she got a dirty drug test. Wouldn't Toad just crucify her even more?

And her big, important Legacy Dad, so high up in the Forest Service. He'd be furious.

Milly-cidal even.

Distracted, she almost misses the topic of the ranger's next comments.

"I got a call from the Deputy Regional Forester for Natural Resources in Juneau," he says, "She's asking for you to help them out with something they're calling the 'Great Land Geo-Challenge.' What a mouthful. They wanted you because of this bear thing, I think. I don't know much about it but it seems to be some kind of race."

73

He beams at Mill who, thanks to her Dad, knows what's coming, "I know that it's a lot to ask coming on top of all your field work and the state's case against you. But, the DRF said you were the one. The actual field work doesn't take place until August or just before. But there's some meetings and special training for the agency people involved. It'll take some time, a lot of it in Fairbanks where the agencies will have their command center."

Percy gives Mill a few moments to digest what he has said. "Look, Mill. I know you're worried about getting your projects done before fall. But the Deputy offered to send other district folks from around Alaska for that. You get everything ready and they'll get the work done while you're gone. And wouldn't it also be nice to get away from the Cordova fish cops for awhile?"

Considering the ranger's sales pitch, Mill looks a little less dubious. Percy takes her change in expression as an encouraging sign, "And Mill, I've just thought of another small bonus. You'll have to get up to Fairbanks starting Monday for the first meeting. Because you'll be temporarily reassigned out of the field for the summer, I'll send the drug-test notice back and tell them to check you later when you get back. That'll save you some time and trouble. How's it look to you now?"

Small bonus? No, a way-big bonus!

Curse her father…bless her father!

Mill fights to keep a grin off her face. "Okay," Mill says, "You're right, Percy. It'll do me good to get away for awhile. I'll do it."

Relief blooms inside her.

Panic subsides.

Then, ironically, the old darkness inside her wakes…tugs at her…pulls hard.

Chapter 18 - On the Alsek

Hard Rock Gruber watches through night-vision goggles as crews place the last pallets of concentrated nickel ore into the big, flat-bottomed landing craft. The heavy loads strain robot arms and landing-craft limits.

An unbalanced or shifting load could easily spell disaster in the shallow, tumbling waters of the Alsek or in the wild, wind-tossed, ship-side waters off the coast.

The crews move quietly, carefully.

Gruber nods as the last landing craft completes its load. Ponderous under the weight, the boat casts off and motors up to join the other landing craft moving slowly downriver.

Hard Rock's plan for Alsek Blue Billions has finally come to full flower. After a lifetime of chasing prospects and dodging cops, Hard Rock is on the verge of becoming a millionaire. And if he can keep operating long enough, he might even see a billion tax-free dollars out of the mine's unexpectedly rich ore. Live in Dubai with a harem.

After all, no one knows he is here, mining in an American national park. And no one will be able to track the money because Hard Rock has a hand-shake contract with a trusted minerals broker in Malaysia.

The broker will mix Gruber's nickel into bigger shipments from legitimate mines and sell everything into the lucrative China market. No origin certificates or paperwork needed. Cash on delivery for both Gruber and Si Tan Du.

This first shipment should pay for Hard Rock's investment here. After that, everything is gravy, at least a couple million for each shipment.

August is almost here. This first shipment has moved out well. Another should go as soon as the freighter can unload in Indonesia and get back in a couple of weeks.

Hard Rock looks forward to getting those two shipments delivered. Once the ore is in Chinese hands and payments received, he will pick up production even more and send another shipment.

He'll have to slow down some later. Winter storms will likely drive his small freighter into port. Shipping will only begin again when the storms abate, perhaps as late as April or May of next year.

Hard Rock pats the gun on his hip. He will get the job done…come high water or Hell.

He turns and walks back towards the high, jumbled pile of boulders that, along with a camouflage net over the mouth, conceals the mine's entrance.

A small table rests among the boulders, lit by a kerosene lantern. Casey Summerland looks up from his chair as Hard Rock approaches, a steaming pot of coffee near his elbow and platters of food laid out.

Hard Rock sits down across from Casey and digs in. No food ever tasted better to him than pancakes, ham, and eggs served hot in front of Alsek Blue Billions.

"Satisfied, boss?" asks Casey.

His mouth full of ham, Hard Rock mumbles, "Couldn't be topped, Case. When we get back inside, get a message off to Du that the shipment's on its way."

Casey smiles, "Already done. I sent the e-mail as soon as the last boat pulled out...encrypted like you wanted."

"Good man, Casey, good man," replies Gruber, tipping up his coffee mug and taking a deep swallow, "Gets no better than this."

He waves his hand around the wild, rocky landscape, "Wonder what the poor folks are doing to keep themselves happy?"

Both men laugh.

They munch for awhile more. Then Summerland clears the breakfast things into a tub, packs up the portable table and folding chairs, and takes everything back into the mine entrance.

Time for Summerland to get back to work checking operations, making sure generators got refueled properly, and looking in on a sick driller.

Hard Rock lingers on the surface for a few minutes, enjoying the wind and a rare view of the sun rising in a deep-blue sky. Then he, too, feels the call of work and heads for the adit.

Just as he reaches the mine mouth, Gruber hears the thrumming sound of a diesel boat on the Alsek, coming his way. He walks towards the river bank, steps behind a large rock, and watches as a boat pulls up to the shore.

Two men climb out and walk almost directly towards him.

Gruber pulls the Ruger Redhawk from his holster. He rests the revolver on the rock and takes aim, prepared to shoot if the two come close enough to see him.

Instead, the two men stop just above the Alsek's high-water mark, on the silty-gravelly plateau etched by flood, wind, and rain. They set down their gear, take shovels, and dig.

"What the Hell," thinks Gruber, "Are they U.S. Geological Survey doing soil samples? What?"

He watches them warily. They're digging alright, but not filling sample buckets or doing field geo-chemical assays.

Gruber relaxes a little. He holsters the Redhawk.

The men dig deeply. Then they plant a tall, red-and-white striped pole capped with bright-green flagging.

They drill into the pole and attach a box. Next to the box they screw on a photo-voltaic power source, wire the two together, and screw an antenna onto the box.

"Can it be a transmitter?" Gruber wonders, "If they're not minerals guys, who the Hell are they? Maybe some kind of land surveyors or map team. Or weather guys puttin' in a portable weather station."

The men check their work. Then one man picks up the shovels, walks up river about fifty yards, and begins digging another hole. The other man walks back to the boat, takes out another striped pole and a bag of gear, and marches towards the digger.

The two repeat the burying and activation process at the new site, check their work, and walk back to the boat. They disappear into it.

Gruber hears the sound of the diesel starting up. It moves out to mid-river and turns west towards Dry Bay.

He moves forward cautiously and tries to catch a glimpse of the boat without being seen. On the stern, in large deep-red letters outlined in black, are the words, "Great Land Geo-Challenge."

This name doesn't clear up Gruber's confusion about what the men were doing on his very doorstep, but at least the words don't hint of a rival mining outfit or a government agency.

Gruber pats his Redhawk once again. If these Geo-Challenge bastards interfere with Alsek Blue Billions, Hard Rock will figure out how to deal with them.

He decides he doesn't want to knock the gaudy poles down and throw them in the river…at least not now. The guys would probably just come back, fix them, and look around for who'd done it.

Look around and maybe find the entrance to Alsek Blue Billions.

Still, he has to know what they're up to. He'll get Casey researching this "Geo-Challenge" thing on-line.

Find out what they're up to.

Stop 'em dead if need be.

Chapter 19 – Fairbanks, Bear Flanks

Mill leaves Cordova on Alaska Airlines 61, bound for Fairbanks with a change in Anchorage. Onboard, she looks at the Geo-Challenge agenda for the next few days. Lots of policy, planning, and permitting.

Hmmm.

Plenty of coffee needed for this stuff!

The start looks good. The Geo-Challenge producers will kick it off with a program "pitch" like the ones they do in Hollywood. They've promised some glam, a full briefing, and video clips from past "reality" shows they produced.

Way cool!

After the pitch, the producers will explain their field methods and expectations in more detail.

Way interesting!

When the week is over, Mill will go to Anchorage again for another Wild Girl hunt.

Just thinking about it summons the hunger…the darkness. Mill stuffs the feelings—her fears, her anger down…down deep. She has to wait, even while grim lust grows in her core.

Mill checks into the downtown Fairbanks Hilton, a basic-box nicely decorated inside with Alaska Native motifs. A tall totem pole stands in the lobby. The light-tan walls display muted, dark-brown pictographs of native life—hunting, food preparation, long houses. The effect is interesting and soothing.

When she opens the door to her third-floor room, Mill sees that it's also decorated in the same native-lifeways motif.

In addition, two nice photos of Fairbanks in the winter hang over her bed. The queen is covered with a walking-moose-and-willow spread, topped with six fluffy pillows. Window curtains match the bedspread.

Alaska nice and homey!

About the time she finishes hanging clothes, Mill's stomach rumbles dinner time. In response, she grabs her backpack and walks down to the dining room.

She doesn't fancy hotel eateries as a rule. But she is tired, still shaking off the hypothermia, and figures it's too late to go exploring. The dining room turns out to have nicely figured wooden tables, a wide river view, and muted lighting.

Very tasteful.

A waiter whisks her to a corner table with a nice view of the dining room, bar, and river. He snaps the menu open for her and moves away. It offers good, basic fare. Good enough for tonight.

Mill gestures for the waiter to approach and orders. Then she looks around, playing "spot the bureaucrat," a game she enjoys in lobbies and restaurants at the start of any government meeting like this one.

Can she figure out who the government people are or, this time, maybe the folks from Hollywood? The rooms aren't very crowded, making her game easier.

Mill spots a few people looking at files they brought with them to dinner. These folks definitely could be government nerds like Mill, but she recognizes no one.

She also sees some people way overdressed for Bear Flanks sitting at a table near the bar entrance, drinking wine and making plenty of noise. Could they be the producers and crew from Hollywood?

One of the men in the group is strikingly handsome, tan, and buff. An actor? Who could he be?

Conscious that she often stares rudely, Mill scans back and forth across the room. Every time her eyes hit the handsome guy, though, they get hung up.

And each time her eyes get hung up, they linger longer.

Finally Mill gives in and just stares. After all, he is not looking at Mill or even in her general direction, just talking to his friends. Why not memorize every detail?

Without warning, perhaps in response to a remark from one of his companions, the handsome guy looks up and directly into Mill's eyes. He winks.

Mill instantly looks away. Her face flushes with embarrassment. She has been caught star-struck.

Mill groans inside. How embarrassing...terrible!

Looking down, she studies her silverware as if it holds the secrets of her future.

She decides if she could hide under the tablecloth and not look even more ridiculous, she would.

Next to her right ear, a quiet voice says, "Gorgeous, isn't he?"

Startled, Mill drops the salad fork she had been admiring and looks up. Mill sees a pretty blond woman smiling down at her.

Blushing again, Mill answers, "Yes, he is. And I'm afraid I've made a fool of myself ogling him! What could I be thinking?"

The woman laughs warmly, "I know. I was watching you two from my barstool. Some people should be put behind one of those one-way mirrors so you can drool over them being seen. It's rude of them to go out in public just to be admired."

The two women laugh.

The woman steps around to the opposite side of Mill's table. "May I sit down?" she asks.

Although Mill usually warms slowly to strangers, she smiles a welcome, "Yes, please do and block my view of Mr. Gorgeous over there."

As she seats herself, Mill sees the woman is slender, fit, and beautifully turned out in a light blue-grey summer suit and muted gold jewelry.

She sits across from Mill. Her torso blocks the Mr. Gorgeous bunch from Mill's wandering eyes.

"My name is Tilly Corcoran," she says, reaching across the table to shake hands.

"Mill Meacham," Mill says in response, grasping Tilly's hand firmly, "Thanks for saving me from myself."

Tilly laughs, "I'm not sure you needed saving. The way he looked at you, I thought Mr. Gorgeous might be headed over to keep you company."

Mill shakes her head, "No, not interested. I'm here on business. I don't need any one-night entanglements with any Mr. Gorgeouses. He's definitely trouble wrapped in Christmas paper!"

Tilly laughs and takes a quick glance over her shoulder at Mr. Gorgeous. "Yes, he is," she muses and then turns back to face Mill.

Changing the subject, Tilly asks, "What kind of business are you in, Mill, if you don't mind me asking?"

Mill decides there's probably no harm in telling this stranger why she is in Fairbanks. "Well," Mill answers, "I'm a Forest Service employee here to work on a reality show that's planned for public lands. I'm here for our start-up meeting. I get to help with the field part later on. So, some of this meeting probably won't apply very well to my work. Still, I'm glad to get the whole picture before my part happens in late-July and August."

Tilly smiles broadly, "Well, nice to meet you for sure. I'm a part of the Great Land Geo-Challenge, too. In fact, I've been tapped to be project manager for it. I'll be trying to get all those parts and pieces you mentioned pulled together--environmental analysis, permits, field stuff. And then there's the schedule. We'll have this three-month window to get the whole environmental-assessment thing done and get the permits out. No matter which way to slice it, we're going to be busy women, you and I."

Mill looks at her with sympathy, "Wow, Tilly, big job. What outfit do you work for?"

Tilly replies, "The Bureau of Land Management, out of the District office here in Fairbanks. I haven't been here that long but I guess they wanted some kind of a local to head things up. The local thing gives us an edge when it comes to knowing the ground and resource concerns. We also have a lot of transportation resources like the Alaska Air Service to help us get around. So, here I am, eating dinner with a teammate who's infatuated with Mr. Gorgeous. Couldn't be better!"

Mill laughs, "So, I guess you'll be my boss then. I should start sucking up!"

Tilly smiles, "No, not your boss. I'll just really be coordinating everything, making sure everything gets done on time. We should hear tomorrow who is going to coordinate the field teams."

Tilly smiles reassuringly, "I've been hearing it'll be a wildland fire commander, someone used to fast-moving field operations in Alaska. Those fire guys make sure everybody gets where they need to go, gets the right support, and comes home safely. So they're a good choice."

"Okay," Mill says, "Sounds good. I like wildland fire guys."

Mill asks, "Tilly, where are you from?"

The two women settle into a comfortable conversation about their pasts.

Tilly tells Mill about growing up in suburban California, the daughter of an aero-space designer working for McDonnell-Douglas. She talks about her college life, first at Stanford University in California and then later at Western Washington University in Bellingham. She earned a Bachelor's in Business and later a Master's in Environmental Management.

82

Mill tells Tilly about her life as a Forest Service brat, running a little wild in the Idaho and Utah forests. She tells her a little about her education and adult life, mentioning her fish-squeezer profession. She is careful to conceal her Legacy status and that other, hungry life lived in Anchorage.

At a certain point in the wine drinking, Mill tells Tilly about losing her mother at age seven, about never hearing from her again. Even though she keeps her tone dry, unexpected tears come to Mill's eyes.

Tilly looks at her with concern.

She reaches across the table and takes Mill's hand, "Still hurts, huh?"

Mill feels surprise at the empathy, "Yes, I guess it still hurts. Probably always will. I'm sorry to be such a baby. You didn't come to dinner to hear my sad story."

Tilly continues to hold Mill's hand gently, care in her eyes.

As Mill's emotions settle a bit, she becomes more conscious of Tilly's touch. Tender energy seems to be flowing between them through their hands…eyes…nice, gentle, kind energy, almost loving.

Mill smiles, "Thanks, Tilly. Nice to know someone cares."

Tilly gives her hand a gentle squeeze and releases it, "I do. Anytime you want to talk, look for me."

Mill's now feeling a little embarrassed at having been so vulnerable to a stranger. Yet, she and Tilly seem to have a connection, a kind of recognition between them, something shared…living. The light touch of Tilly's hand had been warm, intense.

Mill feels a sudden pulse between her legs. Her nipples tighten.

Sex? Sex with Tilly? What a stupid idea!

Mill has a new assignment and she wants sex with the boss?

This surprising attraction is crazy, unwelcome! Where would her body take her if she let it?

Mill keeps sex out of her life, public and private, except for Anchorage. And there she keeps it hidden in darkness…not out in the light.

Mill looks away from Tilly's face, away from her deep-blue eyes, away from Tilly's small breasts beneath her blouse…away. She firmly shoves her sexual feelings for Tilly down…down.

The little pulse between Mill's legs goes on for a while, nagging her, until it finally quiets. Mill is conscious that her lust waits, ready to pulse again if Mill's thoughts turn towards Tilly.

She tells the pulse silently, "Not here. Not now. Not ever. Too close to home. Forget it."

Chatting about nothing in particular, the two women finish dinner.

Mill ventures a quick glance around Tilly at the Hollywood table.

Mr. Gorgeous is gone. She had not seen him leave. Her lingering embarrassment fades.

After saying goodbyes, both women head back to their rooms. They both have work to do before tomorrow's meeting.

Mill sleeps restlessly that night, dreaming of faceless men and women…lovers…wanton…mysterious…bodies tangled in darkened rooms.

Chapter 20 - The Pitch

A few minutes before eight the next morning, Mill arrives at the Hilton's meeting room: a windowless, dusty box deep in the dry, over-heated bowels of the hotel.

She is dressed "business-casual" in a short-waisted grey damask jacket, mid-cut white blouse, and black pants. She carries a brown, stressed-leather, shoulder-bag briefcase.

Carefully selecting a spot at a table in a far corner of the room, Mill puts the briefcase down to mark her meeting-place. Looking around, she spots Mr. Gorgeous and the rest of the Great Land Geo-Challenge presentation team.

One spotter-point for Mill!

After a quick glance, Mill keeps her eyes away from Mr. Gorgeous. She worries that he might remember her star-struck stare and tease her in front of the group. The thought causes her cheeks to redden.

She looks around for a safer view.

Tilly is also there. Mill's eyes follow her as she bustles about, taking care of the presenters.

Tilly is wearing a simple dark grey business suit, impeccably cut to her figure. Her skirt ends just above her knee and has side-slits several inches high. As she walks, the slits open and reveal slim, well-toned legs. Under the suit jacket, she wears a light- yellow blouse with small ruffles at the high neck and along the collar.

Tilly's blouse fits her perfectly, emphasizing her torso and breasts without creating a sexy look.

Impressed with Tilly's style, Mill guesses that she works hard at looking good. And yet somehow she also manages to make her good taste look uncontrived, even accidental.

Mill could definitely use a few lessons in such things.

Mill also watches Tilly's pleasant but firm approach to dealing with the hotel's staff. She seems to be able to crack the whip without making them resentful. Clearly, Tilly's drive and diplomatic skills are among the reasons she got the Geo-Challenge assignment.

Mill realizes her eyes are darting back and forth between Mr. Gorgeous and Tilly.

Mill can't decide which one is more attractive. Both are slim and energetic. And what great butts! Graceful movements. Slender hands.

Mill begins to think about the three of them together in her big Hilton bed....

"Whoa, girl!" She admonishes herself, "Not going there, remember?" Mill quickly looks away, searching for something less bi-sexy erotic.

Ah, there's the coffee. Mill walks over to the coffee bar and pours herself a big mug. She takes a small plate and plunders a couple of beautifully sprinkled donuts.

She walks back to where she had left her briefcase and sets the food down. Before tasting either, she will let the coffee cool and the aroma of the donuts tickle her nose.

While she waits, Mill opens her laptop computer, plugs it in to a wall outlet, and sets up her mouse.

Other people walk in. Some greet others in the room. Back slaps and smiling handshakes remind Mill that she is a relative newcomer to the Alaska scene. She may have an aristocratic pedigree in the Forest Service but she is an unknown among this group.

Mill takes a tentative sip on her coffee.

Tilly walks to the front of the room. She takes a microphone from a lectern there and turns it on. Speakers in the ceiling start to buzz.

Tilly taps the mike. A loud thumping fills the room. She reaches into the lectern and the buzzing diminishes. She puts the mike to her mouth and blares, "Okay folks; take your seats, please."

Some of the talk quiets as people top off coffee cups, grab donuts or fruit, and head for their seats. A few people keep talking rather loudly at the entrance to the room.

Tilly taps the mike again. Raising her voice she says, "I mean *now*, folks. There'll be time later to catch up."

A few of the talkers look up at Tilly. One calls, "Okay, teacher, we're sitting down!"

Tilly retorts, "You better, Willy, or you'll have detention all the way through happy hour."

Some people laugh. The last of the herd heads for their seats.

Tilly starts the meeting, "Good Morning. I'm Matilda Corcoran with the Fairbanks office of the Bureau of Land Management. Please call me 'Tilly.' We'll do group introductions later this morning after the Great Land Geo-Challenge producers make their pitch."

She looks out over the group, a smile on her face, "I can't remember when I've been pitched at before...reminds me of baseball. So,

I have some advice for all of us government types used to long, technical presentations. Notice I didn't use the term 'boring.'" The group laughs.

"Anyway, get ready for a fast pitch. Let's try to keep our eyes on the ball. And, let's hit this one out of the ballpark for the producers and the American people. Whatever happens on this project, we work as a team and we have fun!"

With that, Tilly turns off her mike and sits down near the front of the room.

Mr. Gorgeous steps to the side of the lectern. Without seeming to, he strikes a pose—body straight, chin up slightly, one hand on the lectern.

Mill suddenly wishes she had brought her camera. Then she chides herself for being so silly.

What is she, fifteen again?

Mr. Gorgeous switches on his hands-free microphone. His rich baritone voice fills the room, "Hi, everyone. I'm Tom Burrows, one of the producers of the Great Land Geo-Challenge. If you're wondering, yes, I used to be an actor. You may remember me from shows like 'Surgery Center' and 'Hot Bullets.'"

No fan of TV, Mill has never heard of these shows. But she glances around the room and sees several faces smiling and nodding recognition.

She thinks to herself, "So Mr. Gorgeous Tom Guy is not only beautiful but famous. Hmmm. And here he is talking to us little 'ol feds way off in Bear Flanks, Alaska. My, my! Lucky us!"

Mill tunes back in to what Burrows is saying, "….but now I like to produce and direct shows like the Geo-Challenge. Acting's hard but producing a fast-paced reality show in wild country is much, much harder. You people can guess how hard. You live and work here all the time. Most folks like me in the lower-48 don't have a clue."

Burrows checks some cards in his hand and then says, "Okay, first I'm going to give you a video overview with an Alaska emphasis. When we get to the pitch video though, you'll notice it's not specifically focused on Alaska. That's because we didn't know where we might be filming when we developed the proposal. It's what we put together last year for potential backers, the money people. They loved the concept and invested even without Alaska in it. So watch the show. It'll take less than ten minutes. Then I'll answer any questions you have and we'll dive right in to other things you need to know."

Burrows looks around the room, "Everybody ready? If you are, let's hear a 'yes'!"

Surprised by his desire for audience participation, the government nerds only give Burrows a few halfhearted "Yeses."

Burrows cups his ear theatrically and turns his head towards the group. He asks again, "Okay...ready...let's hear it now. Are you ready to hit my pitch out of the ballpark?"

This time, caught up by Burrows' charisma, at least half the bureaucrats, including Mill, yell, "Yes."

Smiling and offering the group a thumbs up, Burrows keys the projector. As the screen lights up, one of his colleagues turns down the ceiling lights.

The title comes on the screen, "The Great Land Geo-Challenge: The Most Extreme Race Ever." Behind the words flashes a colorful topographic map of Alaska. Music swells. Tom Burrows' voice fills the room, his already mellifluous tones electronically deepened and enhanced.

Mill thinks, "No wonder they picked Mr. Tom Gorgeous as their pitchman. He can get a bunch of feds shouting 'yes' to taking on more work. Now he's seducing me with music and his voice. That's real ability."

——————————————//——————————————

An hour later, Tilly thanks the producers for their presentation and time. As Burrows and his team gather their materials to go, Tilly calls a 20-minute break.

Some feds and a couple of hotel employees bustle up to ask for Burrows for his autograph.

He kindly fills their requests and chats with them about his acting career, the programs, and his co-stars.

Watching him, Mill decides he is really rather a nice person, despite being "Mr. Gorgeous," glamorous, and all that. After all, he can't help being handsome and articulate, cute and sexy, can he? Well, maybe.

And besides, the rational part of Mill knows that Hollywood stars have a plain life, too--one filled with everyday things like dirty baby diapers and unpaid bills.

Still, like most Americans, she would also like to think they're special somehow--glamorous princes and princesses living exceptionally powerful and productive lives. Mill shakes her head at her foolishness.

Chapter 21 - The Geo-Challenge Explored

Burrows and his team leave the meeting room.

Mill turns her attention to her computer and starts typing furiously, intent on getting her impressions, ideas, and questions down before Tilly reconvenes the group.

The next several presenters have lots of legal and permitting issues to cover. That bureaucratic stuff is likely to turn down the brightness of Mill's mind to the nodding-off point. She doesn't want to lose anything she has gathered so far if she goes into meeting-coma.

Mill looks at the expertly designed, glossy, four-page color handout Burrows' team had passed around the room. Across the brochure's top are miniature playbills for the successful programs that Burrows and his group produced before.

Below the tiny playbills are the words, "The Great Land Geo-Challenge" in a bold, art-deco, 3-D typeface. Elsewhere, spread attractively across the four pages, the designers box and package information according topic. Inset diagrams, maps, and photos cleanly and succinctly support the text.

Mill had scribbled notes in her brochure's margins and underlined certain parts while the video ran and questions were asked and answered. Now, she wants to capture the ideas and questions from her scratches. She turns to her computer and starts typing.

A deepish male voice intrudes, "Excuse me. May I interrupt you for a minute?"

Mill looks up. It's a guy from the next table, kind of a cute guy with nice grey eyes. Suppressing a mild feeling of annoyance, Mill says, "Sure. What can I do for you?"

"Well," he replies, "I couldn't help but notice that you've been making notes all through the presentation. Are you an official part of the Geo-Challenge?"

Mill smiles, "Yes, I'm one of the agency reps that will travel with the racers. Mill Meacham, Forest Service."

Mill extends her hand and he shakes it, "Fritz Sawyer, Fish and Wildlife Service. I'm Group Leader for Conservation and Mitigation here in Alaska."

Mill asks Fritz, "Not to be rude, but why are you here? I thought I heard that the BLM would be representing you guys."

Fritz smiles, "Yeah, the BLM is going to handle all the permitting and race coordination, but the Service still has a big interest in the ecological effects across Alaska and on how the race will be run across the Arctic National Wildlife Refuge which we manage."

"Okay," Mill says, "I get it. So, what can I do for you?"

Sawyer points to the brochure, "I guess I just wanted to talk some things over. And, really, here's my problem. I'm totally color blind. I just see shades of grey, no colors at all. I can read the text just fine. But some the charts are really hard for me to figure out, and I don't get the map. Could we just sit and run through a few things together, maybe get a few of my questions answered?"

"Sure, I'd be glad to help," Mill answers.

She notices Fritz' eyes can't seem to settle on her face. They veer south to her breasts every few seconds. She wonders briefly if Fritz is really color-blind or just interested in a roll in the hay. Either way, it's a free country. His wandering eyes might be annoying, but whether he knows it or not, all Fritz is going to get from her is social, not sexual, intercourse.

To divert his eyes from her cleavage, Mill points to a box of text. She says to Fritz, "Looks like the Great Land Geo-Challenge is a real race. It's a reality show like so many others but what makes it different is that the race will be run in the Alaska bush, real wild backcountry like your ANWR. And, even more unusual, the racers are gonna be guided by Global Positioning System hand-helds."

Fritz murmurs, "Yeah, that's definitely different. Most of those reality shows are on an island or make use of transportation you might see anywhere."

Mill points again, "See here, the brochure says we will be using the kind of GPS I have, the Garmin *e*trex. But we'll be getting a much more advanced model, the *e*trex Vista HCx, especially modified at the factory for two-way communications. In fact, I don't think even the regular HCx has been released to the public yet."

Mill asks, "Do you have a GPS?"

Fritz shakes his head, "No."

She says to him, "I love my *e*trex. It's a little yellow gizmo that fits in my pocket or hangs around my neck. Once I give it a destination, it shows me how to get there and how far away it is. And as I roam around, it keeps track of my path so I can backtrack if I want to. One time I left my binoculars at a lunch spot, and the *e*trex took me right back there. This

90

updated Vista model's a little heavier and colored grey, but just as compact. I'm really looking forward to figuring it out…lots more features…topographic maps for example."

Fritz says, "I've seen etrexes but I don't have one yet."

He pauses and looks a little bashful, "This is really nerdy, but did you know that a science fiction writer, Issac Azimov, first proposed GPS in like the 1930s. He was quite a guy. I had a technology course a few years back that covered how a bunch of his wild ideas became things we use all the time—GPS, radar--stuff like that. It was his idea but the U.S. military gets the credit for making the miracle happen."

Fritz goes on to describe how, over many years, the Pentagon placed twenty-four satellites in fixed orbits above the Earth. Each satellite holds transmitters controlled by ultra-precise atomic clocks.

Mill's little etrex can tell where she is to within a couple of feet. To do this, Fritz tells her that the etrex calculates the difference in the time it takes for signals to reach it from two or more satellites and the direction the signals come from.

Thanks to computing power in her etrex, Mill can see where she is on Earth with remarkable precision. By comparing Mill's location with a destination, it can tell her what direction to go; it even points the way with an arrow.

Mill has heard and experienced some of this before, but she tells Fritz, "You know, that's really cool. I mean I saw my screen say 'acquiring satellites' but I never thought there were so many."

"Yeah," Fritz answers, "I don't understand the math, but I think the number has to do with how far out the satellites have to be placed to stay fixed orbit. That's all I know. Anyway, this whole GPS in the race thing sounds exciting. I hope they've field tested them thoroughly."

Mill laughs ironically, "Yeah, me, too. Me even more so. This brochure also says the Vistas will also be fitted with transceivers to allow race controllers to follow our routes and progress. Race controllers? I thought we agency folks were the race controllers."

Fritz smiles and points, "No, this says that while you're dodging moose and swimming rivers, the race controllers can change things in your GPS units--maps, coordinates, directions--to confuse the racers, challenge them. The brochure calls these changes "inputs" and says you'll have to deal with up to three of them on each stage."

Mill sighs, "I guess I have more questions to ask about these 'input' thingies." She makes a few more notes in her computer.

Mill picks up the brochure again, "Well, I guess this goes together with the GPSes, but the Geo-Challenge uses the idea of geo-caching, too. Have you ever done that? I have a bunch of friends who do it all the time, but I never have."

Fritz shakes his head, "No, but I've read about it and I know the Service has some sort of policy about doing it on refuges…not really in favor of it, I guess."

Mill knows her friends use GPS units to locate places with hidden containers, called "geo-caches." The geo-caches might be ammo boxes, plastic pipes, or tins—anything that can be sealed against the weather. Inside the caches are little souvenirs or tokens, a log book, maybe an ink stamp unique to the site, or information about the site and area. Geo-caches can be anywhere—on the backs of big-city street signs or on backcountry mountaintops.

She replies, "Yeah, no wonder the Forest Service and Fish and Wildlife Service don't want geo-caches on public land. It's probably too easy for caches to become garbage dumps. Still, I've got to wonder if both agencies wouldn't get a lot more public support if we embraced geo-caching…made an emphasis out of it. For the Forest Service, the recreation and wilderness programs are always way short of money. Wouldn't geo-cachers' support help that?"

Fritz nods, "Probably. I think the Service suffers from having a lot of really small refuges in the lower-48. Because the small ones get people-hammered a lot, the whole agency mentality is to mostly keep people out. I don't see geo-caching fitting in with that very well."

Fritz points to the map in his brochure, "This map is awfully small and it's kind of a grey blob to me. I can read the text, but how does the map fit with the text and graphics?"

Mill flips the page to look at the race description and the accompanying map. The Great Land Geo-Challenge will start on the Beaufort Sea on Alaska's northern coast, south of the Arctic Ocean. Three teams of two people, all tri-athletes and experienced in the outdoors, will start the race in traditional Eskimo umiaks a couple of miles offshore. Using their GPS units to guide them, they will paddle to the shore and find their first cache.

Mill checks her notes and points to the map, "Fritz, can you see…well, for me, this red line on the map? To you, I bet it'd be light grey."

Fritz looks where her finger's pointing, "Yeah, I see it now, but it's not much darker than the background, not much contrast, you know? So I couldn't figure out what it was. Looked like a smudge or something."

Mill traces the route for him, "Race starts here at Demarcation Bay on the Beaufort Sea part of the Arctic Ocean, runs down to the Sheenjek River. That's the Brooks-Romanzof Trek part. That's mostly within ANWR, right?" Fritz nods.

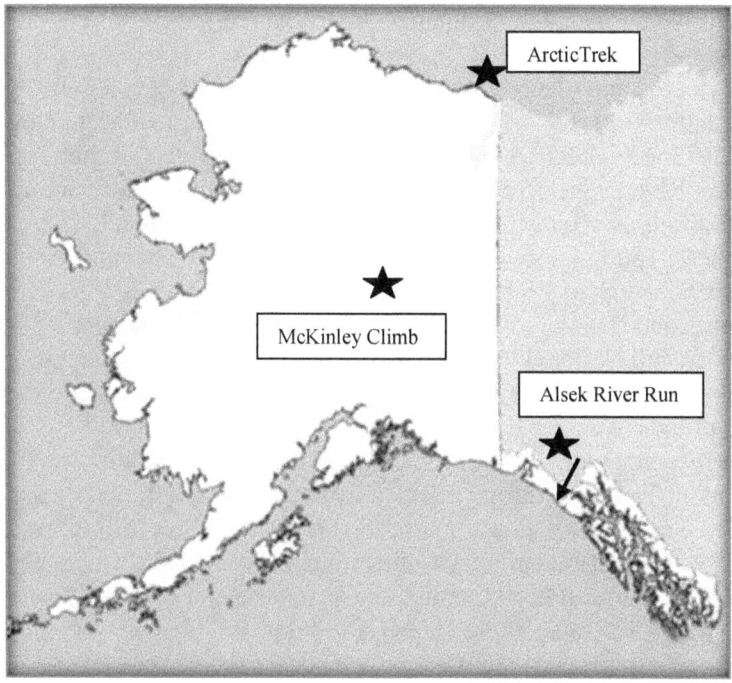

"Okay," she continues, "You Fish and Wildlife guys host that. Then this little star covers the McKinley Climb. That's in Denali National Park, so Park Service hosts it. Okay, and down here in the lower right is the Alsek River Run...starts in Kluane National Park up in Canada and goes down past Glacier Bay National Park to Dry Bay on the Tongass National Forest in Southeast."

She checks the simple map for more details. But almost all of the places mentioned in brochure aren't shown. She tells Fritz, "This map's too large-scale to show what they talk about in the write-up. We'll have to go on-line or find an Alaska Gazetteer with its smaller-scale topo maps to nail down any more details."

Fritz answers, "I'm okay for now. In a few weeks I'll get all the topographic maps that Tilly Corcoran and her staff have to make for the environmental assessment. I'll have more than enough detail then."

They both laugh. The amount of detail in the environmental assessment will be overwhelming. No mere mortal could read it all, let alone understand it. But the route maps will be detailed and useful. No one does maps better than Tilly's agency, the Bureau of Land Management.

They both study the brochure intently. The first stage is a trek from Demarcation Bay across the Brooks Range and Romanzof Mountains to a site on the Sheenjek River, one of the northern headwaters of the mighty Yukon River. The brochure says the distance between the start and finish is 137 air miles. But Mill figures the ground actually pounded would be at least 160 miles depending on what route the racers choose, four or five days march at a fast pace.

The second stage involves climbing to 18,000 feet on Mount McKinley in Denali National Park. Compared to the Brooks-Romanzof challenge, the McKinley stage is short in miles but horrific in vertical change and altitude.

The final stage is a kayak trip down the Alsek River from Canada's Yukon Territory, through British Columbia, to Dry Bay near the Alaska coast. The brochure doesn't describe the distance, but Mill thinks it looks straightforward enough on the little map, maybe 150 miles. She figures the kayak trip could be done in three or four days if everything goes well, but then she looks more closely a footnote on the map.

It says, "A portion of the Alsek is considered too dangerous to navigate. Teams are required to make a glacier crossing to avoid the section known as Turnback Canyon, a deadly section of the Alsek only navigated by a few expert kayakers in the past."

She thinks of some of the videos she has seen of wild Class V+ white-water and of her experience flying over the Bering Glacier with its deep crevasses and deep-blue surface lakes. A shiver runs up her spine.

"Hey, Fritz," Mill asks, "Do you know anything about the Alsek River? Look at this footnote. It talks about a 'deadly Turnback Canyon' and a 'glacier crossing.' Sounds pretty tricky."

Fritz studies the footnote, "No, I've never been anywhere around the Alsek. We have some island refuges down in Southeast but I've not been down to visit them. It does sound dangerous. Could be fun though…different."

Mill looks at another part of the race description. She points to the text, "And here's more to add to the anxiety index. Did you see this, Fritz? For the whole trip, racers have no maps, no compasses, no radios, just the GPSes. Agency reps like me will have the one means of outside communication, a satellite phone. What do you think of that?"

Fritz runs his hands through his hair and leans back from the table, "Sounds like a recipe for disaster. What if you have an injury, multiple injuries, and the sat phone isn't working?"

Mill smiles grimly, "Well, I guess we just pioneer through and hope that the GPSes get us home."

She continues to read tidbits to Fritz, "The winning team is the one that completes all three challenges in the least time. Both team members have to finish before the clock stops. That seems straightforward enough."

Mill reads more of the text below the route description. Transportation will be provided from the end of one challenge to the start of the next. Mill mentions this to Fritz, "Thank God for that or we'd be a lot more than a month or so running this race."

He answers, "As it is, the teams have a lot of territory to cover--all of it wild and much of it seriously up and down. I envy you the trip but it's gonna strain everybody to the max."

She smiles, "Well, at least I don't have to make the McKinley climb. One of the Park Service Mountain Rangers will go up with the racers. That climbing's too specialized for me. I get to stay at the base camp and get ready for the Alsek River Run."

Fritz replies, "Yeah, I guarantee you'll need some R and R after the Trek."

Mill wags a thoughtful finger at Fritz, "You've been up in ANWR a lot. I bet it's got a lot of tough ground." He nods.

She smiles grimly, "You're making me begin to wonder whether I'm fit enough to keep pace with the racers and the camera and sound crew. Burrows called them the 'tech crew.' I imagine they'll be in as great a shape as the racers. Damn, just what I wanted—a training program to make me into a world-class athlete in a couple of months…as if that could ever happen!"

Fritz laughs at her, "Yeah, I don't envy you getting ready for this. And, if I read the race schedule right, you have to be ready by the end of July."

Mill shakes her head ruefully, "What have I gotten myself in for?"

Turning to the final page of the handout, Mill reads the section on geo-caching again. "So, Fritz," she asks, "Did you see read this part about the field caches? Each team will have a designated cache at landing site in Demarcation Bay with a lot of gear in it—clothes, packs, tents, and all that. Then, later caches will add more equipment, food, batteries, and other things kinda tailored to upcoming parts of the race. That's cool, but then it gets complicated."

"If I'm reading this right, sometimes the race controllers will reveal a cache's location to only one team. Sometimes a cache will be assigned to one team but its location will be shared with one or both of the other teams. Sometimes everyone will be directed to converge on a single cache site. There might be "bonus" caches awarded to teams that complete a stage or difficult part first. So, from a cache standpoint, we have one of those 'yours, mine, and ours' things going."

Fritz replies, "It's a little complicated for sure. But, Mill, think about this. Whoever gets to a cache first can take the stuff, hide it, or even destroy it. Who's gonna stop them? So you could work your rear ends off getting to a cache, only to find it empty. It might even be one designated for you that some other group stumbles across. Hope you don't have to count on one particular cache for survival."

Mill shudders a little at Fritz' words, thinking back to her recent bear encounter along the Copper River. What if someone had removed the flares from her float coat? She would probably be dead now.

Fritz thinks for a moment, "Mill, if I were you, I'd be asking a lot of questions about safety and backups before the race starts."

Mill answers, "You're right about that. I have a list going of things like that on my laptop. But this says that at least they've thought of some obvious things. Each racer and team member can order the equipment and food that they want. The producers will make sure those things get placed in the right caches. And they've given support people like me the use of the same equipment outfitters and sports nutritionists who are available to the racers. I can't imagine that they really want to spend the money on us, but the producers probably want to make sure that the racers don't get held up by some funky malnourished or ill-equipped government employee."

"I mean look at this. It says I should plan on consuming six-to-eight-thousand nutritionally dense calories a day.' Nutritionally dense? What's that? Fruit cake? I guess I better plan on several talks with the nutrition people."

Wow! What would eight thousand calories a day do to her girlish figure? But then, thinking of the physical challenges, Mill realizes she will probably lose weight…in sweat if nothing else.

Tilly calls the group back together.

Fritz leans forward, his eyes locked once again on Mill's breasts, "Mill, would you like to get together for a drink later?"

Mill thinks, "A-ha! The doggy wags his tail and salivates."

"No," she replies tartly, "I'll be too busy starting my Geo-Challenge exercise program."

The government part starts.

Mill steels herself firmly against yawning.

After five minutes, she falls into a meeting-coma and yawns anyway.

Oh well…a nap may come.

Respect the need for mental health.

Chapter 22 - Wild Girl Goes Back

Mill settles into a bulkhead seat on Alaska Airlines flight 188 to Anchorage--cushiony and plenty of leg room.

The Geo-Challenge meeting had finished up on Friday at 1, giving her a comfortable amount of time for travel to the Fairbanks Airport. And thanks to the slow pace of the week, Wild Girl is feeling pretty well rested for her first-night hunt. She should be done dressing and primping and on the way to a club by 7.

Just right.

The anger-hunger grows in her belly.

Through the week, unwanted, sexy thoughts of Tilly have put Mill in the mood for girl skin next to her skin…girl touches…girl tastes.

Closing her eyes and resting her head on the seat's cushions, Mill imagines Tilly's slender body in her arms, mouths touching, kissing…fingers sliding over smooth skin to warm, slippery places…. Tilly's glad orgasmic coo.

Mill shudders.

Any more of this and she would have to go to the restroom and find some relief for her pulsing girl parts.

With an effort, she gets control of her imagination. "Think about something else,' she urges herself, "At least until you get to a club and can find someone."

Mill wonders if there's an upscale lesbian watering hole in Anchorage. Maybe she can find someone to fill in for Tilly. It should be easy to find out.

"Okay," she counsels herself, "Calm down and move on."

Desperate to change focus, Mill thinks back to the last day of the meeting and work with the fire commander, Joe Schmoker, who would be handling the agency reps in the field.

Because of his last name, many fire fighters referred to him as "Smoky Joe." When Mill checked around, she found that Joe Schmoker really didn't like that nickname. She resolved not to use it.

But of course, once she heard it, she couldn't get the nickname out of her mind. For the whole day, she had "Smoky Joe, Smoky Joe, Joe's so smoky" and things like that running through her mind.

Considering her past history, she would likely slip up and call him Smoky Joe at some point. Mill sighs. Well, she would just be ready to apologize.

As he briefed the agency reps, Smoky Joe…ah…Joe Schmoker had covered a long list of items: their joint mission, personal roles, communications protocols, equipment, food, logistics, and transportation. Most of all, Joe covered safety and then covered it again.

It had been Joe's safety concerns that had kept Mill and the other agency representatives off McKinley. And his safety concerns would keep a helicopter within a two-hour flight of the reps.

Of course, any aircraft rescue would depend on that most fickle of things, Alaska weather.

Still, Mill is reassured that a "dust-off" helicopter would be standing by and that Joe could be in frequent contact via satellite phone.

Mill thinks, "Well, he sure covered the basic stuff. But I still wonder about the racers…the video and audio guys. What about them? Who's gonna cover their asses."

When Mill had asked Joe that question, Schmoker had given few answers. He simply said that safety for the Geo-Challenge people was up to the producers and that he would work closely with them when they were ready to share their plans.

Now on the plane, Mill retakes her vow to find out more, a lot more, about those things. Her mind goes to the deep, dark eddy in the Copper, diving for her life, coming up behind the bear….

Mill shudders again--fear, not lust, touching her spine this time.

As if in sympathy with her mood, the plane begins to buck and sway. First the flaps and then the wheels come down.

They're on final approach.

Watch out, Anchorage! Wild Girl Hunting is back for more.

About 20 minutes off the Fairbanks flight, Mill reaches her haven. The little gold vibrator sits where she had left it in the middle of her vanity, its tiny image mirrored to her--right, left, up, down.

A slight pulse starts between her legs.

Now?

A quickie to start?

No, not now.

She might lose the edge…miss the vibe.

Suddenly tired, Mill sits down on the vanity's little bench. She stares into her mirrored eyes. She tries to conjure Wild Girl Hunting's fiery, determined eyes.

For a moment, her eyes glow. But then they go cold…passionless.

Darkness creeps closer to her from the edges of the room, diming the bright vanity lights. Mill shivers along the base of her neck. Fear scuttles little fingers down her spine.

Where's Wild Girl? She tries to shrug off the mood.

"Come on, Millicent," she says weakly, "Time to hunt!"

Nothing.

Desperate to conjure Wild Girl, Mill stands up and whips the wardrobe open. Sniffing the nice cedar aroma, she reaches into the back and takes out her lockbox, opens it, and peers inside.

She locates her little hash pipe and some Matanuska Thunder Fuck, the strong, locally grown marijuana.

Putting the dope and pipe aside, she opens an aspirin bottle filled with Ecstasy and picks up her pill cutter. Mill cuts a tab of E in half and downs one piece with a gulp of bottled water from her bag.

As she waits for the E to lift her mood, she looks thoughtfully at the pipe. Mill tries not to smoke any place where someone might detect the distinctive smell.

But now she wants the dope's mellow freedom to lift her mood, to come over her with the E, build together into a Wild Girl liberating high.

Mill grabs the little pipe and stuffs it with dope. She reaches into the left vanity drawer and finds a little gold lighter. Snap. There, fire in the bowl.

She draws the smoke deep into her lungs, holds it…holds it. She remembers the deep cold of the pond, diving, holding her breath.

Mill holds the toke deep…long. Her ears begin to pulse-thump. Comes a slight buzz.

Able to hold the toke no longer, Mill breathes-coughs the smoke out. Almost clear. Good.

The Thunder Fuck's already beginning to penetrate, rush into her and blend with the E. She sucks the pipe's grey-blue smoke deep again and holds it…cold Copper…holds it.

Mill's head spins when she lets the second toke go. She feels the high coming on fast, E and Thunder Fuck taking over. She can tell this will be a good one, a long one…hours long.

Mill's power rises. It pushes back the darkness. She feels strong.

This high *could* last forever and, if there was any mercy in the universe, *it would*.

Mill looks in the mirror. Hunter eyes stare back, hungry eyes, the bear's eyes.

She killed the bear.

Wild Girl owns his power.

Wild Girl stands and strips naked, dropping her Cordova clothes into her open suitcase. She turns to the wardrobe and takes out a light tan, almost cream-colored, leather outfit. The skirt and jacket are beautifully stitched and tailored finely to her figure. The skirt is slit up both sides several inches.

For a moment, she remembers Tilly's slender-strong legs that first day in Fairbanks. She lets the thought linger…feels the bear-hunger of it…then lets go.

She tries several shirts and blouses with the suit, settling on a plain light-blue blouse with small horn buttons.

Wild Girl takes out bra and panties. She puts them on, takes the push-dagger from the lockbox, and slides it into its panty sheath. Then she takes out patterned stockings and pulls them on. The stockings cling snugly to her upper thighs.

She doesn't like bulky, bumpy garter belts. And pantyhose get in the way of eager fingers, penises, and tongues.

She puts on the blouse and slides into the leather skirt.

She searches her jewelry and decides on three plain gold chains of different lengths and small gold disc earrings. Her hair will do as it is, once she runs a quick brush through it.

She puts on the leather jacket and matching shoes with two-inch heels.

She turns and studies her image in the long mirror. Perfect. She looks like a lawyer or successful businesswoman out for some fun.

Mill's mind drifts to Tilly…to Tilly fun. Yes, Wild Girl will be a successful woman out for some lady fun, for girl sex.

She feels the pulse again. Not yet. Later this night, Wild Girl will bear-hunt the vibe.

She slides her rat-hole money into the hidden pocket in the skirt's waistband. She takes the grey silk windbreaker from the wardrobe and puts some cash and her fake ID in the right pocket. She walks to the door, opens it, and steps out into the dimly lit hall.

She snaps off the lights and closes the door. It locks automatically.

A man's voice rasps, "Good evening, Miss."

Mill jumps an inch and drops the windbreaker. She instinctively turns to face the voice and shifts into fighting stance, right foot back, ready to defend herself with expert karate. Her hands take defensive positions, one blocking at throat level and one at her waist, poised to strike.

"Whoa, Miss," the guy moves from the shadow of a doorway and shows her his empty hands, "No need to be that way. I won't hurt you. I was just waitin' here to see if you was comin' out." He steps forward under the ceiling light, hands held wide.

Mill sees that he is older, probably in his fifties, a foot taller than she is and ruggedly built. With the light directly over his head, his eyes are dark pools.

He offers her a crooked smile, "No, Miss, I won't hurt you. And I'd like to make sure you don't hurt me!"

He laughs, "You're ready for anything, even in a dark alley, ain't you, Miss."

Mill realizes she looks a little ridiculous, ready for combat in a dusty rental-space hallway. Still watching the man closely, she relaxes a little, picks up her coat, and stands normally.

"What do you want?" she asks, "I'm on my way out to dinner."

He shoves his hands in his pockets, "I was just walkin' my rounds. I smell something funny…smoke maybe. I saw light under your door…almost knocked. I wondered what was goin' on but I dint want to bother no one. So I waited to see if you came out or if I needed to call the fire department."

His voice takes on a defensive tone, "See, people can forget and leave something on. Can't have a fire in a place like this, you know."

Mill feels a little panic. The Thunder Fuck, of course! Could he guess?

Regaining her tough composure, Wild Girl Hunting says gruffly, "Nothing wrong here. I just lit a cigarette. I put it out a while ago." She takes a step back and starts to turn away, "I have to go now."

"Dint smell like no cigarette to me," he says solemnly, a little menace slithering into his tone.

But then, with nothing left to ask, he shifts his weight a couple of times and says, "I guess I better go finish my rounds. You want me to come out to your car with you, Miss?"

Still a little flustered by how close she had come to getting caught, Wild Girl answers quickly, "No need. Thanks."

She can't be delayed by this goon now. She has to score soon. Her rage rises. The shock of this encounter, the extra jolt of fear, has just made her anger-hunger stronger. She turns quickly and heads out of the building to the cab stand.

A watchman doing his rounds! Wow!

She had never seen anyone around her storage unit before. Besides a few cameras at driveway and door entrances, she had no idea they even hired security. Someone walking the hallways of storage units just seems like overkill.

Besides, the man's presence hadn't conveyed any comfort to Mill, just floating menace, a calculating interest.

Back in the building's rental office, Drag Carlson watches Mill walk toward the cab stand.

He has plans for her. Leather outfit…nice hair and figure. She has money, that's for sure. She looks good.

Drag isn't sure what he wants from this little tighty yet. That karate stuff she did looked real. No matter how much bigger Drag is than this little split-tail deer, she looks like she could give him a bad time if he wasn't careful. But, with the right moves, he can definitely get something off her. What could that be?

Drag knows dopers, heads, hypes, and crystal-sniffers, poon-hounds and hump-whores. He has known them all his life, all around Anchorage. And he had gotten to know them even better when he did his three-year stretch in the state pen down in Juneau.

Most importantly, Drag knows how to trap them and tap them, ripen them and rip them off.

Drag once chained up two women heroin users in his spare bedroom. A little bit of black tar had got them in there and, along with threats and beatings, a little more had kept them quiet for three months.

Drag had banged their cold tails without mercy before finally getting tired of them and letting them go.

One of them had turned up pregnant but that was none of his concern. When she showed up on his door step, he ran her off with his .45.

Drag couldn't count how many men and women he had ripped off. Blackmail. Theft. Burglary. Forced sex. They had all given it up once his size and words had made clear what their choices were.

He really liked to work the ones with money and status. They had so much more to give.

And so many more reasons to stay silent after he did them.

He began to think more about this nice-looking karate-doper, fallen so conveniently into his hands.

He would get something off her, but what would it be?

She looks like money but not lots.

He takes out her registration card. It states that she is Lucy Moore from an address in Seattle.

"Okay, Lucy-twist," Drag says to the air, "I got you. You're Drag's. You gonna do just what I want…you just don't know it yet.

Chapter 23 – Lady Slippery

The cabbie that earlier drove Mill from the airport had looked at her in his rear-view mirror with disbelieving eyes when she asked about lesbian bars and night clubs. Of course, she had been discreet in how she asked but he got the point readily enough.

"Why would a pretty girl like you be interested in that scene?" he asked, "There's plenty other things going on in Anchorage besides that dyke stuff." His words were gruff-sounding, even fatherly, but he hadn't seemed hostile.

Mill replied, "I just want to see what they do. You know, check 'em out."

"I've never gone to a place like that," she lied, "If it's too weird, I'll just leave, you know, right away."

The cabbie nodded his head, "Okay. You're just checking it out, huh? Well a nice person like you should stay away from the tougher places. There're a couple of hard-case joints over by Merritt Field. No, I'd go to The Lady Slipper if I was you. It's a pretty nice place…quiet…in the first floor of an office building downtown. It overlooks Cook Inlet and the docks, so you'll get some interesting scenery. There's never no trouble there I ever heard of."

Mill had thanked him with an extra big tip.

Now, after leaving the storage building, Wild Girl takes another cab to downtown Anchorage. She has the cabbie drop her a few blocks from The Lady Slipper.

After walking past the place to check it out, she turns back and walks in under its canopied entrance. A tall doorwoman in a tuxedo greets her. Bowing slightly, she smiles warmly, opens the door, and waves Wild Girl in. Beyond the door, a large male bouncer sits in a darkened alcove watching the door. He, too, waves her past with a genial hand.

Beyond him, a dark interior beckons. Soft piano music plays.

Wild Girl walks past a few decorative screens and large pots of plants which shield patrons from any prying eyes peering in from the street.

A woman in a severely cut four-button business suit smiles at her from behind a podium. Her plain white blouse is brightly accented by a floppy crimson bow-tie. She has a chrysanthemum in the same crimson shade wound into the side of her French braid.

"One for dinner? Or just drinks this evening?" she asks.

Wild Girl answers softly, "I think I'll start with drinks and see what develops."

The maître'd looks into Mill's doped eyes and lifts an eyebrow, "Will others be joining you?"

Wild Girl is afraid to speak. The dope has thoroughly lowered her inhibitions and this place is so tantalizing. Her up-thrusting anger-hunger might come through in her words…send a warning to this woman…and there's no vibe yet.

She shakes her head "No."

The maître'd smiles broadly, "Well then, perhaps you'd like some company?"

Wild Girl nods her head, "Yes."

The woman gives Mill a slight wink, "I'll pass the word. Just be open to who comes to you. Everyone here is nice, discreet. Trust us."

"I already do," Wild Girl whispers hoarsely.

The maître'd bows and gestures towards the bar.

Wild Girl walks into the bar room, aglitter with glasses and bottles, mahogany surfaces gleaming softly. Two women tend the bar. A waitress dressed like a ballerina in a leotard, short jacket, and long skirt takes drink orders at one of the tables in the center of the room.

Around the outside of the room, a half-dozen lesbian couples sit in mahogany booths finished in dark-green leather.

Wild Girl takes a stool under a hanging spotlight with a bright copper shade. She lets the light spill over her left side. Her leg gleams from inside her stocking, a near match to the creamy leather of her outfit.

She orders a TNT, downs it quickly, and orders another. The little pulse has begun to beat and Wild Girl tells it to build.

After ten minutes or so, a well-dressed, fortyish woman approaches from the dining room. Her blond hair is cut close to her elegantly shaped skull. She wears a dark-blue, banker's-stripe pants suit and tasteful diamond jewelry in filigreed yellow gold.

"Maggie said you were looking for someone to talk to tonight," the woman smiles at Mill.

Wild Girl looks into the woman's eyes. She sees humor and calm assurance there, "Yes, I am. Please sit. I'll buy us a drink."

The woman gestures towards one of the booths, "How about over there? It's a lot more comfortable…and private."

"Sure," Wild Girl replies, "Looks nice."

She drops down off her stool and finds that the woman is almost exactly her height. Her eyes are a soft, pansy blue. Her skin is smooth, flawless except for a few freckles scattered across her upper cheeks.

The woman offers her hand to Mill, "I'm Charli Jenkins. What's your name?"

Wild Girl shakes Charli's hand, "I'm Lucy, Lucy Moore, from Seattle."

They shake.

"Well," Charli grins, "Nice to meet you, Lucy Moore from Seattle." They turn towards the booth.

Walking side-by-side, Charli gently takes Mill's hand again and squeezes it. She leans towards Mill. "So nice to have you here," she whispers into her ear.

They slide into the booth and sit close together. They chat for a few minutes. No vibe...not yet anyway. Then fresh drinks arrive, Wild Girl's TNT and a colorless drink with a lime slice floating in it for Charli.

Wild Girl points at Charli's simple glass, "Just plain soda?" she guesses.

Charli nods her head, "Yes, I got to liking the booze too much about twenty years ago. I was married, had a couple of kids, and was thoroughly out of touch with who I was or could be. I drank too much so I could stay stuck, stay someone I wasn't cut out to be, doing things I was bad at."

Charli grimaces, "One day I decided to stop being such a stuck cluck. I got sober, ended my old life, and started fresh. Along the way, I dropped thirty pounds, went to school, and became a real estate broker. Now I go out, have virgin drinks, and seduce beautiful younger women. How's that for a life story?"

Under the cover of her bantering confession, Charli looks searchingly at Mill. Charli can see Mill is high, maybe on the edge of out of control.

Charli tries to gauge how much to tell her...how much reality the younger woman can grasp. Maybe some.

After a mental shrug, Charli clears the air, "Lucy, you look high tonight...not just booze...other stuff."

Seeing the defensive look on Mill's face, Charli raises a calming hand, "I understand. I've been where you are, or at least near where you are."

Charli gently squeezes Mill's hand again," After I divorced my husband, I went more than a little wild. For more than a year, I tried to drive out my demons with men, booze, and sex...some drugs. It didn't work."

Charli's speech is not what Wild Girl expects to hear on a first-night hunt. She begins an indignant protest, rage starting to erupt to the surface, unwilling to be denied release.

But Charli puts a tender finger to Mill's lips, "No need to say anything, dear." She smiles warmly at the amped-up younger woman, "I'm not your judge. You can do what you want with your life...with me tonight. I'm just saying that you may not have to get high to be yourself, to let your true self out. And your true self is what you want other people to love, to make love to, not you on booze or drugs."

Charli slides one hand under Mill's skirt. Her warm fingers find Mill's strong upper thigh and gently caress it. She leans across, puts a hand behind Mill's neck, pulls her towards her, and lightly kisses Mill's mouth. She puts her lips next to Mill's ear so her breath just barely tickles Mill's skin.

Charli murmurs, "So, listen, why don't you finish your drink, dear Lucy, and we'll head over to my little place. I'll fix us some food. We can take some time to know each other better."

Charli lightly kisses Mill's ear and nibbles her ear lobe. She moves her hand over to Mill's labia and touches her lightly there.

The little pulse screams to be taken.

Wild Girl spreads her legs slightly to give Charli deeper access. But Charli withdraws her hand.

Charli chuckles, "You see I want to please you. I know you will please me. We can do whatever you want in bed or in my big whirlpool bath...whatever... wherever."

What Charli offers is not what Wild Girl expected on a first-night hunt. She had envisioned sweaty, hard-driving sex with a woman she would barely remember the next day and not at all the next week.

She wanted the strong vibe.

Mechanical passion.

Orgasm motion.

No caring...just mutual release to push back darkness. To answer the bear's anger-hunger.

Now Ms. Wild Girl Hunting suddenly feels less sure, less in control, more vulnerable.

This is not her normal first-night feeling. Is Charli wrong? Too real?

Why shouldn't she just leave and head for one of those dyke dives the cabbie had told her about near Merrill Field? She could be totally Wild Girl there, in control, tough and taking.

But Charli's touch has conveyed such a promise of fulfillment.

And the little pulse is pounding, huge.

Wild Girl says gruffly, "Okay. Let's go to your place. But, I'm throbbing down there where your hand's been playing. I have to get off soon or I'll explode. So, sex first, then food, then more sex. Okay, Charli?"

Charli laughs out loud, "Sure. Sex first…lots of sex."

Charli thinks, "Something to be said for bedding lusty young women amped up on drugs and alcohol. Still…somehow, this one's better than that."

She leans forward and kisses Mill long and passionately. Wild Girl's arms go around her.

Charli ends the kiss and leans back, "Lucy love, you take my breath away. Let's go. Really, let's go now, darlin' Lucy."

Wild Girl moves urgently out of the booth on her way to satisfy herself in Charli's arms. Yet, she can't shake an anxious feeling that there's something threatening about Charli.

It's not like Charli isn't offering what Wild Girl Hunting craves…sex, lots of sex…and she wants release now. But where's the vibe? She wonders if maybe Charli knows the darkness, how to make it fade, even go away. Is that the disturbing difference she feels? How could that be bad?

Does the darkness somehow define Wild Girl…make her possible? And if Charli is offering to share something, something lighter, is that the threat? Does Mill want that?

Too confusing. Well, Wild Girl can always walk away.

Charli takes Mill's hand and Wild Girl feels the lightness in her touch. Deception doesn't belong in this here and now.

Mill turns to Charli and looks at her levelly, "Charli, my name is really Millicent and I'm from Cordova. You can just call me 'Mill.'"

Charli replies, "I wondered about the name. 'Lucy' didn't seem to fit you. Okay, nice to know you 'Millicent' or 'just Mill.' And nice to be with another Alaskan."

Charli kisses Mill again.

She gently touches her left breast, "Let's go, darlin' Mill."

Chapter 24 – A Different Waking Place

Mill wakes in Charli's arms in the middle of Charli's king-sized bed. When she opens her eyes, Charli kisses her temple, "Good morning, darlin' Mill."

Mill's forehead is pressed into Charli's slender chest. Charli's arms hold her gently but tightly.

Mill puts her arms around Charli and gives her a hug, "Good morning to you, darlin' Charli!"

Mill looks at her newest lover, one eyebrow raised, and her mouth twists ironically, "Don't we just sound like suburban newlyweds!"

Charli pokes Mill's ribs with an index finger, "Not a couple my mother would have called 'proper' but darlin' nonetheless. Still hungry?" They both laugh.

Last night, after first making love, the two women started out on a mission to prepare food. That hunger quickly turned into a shared joke as they bypassed the kitchen to made love on Charli's overstuffed couch, then in her whirlpool bath, and then on her bed.

Time after time, they agreed to take a break and cook something. But, these intentions rapidly dissolved into more sex…surging, powerful sex…slow, easy sex.

"Still horny?" Mill asks hopefully.

Charli smiles and winks at her. She stretches over Mill, brushing Mill's lips with her nipples. She lingers for a moment letting Mill taste. Then she takes a glass of orange juice from the night table.

She hands it to Mill, "Horny for you…always."

They had spent most of the night in Charli's master suite. So Mill has seen little of Charli's "little place." But now, after a few sips of orange juice, Mill jumps out of bed.

After using the bathroom, Mill steps into the main house and takes a quick look around. She notes that Charli's little place is not "little." It's a large, two-story loft in a converted industrial building standing on rocky bluffs overlooking Cook Inlet.

White walls and large windows give it a profound sense of openness. A two-story fireplace beautifully crafted from tan native stone, some well-placed lighting, and matte-finished hardwood floors convey a sense of warmth and integration.

Colorful paintings and sculpture with a Pacific Island feel deliver an upbeat mood.

The modern kitchen has every useful appliance. Off the kitchen, a breakfast nook looks out on Cook Inlet through a window-wall.

Every element of the loft reflects Charli—light, easy, focused, warm, inviting, efficient.

Mill tells her this when she returns to the bedroom. Charli hugs her close then hands Mill her juice glass "to give you a little energy."

Charli's wink when she delivers the glass hints that she has something sexual in mind. It doesn't test Mill's imagination much to figure out what Charli wants. No, the test is figuring out how to deliver it.

Charli has a really big collection of sex toys, boxes of them. As she said to Mill the night before, she is "a little bit of a nut about them." So, Mill has lots to choose from to satisfy her lover.

Mill sets aside her half-empty juice glass. She reaches for a double dildo on the night table, one with a built-in vibrator. Mill turns on the floppy tool. A low buzz fills the room.

"Okay," Mill says to Charli, "Let's make breakfast...."

Charli chuckles and rolls onto her back, "Sure, I'd like you over easy, please."

Mill slips the buzzing device into Charli. They entwine their legs and Mill mounts her end. They begin to move.

For a long time, their soft cries fill the room.

Then, finally replete, they collapse, kissing, into each other's sweaty embrace.

Mill whispers tiredly, "Will the made please clear the breakfast dishes..."

Mill is ready to leave Charli's at 10 a.m. At the door, Charli coyly presses a business card into Mill's hand, "Darlin' Mill, here's my info. Contact me anytime if you're back in town...whatever. Just call when you want. I'd love to see you again. And I know everybody in Anchorage, a least everybody who matters. So, if you want some help here with anything, finding a place...whatever...I'm your gal."

Mill hugs Charli again and gives her a long kiss, "Thanks, Charli. I'll definitely be in touch. I just don't know when."

They kiss again and hold each other tightly. Turning away, Mill leaves.

She catches a cab to the dry cleaners she uses on Third. "What a great night," she thinks to herself as she settles back against the cab's cushions. Mill hums happily as she rides along.

She feels a lot better this morning than she felt after many first nights. After all, she had been well-laid and, unlike how she feels after so many Wild Girl hunts, she has no hangover. These things are good.

And, best of all, the darkness is far away.

Mill recalls feeling a little nostalgic just as Charli closed her door. *That* feeling is definitely different, disturbing, even threatening.

Her mood lowers. Darkness approaches.

Wild Girl's bear-anger rises.

Wild Girl hunts alone, dammit!

She takes…she leaves.

That's how it works…how it has to work.

Wild Girl forces Charli out of her mind.

Mill picks up her black dress and other clothes at the dry cleaners and goes back to her haven. She changes into casual clothes and puts away the black dress and her leather outfit.

She leaves the storage facility and walks rapidly to a 24-hour diner less than a mile away.

In the security office, Drag Carlson watches Mill come in, a happy smile on her face.

Drag is really just the part-time custodian for the business, not a watchman. But he had figured out how to use his master key to get into the business office after it closes. And he learned how to operate the cameras covering the exits.

At first, he just used them to make sure his boss didn't sneak up on him goofing off. Later he learned to spy on the tenants.

As Mill leaves the building, Drag swivels the street-side camera to watch her quick stride moving away. He thinks, "Nice ass, little tighty. Yes, ol' Drag has plans for you, baby, plans he is firming up."

Drag taps a short piece of pipe wrapped in an old sock against the sole of his shoe. Watching Mill's backside, he smacks the pipe hard, then harder.

Okay, that stroke should knock her down, but not out. It'll do to start things. Drag things. He wants her awake….

_____//_____

Mill eats a hasty lunch at the diner. Suddenly she is tempted to call Charli for another night with her, but Wild Girl Hunting holds her back.

Would a second time work as well? At all?

Probably not. Wild Girl knows one-nighters produce the best passion, the best release, and the least mess…the most safety.

Still, the morning-after sex with Charli had been spectacular and Mill had been sober.

She takes out Charli's card. Should she call? No, best to leave it alone while she sorts out her feelings about actually knowing a lover, about more than one-night stands.

Besides, Wild Girl Hunting is ready again…bear-hungry.

When she gets loose, Wild Girl will satisfy.

She takes a cab from the diner to a motel in Spenard, a different place than she had used with Wyoming a month before.

Best not to be conspicuous, known. She wouldn't look for Wyoming this time. She would try a few other bars. But if he showed up at the other places, well, he might turn out to be the perfect second-nighter again.

A thought of Charli, then another of Tilly, push through her mind.

She drives the thoughts away.

Mill sighs.

The little pulse between her legs starts up. She begins to think about rich Thunder Fuck smoke filling her lungs, a rising tide of E.

Three more hours and Wild Girl Hunting can start her stalk.

She drops her clothes and steps into the old motel's clean shower with its cracked and patched yellow tile. She turns the water on hot, steamy. She draws the moisture into her lungs.

Good.

She soaps and rinses, toying with the idea of pleasing herself, of sending busy fingers into soapy recesses.

No, better to let the little pulse build, lift it high with dope and E, and send it raging out with Wild Girl.

At five, Mill takes a cab back to her haven to change. As she walks to the storage room, she looks around for the big man who had accosted her the day before.

No one on her floor. Silent.

Mill opens the door to her storage room and snaps on the lights.

What's this?

She sees her lockbox on the vanity, the contents spread across the surface.

Cold shock hits her. Surely she left the lockbox in the wardrobe.

116

Son of a bitch! That bastard must have waited for her to leave and then broke in!

Anxious, she strides forward.

She barely catches a glimpse of Drag's swinging arm in the vanity's mirror. Before she can react, his practiced hand smacks the pipe against her head just behind her right ear. Thunk!

Mill folds up and drops to the floor, half conscious, unable to move or speak. Her head is whirling, ears roaring…ringing.

A metallic taste fills her mouth.

Drag grabs an armload of her clothes from the wardrobe and drops them to the floor. He rolls her on top of the pile, face up.

He seizes her hands and ties each wrist above her head with a rope wound around a wardrobe leg.

A snarl on his lips, Drag rips open her blouse and bra, exposing her chest. When she doesn't move or protest, he reaches down and strips her naked below the waist.

She tries to move but can't. She tries to yell but makes no noise.

Drag runs his hands up and down her body.

Staring into her unfocused eyes, Drag pinches her hard between the legs. She whimpers but the sound is lost to the roaring in her head.

"I'm gonna make it hurt, Lucy Moore," he says, "Unless you do what I say when I say it."

He twists her nipples. Mill whimpers louder. This time she hears her pain.

Then, for no reason befuddled Mill can understand, Drag stands up. He waves what must be a piece of wood or pipe in a sock at her threateningly, "You stay there and be quiet. I'll be back to deal with you in a few minutes."

He opens the door, glances up and down the hall, and slips out.

Mill wonders groggily where the bastard is going.

She can't know this, but Drag has to make sure no one else is around. A quick check of the security cameras will guarantee his privacy.

He has promised himself that Lucy Twist will scream…a lot.

Mill hears his heavy steps recede down the hallway.

Now Mill's fear and adrenaline are firing all her circuits. Her mind clears.

Mill was raped at fourteen. She knows that teary place of total, crushing helplessness and violation.

Is that what Drag has planned? If so, he could have taken her while she was half knocked out. So, maybe not.

Then what does the jerk really want? Rip her off? Blackmail her? Kill her?

Most urgently, how long he'll be gone?

No matter, she will have to act fast. Whatever he has planned, that shit isn't going to happen to Mill Meacham, not today, not ever again.

Her rape experience tells her that she has to get free…move, run, escape, attack…whatever, now.

She tries her strength. It's back.

Her wrists are bound tightly against the wardrobe's leg. She pulls against her bonds and slides her face close to the knots.

After an unsuccessful struggle to pull the knots loose with her teeth, Mill realizes she is taking too much time…almost panics. She calms herself and checks the rope. Her probing fingers follow it under the wardrobe. They tell her that the leg isn't uniform—two blocks with a hollow behind.

Mill squirms onto her side and shoves her hands under the wardrobe. Scraping some skin, she gets her right hand all the way into the hollow.

She touches the knot on her right wrist and realizes she is touching a double half hitch. She digs the fingers of her left hand into it and urgently pushes and pulls. She gradually feels it loosen a little, then more.

Now, pull! Her right hand slowly slides out of the knot and pops out from under the wardrobe, costing her some more skin.

Free!

She pulls her left hand out. But what next?

She listens for a moment…no sound of the goon.

She touches the rising lump behind her ear. He could do more and worse than this! What should she do?

She resists her strong impulse to dress, grab her valuables, and run. Looking at the open lockbox, a re-found horror strikes her. He had gone through her stuff. He probably knows about the dope, the Ecstasy.

She can't run and still hope to be Wild Girl Hunting. She has to deal with him here, one way or another.

Footsteps clomp far away. Anxiety spreads through her.

Mill's vision starts to cloud around the edges. She calms down with an effort.

What to do? She has nothing to hit him with. The little panty dagger might cut him but, returning like this, he will be wary, maybe have a gun.

No time to look for the dagger anyway. She will have to surprise him and take him down somehow. She'll have to fake it…trap him.

Mill quickly wraps the rope back around the wardrobe leg like Drag had done. She lies down, opens her blouse widely to expose her breasts, and twists her wrists around the loose rope ends until she looks tied again.

She spreads her naked legs and closes her eyes.

Drag enters. He looks down, "Nice. Time to wake up, Sleeping Beauty. Drag has somethin' to give you."

He kneels and reaches down to pinch her, this time on the inner thigh.

At his painful touch, Mill opens her eyes. She sends a long look down her naked body. His eyes follow hers.

A cold smile begins to form on his lips. He moves his hand up from her thigh to her low belly.

He licks his lips, "I think you'd like some of ol' Drag's big buddy…."

"Sure," Wild Girl whispers, "Do me now. I like it rough. Sure."

Drag leans across her. He puts his hands on her hips and starts to slide her closer to him.

He reaches one hand towards his belt buckle, his attention on what lies below her waist.

Now!

Mill's left hand whips out from under the cord. With all the force she can muster from her off-balance position, Mill drives four bladed knuckles into his throat.

Her blade-punch is dead on.

Drag's head whips back against the wall. Thunk! The sound of a slaughterhouse sledgehammer smashing a steer's skull.

Rebounding, Drag falls, eyes bulging, choking, to his hands and knees.

Mill jumps to her feet. She gauges the distance to Drag's head carefully.

Mill spins in a tight circle and crescent kicks him full-force behind his ear, paying him back for the lump on her head.

Drag's heavy body whips around. He sprawls limply, face smacking the concrete floor.

Mill drops into fighting stance next to him, hands defending, ready for another punch or kick. She stays in this position for a time and looks at him.

Will he need another kick? A choke-hold?

Doesn't look like it. No need.

This shitheel, Drag or whatever he called himself, is down and out cold.

Mill's heart is trying to beat its way out of her chest. She stands and leans against the wall, a little dizzy from excitement, Drag's blow, and the exertion of putting him down.

She squats, back against the wardrobe, until the dizziness passes.

Calmer after a moment, she wonders, "Do I call the cops? Then they'll have my name, maybe find the dope. Figure out what I'm doing." Not a good plan. "What if he dies? Now, there's a bad future."

She wills Drag to live...as a vegetable. He obligingly makes a snoring noise. Good.

Wild Girl sneers at Drag, "Look, loser shit bag, you probably won't talk after getting your ass kicked by a girl. But how do I know? Maybe you *should* die."

Mill calms down even more, "No, not good."

So, what should she do with him until she can clear out of here, vanish?

Looks like the best thing will be to hide him, keep him locked up or something until she can disappear. What about one of those big green garbage containers out back? Tie him up and dump him in one of them like the trash he is. No, too public.

Better dump him here inside the building. A utility room? An unused storage room? But, how to move him?

Mill thinks of the flat-bed dollies the storage company provides for patrons. Okay.

Mill ties Drag's hands behind him with his rope and checks his pockets. She finds some of her jewelry, the dope, E, money, dagger, and her fake IDs.

Mill suddenly worries about her real ID hidden in the lining of her Cordova suitcase. She jumps over Drag and pokes around in the rolling case. Her ID and credit cards are where she left them.

120

Had he seen them, touched them, maybe even copied down the information? Mill doesn't think so. They're in the same place she remembers leaving them.

And why would Drag leave the real goods in the suitcase and put her fake IDs is in his pocket?

Reassured, Mill dresses quickly in her Cordova clothes, then checks to make sure Drag is still out. No surprise, he is.

She runs down the hall for a dolly. Hauling it back to the storage compartment, she tugs and rolls Drag's unconscious body out into the hall and up onto the dolly's flat surface.

Once he is on board, Mill can roll his considerable weight around without too much strain. She sees that Drag's feet and legs hang over the edges quite a bit but it doesn't look like he will fall off. She looks at his sprawling limbs and decides she really doesn't care if she runs them into a few sharp corners.

Mill drags the dolly down the hall to the elevator. When the door opens, she tugs it in.

Where to now? She punches the top floor button. The elevator jerks and then rises. When the door opens, she sees a row of empty storage compartments, doors open.

She rolls the dolly to the first unused compartment, a big room with a roll-up door, tugs the dolly inside, and shoves Drag off. His face smacks the floor again. On impact, he makes snorting noises, so she knows he is still alive.

Good! Even if he deserves it, the bastard hasn't died yet.

She is leaving him alive, on his own. No fault, no foul on Mill.

She re-ties his hands tighter just in case the knots loosened on the way up. Suddenly inspired, she ties his shoe laces tightly together and says, "Okay, useless prick, I hope it takes you a month to get loose and a month more for someone to find you."

Mill pulls the empty dolly back out into the hall and rolls down the door. It has a crude latch that accepts a padlock. But Mill doesn't need a lock. The latch is made so it can only be operated from the outside. A guy inside with his hands and feet tied doesn't have a chance of opening it.

And once Drag wakes up and somehow gets loose, with luck he will have to kick and rattle the door or yell for days before anyone hears him. Mill checks to make sure the lock is all the way closed and the little security tab holds the lock handle is in place. Tight!

She heads for the elevator with the dolly.

Back at her compartment, Mill parks the dolly in the hallway and scrubs a little Drag blood off it with tissues and water. She piles her suitcase, clothes, and personal items on it, burying her lockbox under the rest.

Going back inside, she uses the tissues and water to clean up a few drops of Drag blood from the floor. No need to leave a trace of anything for the building owners to wonder about.

Then she takes a final look around the little room, checking to make sure everything that can go with her or might identify her is loaded. She has to leave the nice big wardrobe, vanity, lamps, and mirror behind.

She likes those things.

She sighs.

The door locks behind her as she leaves.

Mill feels a little tear of rage and regret trickle from her right eye. Stupid fat fucker ruined her safe haven! So unfair!

She should have kicked him again, hard, in the balls, just for spite! Shaking her head, she hauls her dolly-load to the elevator. Waiting for it to arrive, she flips open her cell phone and calls a cab.

The elevator jerk-stops on the first floor. She will overnight in the run-down, edge-of-Spenard motel she rented earlier. Tomorrow morning she will have to find another storage place for Wild Girl Hunting's gear.

_____//_____

Alaska Airlines Flight 66 blasts down the runway with Mill on board.

The tail art on most Alaska Airlines planes displays the face of a smiling Alaska Native. According to Alaska lore, the image belongs to Iditarod Sled Dog Race founder, **Joe** Redington, Sr.

In his day, the airlines and Joe denied it. No one knows for sure

Mill doesn't especially care about the Screaming Eskimo's identity. Seated next to the 737s engines, Mill says to herself, "The Screamin' Eskimo sure has a big mouth tonight!"

The loud noise is especially irritating to Mill after her chaotic Anchorage weekend. The engine noise drops as the plane climbs into the clouds, levels out, and heads for Cordova.

Mill gets a little less grumpy.

122

She feels more tired than she has ever been after an Anchorage weekend.

First up so high, so fun with Charli. That first night so different, such strong sex and such strong connection.

Then dropping so low, so down with that watchman guy. What had he called himself, "Drag?" Well, that was certainly a good name for him. He definitely had been a drag on Mill's weekend, her whole life for that matter.

Then after Drag, what a bad second-night.

Mill too afraid to go out. No dope. No hunt. Just the golden bullet in the seedy motel. And even after several orgasms, no sleep. So anxious.

Damn him again! She has to piece her Anchorage life back together. Build another haven.

How frustrating!

On Sunday morning, she had stuffed her Anchorage things into a new storage-space rental, a temporary fix.

Mill wonders if she should rent an apartment or a room. And yet that could be so expensive, ultimately so unsafe. She'd be tempted to bring lovers there and take easy risks. Then, people like Drag would be able to find her, pin her down.

Maybe a bigger storage room, even one in a private home or a garage.

But wouldn't Drag be checking all angles, looking for her to get even? Damn that bastard!

Would there ever be a safe place for Mill and Wild Girl Hunting in Anchorage again?

Mill is suddenly struck with a terrible thought. Who *really* had been the hunter? Maybe while Wild Girl thought she was hunting, other, bigger predators like Drag had been trying to take *her* down. Had they just missed until this weekend?

Maybe she had always been the *prey* and not the hunter at all…not a bear but a fawn.

A deep chill runs down her spine.

Wild Girl Hunting could easily be Millicent Meacham, dead meat.

Her vision clouds with anxiety. She can barely see the seat back in front of her.

Could Drag, or someone even worse, know about Cordova, about her real name and her real life? Could a deadly predator be on her trail right now?

Mill had escaped Drag.

But maybe he has ruined Wild Girl Hunting anyway.

She breathes deeply several times and relaxes her body.

She reminds herself that Drag can't know. No one can know. Her real ID remains hidden.

No Drag on this flight.

Anchorage trouble behind.

Cordova home ahead.

Exhausted, Mill's head sags back onto the head cushion. She drops into a sleep so deep that she doesn't wake until the Eskimo screams down the Cordova runway and bang-jolts to a stop.

Chapter 25 - Ready, Steady, Go

A day back from Anchorage, Mill faces another instructor practicing kicks, blows, and evasion at the Cordova Martial Arts Academy.

She bounces on the balls of her feet, holding a vision of Drag in her mind. She screams, "Taaah," and launches a spinning kick at Jersey Jerry's head. He grins and ducks, retreating.

Compared to Mill, Jerry is huge, an easy match for Drag in size. But big or not, Jerry uses his sharp quickness to evade her kick. He doesn't want any of her blows to land, no matter how lightly she throws them.

As an instructor here, Mill has already led two classes this morning, one for beginners and one for intermediates. Those classes are fun for her...eager kids and young adults, all trying to get it right...earn their belts...be top doggies.

While she teaches them, she has to watch their erratic feet and elbows, clumsy throws and holds. More than one instructor has been hurt by students.

Mill had no trouble taking Drag down with an unexpected attack. Yet she had been painfully knocked off her feet twice today by ungainly and too-forceful students.

Mill was originally attracted to karate-jutsu as a teen because of her desire to protect herself. And she stayed with it because it brought order and a kind of serenity to much of her life.

Although martial arts are intended to ready students for personal "war," they are more about life and living it than killing or hurting others, more about conquering self than opponents. If students achieve self-discipline, Mill knows the actual martial-arts techniques come much easier. So, as Mill leads her students through their karate-jutsu exercises, she reminds them regularly about focus, discipline, and the importance of building strong life-energy, called "chi."

Jerry moves in quickly and throws Mill over his hip. She lands easily on the wrestling mat and bounces back to her feet. Just as she is adjusting her gi for another round, a gong sounds, signaling the end of the hour set aside for sparring.

Relaxing, the pair walks off the mat into the break area.

Jerry says to Mill, "You're working me hard today, girl. Are you training for a meet... Olympics...what?"

"No, not really, Jerr," Mill smiles. Grabbing her hand towel, she wipes sweat from her face, "No, I'm going out as Forest Service rep on a reality show. It's a kinda race called the 'Great Land Geo-Challenge.' If I don't get in shape for it, it'll surely kick my butt."

"Wow," replies Jerry, "What's this all about? Maybe I want to enter." Jerry is a competitive guy. Races of any kind interest him.

Mill begins to fill Jerry in on the Geo-Challenge. Other instructors drift over to listen and join the discussion.

The attention embarrasses Mill a little. After all, she isn't a Geo-Challenge contestant, just an agency nerd...nobody important. She fills everyone in about the race and then answers questions.

After her explanation, Mill enjoys listening to them kick around the craziness of the three stages and the geo-caches, but mostly the insanity of sending the cheechako racers unarmed into bear country.

After promising to help Mill any way they can, the group breaks up.

As Mill packs her sparring gear, one of the quieter instructors, Jared Springer, approaches her. "Mill," he says, "You know Melony and I like to run cross-country. If you'd like to join us for the next couple of months, we'd be glad to have you go along. Melony's always complaining that, since we got married, I leave her behind when we run any distance at all."

Jared looks a little sheepish, "I guess she might be right. When we lived apart, I wanted to spend all my spare time with her. Now that we're together all the time, I feel more like breaking away. I guess I'll never get it right. Yeah, I'm sure Melony'd love to have someone to run with...talk to."

Mill looks at Jared. This was the longest speech he had ever made to her. Clearly a shy guy, she appreciates that he is willing to support her now. Plus Melony is a top runner and does a couple of marathons a year-- just the person to stretch Mill out and build up her endurance.

"Jared, that's the nicest offer of physical punishment I've had all week,"

Mill dimples up at him, "I'd be pleased to join you and Melony. Just be merciful on an out-of-shape bureaucrat."

They both laugh. Jared writes down Mill's phone numbers. He promises to get back to her as soon as he talks things through with Melony.

They leave the Academy and head for home.

Mill smiles as she lets herself into her snug little Cordova apartment.

She had held mental fingers crossed as she told Jared about that "the nicest offer in the last week" business. After all, although her first-night with Charli could hardly been called "punishment," it definitely had been physical...and a lot nicer than running cross country around Cordova.

Now in her shower, Mill lets the pleasant memories of Charli's lithe, strong body wash over her. Charli's quick fingers and darting tongue had been all over her like warm water.

The ever-ready pulse between Mill's legs flickers and then beats. This time Mill doesn't drive the passion down and away. She steps out of the shower and towels off.

Moving in a controlled walk, hips swaying, she goes to her luggage and finds the golden bullet. Turning it on, she raises it in a buzzing salute to Charli's boxes of sex toys.

She sits in her easy chair, legs wide and presses the bullet in...there...right there...now.

An hour later, curled up in bed, dreamless sleep takes Mill down, away.

Chapter 26 - Armando Suemez

On Wednesday, a tall man wearing a navy blue sport coat and neatly pressed tan slacks appears at the door to Mill's cubie. Outside of church and few official events like city council candidates running for office, Mill could not recall seeing anyone dressed so formally in Cordova.

She smiles up at the man, "You're not from around here, are you?"

He chuckles, "Funny, that's what the receptionist said when I came in."

He takes one careful step into her crowded space and holds out his hand, "I'm Special Agent Armando Suemez from the Southwest Region in Albuquerque. Are you Millicent Meacham?"

Mill looks more closely at Suemez. She notes a lean brown face, sun- and wind-scarred, slightly damaged by youthful acne. Suemez certainly looks like he hails from the Southwest.

Suemez' mouth is more a crease…severe, almost lipless.

But, as he meets Mill's inquiring gaze, his mouth stretches up and wide into a beautiful grin. His slightly crooked, white teeth beam out at her.

Along with the smile, his twice-broken nose gives his face an almost tipsy, rough appearance. In different clothes he might be taken for an amiable barfly or somebody's scruffy fishing buddy.

But Mill looks into his bright, intelligent eyes and sees a relentless curiosity and resolve. He has the appraising eyes of an old-west sheriff, warm to people needing help and merciless to lawbreakers.

Smile or not, anyone underestimating Suemez would be making a big mistake. An uneasy thought flashes into Mill's mind. Perhaps Suemez is here because of her Anchorage life.

Did that creature Drag die? File a complaint?

No, Suemez wouldn't be here for that. It would be Anchorage cops or ASP that stood before her if the visit was about Drag.

Her fear subsides.

Suemez watches as emotions flit across Mill's face. Her initial fear is apparent.

He thinks, "Does this girl have something to hide?" Then when her fear fades quickly, Suemez grows less concerned.

Suemez believes every normal person has a "guilt list," things they've done wrong but never confessed or reconciled. So, when confronted by law enforcement, a person mentally checks the guilt list. They ask themselves, "Who told on me?" or "How did he find out?"

But once they come up with nothing that could be known or at least not actionable, they relax. Yes, Meacham has some things on her guilt list, but nothing she fears Suemez over and, based on her reaction, her list might be fairly short.

Suemez knows not to judge potential criminals by initial impressions. But like every experienced investigator, he knows his gut often gives him his first read on someone's credibility and honesty.

Everyone has things on their guilt list. But people give off signals and Suemez has learned to read those "tells." In fact, he has taught trainees how to detect lies and evasions by reading facial expressions and body language at the Federal Law Enforcement Training Center in Georgia.

Mill holds out her hand, "Yes, I'm Meacham. Please call me, 'Mill.' Nice to meet you Special Agent Suemez! What can I do for you?"

Suemez smiles thinly, "Well, first, please call me 'Manny.' And speaking of work, it's more what I can do for you."

Manny looks at Mill seriously, "I travelled here at the Alaska Region's request to look into this bear-take issue between you and Game and Fish Enforcement. I'm wondering if you have a few minutes to talk to me this morning."

Manny watches her closely to see if she has another fear reaction. Instead, he sees her smile confidently and begin to look indignant. His concern about her guilt recedes even further.

On her part, Mill is quite surprised that Suemez has come to Cordova so quickly. Mitch Mendenhall had only sent the request in a week ago.

But she also knows how Forest Service Legacies network and how the Green Creed works to protect Legacy employees and children. So, she imagines that arrangements were being finalized before the attorney's formal request came in.

No matter how Suemez has gotten here, she is glad to see him. "Okay, Manny," she grins, "I'm sure glad to see you. What do you need from me?"

"Well," Manny replies, mouth once again a tight crease, "Why don't we find a private place to talk and we'll get down to business."

Mill nods. They head down to the district ranger's office. Percy has gone to Anchorage for a forest leadership team meeting, so Mill figures she and Manny can commandeer Percy's space.

They get coffee and settle in.

Manny opens a file he has been carrying, "Just some background first, Mill." His slight Hispanic accent changes her name to "Meel."

She finds it charming. He takes out a list and begins reading from it. It's made up of dates, times, and events that cover the whole bear incident, ending with Mitch telling Mill, Dill, and Percy to leave the fish-cop office and to have no more communication with them.

Suemez looks at her, "That sound like everything that's happened to date?"

Mill replies, "Yes, I haven't heard a peep from anyone since."

She looks at him curiously, "So, before we go any further, I'm dying to ask. Why *are* you dressed like you're headed out for a big-city night on the town."

Suemez looks a little sheepish, "Well, I wanted to interview the Game and Fish Enforcement guys and look at any evidence they would let me see in Anchorage before coming over here to Cordova. My luggage got lost between Seattle and Anchorage…go figure where…and it hasn't caught up yet. So, although I feel kinda like a fish outta water…or a bear at a barbeque…whatever you Alaskans say…I thought I'd just soldier through my fashion fox pass."

Mill laughs at his explanation, "Hey, if I were you I'd just walk through town looking proud. It'll be a week's worth of gossip if you refuse to tell people who you are!"

Suemez laughs shortly then turns to serious business again, "Okay, enough about why I look like a *girasol* in a fireweed patch."

Suemez takes out a legal pad and a pencil. He also takes a small digital voice recorder from his pocket and sets it on the ranger's desk, "Please just forget the recorder's there. I'm not taking a formal statement from you. It's just there so I can listen to what you say later and make sure I didn't miss something. Okay with you?"

Mill replies, "Yes, fine with me."

Suemez turns on the recorder, gives the date, his name and badge number, and states he is interviewing Mill Meacham concerning a bear-take incident. He looks at her expectantly, "So, Mill, please state your name and then tell me your story. Just start at the beginnin' and tell me the whole thing the way you would to a friend. Try not to leave anything out. I won't interrupt but you should figure on a bunch-a questions at the end. Okay with you?"

When Mill says "Yeah, sure," Suemez sits back in Percy's chair, face neutral, and listens carefully.

Mill begins with her name and position on the Cordova Ranger District. She starts her story with a brief description of the overall fisheries work plan for the summer. Then she explains the field work she and Dill had done all that long day along the rolling Copper River.

As she starts on the bear attack part of her story, quite unexpectedly, Mill's voice breaks and a few tears shine in her eyes.

Manny says, "Just take your time, Mill. Do you need a break or something...water, maybe?"

Mill shakes her head "No." Suemez' supportive words help pull her past the rough spot.

Mill goes over the attack in detail—the bear's initial charge, his relentless pursuit, their struggle across the Copper, then finally the showdown in the pond.

She talks about her feelings—the fear, her panic, her numb, fierce, to-the-death attack on the bear, her near-death lethargy after killing him, her joy at being rescued by Dill, and the warm feelings she had towards the district employees and their families who had come out to the landing to welcome her soggy butt home.

As Mill explains the last bit about Dill's rescue and the warm embraces at the landing, she breaks down. She cries for a long time, unable to muster enough control to continue. Finally, she whispers, "I really don't have anything more."

Manny has been watching her and listening closely, making a few notes. His gut check tells him Mill's being completely honest. Although he had let nothing she said change his expression, hairs stood up on the back of his neck a couple of times while she told her story.

"*Jodame!*" he thinks, "*Que chica valienta*...what a tough little gal."

Suemez looks down at his notes. "Okay, Mill, I have some specific questions for you. Ready?"

Feeling calmer, Mill wipes her eyes and smiles at him, "Sure, go ahead."

Suemez asks, "So, what about the rifle. Did you handle it that day?"

Mill thinks back, "Yes, taking it in and out of the boat."

He nods, "Alright, what about opening or closing the bolt, loading ammunition in the magazine, taking it out, or pulling the trigger to dry fire it? Do any of those things?"

Mill shakes her head, "I might have worked the bolt to chamber a round or to make sure it was empty. But Dill loaded the weapon before we left. And he took care of the ammo when we got back. I never touched the trigger or even the trigger guard except to check the safety, that's all. Why are you asking about the rifle?"

"Well, although Game and Fish Enforcement didn't say it, I think their theory is that you used the rifle to kill the bear. I mean, in their view, any other theory would be ridiculous. They probably figure you couldn't beat a bear in hand-to-hand combat. They would ask themselves did you use the rifle? A knife? The boat anchor? I don't know what they think, but it's not that you drowned the bear or I wouldn't be here."

Suemez shrugs, "So, I'm just trying to get more information about the use of the gun. Who handled it and when or shot it…that stuff."

Mill says, "Okay, well, I can't prove that I didn't fire the rifle. But I didn't touch the ammunition."

Manny looks thoughtful, "Did Game and Fish Enforcement seize the gun as evidence or test you or Mr. Dillard for gunshot residue? That would have been swabbing your hands, your forearms, and maybe your face on the side you normally mount a rifle."

Mill replies, "No, none of that."

Suemez continues, "One final thing, a different topic. Do you think Mr. Dillard's story will match yours?"

Mill nods, "Yeah, I'm sure it will. I mean he had control of the rifle in the boat the whole time I was trying to deal with the bear in the river. I'm sure if he had seen the bear trailing me across the Copper or trying to attack me in the pond, he would have used the gun to scare it or kill it. I'm sure he'll tell you that."

Suemez looks thoughtful, "Okay, I'll interview him tomorrow. So, just so everything stays cool, don't tell him what we discussed or what questions I might be asking between now and then. In fact, if you can, don't have any contact with him at all. Okay?" Mill quickly agrees.

Suemez looks at his notes again, "Is there a bear expert on the district? The reason why I ask is that Game and Fish Enforcement has already contacted the official Alaska bear biologist for an expert opinion about whether you could have drowned this bear. Little Mill, big bear…all that. I'm guessing that no matter what the bear guy really thinks, he might be pressured to roll over to their view of the facts. So, I'd like to have a second opinion from an expert…maybe have our person go over the necropsy report."

Mill shakes her head, "No, no one on the district. Our wildlife bio is Carrie Muir but she works mainly with bird species like the Dusky Canada Goose and those millions of Sandpipers that come through here every year. Maybe she'd know someone, though."

Suemez smiles his bright smile, "Okay. I'll talk to Carrie. And…I think that's all for Mill today. You did really well. Thanks for your cooperation. I'm sure I'll have more questions later."

Mill smiles back mischievously, dimples showing, "Special Agent Suemez, aren't you going to tell me not to leave town?"

Suemez scowls and tries to look stern. Then, unable to hold his expression, laughs, "No, no, only cops on TV tell people that crazy stuff. No better way to signal that you think someone's a suspect than say 'don't leave town.' If real cops told someone that, many of 'em would rabbit or dump evidence. Hey, I'd rather say 'Looks like that's all we'll need from you. Everything looks okay.' And then put surveillance on them or surprise them with a search warrant. That works!"

They both laugh.

Suemez stands and says, "Mill, I think I'll be able to wrap everything up in a week or two. After that, it's up to the attorneys. I can't speak for them. But I'm sure they'll be in touch after my report gets to them. Again, thanks. I'm glad you made it home safe."

Manny offers his hand, they shake, and he heads out the door.

Mill knows things could still go badly. She could lose her job, pay big fines, or even go to jail. But, come what may, she feels like she has a pro working on her side.

Mill leaves the ranger's office with a profound sense of relief.

Chapter 28 - Up and Down, All Around

Two weeks later, Percy calls Mill and Dill into his office for a teleconference with Mitch Mendenhall.

There, Mill finds out that Manny Suemez had been as good as his word. Mitch explains that Manny's report arrived two days before and that he has reviewed it thoroughly, "So, let me cut to the chase right off, Manny believes the state's case is strictly circumstantial. They have no evidence of wrongdoing whatsoever. So, unless a witness comes forward or some other evidence appears, their case will be based just on expert testimony and outright speculation."

Mill, Dill, and the ranger all start to grin widely. Mill and Dill do a soft high-five.

Mendenhall's voice changes to a lower tone, "That was the good news. So here's the bad. Special Agent Suemez also believes they fully intend to prosecute you and they may even get a conviction."

The three now look stricken. Percy asks, "How can that be, Mitch? I mean you said 'no evidence of wrongdoing,' didn't you?"

"Yes, I did," Mitch responds, "But in Alaska they don't always need physical evidence of game violations to get a conviction. Let me take a quick minute and tell you why. Here's what I think I've figured out by talking to old-timers and some of our current employees."

"Way back, before Alaska became a state in 1959, residents fished and hunted pretty much as they wanted. Out-of-state hunters ditto. There were federal regulations that covered the Alaska Territory but enforcement was pretty lax. Alaska was America's "Serengeti," a vast reservoir of hunting and fishing opportunities."

"After statehood, the new Alaska government acted to protect resident hunters and support state-licensed guides. Then over the years, they created a complex system of requirements for out-of-state hunters and fishers. For example, in some places, out-of-staters had to bring meat back to town with the bone in and residents didn't. Out-of-state brown-bear hunters had to be guided but residents didn't."

"The reasons for these requirements were honorable enough on the face of it—to prevent the wanton waste of meat in the first case and to keep tenderfoot hunters safe in the second. But in addition to guaranteeing guides a livelihood, the effect of the state's regulations was to create more violations for out-of-staters and, therefore, more cash flow to the state."

The three people in Cordova are beginning to wonder what this has to do with them.

As if reading their minds, Mendenhall remarks, "Okay. So, you're not out-of-staters. But let me finish and I'll get back to your case. The state gradually raised fees for the out-of-state folks. Today, outsiders pay about ten times what residents pay to hunt and fish. So, all in all, totaling up fees and money from violations, the state gets a lot of income from out-of-state hunters and fishers. I can give you the numbers if you want, but that's not really germane."

He continues, "For a long time, Game and Fish enforcement stayed focused on nailing out-of-staters. Hey, it was good money and the local people supported the whole idea of making strangers pay through the nose. Not very hospitable, but also not much different than anywhere else."

"Then, in the late 1970's or thereabouts, things began to change. Big-money oil development on the North Slope changed relationships all over and the state's interests started to diverge from those of rural people and traditional Alaskans. Gradually, where once they had close ties, state agencies started to mistrust and then later attack rural folks.

"Things were especially hard on the Alaska Game and Fish Department and ASP's Game and Fish Enforcement because they lost effective control on federal lands due to federal legislation and its conflicts with the Alaska Constitution. The whole business really pissed them off. Things went rapidly to the political dark side."

"So, here's the punch line. What the fish cops used to delight in doing to out-of-staters, they began to do to residents. They began to use enforcement for political purposes. Rural people and their supporters in cities often lined up with federal agencies to protect rural hunting and fishing rights. Game and Fish Enforcement targeted those people, partly for lining up with the feds and partly because they had few votes and little political clout. Eventually federal employees involved with fish management were also targeted."

Mendenhall laughs ironically, "I bet you're getting my point now. Let me add a couple of other worrisome things. Game and Fish Enforcement actually pays their own prosecutor. They say it's to give violators a speedy trial but it also helps them avoid prosecutorial constraints on their actions. The fish cops also appear at trial in uniform, not just to testify or sit in the public seating, but to sit at the prosecutor's table. They say they're present to offer advice to the prosecutor. True enough, but they are also there to stare down the judge if a trial's not going their way. That near-intimidation is something that no court will permit at any other kind of trial."

"And to make matters even more interesting, the lack of evidence in your case is somewhat of an advantage for them. Because wild foods get eaten and evidence disappears, judges are used to speculative cases where the prosecutor presents little or no material evidence. So, to prove their case, prosecutors rely heavily on carefully prepared expert witnesses. Judges listen to those experts and after many trials get know them...believe them."

By now, Mill and Dill are truly alarmed.

A dry-mouthed Mill stutters, "Well...Mitch...ah...what can we do? I mean seems like we're sitting ducks, Dill and I. We have a lot to lose. What should we do?"

Mitch's voice comes through the phone drily but with a hint of compassion, "Yes, you do have a lot to lose. But so does the federal government. Although it's up to Alaska to clean up their game and fish enforcement system, the federal government can't put up with state employees targeting feds for political purposes."

His voice changes to a grim tone, "So, I've made a proposal to the U.S. Attorney in Anchorage that, based on Manny's work, we bring in the FBI to investigate. I don't know a lot about this branch of law, but what the state seems to be doing is something like state-sponsored extortion. You know, like those places with speed traps where one mile over a speed limit of seven miles an hour gets you a hundred-dollar fine. The corruption, if any, could run deep. It may even extend to judges and some trial attorneys. It could be a big deal, I guess, if the USA decides to act."

Now Mendenhall sounds tired, "I can't tell you what the USA might decide. This stuff is big politics—could upset the balance of power between states and the federal government and all that. So, you shouldn't expect anything soon. Just sit tight until we get an answer. And absolutely do not discuss this with anyone, including each other. If word gets out, it'll create big problems for the U.S. Attorney and the FBI'll have a hard time getting anything done. Okay, I'm finally out of breath. More questions please?"

The call goes on for another half hour until Mendenhall has to leave for another meeting. His parting shot, "Remember, no talking to anyone, not even each other, unless it's me or someone from the U.S. Attorney's office. Clear?"

The three agree and hang up.

They leave the ranger's office shaking their heads.

Walking to her cubie, Mill thinks, "Whoo, what a roller-coaster ride that call was. Bad…good…bad…wait… talk…don't talk. This country girl is not prepared for such craziness!"

She sits at her desk for an hour, unable to work, anxiety crowding and blurring her vision. Her sight finally clears after she stares out at the sunny waters of Prince William Sound, beckoning her out to adventure.

She turns to her computer keyboard and starts typing. She has a bunch of things to get done before a team comes in to work with Dill on the summer projects. Mill works quickly because she is due to leave tomorrow to begin full-time preparations for the Great Land Geo-Challenge in Fairbanks.

The three agency representatives will spend two weeks training on equipment and preparing physically. Then the tech crews will join them for a week or ten days so they can learn to work together.

Mill will spend the training time where she likes to be—outdoors.

And she will be learning new stuff, including use of the satellite phone and the advanced etrex GPS unit.

At last, she smiles.

Almost time to go!

Chapter 29 -- Back in Bear Flanks

Mill had been told someone would meet her 9 a.m. flight and drive her to the Alaska Fire Service Center. When she enters the terminal, she is a little shocked when her driver turns out to be Smoky Joe, master wildland firefighter.

His big grin and welcoming hand quickly ends any shyness she feels, "Great to see you, Mill. I'm glad you're going to work with us."

They make small talk for a moment, and then Schmoker asks with concern in his voice, "I heard about a bear incident you had a few months ago. Are you over that yet? Still having nightmares about it?"

Mill marvels that Joe cares about her well-being. Surely this important guy has a lot more on his mind than whether Mill still has nightmares about bear attacks. She does.

"Yeah, I'm pretty well over that business, Mr. Schmoker. I still wake up to noises in my apartment, wondering if it's a bear sneaking up on me. But I started with about ten sleep interruptions a night right after the incident. I'm down to maybe one or two a week now. My doctor in Cordova says that's pretty typical, so I must be doing okay. And…thanks for asking. I didn't even know you knew."

Smoky Joe smiles, "Well, I like to keep track, you know, of my team. I've been in the fire service so long, I know that every team member has to be in good shape or mistakes get made and bad stuff happens. So, I like to check. I'm not trying to be nosy, just in touch. Okay with you?"

Mill appreciates his consideration. Her luggage arrives and they walk out of the terminal to a white van emblazoned with the words "Alaska Fire Service" in fiery orange letters outlined in black. The bright words are accompanied by black-highlighted orange stripes that extend around and over the van. The whole color scheme is professionally done but really stands out.

"Wow," says Mill thinking of the small Forest Service shield and tame green stripes on her agency's white fire vehicles, "You can't miss who owns this rig!"

"No," Joe answers, "You really can't. It's pretty wild sitting next to vehicles here at the airport. But out in fire camp, there're sometimes hundreds of vehicles parked together in the staging or parking areas. Lots of them white. So, we put these fire-fighter stripes on our rigs. You can spot 'em from any direction, even flying over."

Mill throws her bags into the back of the van, "Good thinking!" She is instantly embarrassed at offering her opinion to such a high-ranking guy. Her cheeks flush.

Guessing at the source of her discomfort, Joe says lightly, "I'm glad you approve. A proper bureaucrat would refuse to ride in a pimped-out truck like this. I'm glad you're not proper."

Relieved, Mill laughs and Joe joins her with a chuckle.

Schmoker starts the rig. They drive towards the gate.

Mill studies his profile. As she noted in the previous Geo-Challenge meeting, big Schmoker's fiftyish physique is rock solid, no paunch. His face is craggy with big grey eyebrows and shock of grey-white hair. He has a smooth burn mark on one weathered cheek and a deep tan that contrasts sharply with his light-blue eyes.

Joe carries himself with the air of a battle-tested field commander, sure of himself and his subordinates. He is classified as a Type 1 Incident Commander in the wildfire services nationally, the highest leadership rating.

But he is more than that. The wildfire leadership brings Joe in for the really bad ones--fire, flood, or other natural disasters...even terrorist attacks—the catastrophes that drive hope out of the most hopeful soul.

Last year, after the September 11th Al Qaeda terrorist attacks on the World Trade Center, Joe's face had become immediately recognizable on the streets of New York. Dressed in his fire service bright yellow shirt and dark green pants, off-duty Joe had walked the streets comforting New Yorkers.

Within a few days, other wildland fire service people were doing the same. It wasn't long before when New Yorkers wanted to know something about the salvage and recovery operations at the Twin Towers, they told one another, "Ask the green pants. They always know what's going on"—a tribute to Joe and the other wildland firefighter serving there.

These seasoned veterans of catastrophe knew that the bigger part of any recovery is human touch...a caring word...eye contact...a hug...honesty.

Joe steers the van out onto the highway, "Meacham, I've gotten a couple of calls from your dad, W.A. He spent a fair amount of time yelling at me over the phone, telling me what I should and shouldn't be doing on the Geo-Challenge. Seems your dad had some role in setting the thing up, some sense of ownership."

140

Joe shrugs, "Okay, I can understand that feeling. I had a hard time letting go of some of the incidents I've been on when it was time for me to stand down…same sense of ownership."

Mill replies, "Yeah sure, I get it."

"Well," Schmoker continues, "Once W.A. wound down on the Geo-Challenge, he had some advice for me about you. I won't tell you what that advice was but I kinda need to know. Does your dad speak for you? Or are you your own woman?"

Mill's habitual slight frown deepens, "Mr. Schmoker, I don't need my Dad to speak for me. I know he mostly means well. But sometimes he comes crashing into my life, roars out again, and leaves me with a mess. Looks like he's done that again by calling you."

She turns to speak directly to Schmoker, "So, please just know that I simply want to be a member of the team. I'm fit. I like hard work. I like to learn new things. I'm pretty self-sufficient, indoors and out. I think my field experience will be useful to you. So, does all that answer your questions?"

Joe grins, "I was hoping you'd make a speech like that. Say no more. You're on my team. Some people think being on my team means a lot. And, no more 'Mr. Schmoker,' okay? Call me 'Joe' please."

Mill's face dimples, "Okay, Joe."

He turns to look at her, "You're going to hear me called, 'Smoky Joe.' People say I don't like that and that's true. But probably not for the reasons you think."

He turns back to his driving, "It's really kind of a compliment. But I don't want that nickname. It's the kind of things people in the media love to throw around. I have no desire to be a media star. And, nicknames like that can be hard on morale. A lot of wildland firefighters have to eat smoke on the fire line and sit in smoke for weeks back at camp. Terrible colds and lung problems result…lung cancer even. And, along with the fire causing it, smoke is what we're there to get rid of. So I don't want to be known as 'smoky' anything."

He smiles, "If I could be called 'No-Smoke Joe,' I'd be a happy man."

Mill smiles back, "I'll just stick with 'Joe' and thanks for your explanation. And I think I'd like to be known as 'Bears-Nowhere-Around Mill' for the Geo-Challenge."

"Amen to that," Joe replies.

At the Fire Center, Joe takes Mill to join her two federal colleagues who are waiting in a classroom. He makes introductions, "Mill Meacham, meet Art Childs and Cal Freiberg. Art and Cal, meet Mill. She's Forest Service, fish bio up from Cordova. Mill, Art's BLM from Fairbanks, wildlife bio, and knows Tilly Corcoran. Cal's Park Service, in from Grand Teton National Park in Wyoming, deputy in the Mountain Rangers there."

The three exchange handshakes.

The two wiry, scarred outdoorsmen look Mill over carefully. Beyond her beauty, they see her strong body and guess at the mental toughness behind it.

Art has already shared with Cal what he knows about Mill's growing legend and how she is rumored to have drowned a three-year-old brown bear.

They nod at her showing they accept her. The three take their seats.

Joe turns on an overhead projector and outlines the next two weeks work for the team, "Physical training will occur first thing in the morning for two hours and last thing in the afternoon for an hour. In between, you three will learn every 'who-what-where-when-how' of the race until you can repeat the details without notes, start to finish."

"And, because of your roles as federal representatives, you will memorize the environmental-protection requirements that the racers and producers have to meet...land and waters, fish and wildlife...everything. Questions?"

Mill asks, "Each of us seems to have different skills, fish, wildlife and recreation. Do we work together on stuff or are we going to be assigned some way to match subjects with skills?"

Joe answers, "Good question. Because of your areas of professional expertise, as we discuss the protection measures, you will supply your teammates with anything you know that will make their jobs easier, particularly in the field. You have two days to study the protection requirements before we get together to hash them through."

"Mill, you will cover fish and aquatics, including plants and wetlands. Art will explain wildlife and wildlife habitats. Make sure to cover all threatened and endangered species likely to be encountered

142

thoroughly. Cal, I want you to discuss and demonstrate leave-no-trace camping and low-impact rock and technical climbing. Everybody clear?"

The three answer, "Yes."

Schmoker continues, "Alright, moving on. You guys will also spend at least an hour a day learning what you need to know about your race equipment, everything from boots to batteries, socks to satellite phones."

The three smile. It's always fun trying out new gear.

Joe ends his presentation.

After a few questions from Mill and her two colleagues, Joe points to two people who've come into the back of the classroom. He introduces them as "your new best friends," and explains that they will direct exercise programs for the next three weeks, two weeks with the feds alone and one week with agency reps and the tech crews combined.

The two incredibly fit exercise trainers walk to the front of the room. The tallest, a woman, explains, "Our program focuses on good nutrition, exercise, and flexibility. It's only a little less rigorous than the traditional smokejumper regimen, one of the toughest training programs in the world. Our program is for people like you who have to take on wild nature under extreme conditions. We will challenge you but, know this, you will survive. Almost everyone does."

The woman smiles as she utters the last sentence.

The three bureaucrats groan. "Thank God I've been working out with Jared and Melony," Mill thinks, "I may actually be able to 'survive' this."

Little did Mill know that the flex training would be the greatest challenge for her tough body. Years of karate, running, and weight-lifting have left her muscles and tendons tighter than she imagines.

The trainers finish their talk and take the three reps to a room filled with weight machines, mats, and a 'torture rack,' the apparatus for flexibility exercise. The three change into exercise gear, get a sports physical, provide specimens to the Center's nurse, and answer a detailed questionnaire.

Mill gulps nervously over a couple of the questions concerning drugs, alcohol, and exposure to sexually transmitted diseases. She lies outrageously on the form but figures she is pretty safe from being discovered.

She knows that, under federal rules, the urine and blood samples she has given to the nurse can't be analyzed for drugs without prior notice. Slim protection for her secrets but all the protection she has.

The three get a tour of the exercise center. Each gets a personalized program, one tailored to their personal strengths and deficits. Mill's emphasizes upper body strengthening, particularly vertical lifts.

Then she is shown to the torture rack, "Okay, Mill, you'll want to start out easy with floor stretches, then work up to using every station on the rack. For us gals, the toughest parts are usually the back rolls and holds followed by the slow ab crunches. Here, I'll demonstrate."

The lithe trainer quickly wraps her body around the bars. She goes through several movements, including one where she crosses her arms, locks her shins and knees into padded bars, and bends over backwards until her head almost touches the mat below. She holds that position for ten seconds or so. Then she reverses her motion and returns upright using only her stomach and abdominal muscles.

Mill looks a little grim.

The trainer smiles, "Look I'll be here to help you every day for the first week." She pats Mill's shoulder, "Don't worry, you'll get through it and be a better person for it."

Mill wonders darkly, "I might get through it. But unless 'better person' means someone doomed to look backwards forever, I might not qualify." Okay, maybe Mill would get six-pack abs out of it…well, more likely a four-pack with surgical scars.

The trainers round up the three reps and head off to lunch.

Still in a dark mood, Mill expects "lunch" to be a leafy green salad, a single crouton, and an anemic cherry tomato. She is pleasantly surprised to see three generous courses waiting for her—a big bowl of soup, a huge sandwich with chips, and a massive chunk of gooey berry pie. She samples each item.

The pie is good.

She eats that first.

When you were born with a pie hole in your face, why waste time on other food?

Chapter 30 -- Techies

Two weeks later, the tech crews show up.

Joe Schmoker quickly assigns each of the now-buffed feds to one of the teams.

Mill is pleased to be with the only tech crew with another woman on it, Melissa Bagley. They quickly exchange information.

Melissa says, "I work the sound equipment...all the parts and pieces. I try to be as inconspicuous as possible while keeping the talent wired for sound."

Melissa explains that by 'talent,' a Hollywood term, she means the racers. "I'm also supposed to get as much wild noise as I can. You know, capture the sounds of animals, birds, wind, and water as we go along. You can help me with that and let me know when some opportunity comes up."

Mill nods, "Sounds challenging. Fun even." Melissa pats her arm in thanks.

Melissa's partner and apparent soul mate is Enoch Saarinen, a tall, slender guy with an auburn ponytail. He runs the camera equipment and lighting.

Mill shakes hands with him, "So you like running around the wild country shooting video, huh?" Ever-serious, Enoch replies, "Absolutely...."

Both Melissa and Enoch are EMTs. Melissa also served in the military as a medic.

Mill starts to feel lots better about their safety situation. "Two EMTs on my team and a dust-off helo on call. Nice," she thinks.

Joe calls the chatting group to order, "Hey, people, you'll get a chance to talk on a break. One should be coming up soon. I've got several things to go over with you. But first I want to introduce the overall program coordinator for the federal environmental work, Tilly Corcoran. Tilly, please say hello to these folks."

Mill had not noticed when Tilly entered a minute or so before. Now, Mill's eyes go to her irresistibly.

Tilly looks like a sexy camp counselor—smart brown boots, close-fitting grey brush pants, and a deep-blue Abercrombie and Fitch pocketed safari shirt with roll-up-and-button sleeves.

The field shirt is the color of her eyes. Hanging down her back is a bush hat in the same shade of grey as her pants.

Mill is enchanted once again.   Tilly looks fabulous.

Tilly steps forward and asks the group for introductions. Everyone gives their name and job.

When it's Mill's turn, Tilly looks her in the eyes, smiles widely, and nods, acknowledging their past connection.

Mill feels her cheeks flush.   She sees a touch of color come up in Tilly's cheeks, too.   Their eyes stay connected for a moment even after Melissa begins to introduce herself.

Mill wonders, "Does Tilly feel something, too?   No way."   She tries to take hold of her rising feelings, "And not Tilly.   Remember, Idiot Millicent, *not* Tilly.   Wrong time, wrong place, wrong woman…wrong everything!"

Tilly tells the group that the environmental analysis is done and a decision has been sent out for public response.   She expects few comments because the impacts of the Great Land Geo-Challenge on wild things and places are so few.

Still, she cautions, the permit could be held up for weeks if someone raises a big protest.   Tilly smiles, "But don't worry too much. Things are right on schedule.   We've talked to everybody we could think of about what we're going to do.   Everyone seems to be on board.   The actual environmental impacts are minor and the mitigations simple and straightforward.   The permit will very likely be out on time, right around July15th.   And you'll be off on the Geo-Challenge by the 28th."

The group claps.   Hands go up with questions.

In answer to a question from Melissa, Tilly tells the group that she doesn't know any names or backgrounds for the racers other than they're all experienced outdoors-folk.

She says, "Oh, and I guess you tech crews know this already, but you federal employees have to sign a non-disclosure agreement.   It will be in force until the last segment of the program has aired.   I don't have a clue when that will be but figure sometime late this fall, maybe early winter. The agreement got hashed out between the U.S. Solicitor General's Office and the producer's legal staff.   It's good to go.   You feds have to sign to participate.   I have the forms for you."

The three nod.   Of course they will sign.

Art knows Tilly from the BLM's Fairbanks office.   He asks with an air of familiarity, "Tilly, I know you like to drive things ahead and I admire that.   But are there any glitches you see coming up that we should be aware of…things that might slow this whole thing down or make our field work more difficult?"

Tilly winks at Art, "You know me too well, Mr. Hill. Yes, there are a few things…nothing major. The Athabaskan Gwichyaa Gwich'in people in Fort Yukon had some concerns about effects of the race on the Porcupine Caribou Herd. At first they seemed to be worried about the presence of people moving cross country in the Arctic National Wildlife Refuge while the herd is dispersed in family groups."

"But when we parsed it out with them, the real concern seemed to be two things—the use of hovering helicopters for filming and the need for the Geo-Challenge program to convey a conservation message about the caribou. So, we worked with the tribe and the Fish and Wildlife Service. Right now the producers are looking at the solution we've offered."

"We said no helos on the Brooks-Romanzof Trek except for one high-altitude fast-pass a day. And we agreed to script at least one minute of commentary about the caribou and ANWR into the program."

Tilly looks around the group, "I've heard that helo restriction is a much bigger sticking point than script content to the tech folks. I guess you tech guys will have to do a lot more running around to get your shots." She sees a few heads shake and ironic smiles meant to agree with her conclusion.

The tech crews are used to having it tough but this restriction could double their work on the Brooks-Romanzof Trek. Without helicopter coverage, they'll have to outpace the racers many more times than planned. They'll have to move to high places to get the down-angle shots that the helos could have covered. And once shots have been taken, they'll have to work back to the racers along oblique angles that could double or triple the miles they go compared what the racers have to travel.

Their rueful smiles show Tilly and the other feds that they're used to going those many extra miles. It's just part of their jobs but not any kind of fun.

Tilly looks around the group, catching each techie's eye, "Sorry about the extra work. I'll make sure the producers get some extra treats to you in the field."

A few of the tech people smile a little at her kind words. Once again, Tilly has taken some of the sting out of a tough situation.

Listening to her words, Mill admires Tilly even more. She smiles shyly at Tilly. Tilly returns the smile.

A week later, Mill, Melissa, and Enoch toil up a huge glacial moraine east of Fairbanks. They're panting with exertion, but the weeks of training have paid off. None of them is feeling any pain.

Although Enoch has point for the moment, the two women glance at the *e*trexes hanging around their necks from time to time. They are closing rapidly on a simulated cache site.

Because they've broken clear of the moraine's treed and brushy lower slopes, Mill thinks they will easily beat the time the course-layers have set for them to find the cache.

In the week they've been together, the three have knit close. Turns out Enoch and Melissa are soul mates of a kind, just not the kind Mill thought initially.

Enoch is Melissa's partner but definitely not Melissa's lover. He is gay, tough as nails and highly disciplined, as macho as anyone working the Geo-Challenge. But Enoch and Melissa definitely share a love—the outdoors, wild country, shooting nature programs, meeting physical challenges.

Although they don't sleep or run a business together, they're partners in the sense that they adore working with one another. If one of them is asked by a prospective employer who they'd like to work with, the one asked always requests the other. Their reputation as a pair is so great, producers fight to hire them, sometimes offering five-figure bonuses to get them for longer shoots.

Mill yells encouragement to her team mates, "Hey guys, we're doing great. I think we're definitely going to beat the other crews!"

Enoch yells back, "Yeah, let's pick 'em up and lay 'em down. Let's show those macho guys who's the best team on this mountain...us ladies!"

Their laughs come out in puffs as they push harder.

Mill looks at the bulky outlines of Melissa and Enoch ahead of her. All three are wearing identical waist-length saddle-cloth rain parkas in light green. When they join up with the racers, they will be called "the Green Group" by the Geo-Challenge production team.

The other teams are outfitted in different colors, one blue and one brown.

Over their parkas, the three are strapped into identical grey and yellow, frame-in packs, each one individually sized and carefully adjusted. In the center of the each pack's back flap is a big, round "Great Land Geo-Challenge" patch--black words over a light blue Alaska outline. A dark red line on the patch traces the three race stages. A big gold star rests in the lower right corner, marking the finish along the Alsek River, near Dry Bay on the Tongass national Forest and Glacier Bay National Park.

With full water bottles, each pack weighs about forty pounds. About fifteen pounds of each pack's contents are the same…knife… water…quick rations…batteries…first aid kit…compass…whistle…flares. These items are stored in the same pocket or pouch in each pack. The idea is that if any team member needs an item in an emergency, they can grab any pack and immediately find what they need.

Each person's pack also carries unique items weighing about twenty-five pounds. Mill's pack holds a flat bundle of documents, each laminated in plastic against the elements. The laminated documents include topographic maps of the race route in case the etrexes fail. And there's also long lists of environmental-protection guidelines each racer and support team has to meet.

In some cases, photos and drawings of sensitive, threatened, or endangered species are shown to help with field identification. Many Alaska Native sites are also shown with detailed instructions about avoiding them or how respect is to be paid them.

Mill also has the satellite phone with two spare batteries and a set of bizarre, hieroglyphic user instructions. Mill's three weeks of practice with the tricky phone have proved to be the best teacher because, after studying the instructions frequently, she still can't figure them out.

She also carries a solar-powered battery charger. Lashed atop her pack during the long days of July and early August, she will be able to charge batteries for the satellite phone, radios, flashlights, or any of Enoch's or Melissa's equipment. The Green Group's appetite for batteries won't be fully met by the ones she charges, but anything the group can do to reuse and cut weight throughout the Trek will help.

On being assigned the battery-charger job a few days earlier, Mill held up a finger, cocked her head, and remarked with dimples, "What an electrifying experience I will have!"

Then she had to pledge to the groaning Enoch and Melissa never to pun again. Otherwise, Enoch said he would "commit battery upon her."

Mill threw granola bars at him for being "way too punny." Good team.

Enoch's pack is loaded with camera gear. He carries three custom-made, multi-lensed, digital video cameras. They're ultra small and light, about the size of one of his big hands. Each records directly to digital storage media.

He also carries three GoPro button cameras. The GoPro's aren't as sophisticated as Enoch's custom cameras. But Enoch can clip the small, light cameras on a racer's cap or clothes. Then the GoPros' wide-view lenses will record each racer's bouncing movements across rock, field, and water for about five hours before batteries and recording chips have to be replaced.

Melissa's gear includes a whole bunch of mikes, some tiny ones to plant on racers, or in tents, and one with a small parabolic dish to catch race and wild sounds across longer distances.

Her gear is radio linked to Enoch's so that sound and video tracks are laid down simultaneously. Enoch's cameras can record up to six separate audio signals while shooting video. That way, the studio team doing the video program can mix the field-synchronized sounds whichever way they want.

In the field, Melissa and Enoch help each other out, swapping cameras and sound equipment back and forth, making each other's job easier and the team more efficient.

At Mill's request, both of them have trained her to do some of the basics for them, too. She can now, without thinking, turn equipment off, pack it properly, hump it to the next recording site, set it back up, and start it working again.

The sweaty team reaches the broad top of the moraine.

Enoch yells, "This way" and rushes off to the right. Following him, the two women race forward twenty yards only to find a shocking-pink cooler resting on a boulder.

Enoch opens it. Inside are three quarts of bright blue Gatorade and a bottle of champagne.

A note in Tilly's handwriting says, "Congrats, Rock Rats! Drink the Gatorade first!"

The three laugh and open their power drinks. After looking down the steep slope they will have to traverse to get back to their jump-off point, they agree to drink the champagne back at the motel.

Mill raises her Gatorade jug in a toast, "Here's to the EMM team. Next time we meet, we'll be freezing our asses off on the Beaufort Sea!"

They bump plastic bottles together and smile, ready for the Arctic.

Chapter 31 - Anchorage Haven

Enoch and Melissa are back at their places in Port Townsend, Washington, to tidy up and shut things down before starting the six-week Geo-Challenge shoot.

Mill returns to Cordova for much the same purpose.

She doesn't have plants or pets to worry about like the other two do. But she does want to check in with Percy and Dill to find out how the summer fisheries work is going. She doesn't want to interfere, but, really, it *is* her program.

When she gets to the office, as it is with Forest Service districts all over Alaska in the summer, there's no one around. Everybody's in the field and not expected home until late. Even Percy's out with a survey crew looking at a bridge damaged by winter ice.

Mill reads some field notes Dill has left her.

She is both pleased and a little miffed that everything is going well. After all, it's nice that the team the ranger brought in is meeting Mill's schedule but it would also be nice to be missed and needed a little, too.

She turns on the Aqua data base and enters Dill's field data. Now she feels a little better for a least doing this small part.

She makes a note on Dill's forms that she has done the entry work and sets them back on his tidy desk. "That'll surprise him," she smiles.

Mill looks for anything more she can do for Dill but finds nothing. She shrugs and turns to a small heap of phone-message slips on her desk.

She sees one telling her to call Chick Sorensen and another for Mitch Mendenhall. And there's a third for Jerry Spencer, Mill's attorney for the fish-cop issue. That note reads, "Fish cops tried to serve you at my address. Return any registered letters you get from them. Sign nothing."

Mill gets the point. Even though Mitch had been clear with the fish cops, they are still trying to have her sign a citation for killing the bear.

She knows the fish cops can actually sign the citation themselves, certifying that she refused to sign and turning it in to the prosecutor that way. But they really seem to want her signature for some reason.

Well, if she can get out of town before they catch up with her, it might be a long time before the fish cops actually serve her.

Maybe never, if the USA moves fast enough.

She picks up the phone and calls Chick Sorensen. He answers on the first ring, a real surprise because he, too, is usually so busy in the field during the summer.

"Hurt my ankle," he growls when she asks why he is in the office, "Can't go back out for another week. Damn nuisance. Frickin' paperwork."

Chick's voice drops almost to a whisper, "Anyway, I was calling to give you a heads up on your bear-kill thing. One of those times I just couldn't *not* call, you know what I mean? Anyway, I was in Toad's office early yesterday, out in the waiting room. I overheard him talking with someone in Anchorage, probably ASP headquarters. They were arguing about whether to arrest you or not. Book you and all that."

Chick laughs bitterly, "They know they can't hold you. But if they bust you and fingerprint you, they can formally serve you with the citation, make you take it. They want to jail you, before witnesses. They liked that idea."

"But what really got them crowing was the idea of paying the federal government back for refusing to kowtow to them. They plan to have photos taken, maybe video, do a formal press release, and put the story of your arrest up on their website. Then the Alaska Rights Committee's gonna march that story all around Washington, DC, to pressure the Forest Service to shove you out in the cold, and make you answer their charges personally. Pitiful bastards."

Mill is stunned. She begins to stutter her thanks for the warning. But Chick says, "My pleasure to help out."

As if he now fears being overheard, his whispery voice gets even lower, "But I can't say any more. Gotta go."

Chick hangs up.

Mill stares for a moment at the quiet phone. She clears the line and calls Mitch Mendenhall. Mendenhall's phone rings through to voice mail and she leaves a message with the information Chick's just given her.

Then she calls Jerry Spencer who answers, "Hello, Jerry Spencer here. Have legal problems? I'm the solution!"

Mill's habitual frown deepens, "Jerry, this is Mill Meacham. I definitely have a legal problem...."

Spencer responds in a feisty tone, "Yes, you do seem to have ticked off the fish cops a little. They were pretty upset when I refused to accept your citation for you. Toad said some inappropriate things, sorta threatened me. I told him he should go away and he did. No one threatens an officer of the court even here in little 'ol Cordova."

Mill starts to feel a little better at the image of small-statured Jerry standing up to lumbering Toad Craven in his brass-bedazzled fish-cop uniform. "So, Jerry, here's some information."

Without revealing her source by name, she quickly fills Jerry in on what she had heard from Chick. Mill knows Jerry is smart enough to guess her source and to make use of the information without it leading back to Chick.

"Hmmm," Jerry muses, "Well, you're not a fugitive in any way. You've been fully compliant with the state on a misdemeanor charge. On advice of counsel, you've refused to sign the citation. That's all. No judge will give the fish cops a warrant for your arrest given the facts in dispute."

"So, I guess you have two choices. You can march down to Toad's office with me and sign your citation. Or, you can get out of town for awhile to avoid harassment while I keep working on things with Mr. Mendenhall and ASP. Can you do that? Leave town, I mean?"

Mill laughs a little harshly, "I just got back here from Fairbanks…barely unpacked. But, look, I'm on temporary duty, assigned to a project that will take me all over the state. Can the fish cops compel the Forest Service to say where I am?"

Jerry thinks for a moment, "Well, you'd probably have to ask Mitch for a definitive answer. But, on the facts, I'd say 'No, they can't.' I mean the federal government is rejecting the charges against you, so they logically wouldn't accept the idea that you were somehow a fugitive. No fault, no fugitive…so, no information."

"Cool," Mill says grimly, "I'll be out of here in a few hours, take the ferry to Valdez, and then stay out of sight. How often do you want me to check in with you?"

Jerry answers, "Call every week or two. I'll send you a little e-mail from time to time and you can reply. But no rush on anything. I'm sure these state-federal feuds take awhile to get through."

Jerry laughs, "Enjoy your temporary duty. We used to call it, "TDY" in the Army. My temporary assignments always seemed to eventually involve bad beer in worse bars. They were anything but TiDY. Bye, Mill."

They hang up.

Mill quickly hand writes a note to Percy telling him she will be on personal leave until the race starts and puts the note and a signed leave form on his desk. He has her cell phone number and home e-mail address so no sweat staying in touch.

Mill grabs a few things from her desk and throws them in her backpack. She heads towards the front door.

She jogs down the stairs but pauses at the entrance. She looks up and down the street, wondering if the fish cops might be lurking outside ready to scoop her up.

Is that the ASP's Cordova SUV parked on that side-street?

Scared now and feeling like an idiot, she trots back up the stairs and exits the building through the back.

She can see her truck is in the district parking lot. No one's near it but she doesn't approach. Nothing in there she needs.

She locks it with the remote. First time she has ever left her truck at work so close to the several bars down the street. She shuts concern for her pickup out of her mind. She has bigger things to worry about.

She almost giggles with tension.

What a weird situation. Fish-bio bureaucrat on the run!

Mill walks down the alley and turns east. Three blocks' walk and she enters the back door of her apartment.

She has a little more than two weeks before the Geo-Challenge begins. She takes her time loading two rolling suitcases, one for her "vacation" and one for life in the wild.

She looks out her front window and sees the chubby "Blue Canoe" Alaska Ferry going by in the Sound. It's headed for the dock three miles up.

It must unload passengers, vehicles, and freight first, so it won't be ready to board for at least a couple of hours. Mill checks the schedule on the ferry website and pegs departure at three hours fifteen minutes from now.

She will walk on board at the last minute and buy a ticket to Valdez with cash. She calls a friend and asks for a ride to the Cordova Ferry Dock. No problem.

She has a few minutes to unwind. She drops onto her bed and covers her eyes with her forearm.

Where should she go from Valdez?

She could run up north to Fairbanks and wait for the Geo-Challenge to start, maybe explore the country a little.

Or better yet, she could go back to Anchorage and do a little Wild-Girl hunting, maybe act a little more discreetly than before.

She checks for the darkness within. It's there, but somehow withdrawn, waiting, no longer as fierce or driving as before.

So, maybe Mill could put off Wild Girl's next hunt for awhile.

What about Charli? She had said "anytime."

Should Mill risk more with Charli, get closer? Drawing a deep breath, Mill finds Charli's business card and opens her cell phone….

Three days later, Mill sits in Charli's breakfast nook. Cook Inlet stretches out below them, a calming chaos of wind, wave, and wash.

After a delightful night of love-making followed by this morning's country breakfast, a replete Mill has just finished telling Charli about her fish cop mess.

She hadn't planned to burden Charli with the story. In fact, she worries that she shouldn't have told the older woman anything. Yet, as Mill said to herself before beginning to talk, "My pussy's purring, my belly's full, and I'm safe. I really want to talk this over with someone I trust."

Charli looks at her, face cocked to one side, "So, darlin' Mill, can your friend Charli do anything to help you?"

Mill smiles at her gratefully, "Well, you know, I just hadn't thought that far, Charli. I guess all I really wanted to do is tell you my story. Get some sympathy maybe?"

"Okay, love," Charli replies, "I heard a wise saying once. 'Inside every fear, there's wish trying to come true.' So, Mill, what's your fear and what wish do you want to come true?"

Mill looks at her lover in a new way, "Charli, I had no idea you were a fairy godmother!"

They both laugh.

Charli flicks her tongue lasciviously, "Well, I could hardly be thought of as your 'mother' in any way. 'Fairy' maybe. But seriously, Mill, what are you afraid of and what do you wish would happen as a result?"

"Okay," Mill says thoughtfully, "I guess I'm afraid of my secrets being revealed. About you and I and, you know, that I use drugs and stuff. That I go a little wild from time to time."

"And I'm afraid that I'll lose my job. I've worked so hard for it, so hard."

"And, in a much smaller way, I'm afraid that my Dad won't be proud of me, or worse.... This is bigger, older...that my Mom might never come home because she heard what a mess I've made of my life."

Mill's voice gets progressively sadder as she tells Charli her fears. Although she doesn't cry, her constant frown deepens.

Charli knows a little of Mill's young life, about her mother leaving when Mill was seven and disappearing. She reaches across the table and takes Mill's hand gently. "Okay," she says softly, "If those are your fears, what are your wishes?"

Mill takes a long shuddering breath, "Wishes? Okay. Let's see. I wish that my secrets might not be revealed, that I keep my job and keep doing neat stuff, and that my Dad be pleased with me. And that...that...my mother comes home to me. How's that for impossible wishes?"

Mill's face has gotten happier as she states her wishes, ending on a slight down note as she asks for that near-impossible thing, her long-lost mother's return.

Charli pats Mill's hand again, "Okay, I think Fairy God-lover Charli can help you, at least a little. Let's spend a little more time talking about your secrets so I'll know how best to help you protect them. And then we'll talk about your job and how to make sure you keep it. The Mom and Dad part may be something your Fairy God-lover can't tackle, at least for now."

An hour later, back on Charli's bed, Mill wraps Charli in her arms. They kiss long and lovingly.

After a time, Charli disentangles herself. She rolls to the side of the bed and reaches down into one of her boxes full of sex toys. She pulls out a solid glass dildo with two heads, one for vaginas and one for bottoms.

Mill frowns, "Charli, I don't want anything in my bottom. You know...the rape."

"No, Mill," Charli says, "I would never do that to you. This is for me. Be a dear and get a bowl full of hot water. You'll warm this and use it on me vigorously. That way, you can give your fairy God-lover three orgasm-wishes."

They both laugh. Mill jumps out of bed and heads for the kitchen, a large bowl, and hot water.

158

Chapter 32 - Surprise Party

Two days later, Mill comes in from a morning ten-mile run to find Charli on the phone, talking to a friend about a small party at her loft planned for this Saturday night.

When Mill and Charli had talked about the party that morning, Mill expressed concerns about wanting to keep a low profile while in Anchorage. She told Charli a little about Drag and, of course, how the fish cops might be hunting her.

Charli reassured her that the party would be small and discreet, "Believe me, darlin' Mill," she said, "All of us know how to stay out of sight. This will be a small gathering of friends, first names only…and you can pick whatever first name you'd like. How's that."

Mill laughed at that point, thinking about how using the name "Lucy Moore" had both helped her to escape Drag and almost stifled honest communications with Charli.

Mill hugged Charli and said, "Okay, whatever you think will work. I'll stick with 'Mill' I think. Even as small as Alaska can be socially, I'd bet no one at this party will recognize me or my name."

Charli agreed that she would serve as bartender for the first round of drinks, coffee, tea, water, or whatever. That way, she could help Charli, get to know each of Charli's other guests without a formal introduction, and keep the whole identity business casual.

As 'bartender,' she might not even be asked where she worked or how she came to be at Charli's loft in Anchorage. Most of Charli's friends knew not to pry anyway, but playing bartender should put a further damper on the guests' curiosity.

On Saturday night, Mill finds out how wrong she can be about social circles in Alaska.

As she serves up a perfect vodka martini for a tall woman named "California," Mill looks past the woman's shoulder and sees…Tilly…Tilly Corcoran, for God's sake, next in line.

Mill almost drops California's martini on Charli's finely polished, maple-topped breakfast bar. She covers her amazement with a few polite words to the woman.

And then Tilly stands in front of her, a wry smile on her perfectly made-up face.

She looks wonderful in a simple v-neck cranberry sweater and black wool skirt. Her small diamond earrings twinkle under Charli's bright spotlights.

"Hi, Mill," the clearly flustered Tilly says quietly, "I bet you're as surprised to see me as I am to see you. How's that for the mother of all understatements? How have you been? I've been fine. I just got in from Fairbanks."

She checks herself, "Listen to me babbling on." Seeing the alarmed smile on Mill's face, Tilly plunges back in, "Look, Charli told everyone not to pressure you for information. I sure won't do that!"

She gives Mill a worried but compassionate look, "Do you just want to pretend we don't know each other for now? Maybe talk later?"

Tilly understands what hurdles lesbians face trying to "come out of the closet." So, she is giving Mill plenty of room to feel comfortable about what may be Mill's changing life.

Mill nods gratefully, "Look, Tilly, me being here is more complicated than it seems. So, yes, if it's okay with you, we won't get into my situation this evening. Can we do that later, maybe on a break from the Geo-Challenge?"

Tilly looks at Mill thoughtfully. A bright smile touches her lips, "Yeah, getting together in a couple of weeks would be great. Let's get coffee or drinks when we can."

Mill feels relieved at not having to review her recent life history in the midst of a lesbian dinner party.

She dimples, "That would work for me. Okay, until then." Mill holds out her hand and gives Tilly's a firm shake.

At the touch, the warm tingle she first felt from Tilly in Fairbanks flows up Mill's arm again. Mill drops Tilly's hand.

She picks up a lime slice and holds it under her nose for a moustache. She puts on her best Alaska sourdough faux-frontier dialect. "Okay, Mzz. Tilly, belly up to the bar. Whatya have? A shot of Red Eye?"

Tilly laughs delightedly, "Sarsaparilla, please, barkeep Mill. No, make that orange juice. Sarsaparilla gives me a hangover. Oh, and I like your green mustache, very Alaskan. Couldn't tell you how many of those I see in Fairbanks!"

Mill pours orange juice with a flourish.

Tilly takes her glass and turns away. She walks a few feet, stops, turns slightly, and gives Mill a smile and a wink over her elegant right shoulder. Then she strides, hips swaying, toward Charli's crescent-shaped, sunken living room.

Mill watches Tilly's graceful movements until she disappears into the little knot of chattering visitors surrounding Charli.

Then Mill lets out her breath.

Chapter 33 - Jump Off

July 26.

Mill sits in the Anchorage airport departure lounge waiting to board the flight to Kotzebue. When the plane gets to that remote, western-coast Inupiaq town thirty miles above the Arctic Circle, she will shift to a smaller Baker Aviation plane for the trip to Demarcation Bay.

She figures some of the support team members might fly with her, maybe Art or Cal.

The racers are coming in to Demarcation Bay by charter plane. They're not supposed to mix with the support teams until a day before the race.

Other support folks will be waiting at the fuel and cargo stop in Kaktovik. Enoch and the other camera techs have been in that tiny, remote town for a few days taking lots of background footage. Because Arctic weather is always unpredictable, they wanted plenty of time ahead of the race to get shots of the seashore, birds, and animals, and to record day changes like sunrises and sunsets or wind-driven clouds.

Mill takes out the thick "shooting script" package the producers sent her by courier yesterday. Calling it a script seems odd because the program is pretty much unscripted. She wonders how you could write dialog and stage directions for a mad scramble through wild country.

But the script package contains a lot more detail about the route, geo-caches, and schedule. So, Mill is glad to have it.

A thick rubber band pins the script to her federal race-operations guide. She separates the two files.

She has just opened the script when her cell phone rings. She grumpily roots for it in the deepest, most crammed pocket in her Geo-Challenge parka.

She grabs the phone out and flips it open on the last ring, "Mill here!"

Mitch Mendenhall's urgent voice comes through clearly, "Mill, this is Mitch in Juneau. Can you talk?"

Mill looks around and sees no one close by. She grunts, "Yes."

He continues, "If it's okay with you, I'm going to join us both to a teleconference I've been on for the last half hour. We've started talking about your case. The group thought it'd be better if we could bring you in to the conversation. You okay with that?"

Before Mill can ask who she will be talking to or even answer "Yes" to Mitch's rapid-fire question, the phone clicks and takes on a hollow sound. Mitch has connected them.

Introductions are quickly made. Mill's guess that the people on the teleconference are federal attorneys proves correct.

She is also pleasantly surprised to hear Manny Suemez voice say, "Hey, Mill, how'ya doin'?"

And she is a little surprised when an FBI Agent named Mary something-or-other speaks up. "Mary," Mill asks, "Could you give me your last name again, please?" "Sure, Ms. Meacham," Mary Wrangel replies calmly, "It's 'Wrangel' with a 'w' like the Alaska town...one 'l.'"

Mitch's voice cuts in, "Okay, ready, Mill?"

"Yeah, sure," she replies, "Let's go."

The Assistant U.S. Attorney begins, "Ms. Meacham, let summarize where we are. We know the facts of your case. I know you've been waiting to hear from us. I apologize for the delay in getting back to you but we have a large case load and we had to gather some additional information before we could make a final decision about what to do."

Mill feels a smile lift the frown off her face. The AUSA continues, "We've found enough evidence to proceed with a case against ASP, more specifically individuals within ASP Game and Fish Enforcement. So, we will continue to handle your case versus letting you work solely with your personal attorney, Mister Spencer, or just supplying information to help him."

"And please don't stop working with Mr. Spencer just because we have decided to represent you. Mr. Spencer is far better versed in Alaska game and fish law than any of us are. In fact, if you'll give us your permission to do so, we'd like to bring him in from time to time to consult with us."

"Yes, of course," Mill responds immediately, immediately wondering how much Jerry's "consulting" will cost her.

She gets her answer when the AUSA says, "Oh...and we will cover Jerry's charges when he's working with us, if they're reasonable."

Mill makes a mental note to make sure Jerry understands "reasonable" when working with "Uncle Deep Pockets" as the federal government is often called in Alaska.

"Okay," the AUSA concludes, "Why don't we hear from Special Agent Wrangel who's been in touch with the colonel in charge of ASP?"

164

Mary clears her voice and begins to talk in a smooth, professional tone—one that contains a certain undertone of suppressed excitement.

"What this group may not know," Mary says, "is that Colonel Jim Lowell is a former FBI agent. He got tired of Bureau politics and moved on some years ago…went through a divorce about the same time, too. He's definitely over whatever bothered him about the Bureau back then, maybe not the divorce."

"When I sat down with him I expected him to be defensive. He was. We had a 'spirited discussion' as they say in DC."

People on the teleconference chuckle appreciatively.

Mary continues, "In fact, he was so unwilling to cooperate, I backed off. I said I'd come back to see him in a few days. I figured I better give him time to calm down and reconsider. In fact, I thought my actual chances of getting another appointment with him without a warrant or subpoena was pretty slim."

Mary's voice changes, "Imagine my surprise when he called the next afternoon. Somehow he had a change of heart. Turns out…at least according to Lowell…that he's had some of the same concerns about performance within the ranks of ASP's Game and Fish Enforcement as we do. He's caught up in the same mess Meacham is…Alaska politics…bush versus city…state versus federal."

"After some verbal dancing around about how far to go, Lowell told me he'd appreciate having some 'help getting ASP straightened out.' But he also doesn't want a scandal to rip his organization apart."

"So, he's agreed to let my team come in undercover and off-hours to review records, including e-mails. We can conduct discreet interviews with people that Game and Fish Enforcement previously cited, talk quietly to judges… whoever, whatever. And, most importantly, we can wire-tap or bug Game and Fish Enforcement officers as needed."

"He knows we could do all these things without his permission. But he's very anxious to make sure we focus only on the bad apples and get the job done as quickly as possible. Otherwise, it'll be his neck on the chopping block with his rank-and-file holding the ax and the politicians holding his arms. So he supports a neat and clean approach, fast in and fast out…low profile."

Wrangel's voice changes, "Here's a tricky part. As mentioned, this investigation is very risky business for him politically. He'd like some cover when the deal goes down. So, he'd like us to state publicly that he asked us for assistance based on concerns he'd been hearing from rural

Alaskans. He doesn't want us to mention that we initiated the contact. Do you think we'd be willing to do that in exchange for his full cooperation?"

The phone is silent for a few seconds. Then the AUSA's voice comes through drily, "So, he would like us to give him credit for something we could do with or without him?"

He laughs, "Okay, we can as long as he gives us full access. We get to go everywhere…look at everything.

"He wants a speedy investigation? Well, as long as speedy also means thorough. Colonel Lowell knows it will take us longer if we have to infiltrate secret ASP cults and slay sacred fish-cop cows. So the bargain he's offering us makes sense. Okay, Mary, make sure Colonel Lowell understands what we require. If he agrees, go to work."

The group talks about a few more particulars and then the call ends.

The grin on Mill's face lingers for several minutes.

But then worries crowd into her mind.

What if the FBI investigates her and finds Drag or Wild Girl Hunting and her drugs?

Her frown returns.

She shrugs.

Nothing she can do about any of it now.

She opens the shooting script again and starts to read.

Chapter 34 - The Great Land Race Begins

The Green Group's umiak leaps in the wild, wind-whipped Beaufort Sea.

As they edge toward Demarcation Bay, Mill takes a bucketful of cold saltwater in the face and sputters it clear, cussing.

She wonders for the hundredth time today why in Hell the producers decided on a sea landing for the start of the race. At least they had changed the script and allowed for outboard motors. Otherwise the racers would be rowing the bulky boats ashore.

Mill holds on. The umiak circles for awhile, as the racer driving the boat dodges chunks of pack ice broken off from ice masses to the north, searching for the Green Group's start point.

Finally a factory-installed light on the racers' *e*trexes blinks green, a signal from the race controllers that the umiak has reached its start coordinates.

At the tiller, Reggie Bonet sees the green light. He pushes hard on the outboard's handle to turn the clumsy boat towards Demarcation and cranks it full throttle.

Under this clumsy impulse, the umiak rolls into a large wave and almost broaches as it turns. A mass of water rolls over the umiak's port bow quarter. Perched as she is under the bow, Mill has another bad moment as the freezing wave floods over her.

Reggie rights the boat and drives it sluggishly over the next wave.

"Looks like we'll make it, this time," Mill thinks morbidly.

She flips Reggie the bird as a reward for his soggy seamanship. He grins at her, flips one back, and yells something to her, his words blown away by the wind and buried under the noise of sea and engine.

Umiaks are the traditional fishing, sealing, and whaling boats for Alaska's Eskimo peoples. They make them out of walrus hide cleverly stretched over bone and driftwood frames. In modern times, fishers and hunters have largely replaced umiaks with stout aluminum work boats. So, umiaks are becoming scarcer and more highly prized by more traditional people and communities.

In the months before the race, the producers had a hard time convincing traditional clans and villages to let their umiaks be used in the Geo-Challenge. Still, the promise of money, the chance for family members to see their boat on TV, and the producer's agreement to share Inupiaq culture with the world carried the day.

Three umiaks were eventually leased to the Geo-Challenge and now face the running seas in the hands of inexperienced, urgent racers like Reggie. Considering Reggie's record so far, Mill wonders if the Alaska Natives had made a bad bargain.

Water drums noisily against the umiak's taut hide hull. The outboard whines and thump-shudders over steep waves.

"Maybe it'll make for good reality TV," Mill says to herself, "But Melissa's gills are green. So are mine. If she barfs, I'll barf, and neither one of us is about to stick our heads over the side to do it!"

Mill looks enviously at Melissa perched at the side of the boat where water over the bow mostly misses her. Melissa is filming the racers in the umiak for Enoch-- Reggie driving and steering the boat with the outboard—and the other racer, Marie Skinner, bailing water over the side like a maniac robot.

Even after Reggie's nearly successful attempt to swamp them, Marie is actually holding her own against the spray and slop. After five minutes more of heroic efforts by Marie, only about eight inches of water surges back and forth along the umiak's ribs.

The boat pitches wildly up and then fishtails down a tall wave.

Why did Mill even have to be on this boat? Mill could have just waited ashore with Enoch.

Enoch is already there to record their landing. She will just be in the way when they land. She and Melissa have to jump out, push Bonet and Skinner off for a redo landing on their own, and hide from the cameras and microphones.

Water cascades off her hat. Mill wonders if she can get any wetter? Probably not.

Yes, shore duty would have been nice, but Mill's responsibilities out here are clear. She is on the boat to make sure the racers don't harass marine mammals or disturb sea birds. She can even make them re-route if necessary.

Mill muses darkly, "Hell, in this wild water, we'd have to run completely up on a whale's back to even know one was around! Christ on a crutch! And sea birds! Every bird in the air is being blown backwards! How could we disturb them more than they already are?"

Okay, now that she has reminded herself about her job rather than obsessing over her sea-sloshing stomach, Mill figures she should steal a glance ahead of the boat to check for marine mammals and birds. She pops her head up long enough to see that nothing living seems to be in the umiak's direct path. For her trouble, she takes another face-full of water. But she does see something positive.

Mill drops down and yells to Melissa, "Hang in there. We're almost back in Demarcation."

Melissa waves one hand acknowledging the good news as she tries to hold the camera steady on the weaving, bouncing racers. The tiny camera has a decent image-stabilization feature but it can't keep up with the Beaufort Sea's wild gyrations without Melissa's steadying hand.

Mill knows that being in broad Demarcation Bay won't mean that waves and wind drop much. But being back in the bay means that their landing is coming…that's *land*-ing…her boots will soon be on solid ground.

Mill ducks as another wave throws ten gallons of water over the bow and onto her head.

She thinks more dark thoughts of Reggie. She glares back at him. He waves….

_____//_____

From above, maps of Demarcation Bay show that roughly circular, pock-marked look that Mill identifies with a meteor crater. The bay is bounded by land to the south and opens to the Beaufort to the north.

Once ashore, she sees that if a meteor had slammed in here millions of years ago, erosion by water, wind, and frost, along with post-glacial land uplift, has wiped away any conspicuous signs.

After helping to push the umiak off, Mill stands behind Enoch with Melissa as Bonet and Skinner make a fast landing on the rock-ledged shore.

As instructed, Reggie reverses the fast-moving boat at the last moment and brings the umiak in gently. He and Marie jump out, check their GPS units, and run off-camera, haring off to their first, highly important cache.

A recovery team grabs the bouncing umiak before the wind drives it back into the small surf.

Enoch pans his camera to follow the racers. He gently lifts it off its bipod and runs after the pair. Enoch has to use all his skill to keep the racers in view and centered as he leaps over the scabby beach and across browning shore grasses.

Mill finds she has to parallel the racers at a distance that keeps her out of Enoch's lens. This is something Enoch, Melissa, and she rehearsed many times back at the fire center in Fairbanks.

Keeping the right distance had been tough there. Here, as they run inland beyond the shore, staying out of Enoch's lens is proving to be a lot tougher.

Little salt marshes, partially frozen, pull Mill's feet down…slow her…trip her. "What a workout!" she fumes, slogging through frigid mud and muck.

Then, beyond the marshes, wet tussocks—wobbly stacks of grasses encircled by ice-topped mini-ponds—stretch, it seems, for miles to higher, drier ground. Mill teeters drunkenly across the tussock tops. She falls over and over, plunging arms and legs into the icy water.

Once, her face slams down and her plunging hands find no support. Her head goes under, ear-deep.

Water floods into her panting mouth. Bleechh! Cold, cold, cold! Flailing, she grips some tussock tops and surges out of the wet.

Worse than the stinky, brackish water running off her face, Mill can't cuss. Melissa's mikes might pick her up.

Mill decides she will save the cussing up for a time when the mikes are due to be off for at least an hour. Surely it will take that long to set free all the cuss words she will have stored up by then.

Ahead, Reggie and Marie finish struggling through marsh and tussock.

Their GPS units take them to their first cache. Reggie gives a triumphant whoop. Near Mill, Melissa looks at a meter clipped to her rain shell and nods her satisfaction. The lapel mikes she placed hastily on the racers in the umiak are still working.

Enoch records the racers opening the cache, pulling out their equipment and supplies, and assembling their packs for the first long leg of the trek.

Enoch knows that the Great Land Geo-Challenge is a timed race. This means the racers will move swiftly, even frantically, across the race course. They will minimize the time spent on breaks and at caches like this first one. The tech team has to match them, even beat them.

The team that uses the least time for all three stages will win $100,000 each plus major sports-equipment endorsement deals. $10,000 prizes will also be awarded to the winners of each stage: the Brooks-Romanzof Trek, the Mount McKinley Climb, and the Alsek River Run. If a team wins all three, each person stands to make $130,000 plus endorsement contracts worth perhaps millions.

The money is good but it's also about entering sports history as the winners of "The Greatest Race Ever."

The teams are eager indeed. After green lights on the Beaufort, their race clocks were running. And, a few weeks from now, seconds saved along the route could spell the difference between wealth and fame or empty pockets and obscurity.

Marie and Reggie have worked very hard to be here. Tri-athletes with many trophies to their names, they spent months working out their approach to each stage.

For the Brooks-Romanzof Trek, they plan to use a "runner-packer" approach. The "runner," ranges ahead with a light pack, moving quickly and looking for the best route across the Kongakut River, over the eroded, rocky Brooks Range and Romanzof Mountains, and down to the Sheenjek River finish.

Behind the runner, the "packer" will hurry along under a heavier load, following the route the runner pioneers.

In the steeper mountain reaches, the two will pair up again, distribute weight according to their strength and stamina at the time, and press on as fast as possible.

Once they reach gentler slopes again, they will return to the runner-packer method.

Reggie and Marie know each other well. They will switch off runner and packer roles at any time, without hesitation, if the change will speed them up as a team.

Since the EMM team also has to reload from separate caches at the same sites, Mill, Melissa, and Enoch have practiced what Enoch calls "rip-jamming." EMM can't be left behind when the racers move out.

No, they have to be ahead of the racers to video their movements. So, one EMMer will open and rip out the supplies as fast as hands can move. The other two will jam supplies and gear into packs.

Race rules allow for a twenty-minute time break at each cache to allow the racers time to open the cache and get organized. If racers take less time to load, they get a time bonus of the unused break minutes. Mill expects the racers to almost jog through the cache sites, pausing only long enough to pop the drums open, load, and go.

Sure enough, Bonet and Skinner finish loading after only seven minutes at their first cache.

Marie will run the first leg, a twenty mile stretch to their next cache where water, food, and a tiny backpack stove wait for them.

Reggie will race-walk behind Marie under the heavier load.

The pair shoulders their burdens and moves out.

The EMM team is already five hundred meters south waiting for the racers.

Enoch and Melissa have cameras ready.

Mill has scanned the area for late-nesting birds or other species of concern.

As she waits for the racers to reach them, Mill takes in the scenery, absolutely enthralled by the colors and textures of the land. It's early fall in these latitudes; frost has touched yellow to the willows and the stunted cottonwoods along the rivers and streams. Here and there, valiant, pillow-like saxifrages offer a few tiny, hopeful flowers to occasional sunbeams. Mosses and lichens cover rocks and ledges, food for family groups of caribou grazing in the distance. Blueberry thickets bright with green-red leafs line the banks of streams and arc over wet spots on side slopes.

Mill scans the blueberry thickets with her tiny Nikon roof-prism field glasses. She looks for bears in macrophage, the gorging they do to prepare for over-wintering. There…sure enough…a large, cream-bodied, brown-legged Tolkat grizzly rips berries, leaves, and twigs with two-inch claws and crams the mass into his mouth.

These Tolkat bears might never have seen people before and so might not view them as prey to be killed and eaten.

But, if the EMM team or the racers disturb such a bear while he is stuffing himself near his den, the bear could shred them in an instant.

Mill shudders, remembering the Copper River brown bear. No more of that for her, please!

Mill makes a mental note to tell the racers to steer clear of that bear. The bear is well off to the side of their likely route.

But who could tell what the bear and the racers might do to cross paths? The lack of radios on the trek hampers communications about such things.

The race rules allow Mill to communicate often with the racers and the other members of the EMM team. Since they have no radios, she

172

has to move close enough to shout and point, a tiring and tiresome but do-able thing, then run back the necessary distance to be out of the video shot.

Mill spots a couple of Arctic foxes, fur just turning white. Low to the ground and sight-fixed on something unseen to Mill, they're obviously stalking prey like Arctic hares or ptarmigan.

Similarly, a boldly marked female goshawk circles and then plunges down. A moment later, she labors back up triumphantly with a wiggling young hare in her talons.

The racers and tech team are supposed to avoid harassing goshawks, particularly young ones recently fledged. This female quickly vanishes towards the dun Brooks Range hills. So, Mill figures there's no chance of any of them harassing such a mobile bird or her young from here.

Now Skinner and Bonet hurry close. Mill has to move and soon. But she doesn't yet know where to go. The racers will choose the route.

As they near her, she shouts a warning to the racers and points towards the bear. They change course slightly to the west.

The racers have to cross the north-south aligned Kongakut River, a formidable obstacle on their southwesterly path to the Sheenjek. Here, close to the sea, the clear-water Kong has many braids--wide, deep mini-rivers coursing back and forth across the land.

Higher up, the river is a single, broader flow filled with boulder fields, white-water, gravel bars, and deep, tumbling runs.

The racers can choose to tackle each twisting mini-river hereabouts and risk their lives and gear at each crossing. Or they can move upriver and look for a single crossing and wetting.

The only consequence to the upriver choice is that each step south along the Kong lengthens the distance to the Sheenjek which lies to the southwest.

Mill's sure that Bonet and Skinner have studied the topographic maps of the area closely to identify good crossings.

The Kong passes a lot of water and gravel during the spring. Now at mid-summer, the river is low.

So, Mill bets Marie and Reggie will head upriver and battle across a wide, shallow part in a single trip.

Mill is surprised when the racers stop fifty yards short of the EMM team, clearly planning to cross here where the river is probably the most braided. She is even more surprised when both of them tear off their clothes and stuff everything they are wearing in their packs.

Enoch and Melissa work their cameras in for above-the-waist close-ups and then back out to show the racers' naked figures small against the huge Alaska landscape.

Looking at the naked racers, Mill observes that without female breasts and male genitals for reference, she almost can't tell one from the other. Both are lean, mean, Geo-Challenge racing machines with well-defined muscles and minimum of body fat.

Mill watches as the naked pair dons water shoes. They pull large trash bags out of their packs and stuff the packs into the trash bags. They make sure that each bag holds plenty of air, seal the bags with tape, and carry the puffy objects to the first river bank.

There, Bonet ties twenty yards of rope around each balloon-pack, lashing the rope tightly around each one in a couple of directions, one pack tied to the rope's end and one tied in the rope's middle. Then he takes the loose end of the rope ties it around his waist.

Reggie looks out across the braided river and picks his route. With a whoop for the parabolic microphone in Melissa's hand, he plunges into the first deep-but-narrow stream.

About the time he reaches the first gravelly island, the rope tied to the first pack pulls taut. With Skinner's help, he quickly reels it into the water.

Holding on to the rope just ahead of the second pack, Marie jumps in. She follows Bonet across the water, kicking hard, partially buoyed by the inflated bag.

The two begin to leapfrog across the Kongakut, moving from gravel bar to gravel bar, one racer nearly always on shore. At each portage, both carry the puffy, bagged packs to make sure they don't puncture.

As the racers conquer the Kong, Enoch records their struggles.

Mill and Melissa quickly put away recording gear in waterproof bags and stuff the bags in their packs.

While Melissa finishes that chore, Mill triggers a CO_2 canister on a little, ultra-light, four-person raft she carried here from the first cache near the Beaufort. It inflates instantly and she shoves it into the water.

Each of them takes out and unfolds a small paddle. Melissa and Enoch step gingerly into the little boat and sit down. Mill hands in the packs, pushes them off, and jumps in as the swift Kong current tugs them away from shore.

174

As her foot leaves the riverbank, with an internal flinch, Mill compulsively looks over her shoulder to see if the Tolkat grizzly's charging her. She pushes away both her foolishness and the shore, and then digs in with her paddle.

The three EMMers bob and slide across the river. Their erratic path through the braids and the force of the river's flow pushes them towards the sea. But, with vigorous paddling, the three reach the other side sooner than Reggie and Marie using skinny-dipping to cross the Kong.

On land, Melissa and Enoch shoulder their packs. They jog off upstream to cover the racers' landing.

Once the landing video is 'in the can,' Melissa plans to wire the racers for full-time sound. She is happy at the thought that they have made the wiring process extra convenient for her by stripping naked.

Mill deflates the raft and rolls it up with the paddles inside. Based on what they know about water crossings along the rest of the trek, they won't need the little raft again.

She triggers a radio beacon attached to the raft. Its signal will guide a recovery crew to the site in a day or two.

Each cache has a similar radio beacon. For the Geo-Challenge producers to meet the requirements of the fed-agencies' permit, one of Mill's duties is to make sure the trigger gets pulled as soon as the racers finish with a cache or drop a beacon-attached piece of equipment.

Mill's motto for this part of her job is, "I'll pack it in…if someone else packs it out!"

Mill shoulders her load and moves out. She can see that the racers are clothed and ready to move, too.

The figure that must be Marie takes off at a trot towards the first hills ahead, soft, steep mounds on the doorstep of the Brooks Range.

Mill will have to hump hard to catch up.

She glances at her GPS.

173 miles to go.

It is etrex time.

Follow the arrow.

Chapter 35 – Control Room, Input 1

The race controllers assigned to Bonet and Skinner, called 'Green Control' to match the color of the racers' rain gear and parkas, look expectantly at the Geo-Challenge director.

The controllers expect to make their first "input" any time now. Each set of racers could get as many as three inputs per stage.

The controllers want to make the first input a doozey, although they also want to save the best for last.

The director looks closely at the detailed topographic map on the computer screen and the slow-moving lines that trace each racer.

The director nods, "They've crossed the Kongakut. Go ahead...."

Chapter 36 - Brooks Range

Four hours later, the racers and the EMM team reach the second cache site. This site holds one cache for the racers and one for the support team--twenty-gallon, sealed plastic drums, buried deeply and buried under a few inches of soil.

Each drum's location is marked by a small piece of cleverly hidden flagging nailed to the surface—blue for the racers, red for the support team--hidden to force them to find caches with their GPS units, not their eyes.

Reggie and Marie empty their drum quickly and get ready to head further into the hills. This time, they'll depart with a ten-minute bonus.

After frantically rip-jamming their cache, the EMM team is on the trail ahead of the racers once again.

Mill gulps down some power drink she hastily made from powder. "Tastes like soapy dishwater," she says to Melissa who is setting up a camera nearby, "But some of the best dishwater I've ever had. I'll be a connoisseur of power dishwater by the time this Trek is over."

Melissa takes a slug of it and agrees, "Some of the best."

Mill figures Reggie and Marie will stop for the night at the next cache, fifteen miles ahead, and that they'll make a three-hour cache-dash by headlamp if necessary.

If conditions over the last few miles are any sign of what's to come, the ground between here and there will be increasingly steep, rough, and rocky. Even with headlamps, trekking in the dark could prove costly to ankles and knees.

Mill scans the area ahead. She sees a raptor nest ahead perched in the middle of a small cliff. She runs back and catches Reggie to tell him about it just before he leaves the cache. He is the runner now so he will have to steer a route around the birds.

He nods and takes off. Marie follows at a more careful plod, feet following a deeply incised trail, wary of possible injury under the weight of her sixty-pound pack.

Mill decides to walk a parallel path a hundred yards or so east of Marie.

Using her binoculars, Mill notes again what she had seen earlier, a vast network of braided trails running everywhere and anywhere, going who knew where.

Narrow trails twine along ridge lines and across scree slopes high on side hills. Wider trails wander through dry tussock fields. Trails range along stream ways and through boulder patches. Trails worn into the landscape for millennia.

The trails belong to the Porcupine Caribou Herd, a vast pack of animals whose ancestors have ranged this area for tens of thousands of years.

Here and there, Mill watches small family groups of caribou cows and calves walk along, eating as they move, instinctively avoiding the swarms of insects that have plagued them throughout the long days of the short Arctic summer.

And high along a ridge, Mill spots a dozen or so bulls running gracefully, perhaps fleeing from a bear charge. Their huge antlers gleam in some places and show streaks of blood and dangling skin in others.

The hanging tissue is what nurtured boney antler growth throughout the wintery spring. It's often called "velvet" because of its appearance when intact.

Mill marvels again that such relatively small animals could produce such disproportionately large antlers, some taller than the animals' shoulder height. She can't guess at the adaptive purpose but finds the caribou magnificent—bulls, cows, calves, and all.

Yes, a force of nature, the caribou have hammered these trails into the land. And every other species, including humans, use them.

Mill puts away her field glasses. She checks the roll-up solar-cell bundle clamped to the top of her pack and the leads from the solar cells to the charger hanging at her waist. Right now, it contains a set of Enoch's camera batteries.

Mill lifts her pack and shrugs it on. She starts an easy jog to stay up with Marie.

The brown Brooks Range looms just ahead, the tops of its high hills lost in evening fog, spots of green and yellow tracing the courses of little streams and creeks down hillsides.

She glances over her shoulder back towards the sea. The Beaufort stretches north, grey-dark blue, towards a lost, cold-misty horizon. Low clouds scud over the dark water. A steely chop dots the sea surface with white puffs and curls.

Mill thinks, "No going back. All ahead full!"

She breaks into a trot.

Mill has a team and racers to support.

It's 10 p.m. Daylight fades into a summer-in-the-Arctic dusk. At the cache site, the Green Group shuts down for the day.

Although clouds block its light from the racers, the sun will just barely drop to kiss the horizon before rising fully again. This time of year and under such a dense cloud layer, the night gets too dark to trek safely without headlamps even though it never really gets cave-bottom black as it does during the Arctic winter.

The Green Group busies about the camp site. Three little white-gas stoves hiss. Water for tea or coffee and freeze-dried meals boils in small stainless-steel pots.

Three tents are staked and set up...one for the racers...one for the techies...and one for Mill, sleeping bags and mats rolled out in each tent.

Packs have been reworked for tomorrow and stacked outside the tents.

Food is cached well away from camp to keep hungry bears away from people.

Camp is finally made and the tired trekkers sit on the ground, legs outstretched, food and drink in hand. They chat about the day's march—obstacles, animals, weather.

Reggie remarks, "You know, most people have no idea how much time gets swallowed up by making camp and then breaking it. I swear a fast camp is a real hard thing to achieve."

Reggie's words are met with a chorus of agreement and grumbles.

Enoch laughs, "Yeah, I was on a shoot once in northwest Wyoming, on the Shoshone National Forest and down on some private ranch lands near Riverton. I was with a bunch of pampered actors and movie types who had little or no experience outdoors."

"We shot all of the footage we needed down in Riverton first. That went okay. You know, we were in a ranch setting--no camping, lots of trailers, and cooks with hot food. Like a little three-star resort, really. People complained about the dust and heat, but that was just bitching for effect. A lot of actors do that."

The listeners shake their heads. They can relate.

"A couple of days later, we head out for high country. It's a regular wagon train with trucks, trailers and all that stuff. But then we get to the trailhead where we have to switch to horses and mules. Then the complaining really started. I mean I thought everybody knew the shoot was going to be partly in the wild. And the producers had the whole thing well organized, lots of pack strings and mules for the pack, and good horses and tack for the talent. But it was bitch and moan…moan and bitch…all the way up."

"Well, we finally get to the first campsite. Right above tree line it was. We were going to work our way down. Anyway, the grips and wranglers got everything set up. It took at least two hours, maybe more. And the greenhorns just stood there and didn't help. I figured that breaking camp later would go even slower with so many loafers. I was right, but that's not the point of my story."

"Shortly after we get there, I hear one of the actors tell the executive producer that he'd be damned if he would sleep in a tent, at least one without air conditioning. And the producer had this look on his face like 'how do you tell an idiot that the only air conditioning that tents have is the wind blowing through them.' So, like the smart guy he was, the producer said nothing back to the guy, just smiled and nodded. I guess the actor must have thought the producer agreed with him."

A knowing laugh runs through the group.

"So camp's up and now it's late afternoon, hot, no wind. Thunderheads are building up way off. Real pretty white clouds with grey bellies. We film guys are getting some great footage of them."

Marie murmurs, "Oh yeah, I remember being in the Rockies among those clouds. Incredible, Enoch, almost a religious experience being up there with them."

Enoch replies, "It definitely is for me. Anyway, I walk over to get some equipment and the actor guy is asking the producer where his air conditioner is. Seems he had been over to his tent and couldn't find the controls or something. He seems quite upset."

"The producer opens his mouth, probably to tell the guy off, when an enormous thunderclap shakes the whole damn mountain. You know the Rockies in summer. Well, a second later, wind comes roaring through. Rain and hail come crashing down. In seconds, the tents are flattened. Stuff's flying everywhere, getting soaked."

The Green Group makes sympathetic noises like "Been there, brother" and "Tell me about it."

"I dive for cover. And a few minutes later…the storm's over. I get up and look around. Everything's a huge mess. I couldn't believe it, but the producer and that actor are still standing there, soaking wet and looking a little worse for wear."

"The producer kind of shakes himself and says to the actor, 'I asked special effects to provide you with air conditioning. I guess they overdid it.'"

"And then he just turned and walked away."

Enoch and his listeners roar with laughter.

"I kinda felt sorry for the actor. I mean he was an idiot but he had no camping experience, so what did he know? I helped him get his tent set back up, put his things out to dry, and get some dinner. I was fine with the producer's joke, but I didn't want the guy to give up on enjoying the outdoors."

"He and I have a fishing trip planned next October. We do one every year."

Mill smiles at Enoch…good man…good to have him on her team.

The next morning the Green Group makes a fast break at dawn, 4 a.m.

_____//_____

Mill hauls her weary butt to the top of the latest steep hill of what has become a seeming infinity of steep hills.

She glances down at her *e*trex, "Day three and thirty-three miles to go to the Sheenjek. Nice synchronicity of numbers there."

Along with the four others in her group, Mill is getting a little punchy from the incredible physical effort she has been making. For all the lancing pains she feels under her pack straps and the cold-tired, non-feeling in her legs, Mill is proud of being able to stay up with the racers.

Nothing she had done back in Cordova with Melony and Jared had prepared her for this all-out effort. And the cold, damp, cloudy weather makes rocks slippery and rest stops shivery.

Mill decided on day two that Marie and Reggie were aliens from another planet sent to Earth to humble humans and make us more open to conquest. Each time the racers took off briskly from a cache after a too-brief rest, Mill would think, "Give up, humans, resistance is futile." Then she would stagger back to her feet and jog after them.

Amazingly, after over thirty miles of cold water and tough trails, probably too keyed up to sleep, the racers made love in their tent on the first night.

Hearing their quiet groans, Mill wondered, "Do they know that Melissa is recording every sound? Maybe they don't care."

Outside the tent the next morning at first light, the couple showed no signs of affection. They simply worked together with brisk efficiency by head-lamp light to break camp and get on the trail.

Definitely aliens.

Today, Mill decides Melissa and Enoch are also aliens.

She thinks, "I should probably stop sleeping in the tent next to them. They might turn me into a pod person or something."

Mill giggles and then looks around to see if anyone heard her. No, too far away. Even with hours to go before camping for the night, she is getting punchy. She has to pay attention and watch her step.

At the moment, she is inching her way along a foot-wide caribou trace at the top of a 600-foot scree slope. One bad move and she would tumble to the bottom.

She remembers her time and distance estimates from the Fairbanks meeting. She'd figured 160 miles of ground pounding. According to her *etrex*, they were just under 150 now and at least thirty-three miles to go.

One day? Two?

The distance and difficulty depend on Bonet and Skinner, the land, and, most of all, the marshes, streams, and rock piles—waking nightmares of slogging steps and graceless falls.

Fourth day.

So far they have found three caches--two designated for them and one other, two days ago, open to all three racer groups. The open cache had been empty.

The knowledge that they were beaten to the cache had a telling effect on the racers. Reggie and Marie became grimly determined to not let any other racers be first to a cache again. Leaving the empty-cache site, they hit the trail hard, pushing themselves and the EMM team hard for the next two days.

By this fourth day, their determination to be first is tempered by fatigue and the need to arrive at the Sheenjek in good enough shape to complete the McKinley and Alsek stages. A bad sprain or break would end the race for them. And even their tough bodies have grown weary of endless climbs up and long stumbling slides down.

All through the Brooks Range, the trekkers had raced through the brown grasses and sedges covering mountain slopes. Now, as the Green Group lies sprawled around a flat spot along a ridge in the Romanzofs, the slender, fragile vegetation offers little shelter against the blustery west wind.

Instead, a large irregular rock about the size and shape of a Volkswagen microbus provides them an indifferent windbreak.

Amused by the odd rock, Mill is too tired to point out how much she would like to be riding in a microbus the rest of the way to the Sheenjek.

Mill figures her EMM team has done well. Four days of video and audio have been uplinked to the control room in Fairbanks through the sat phone. Some kind of high-speed data compression programmed into the cameras minimizes call time. Everything had zipped through with no problems.

Mill also figures the editors are already making first cuts on the material because they've already started sending back requests for additional coverage.

Besides all the video Enoch shot of Dall sheep and caribou along the way, Mill had been asked to identify more wildlife and bird species to record. By ranging widely, she was able to find some smaller critters like lemmings and more bird species on the wing. The techies had grabbed that material, too.

Resting by the rock, Mill uplinks some of the new footage--an exquisite video of a mother goshawk fledging her chicks. It had been taken an hour ago with Enoch's mini-tripod-based camera.

"That ought to make 'em happy," she nods to Enoch after the sat phone shows the transmission has gone through.

Enoch smiles back wearily, "Yeah, for now. They'll want more soon and better. I know those guys. They have no idea of how hard it is to get the good stuff and they always want it in their hands yesterday. We send brilliant shots in and then, an hour later, it's 'what have you done for me today?' Hey, we just keep up our end as best we can."

Even resting, he keeps his camera pointed at the racers on break.

Reggie leans back against the microbus-rock.

Suddenly he jerks upright. Looking down at his *etrex*, he yells, "What the *fuck*!"

Marie immediately jumps up from where she has been resting her pack-weary back by lying flat.

She walks over to him, "What's wrong, Regg?"

He spits, "If this piece-of-shit *etrex* is right, we're off course....have been for a while maybe."

Mill looks down at her GPS. Sure enough, something has changed. The direction arrow no longer points south-southwest to where they supposed the race was to end on the Sheenjek. Instead, it points much more westerly, almost due west.

What could have happened?

Reggie guesses first, "The Goddamn controllers, of course...an input. Put us off track using remote control, maybe from the start. I don't know. So we know we're off-course but we don't know how much."

He stops for a moment. Then waving the *etrex*, he says with a trace of fear in his voice, "So, I wonder if we can trust anything we see on this thing at all. We've been following it pretty much blindly, figuring we were on course, but now...."

His voice trails off.

Skinner puts her hand on the back of Reggie's neck and gives him a gentle shake, "Okay, look, we know that the GPSes had us on course the first day. I mean we found the first caches okay. We hit 'em dead on. So, I'm saying we knew where we were when we started out two days ago. And we hit all the caches since, even though the controllers maybe messed with the compass part of the GPSes."

Marie points to the *etrex* in Reggie's hand. "Use the backtracker feature to the first and last caches and then calculate the routes to the Sheenjek from them. We should be able triangulate from our present position looking at the e-maps and figure out if the route we see now is right or not."

Muttering under his breath, Reggie rapidly presses the buttons on his little GPS, "Maybe they could screw up the maps and cache sites separately to further screw with our minds."

"Okay," he says in less than a minute, "good thinking, Marie. As near as I can tell from the maps and waypoints, the arrow is now pointing correctly. But, damn it, we have at least ten, maybe twenty, miles more than we figured this morning.

"And, get this, based on the *etrex*'s topographic maps, the roughest terrain in the Romanzofs are between us and the Sheenjek. The bastards led us way south to make us confront the worst ground so close to the end. They *planned* this, probably even down to where they put the caches. Crap and corruption!"

Marie smiles grimly, "At least we know where to go. And, even though I hate to think of putting that pack on again, we better get going…."

Grumbling, the racers and EMM team get "saddled up."

For sure, they will have to trek by head lamp tonight followed inevitably by a short night of sleep.

Ouch!

Chapter 37 - Rough Trade in Foreign Seas

Casey Summerland walks up to Hard Rock Gruber with a smile, "I got confirmation from Du that the freighter left Malapanbang, steaming for Dry Bay. She'll get here a few days late but she'll get here. Man, what a sense of relief, eh?"

Hard Rock slaps his holster. Chin out, he nods angrily, "Yeah. According to Du, it took every contact he had to get the damn boat out of there and took me at least ten thousand U.S. in bribes. Could anything else have gone wrong?"

Casey shakes his head, "Only if the ship sank."

Seeing his boss' red face, Summerland instantly regrets his words.

He quickly stammers, "But it didn't sink, or even get impounded, really."

His voice falters under Hard Rock's fierce stare.

The whole mess had started when Du sent word that the shipment should reroute from Jakarta into Malapanbang, a small, sleepy harbor. "Good place. All quiet…nice peoples."

At Malapanbang, Du supposedly had the customs officials under his thumb, on retainer. Unloading could go ultra-smoothly with only cursory paperwork. Much better than busy Jakarta harbor where cargo inspections were more thorough and over-worked facilities might delay things for days.

After Hard Rock agreed to off-load the freighter at Malapanbang, Summerland contacted the ship and diverted it to the new destination.

Things looked rosy. With a quick turnaround at Malapanbang, they might get a day or two ahead on their next load of ore in Alaska.

Yeah, sure they would. As soon as the ship docked, local police boarded the ship and arrested the captain. Claiming they were acting on a drug-smuggling tip, customs officials began a minute inspection of every part of the vessel.

Du called Gruber to raise the alarm and to ask for financial support to get the ship out of the bureaucratic vise.

"Goddamn it, Du!" Gruber roared, "You told me you had this wired, no worries, no problems, eh?"

Du started talking quickly in Malay, not a word of which Hard Rock understood. Du seemed sincerely agitated but who could tell?

Hard Rock waited through the torrent of harsh, sibilant words until finally he could take no more. "Du...Du...damn it, *Du!*" he yelled into the phone, "For Christ's sake, speak English...speak *English!*"

After a moment, DU slowed down and started speaking in Malay-peppered English. Gruber found he could more or less follow Du's meaning.

Hard Rock tried to sooth his man in Malaysia, "Okay, Du, okay. I hear you...nothing you could do...new customs man on the scene...suspicious of a North American shipment coming in there...got it...got it. Okay, what do we have to do to get things back on track, eh?"

Gruber would have bet dollars to donuts that Du had set the whole thing up, that he would get at least half of any bribe paid. But what could Gruber make of it other than to try to get out with as little cost as possible?

"Okay, Du, tell the bastard we'll cooperate. For God's sake, get those people off the boat before they figure out what's in those drums. Otherwise, we'll have to pay ten times more. Yeah, yeah, make 'em read the manifest, you know, lubricants...anything. Just get those inspectors off the ship."

And an hour later, the police and customs people had, in fact, left the ship.

Over the next three days, Du and Du's cousin, the Malapanbang customs agent, convivially totaled up the cost of Gruber's 'violations" and estimated how much they could extort.

Du made occasional calls to Hard Rock to tell him how the "negotiations" were going. Safety. Excess oil in the bilge water. Improper sewage equipment. Out-of-date licenses. No visas for three crewmen.

The total penalties kept climbing. Finally, Du and the customs agent decided Gruber would pay no more.

They didn't know Gruber would have paid five times more to get this first shipment through. But he blustered, cussed, and moaned to Du throughout the rip off, "This mine has made me a poor man. I can't pay. The whole thing will go gunnysack if we can't get that concentrate to market," and on and on.

Towards the end, he told Du, "Damn it, Du, I'll look for another partner, one who can get this shipment sprung loose before I pay a penny more. In fact, I'll scuttle that damn ship in the harbor before I pay another cent."

After three days, Hard Rock's cussing and complaining finally worked. Once Summerland wired the money to Du's cousin, crews began unloading the drums.

Back in Alaska, using the RF tags in each drum and monitors on the ship, Casey carefully tracked them as they were signed out into Du's hands by the freighter's crew.

Du had figured correctly that Gruber would tolerate having to bribe Du's cousin as a cost of doing business. But, as he watched the loading, he also knew that Hard Rock would hunt him down and kill him if any of the drums disappeared.

So, once a truck was loaded, an armed guard climbed in the front to control the driver and another sat in the rear with the load. When all were loaded, the trucks ran in a convoy to Du's walled compound thirty kilometers from Malapanbang.

There, Du pulled samples from the drums, authenticated the amount of nickel in the concentrate, and made final shipping arrangements to Hong Kong.

So Du had kept a close eye on the loading and delivery. And now, looking at the rows of drums in his compound, Du muses, "Good the Chinese are so hungry for nickel...."

At the same moment back in Alaska, still scowling at Summerland, Hard Rock Gruber is thinking the same thing.

Chapter 38 – Control Room, Input 2

Once again the Green Control race controllers look expectantly at the director. An hour ago, the controllers saw the Green Group change course to the west, a clear reaction to the geeks' restoration of the proper direction setting on the team's *e*trexes.

None of the controllers feels any remorse for creating such a mess for the Green Group. After all, the racers had known that inputs were part of the race. And, the decision to send the input wasn't the geeks' responsibility. The director had given them the go-ahead.

And really, what a great feeling it was to sit in the control room, warm and dry, while highly trained athletes twist and twitch across monitor screens, battling Arctic weather and wild country. It's almost like a computer game.

The controllers can't wait to watch the video that will come in tonight—the one that will show the moment the racers discovered that the *e*trexes had switched directions. The video editors had promised them that they could watch the segment as many times as they wanted.

The director studies the racer-tracking monitor again to make sure that the Green Group is definitely travelling west. The race safety rules preclude stacking one input on another because tired people in the field might make fatal mistakes trying to deal with two inputs at once.

The director watches the racers wandering line of travel move in a clear westerly direction for another five minutes.

"Okay," he says, "Send the next input."

A Green Geek presses a few keys on his computer, "Done."

The geek rocks back in his cushioned office chair and grins.

Chapter 39 - Sheenjek Bound

Now Mill really struggles to stay ahead of Reggie and Marie as the pair surges ahead towards the last cache where they will load up for the final sprint to the Sheenjek. Bent under her pack, Mill checks back over her shoulder to make sure she is far enough ahead of the racers.

She wants to stay out of Enoch's lens. She knows that the editors can cut her out of the video being captured on the racers' GoPro's. But Enoch's getting the good stuff and she doesn't want to mess him up.

The ground lies so steeply up and down through this part of the Romanzofs that her past practice of staying off to one side of the racers' route no longer works. She simply has to run directly ahead of them --up steep shaley slopes, through barren gravelly saddles, and down slidey faces that slip away from under her mountain boots.

Mill's light walking stick has saved her from many falls in this steep country.

Mill checks her etrex. Three more miles to the cache.

Bonet and Skinner are coming up fast, the tantalizing goal ahead adding energy to their tired bodies.

Mill stops looking back. She has the racers' latest pace figured out. She climbs the last few feet to the top of a crumbly ridge and humps down slope for the cache spot…and rest.

Mill's etrex shows clearly that she should be standing on the EMM cache. But there's no red flagging. When she stamps the earth, she can't hear a hollowish drum-thump.

"Where the bloody Hell is the cache?" she asks herself.

Melissa and Enoch reach her.

Mill says, "I'm having a Hell of a time finding our cache. What do your etrexes say?"

They quickly compare etrex readings.

Enoch says, "Looks like we should be right on top of the caches. Both have got to be within a yard of here."

Marie and Reggie join them and get the news. They all spin around, look back and forth across the mostly barren spot, stomp, find nothing, and then look at each other, faces grim.

Marie says urgently, "Look, we're wasting time. Let's walk a grid with each of us an arm's length apart for…say…fifty yards square or so. Shouldn't take long. But we have to stomp and go slow enough that we don't miss anything."

Mill has experienced leadership from the wiry little Marie before. But Skinner's clarity and direction in the face of her evident exhaustion really impresses Mill now.

The group immediately adopts Marie's plan. The grid-search begins.

A moment later, as they walk along arms out, fingers touching, clogging along, Mill can't help giggling, "Hey, look at us. We're a ballet troop in mountain boots."

They all laugh wearily. They do look absurd.

Twenty minutes later, the search ends. They've found only scaly barren ground.

No caches…and no humor, anywhere, anymore.

Once again, Bonet gets it first. He turns away from a last stomp and faces right into camera Enoch's camera, "You fuckin' controllers! I hope you're satisfied, you bastards. No food for the last push. No fuel for the stoves. And no batteries for the headlamps. We could die for all you care, you pricks!"

He spits on the ground and then says with extra venom, "Screw you. We're still gonna win."

With that, he and Marie turn to the west.

Their eyes scan the horizon towards the Sheenjek. Their GPS units say the finish line is twenty-two miles ahead, an alluring red dot on the little screens, and the tiny GPS maps hint that gentler slopes lie ahead.

They can go back to their runner-packer strategy.

Bonet quickly removes half of the weight from Marie's pack and puts it in his. Now lighter by twenty-five pounds, Skinner moves out briskly, almost jogging.

Bonet follows Marie and strides hard.

The weight on his back precludes jogging but his long strides begin to eat down the distance to the Sheenjek.

Mill launches herself down a parallel caribou trail.

Melissa and Enoch jog past Mill a few moments later, working to outpace the racers once again.

Mill focuses on her breathing. Feeling the strain, she thinks, "No food resupply? We'll never keep up this pace."

She glances at the sky. The long Arctic day is darkening towards dusk, "No fresh batteries either. I'll get some double- and triple-A's on the charger. But no time to charge them all, or even very many. The light's fading. Enoch can shoot with his night-vision cameras, but I bet we won't go too late tonight. Maybe I can sleep late."

She smiles a little. Sleep on the Trek has been a few exhausted hours of rest on a thin mat spread over pebbly ground.

Mill starts taking discharged batteries out of her cargo pockets. She shoves them into the charging station. The little red "charging" light come on. When it turns green, she can put in more.

Mill scans the landscape ahead for environmental issues, doing her other job.

She humps the trail, hard.

Chapter 40 – Alsek Fading Blue

Hard Rock stammers, "A r-race? What do you mean a race? A race here, in our backyard?"

Casey Summerland shrugs his shoulders, "Yeah, strange world, eh? The Great Land Geo-Challenge is one of those reality shows. This one's about a race across Alaska. And, Hard Rock, it's already started. I mean the racers are in the field and the show is being shot…recorded… whatever."

"According to the information on the internet, they're definitely coming here to kayak the Alsek. And, get this, the race ends somewhere around here with a big week-long media operation and awards ceremony at Dry Bay."

Hard Rock's eyes almost bug out of his head as he thinks about the consequences of so many people coming to the area of Alsek Blue Billions.

Racers racing.

Helicopters in the air.

Boats on the river.

People poking around his mine.

Gruber yells, "Goddamn it! That's probably what those candy-cane poles are out there above the beach. They've got to have something to do with the race. I should have thrown the damn things in the river."

Furious, he punches his right fist against the wall of the entry adit, ripping his knuckles on rough granite.

"What can we do about this, Case?" he asks, "Dig up those poles? Move 'em somewhere else? Throw them in the river…still a good idea? We've got to keep people away from the mine, away from where they might see the waste pipe dumping in the river. Hell, they might even be able to hear us operating if they get close enough."

Hands at his sides, Gruber clenches his fists with anger. Blood drips from his torn knuckles to the floor.

Summerland thinks for a few moments. It's weird to hear the normally super-self-confident Hard Rock ask for advice. He clears his throat nervously and lowers his eyes, not sure how angry his volatile and well-armed boss is, "Hard Rock, here's another problem. The freighter's due back here right about the time the race comes by. I mean, I can't be really sure because a lot of the information about the Geo-Challenge is confidential. But it looks like we might be trying to get our second shipment out right on top of this race."

Gruber points to the full storage room and the stacks of pallets and drums once again choking the adit, "Well, what the fuck are we supposed to do, Casey, shut this fucker down and run away while the race people and gawkers swarm the place? I mean, no one can see the mine entrance from the river or flying overhead. But you can't miss it if you walk a hundred yards this way from those damn poles and past the big rock pile! How would we keep people from coming right in here to keep us company, eh? Sit down with us for tea and biscuits?"

Hard Rock yells again, "Goddamn it. We can't *shut down*. We have to *ship*. This is our first *profit* trip. And we can't let people find us or *everything* will be lost, busted...*shut down*."

He had to figure out what to do or Alsek Blue Billions would "steamboat," run out of steam. Hard Rock grips his .44 tightly, blood dripping onto the trigger guard.

Suddenly, he has a plan.

Chapter 41 – Push for the Sheenjek

Midnight.

Darkish, getting darker.

The sun lost below the deep-blue mountain horizon.

The ground lost in a misty gloom.

Above, it's clear for once. If the racers look straight up, they can see a few stars. No moon.

Of the EMM team, only Enoch has a viable headlamp. He turns it on to move ahead and shuts it off to shoot the racers with his night-vision camera.

Reggie's wearing the racers' one functional headlamp. It slowly dims as he paces ahead.

Behind him, Marie has locked her hand into Reggie's pack.

Melissa is similarly holding onto Marie's gear and Mill has wound her hand into Melissa's.

Mill muses, "We're playing blind man's bluff in the Alaskan bush. Crazy."

Hours ago, Reggie and Marie agreed to forge ahead, all night if necessary, to reach the Sheenjek in the morning.

Screw the controllers!

But, worried now, Reggie reminds himself that pushing ahead while exhausted is a bad idea, dangerous.

It's not so much the physical wear and tear or the emotional irritability. Those conditions injure the body and rip partnerships.

No, it's the bad judgment, the mistakes that will *certainly* happen, the chance of injuring someone, even death, because of a muddled mind, a wrong choice.

The group stumbles on another mile.

Or is it only a hundred feet?

Now, Reggie's dimming headlamp only allows him to see a few feet ahead.

What to do? It's fully dark.

Fog tendrils swirl around them.

Bonet slows and then stops.

The women behind him stop stumble-walking.

Enoch moves closer to cover the racers' conversation close up.

Bonet turns to Marie, "Okay, we need to talk. We've got to figure something out…what to do. My light's almost out."

His voice comes out as a tired drawl.

In the dim-yellow glow of his headlamp, Marie's face is lined, her eyes puffed almost closed with fatigue.

Reggie watches her weave dizzily. Or is that him?

The tough little woman attempts a smile but fails, "Look, Reggie, we're all about done in. I know we said we'd push through tonight. The only way it might happen is if we hydrate like crazy and get some rest, an hour or two at least, and then hit it again. Maybe we can turn some of our brains back on, too."

Bonet nods, "Okay."

Mill speaks up, "Enoch, please turn off the camera."

He does.

Mill gazes into the racers' weary faces, "Look, I know I'm not supposed to give you guys any advice about the route or when to race. But my ass is on the line with yours, along with Enoch's and Melissa's. It's up to you to win this Trek but we all want to survive it."

The two racers nod and Marie mutters, "Damn right it is."

Mill continues, "It's after midnight now. An hour or two of rest would be great for all of us. Better, when we wake up, we should be able to make at least slow progress under the starlight until sunrise. We'll put the person with the best night vision in front."

"We can rope the four of us up to keep us together. Then if someone stumbles or falls, even the last in line, we'll know and can help. Like he was doing before, Enoch can work his best camera angles to try and keep Melissa and me out of shots. Does this idea make sense to everyone?"

The racers and other EMM team members think for a minute, fatigue fogging their minds.

Then, without another word, everyone finds a spot to lie flat. If there's a flaw in Mill's plan, they'll figure that out when they wake up and some mind-fog has cleared.

Canteens glug-glug.

Quiet falls.

A distant wolf howl sends little chills up Mill's neck. A blanket of exhaustion smothers her primal fear and excitement at the sound. She drops into a long tunnel…sleeps.

Mill's eyelids flutter open. Her old trick of picturing the words "WAKE UP IN TWO HOURS" just before falling asleep has worked again.

She fights to stay awake. It seems like only her eyelids can move.

With great effort, she raises an achy head on a stiff neck and adjusts her torso more upright, back on pack.

Mill's pack had made a poor pillow. But it worked better than the only other alternative, a lichen-feathered rock.

Not one of them had set up a tent, just spread a sleeping mat and pulled a sleeping bag over themselves or slipped within, boots on.

She looks around. Near her, Bonet's arm pulls Skinner close, the two snuggled for warmth.

Enoch and Melissa lie a few feet away, their bodies, too, close together.

Mill asks herself, "So why didn't the government issue me someone to cuddle up to on this God-forsaken Trek?"

Her sleepy mind goes briefly to Charli; it would be nice if she were here. But no, she reminds herself, Charli is a creature of warm fireplaces and hot rum-cocoas, not nights spent sleeping under the stars on a wind-swept plateau in the Romanzof foothills.

"Tilly…Tilly," Mill thinks, "Now she could do this, but not in her Abercrombie and Fitch safari shirt." Mill smiles a little thinking of Tilly in flannel and cords, lying close to her here on the ground.

Sheer fatigue has knocked any sexual urges out of Mill. But the thought of Tilly's warm body close by is oddly comforting.

Mill listens for the wolves that howled her to sleep. No sound now except for Enoch's snoring. His wheezy rasp comes lightly as he lies there and his breath makes a cloud.

Mill thinks, "Boy, I'd like to tape Enoch right now. Make some good blackmail footage for later." A small smile again chases away her habitual frown for a moment.

Waking further, Mill realizes that she can actually see pretty well in the starlight. Mill shakes her head and blinks sleep out of her eyes.

She looks up to check out the Milky Way and…*Wow! The northern lights*!

White sheets of cold light ripple and wave across the sky. Here and there, red light-feathers creep along the edges of the white waves followed by little bits of deep glacier blue. In the cold, silent air, Mill hears the aurora's crackle and smells the ozone released by billions of solar volts ripping through air.

Across the whole sky-arc above her, the aurora borealis billows and flows, infused with ghostly power and, to Mill, unfathomable intention. The aurora seems to have a clear message for her, but what?

Wait! That's it!

Mill realizes that nearby rocks cast clear shadows. She looks out across the landscape. The land lies naked before her, bathed in the pulsing, wavering Arctic light.

The group can walk easily in this light, maybe even jog on even ground until sunrise several hours away. Muscles and joints creaking, she rolls over and pokes Reggie, "Bonet...Bonet, get up. We have to get going. Look, the northern lights. We can see everything. Really...everything."

She pokes him again harder.

Reggie snorts, shakes himself awake, and stares blankly around. He quickly realizes that what Mill has said is true.

"How long will this last, Mill?" he asks in a hoarse voice.

Mill shakes her head, "I'm not sure, Regg. Probably hours, likely 'til sunrise."

"Fabulous," he husks, "Let's get everybody up and out of here."

In ten minutes they are back on the trail.

Enoch tries to figure out how best to capture the racers moving along under aurora light. Night vision or standard?

Nothing seems to work.

He settles on standard. The video has a ghostly quality he has never seen before.

Racers move as dark shadows against a dim background. It should make great footage for the show.

_____//_____

Daylight.

The racers' reserves of strength are mostly gone. Their two hours of sleep last night are just a fleeting moment measured against today's fatigue.

As they alternate the lead, Bonet and Skinner keep each other on track by talk, grunts, and comparison of etrex readings.

They know they are close to the finish, but they can't see very far ahead. They have dropped down out of the brown, barren Romanzof hills into greener valleys filled with patches of cottonwood and alder, yellow leaves bowing to oncoming fall, and red-leaved blueberry bushes still holding fruit.

Occasionally they startle caribou out of thickets. They watch closely for bears.

Because the trees and brush limit their vision, the racers have to depend even more on the etrexes. The GPSes show five miles to the finish.

It'll take an hour, maybe two, in this environment and at their level of pain and exhaustion to get there. Both racers are wary. They suspect that the controllers might do something to the little GPSes again.

Thinking of the Controllers, Bonet grits, "Those bastards! I swear, Marie, if I ever get a-hold of them, I'll kick their lazy asses from Fairbanks to Fort Yukon. Sons 'a bitches."

Marie looks wearily at Bonet, "So, hey, Regg, we don't know they've done anything, do we? I mean this area looks like the kind of terrain and vegetation we saw in pictures of areas around the finish, doesn't it?"

"Yeah, I guess so," he admits, "but just let those bastards mess with us again…."

The words are no sooner out of Reggie's mouth than something changes on his etrex. A cache has appeared, a half mile or so to the north of their line of march.

For a moment Bonet stares at his GPS, speechless. Then he growls, "See, I told you they were screwing with us. Look at your GPS. Do you see a cache that wasn't there a few minutes ago?"

Marie quickly checks her unit, "No, I don't see anything."

They compare.

Sure enough, Reggie's etrex clearly shows a cache marker where Marie's shows nothing.

"Bloody Hell," Reggie mutters, "Which of these pieces of shit do we believe? And are we on course or off?"

He gathers his tired, tired wits, "Marie, we have a serious problem here. If we bypass the cache and the controllers are sending us away from the finish line, we could be dead meat, no supplies. If we stop and resupply at the cache, provided there *is* even a cache, we'll use up time, maybe lose the Trek."

"And, if we stop and resupply and then wander around for another day or two, we might live…and still lose. What the Hell?"

Marie has had similar thoughts running through her head, "Look, we can't make this choice without the support team. They are as tired and hungry as we are."

Marie turns and waves the EMM team in. They move quickly to join the racers.

Marie looks each of them in the eyes before speaking, "Look at your *e*trexes, folks. Do any of yours show a cache ahead?"

They all look and answer, "No."

Marie smiles grimly, tightening the tired sag of her face, "Okay, well, Reggie's GPS definitely shows a cache ahead, off our route a ways. But his is the only one showing a cache. Mine doesn't show it, yours don't. So, we're stopped here for the moment trying to figure out what to do. If we divert to find the cache and there isn't one, we may be played out and lose the race. If the controllers have us on the wrong course, well, having what's in the cache may mean life or death for all of us, particularly if we get separated for some reason."

Mill holds up the satellite phone, "We can always call for the cavalry with this."

"Yes," replies Skinner, "We can. But the race rules say that if they pull us out, Reggie and I forfeit the whole Geo-Challenge. We will do almost anything to prevent that. We just have to finish after…well, all this."

Tears of frustration well up in Marie's eyes, "What to do, I'm not sure."

Reggie interjects, "Look guys…Marie…what if we accept that the GPSes are accurate. We split up. I think I have a little more juice left than you do, Marie. You take a big chunk of my load and move as fast as you can to the finish shown on your *e*trex. I'll sprint ahead, off-course to the cache, grab basic food and supplies, then hustle to catch you."

As he speaks, he weaves on his feet a little, fatigue assaulting his coordination. Noticing his motion, Bonet straightens himself and grips his walking stick tighter for support.

He smiles and then speaks earnestly to Marie again, "Even if the *e*trexes are off, they seem to be off in the same way. Yours reads just like mine as far as the finish line is concerned. So, once I'm loaded up with stuff from the cache, I'll run to catch you before the finish. If I don't catch you before you get there, or it's not where the GPSes say it is, just wait at what the GPS says is the finish until I arrive. And then we'll refigure what to do if it's a fake."

"We could drop our loads here, but we don't know if the finish line is where the GPSes say it is or not. So we have to keep packing. Okay, anybody got a better plan?"

No one did. "Everybody clear?"

They were.

Bonet unloads half his gear into Marie's pack.

As he turns to go, she grabs and pivots him to face her. Her voice husky, she says, "Stay safe, partner. See you at the finish line."

Skinner pulls Bonet down to her and, for a long moment, kisses him on the mouth. Then she whirls away and starts towards the finish line as fast as her tired body can go.

Bonet shakes his head, sets his *e*trex destination on the cache, and takes off at a sore-ankle trot.

Enoch and Marie quickly split up.

Without a word to Mill, they jog away to get in front of the racers, Enoch following Marie and Melissa on Reggie's trail.

Mill is left in a quandary. Who should she shadow?

She flips a mental coin and follows Bonet. He will be on the trail longer. She should stay with him.

And the thought of getting an energy bar at the cache floats tantalizingly into her mind.

Chapter 42 - Arctic Trek Finish

Marie's *e*trex had not lied. A few hundred yards ahead of her on the banks of the Sheenjek, she sees two striped poles, fifty feet apart, with green flagging fluttering on their tops.

To stop the race clock, she and Bonet have to reach the poles and simultaneously push the red buttons mounted on the solar-powered radios clamped to the poles.

Easy enough.

With the finish in sight, Marie picks up her staggering pace.

Enoch gets out in front of her to capture her final push. He reaches a pole, moves beyond, turns, drops his pack, and kneels stiffly to get a shot of her reaching the finish.

Marie moves up as quickly as her wavering feet and vision will allow. Staggering the last few steps, she clutches the pole, drops her pack, and sags flat to the ground, breathing heavily. For the moment, she doesn't know if she can rise again, even to press the button.

She will do it...she knows this to her core...when Reggie joins her. But where's Bonet?

She will wait. Skinner closes her eyes, letting darkness wash over her.

Enoch turns off the camera. He too lies down...rests his weary head. Just barely able to keep his eyes open, he struggles to stay conscious for the arrival of the rest of Green Group.

His last waking thought is, "C'mon guys...get here."

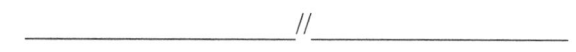

Mill had been so hungry when she rushed up to the cache. The three had grabbed everything they could in a few minutes--food, batteries, fuel. They hastily stuffed packs, filled pockets, and then hurried towards the finish.

Mill had started eating an energy bar before they were twenty feet away from the half-empty cache.

Now she wishes she'd nibbled instead of gobbled. Her guts are rebelling...unh. She'll have to hang on for another three-four miles.

Mill works her stomach muscles, drinks a little water, and breathes deeply to ease the cramps.

Reggie has no more run left in him. He moves ever slower.
One mile.
Two.
Three.
He stumbles crossing a wide, shallow stream…almost falls in the fast water but stays up, cursing.

Melissa's just able to stay ahead of him with the video camera. She matches him step for step.

They cross a little ridge.

There! Mill sees red-striped poles and green flagging…the finish! Marie and Enoch are on the ground.

"Are they okay?" she wonders vaguely. Then she realizes they must be resting, "Good for them. I'll join them soon."

Another cramp cuts into her fatigue a little, slows her steps.

To Mill's right, Bonet croaks wordlessly.

He cries out again as he shambles forward across the grassy river meadow, louder this time, using real words of a sort, "Marie, *Mar-ee*! We're here. Get up! Get up and get a hold of your button!"

Marie lies still, unconscious.

Bonet staggers forward to her side and drops his pack.

He knows that if he bends down, he will fall and stay down.

Reggie nudges Marie with his toe, then harder.

She stirs.

"Marie, Marie, let's go. Get up," he husks.

Her eyes flicker.

Slowly Skinner moves, groans, and finally sits up on one elbow, "Okay, Regg, I hear you."

She tries to stand but her feet won't cooperate.

He reaches down, takes her hand, and pulls, holding on to the pole for support.

Slowly, slowly she rises up to her feet, waivers, and grabs the pole, her hand below his. Her back straightens little by little until she stands on wobbly legs.

"You go," she orders, gesturing weakly towards the other pole with her free hand. Bonet lurches across the fifty yards. He clutches the other pole and turns towards Marie.

He smiles at her with triumph and pain etched equally on his face. He mouths, "We made it."

They push the red buttons.

210

Chapter 43 - Rest at Denali

When Mill finally wakes at 11 a.m., fourteen more hours of sleep haven't replenished her strength or driven the stiffness out of her body. She gets four or five down-days here at Denali Lodge while Bonet and Skinner race up and down McKinley.

To say she welcomes the rest would be a vast understatement.

Rest sure, but she also has to get herself ready for the Alsek River Run that starts in about a week. And she has plenty of work and personal things to deal with, too.

Time to get up.

She rolls gingerly out of bed, walks to the widow, and throws the black-out drapes aside. Sunlight streams into the room.

She stands naked for a moment staring up from her fourth-floor window at Mount McKinley. The mountain's broad white shoulders dominate the blue sky above a fringe of yellowing quaking-aspen leaves that shiver in a sharp breeze.

"Wow," thinks Mill, "And I'm getting paid for this. What a life."

Then she visualizes the last day racing for the Sheenjek--cold, hungry, so tired. "I earned my pay for all of that," she reminds herself.

Mill pulls her eyes away from the beautiful sight of McKinley. She does some leg stretches and pulls on the light-green sweats supplied by the Geo-Challenge.

Walking into the bathroom, she brushes her teeth and drags a comb through her unruly hair, splashing water on a few cowlicks.

"No glam in the mirror for me today," she muses, rubbing at the dark circles under her eyes.

She hesitates and then looks into her mirrored eyes. Calm, brown eyes look back. Mill winks at herself and says out loud, "You finished the Trek, girl, something you never thought you could do. Damn fine effort."

She looks down her torso and shakes her head. She had weighed in the evening before…down twelve pounds after the Trek.

Mill pats her flatter-than-ever-before tummy, "Crazy weight-loss plan, jogging across Arctic Alaska."

The thought of weight-loss immediately leads her mind to food. Her empty stomach growls a loud complaint.

Mill takes her room key and heads down to the Geo-Challenge food service. She eagerly joins the short line of people waiting there for service. She grabs a tray and picks up plates, napkins, and silverware.

Reaching the food, she piles home fries, two large chocolate donuts, and a huge western omelet buried under salsa on her plate, places the plate on a tray, and adds a large glass of cranberry juice.

Mouth watering, she quickly finds a seat in the corner by a large window. A casually dressed waiter comes over to pour coffee.

"Keep it coming," she tells him.

He smiles, thinking that he has never seen hungrier people than this race bunch.

Mill tries to keep her lips from smacking while she shovels food in. But she can't help from saying, "Mmmmm" at the first big bite of omelet.

Twelve pounds.

Plenty of room to grow.

About the time Mill dunks her second donut, she looks up and sees Tilly Corcoran come in. Tilly walks over to the food line, selects a small plate of fresh fruit, and picks up a glass of milk. Turning, she starts towards the door.

Mill calls, "Tilly, over here!"

Tilly looks around blankly for a moment, peers towards the corner, and spots Mill. A big smile crosses her face and she strides towards Mill.

Watching her move, Mill is once again struck by Tilly's graceful walk.

Tilly puts her plate down on the table next to Mill's, "I couldn't see you, Mill. The light from the window's so bright behind you. Thanks for calling me over. I was hoping to run into you before the big status meeting this afternoon."

Mill looks at Tilly quizzically, "Status meeting? What's that?"

Tilly laughs lightly, "Sorry. You couldn't have known about it. You'll be getting a packet of information under your door later this morning giving you all the details. The meeting's mainly just to catch everybody up on the race, see if anything needs to be changed or added for the Alsek River Run, and gives you all an opportunity to turn in your field reports."

Mill quickly asks herself, "Field reports? What field reports?"

Oh yeah, her tired mind now remembers that each agency representative has to file a report about how the race has gone. The reports would be consolidated, given to the Fish and Wildlife Service, and made a part of the Geo-Challenge records that cover environmental protections.

"I thought the reports weren't due until the Geo-Challenge was over," Mill stammers mournfully, hanging her head in mock depression.

Tilly laughs, "That's the way it was, but wiser bureaucrat heads, namely Fritz Sawyer, have decided that the reports should be submitted after each stage. That way, you won't have nearly so big a job at the end."

"Okay," Mill retorts, "But if I have to file my report by this afternoon, you have to buy the drinks tonight...."

Both women laugh and agree to meet at 10 p.m. in the Lodge's lounge for a drink. The drink will fulfill their promise to get together at Charli's party in Anchorage.

Mill feels the little pulse between her legs jump for a moment. She tells it to stop. Slowly it dies down.

They talk a little more.

Then, looking at her watch, Tilly makes her apologies and goes back to work.

Mill contemplates plundering another donut.

Maybe later. She can't begin to think of sitting down at a computer before getting more pack-strap kinks out of her neck and shoulders.

So, first she will grab her red two-piece swim suit for a half hour in the Lodge's big spa and sauna. Then she will get going on that pesky field report.

She'll grab a donut or two on the way back from the spa. Sounds good.

She hurries out of the dining room and back upstairs.

Sure enough, just as Tilly said, a large envelope has been shoved under her door. She drops it on her bed unopened.

She strips off the sweats, puts on her swim suit, wraps herself in the Lodge's terrycloth robe, and goes back out the door.

Two minutes later, she is deep in the spa. Salty, stinky bubbles burst around her.

She rests, eyes closed, and lets the heat soak in....

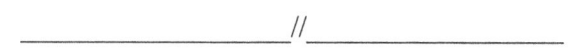

On McKinley's west slope, Bonet and Skinner stand in a warming hut with their assigned Park Service Mountain Ranger, Ben Gibbons. In a few minutes, the three will head up-mountain.

Melissa is outside, making a last gear check and taking the last few bites of an energy bar.

Enoch stands in the corner of the warming hunt, quietly recording the briefing Gibbons is giving the racers.

Gibbons speaks to the two racers, "I hear you two have plenty of experience. Ever do McKinley before?"

Both shake their heads.

"Okay," Gibbons continues, "I won't bore you with a lot of details. I know you're eager to get started. And I'll give you more pointers as we trail up Peters Glacier."

He looks them over carefully. They look fit and reasonably ready for the climb after two days off the Brooks-Romanzof Trek. Still, even though the docs had cleared them for this stage, they both look tired and a maybe a little dehydrated.

The Green Group will follow the West Buttress route up to 18,000 feet on the 20,320-foot mountain. West Buttress is considered the easiest McKinley route by many climbers. It involves a trek across Peters Glacier, followed by a hard but not-too-technical climb up rock faces and cliffs, and finally a steep ascent along a wide ridge.

Climbing in late summer, as it is now, the racers might have to work up wet ice falls and traverse across exposed, crumbling rock-ice outcrops.

Fun climbing, but rarely easy.

He smiles at them encouragingly, "Before we start, I want to remind you to stay thoroughly hydrated and keep plenty of carbs in the engine room. McKinley-West Buttress is only moderately challenging. But you have to be mentally and physically ready for anything. Lots of people have died on this route."

He raises a finger for emphasis, "Weather changes kill most of them. First a sunny day, then snow squalls, icing, and avalanche. It's one of the coldest places on the planet with recorded temperatures of minus 100 degrees Fahrenheit and wind chills of minus 118."

"And you'll be climbing into the dead zone above 15,000 feet without oxygen. It's always a problem, particularly when you're in a hurry like you guys are, racing. Most McKinley climbers aren't racing anything except maybe the weather or a chance to get back down for a beer and bragging rights."

Gibbons looks them both in the eyes, "I'm not saying bad stuff will happen to you. In fact, the next couple of days' weather looks pretty good. But, up here, weather forecasts don't mean much. So stay alert."

"You're only going up to about 18,000 feet, and then I understand you'll get a GPS signal telling you to start back. I don't know how that works, but I'm sure you'll let me know. I'm not going with you as your guide, just there to make sure you follow Park Service and race rules. And I'll be trailing you, not leading. It's up to you to set our route."

Ben turns to a map and runs his finger along the West Buttress route, "Here's what it looks like on this small-scale map."

He points to the etrexes hanging around the racers' necks, "I understand you won't have any maps with you except for what's on the GPSes. That's probably okay because there's not a lot of ways to map changes in glaciers and snow fields anyway. I just urge you to stay situationally aware, know what's going on around you, and where things are. For example, if weather closes in, you'll want to know where you can get under cover and build us snow cave in a drift or whatever. No GPS is going to show you that."

Gibbons smiles at them, "Any questions?"

Reggie says eagerly, "No, Ben, let's get going."

"Okay," Gibbons replies.

He walks over to a small table and gets ready to push a button on the race-timer radio link resting there, "Ready? Set!"

A long pause, then his finger comes down, "Go!"

The two racers whirl around and dash through the door, headed up and then up some more, almost to the highest point in North America.

Chapter 44 – Meeting Denali

At noon, Mill walks into the status meeting with her report ready to hand in.

She had found it fairly easy to write. She had the protection-measures list as a reference, her usual good memory of events, her notes from the Fairbanks orientations, and really not a lot to report.

The Green Group never had a wildlife-disturbance incident, at least that she had seen. The racers and tech crew had been very cooperative in doing what she asked of them even when they had to make a time-robbing course change.

Aside from the Green Group's performance, Mill had written up one lingering concern—trash-removal. She is afraid that the recovery and clean-up crews might leave harmful debris behind. She knows even a plastic bottle cap can kill a critter if it swallows the cap. So she made the clean-up point strongly in her report's "recommendations" section.

As she enters the meeting room, Mill looks for Tilly to hand in her report, but she hasn't arrived yet.

Art Childs and Cal Freiberg are sitting together at a round table near the windows.

Mill smiles at her counterparts and walks over to join them, "Hey, guys, how are my favorite BLooMer and Parkie?"

Both men smile at Mill's fit beauty. "Meacham, you look like you've been run hard and put up wet," drawls Freiberg, drawing on his Jackson Hole background.

Raised in Utah and Idaho, and no stranger to Rockies culture, Mill retorts, "Worked me like a rented mule, for sure."

She pats her shoulders, "I still can't walk without feelin' the collar and harness."

She looks closely at both men. They look like they've had the same kind of experience she did—cold, hard, and challenging, "You guys do okay? Still able to walk and sip whiskey?"

Both men smile wanly.

Art replies, "Bring me more whiskey. That Trek was the toughest thing I ever did, including basic training in the Marines. Not so much the physical part, although that was really difficult. No, for me, it was staying alert enough to make sure the racers, and worse the tech guys, didn't harass the game, stumble into sensitive plant areas and squash 'em, scare fledging birds…all that stuff."

"You guys know what I mean. The tech guys had the hardest part. They had to cover a lot more territory than the racers, half of it looking over their shoulders, falling down. What a job."

The Alaskan shakes his head, "Bottom line? I'm a-lovin' this experience, but I'll be glad to be back at my office and put my feet up on the desk."

Mill looks at the men with concern, "My racers and techies were great. Did what I asked right away and no complaint."

Cal looks at her and frowns," I wish mine had been so good. Got into two arguments with the racers on the first day...intense people, you know what I mean. I think they were mad at me the rest of the trip. But they probably finally figured that arguing me was just time waster and decided to follow the rules."

Cal nods in the direction of his BLM counterpart, "Art had the toughest, though. Two bear encounters and a couple of high falls."

Mill looks at Art, "You okay?"

"Wasn't me," replied Art, "No, each of the techies took a fall...different times...more steep slides than verticals, thankfully. No one really hurt but plenty of adrenaline. Banged up but ready to keep rollin' afterwards."

Mill smiles, "Wow. Lots of adventures. Let's get together after the Alsek Run, have too much to drink, and swap lies, okay?"

Both men laugh and answer, "Okay."

The single Cal already thinks getting to know Mill better is a good idea. He winks at her.

Seeing this, she changes the subject, "So who's winning this wild-ass race?"

As a part of building suspense for the show, the Geo-Challenge producers are keeping certain information confidential. So, the producers share stage times and rankings only with the racers.

"Consensus seems to be that your crew is second, Mill, and Art's is first," Cal replies, "Guess my battlin' brush-busters have earned third place by wasting time arguing with me and getting way off course."

He is about to say more when a group enters the room, Mr. Gorgeous in the lead and Tilly last. From the middle of the pack, Smoky Joe sends the three agency people a thumbs-up.

They grab chairs and sit.

218

Each person introduces themselves--another producer besides Burrows, the director, the director's personal assistant, and the editing chief.

Mill misses the names given in rapid fire but gets the titles straight. She looks with sympathy at the personal assistant who appears to be on the edge of a nervous breakdown.

Pale and seated behind his boss, his hands fidget compulsively in his lap. She imagines the endless running around and details the man must be dealing with.

Incredible stress by the look of him.

Burrows starts the meeting, "Look folks. We don't have lots of time today. Things are moving quickly. The racers are on the mountain now, tech crews in tow. Even though we designed this stage so that they'd probably have to overnight on McKinley, there's an off-hand chance one of the teams might get up and down in one day. We'll see. Hard to believe anyone could complete the Arctic stage, take a couple of days off, and then race forty miles and conquer an 8,000-foot elevation change, up and down in one day. But, you know your racers. They're a tough bunch. So, we'll see if any of 'em makes it back to the finish today. Maybe they all will."

Tom flashes his brightest smile, "Okay. This status meeting is intended to help us with the next stage, the Alsek River Run. Let's get down to it. Editing, you're first."

The chief editor stands, "Congratulations. The video and audio we're getting are very workable. Plenty of material. And you agency reps did a nice job of finding wildlife and scenery shots when we asked for them. I don't have any particular requests at this time other than to help the sound techs remember to keep those little foam wind mufflers on the mikes. We lose audio when they get knocked off. So, please do a visual check of the racers gear from time to time to help make sure the mike covers are on."

She smiles a wan smile, "I know how tired I am. I can only guess how tired you are...how bad it is out there. But it's those little things like mike covers that will make the difference in show quality when we get the Geo-Challenge on the air. And remember, we can dub some voices later, but we'll never get to record the real thing in the field again. This is our only chance to get it right."

The chief editor calls for questions. When there are none, she sits down.

The director stands up, looks at a handful of notes, and begins. "I've heard some grumbling about the inputs we gave you on the first stage. You know safety, comfort, and all that. Look, if what you expected was a walk in the park, you wouldn't be here and neither would your racers. Remember, we can see your locations on our monitors all the time. We see when you stop, where you go. We're getting your audio, video, and daily check-ins on the sat phone. Something really bad goes down, you call, right?"

The agency people nod.

Then Art holds up his hand, "What's the margin here? I mean if we call medivac for a racer, they forfeit. That's understandable. It's the rules. But what if the racers push it, get separated, and lost. Only the agency reps like us have sat phones. No one has radios. Do we call in for search and rescue and get our racers to forfeit when the lost person might show back up at anytime?"

He looks at the director closely to see his reaction and then continues, "Here's my reason for asking. This wasn't a big problem on the Trek. We could pretty much see each other all the time…lack of radios caused everyone to stick together."

"But on the Alsek Run, it'll be different. I've looked at videos of the river. It starts small, then widens quickly. Once it widens, it looks like flowing mud with all the glacial silt in it with lots of braided channels, little shallows, and mud flats. People will get sidetracked easily. Racers could get separated and one could run a lot faster than the other. What about that?"

The director looks at Art calmly, "Okay, good questions. I'll ask Joe Schmoker to speak to some of the safety issues. But my take on the Alsek Run is that it'll be both similar and different than the last stage. One thing is that you'll have to work on with the racers and tech teams before the trip is to set up rallying points. We've set up temporary pylons--six feet high, orange--at five mile intervals down the race route. Those pylons will also be set as waypoints in your GPSes. If you get separated, you can rendezvous at the next pylon down river or the following pylon if someone gets really far ahead."

The director smiles grimly, "That's one way. You can figure out other ways if you want to. Just know this. We *will* be making further inputs on the Alsek stage. None of these, repeat, *none of these*, will change the pylon locations in your *e*trexes."

220

"Also, we will not, repeat, *will not*, change the map coordinates for the entrance to Turnback Canyon. It's too dangerous. No one goes in that canyon. Racers already know that they'll forfeit if they run the canyon to save time. Okay? Clear?"

Art sits back in his chair, encouraged by this information.

The meeting goes on for another fifteen minutes then abruptly ends.

No one has more questions.

Racers are on the mountain.

The Geo-Challenge folks have lots to do.

Whether they like them or not, the agency reps have started to care about the racers and the techies. Looking out the window, Mill thinks of her friends and shivers a little as she looks up at the gigantic mountain, its jagged snowy top wreathed in a tight circle of clouds....

Far above Mill, Bonet and Skinner are approaching 15,000 feet. The snow field around them is blinding white. The racers squint through the darkened lenses of their snow goggles.

It's a perfect climbing day on this, the greatest mountain in North America, bigger in volume, if lower in height, than Everest.

Ahead of the racers, above the steepening broad shoulder of the mountain, the intense blue sky frames McKinley's peak. Out to the blue-banded horizon stretches an endless landscape of trees, grass, water, and wetlands.

Skinner and Bonet were the second race team to start this stage, a result of their standing after the Brooks-Romanzof Trek. The glacier crossing went without a hitch, almost a straight line. The snow held solid under their feet.

The three icefalls took axes well, allowing them to move quickly and stay mostly dry.

After two hours of hard climbing, they overtook Cal's argumentative race team, greeted them, and dropped them behind.

Now, according to the *e*trexes, their first cache lies a few hundred yards ahead.

Bonet and Skinner have a critical decision to make. This 15,000-foot cache holds equipment and food for an overnight stay. A second cache at the 18,000-foot, turn-around point holds minimum supplies, mainly food and water, a stove, and fuel.

If they stop at the first cache, they will add at least ten minutes' time and greatly increase burden. They'll likely have to spend the night, maybe above 15,000 feet in extreme cold and wind, and then try to dig out from under any overnight snow to descend in the morning.

Marie has the lead. Over her shoulder, she puffs, "Regg, we've got to...decide...in the next few minutes...stop, load, and go...or just go. What do...you think?"

Bonet takes several breaths before replying, "I think we...should...pass this...go up. We have...space blankets with us...can use them...for shelter...if we need to. And we have...a cache at...18. Got basic food...water...heat...there. Then...as we come...down ...if we have to...stop...we can...stop here. Risky...but...ahead...of others."

Marie raises her hand above the height of her mountain pack and gives him the thumbs-up. They'll go on up to 18,000 feet, load at the cache, and start back. They've made a risky commitment to the mountain and done the same for Enoch, Melissa, and Ben.

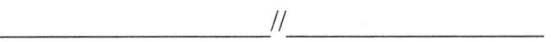

Late in the afternoon, Mill stops by the small conference room where the Tilly and Joe have set up their computers. She is dressed in her bathing suit and borrowed robe for another trip to the spa and sauna.

A phone in his ear, Joe waves a big hand at Mill.

She listens briefly to his side of the conversation. Mill figures that Joe's on the phone talking to his office in Fairbanks, getting an update on aviation weather.

Mill knows that, for a portion of this stage, the racers and support teams will be at altitudes where helicopters can't fly. In addition, neither helos nor fixed-wing aircraft can land safely in the upper elevations—too steep and windy. For that matter, winds can be a problem for rescue aircraft anywhere around McKinley.

Taking all this into account, Joe is checking on what aircraft are available, which ones might actually be able to extract injured people from McKinley over the next two days, and how to staff them to get the job done. He is working closely with the Park Service Mountain Rangers here at Denali...a lot of folks to consult, but something he is damn good at.

Seeing Mill's quizzical expression, he gives her an "okay" with his fingers. She feels better right away.

Tilly is also on the phone. She waves Mill over and motions to a chair. Mill drops into the chair and tucks the edges of the robe around her legs.

Quickly bored, she waits to confirm drinks with Tilly based on this morning's agreement. She eyes the textured wallpaper to pass the time, imagining erotic shapes the designer never intended.

After a few minutes, Tilly hangs up. Leaning forward a little for privacy, she says, "Mill, dear, so nice of you to come and see me." With a slight raise of her elegant eyebrows she smiles, "Anything I can do for you? By the way, I love the outfit."

Mill laughs, "Compliments of the Lodge. Can a girl sneak something home in her luggage?"

They both laugh.

Mill continues, "No, nothing you can do…just wanted to make sure we were still on for drinks this evening. What did we say, 10?"

Tilly looks blank for a moment, "Oh, yeah, that's right…we were going to get together, weren't we?"

Tilly hesitates and then says, "Well, I'm sorry but I got called into a meeting with the Geo-Challenge people. It starts at seven and will go maybe to ten or eleven. Can I get a rain check?"

Mill feels sharp and unexpected pain at Tilly's brush-off. Had Tilly forgotten and then made other plans?

"Sure…sure," Mill says, "Just an opportunity, that's all. We can do it some other time."

To mask her feelings, she shakes her head and smiles, "Got to go and get in the hot tub. So I'll let you keep running the Geo-Challenge without me."

Mill stands and begins to leave. But Tilly takes her hand briefly and then drops it.

She looks into Mill's eyes, "I couldn't do it without you. And we will get that drink soon. I promise." Tilly smiles brightly, leans back in her chair, and waves at Mill as she heads for the door.

Minutes later, Mill bobs alone in the bubbling tub with her arms draped over the pale-yellow-tiled rim.

She can't quite sort out her feelings towards Tilly. Why couldn't she make their drink-date this evening? They had set it up just this morning. How hard could it be? She realizes Tilly has a big job but does she forget that fast, care that little?

And bigger yet, does Tilly want something to start between them or not? Something's definitely there. But who knew what it was?

For years, Mill's love life has been mostly one-night stands--sex, drugs, rock-'n'-roll between the sheets or wherever was convenient. Until Charli, she hadn't made love sober in a long time.

How could Mill consider something with Tilly when Mill's life was such a mess? Just the fish-cop thing alone….

Mill thinks of Tilly's blue eyes, her smile, her slender-strong shoulders, the line of her breasts, her legs. She feels an answering throb down below.

She suddenly feels aroused, drowsy.

She lowers her arm into the bubbles and slips her hand under the waistband of her suit, between her legs.

She closes her eyes…there…right there…now.

Chapter 45 - Checking In With the World

When Mill gets back to her room, a little red light blinks on the Lodge phone signaling that people have called and left messages. She punches in the phone-system's access codes and listens to three voicemails, one from Charli, one from Mitch Mendenhall, and one from her Dad, W.A. Meacham.

Because W.A. is two time-zones away, Mill calls him first, "Dad, it's Mill…."

Before she can get out another word, W.A. starts yelling, "Milly, I keep hearing what a great job you're doing. People are raving up and down about you. I know Smoky Joe. We're old buddies. He tells me my fruit doesn't fall far from my trunk…."

Mill tunes out at this point. She realized long ago that her Dad's ego won't permit him to acknowledge anything she does unless it somehow reflects favorably on him.

W.A. runs at the highest Forest Service levels. And although she isn't interested in becoming a big player in Legacy circles like he is, she knows how fragile support can be for Legacies like him. The high-rolling Legacies can be all camaraderie on the surface and quick knives-in-the-back below.

So she lets W.A. loudly ramble on, praising himself through her, undoubtedly rehearsing boastful stories he will deliver to other Legacies in the future.

Eventually he winds down, "So how you feelin', Milly? Back to normal?"

She begins to speak seriously, "Well, I'm still bruised and stiff, but I…."

W.A. interrupts, "Good to hear it. Good to hear it. Look, I've got a meeting. I'll call again soon. Pretend you're me, do your best on that Alsek River Ramble. Bye."

The phone clicks. W.A. is gone.

Mill drops the handset back in its cradle and says to the empty room, "Well, okay. Nice talking to you, too, Dad. Good catching up." Actually having a two-person conversation with her father is pretty well impossible.

No, his ego talks and she listens.

She rests for a few minutes on the bed, relaxing her still-stiff shoulders. Then she hops off for a bathroom visit. She definitely feels looser in her body and steadier on her feet than yesterday.

Back from the bathroom, she calls Charli's number and leaves voicemail.

Mill is just going through her scattered papers to find Mitch Mendenhall's number when Charli calls back. "Hello, darlin' Mill," Charli purrs into the phone, "How's my Great Land geo-challenger?"

Mill smiles to hear Charli's voice, "Missing you, Charli. I mean, here I am stuck in the Denali Lodge with a huge bed and no one to keep me warm at night."

Charli chuckles, "I'll be right over."

Of course both women know that Charli is hours away and she won't be "right over." Still, Mill feels that sense of warm connection with Charli that she felt before in Anchorage—a connection not as sexual or passionate as before but one with a nurturing sisterhood running through it.

The two women catch up about friends, Mill's progress with the race, and her plans once the race is over. She and Charli had agreed at the end of Mill's last visit that she should come to Anchorage to recover. Both affirm that the trip is still on.

Charli teases, "I got another box of your favorite toys, darlin' Mill. Things with batteries. Things that buzz and wiggle."

Mill laughs delightedly, "Well, you sure know how to grab a girl's interest, darlin' Charli. I'll be so tired, you'll just have my limp body to try them out on to start with. Think of me as a science experiment!"

Charli chuckles, "Dr. Charli, Orgasmic Scientist and Fairy God-lover. That's me, working on the frontiers of science, technology, and magic all at the same time! How delightful."

Mill enjoys this happy conversation, but she has a serious item to check on, too.

"Charli," she asks, "Did you have any ideas, you know, about how you might be able to help me with the bear-drowning thing…the fish cops?"

After Mill asks her question, Charli remains silent for a long moment. Mill wonders if she has offended her, "I mean if you didn't, that's okay. I…I just wondered, you know, if you had."

"No, I'm not offended that you asked me, darlin' Mill, "Charli responds levelly, "I'm just not sure how much to tell you. I mean you have to work with your government people, lawyers and everything.

There might be some things you really don't want to know so that you can always honestly say you never knew about them."

Charli laughs, "I guess that sounds kinda silly when I say it. But I think it's true. I mean about not wanting to know everything."

Charli is quiet for a moment and then says, "Okay, here goes. Back in the days I was running wild, I met this nice man among many, many losers, a guy new to Anchorage at the time. Well, we started a relationship, a hot one by the way. Because I was still pretty mixed up about myself, I even thought about settling down with him. How silly was that? But he was just that kind of person—passionate, solid. He seemed like a safe harbor for me and he really wanted me. So, I almost moved in with him."

Charli's voice sounds wistful, remembering a loving path not traveled, "Turned out to be for the best, of course, that he and I never closed the deal. It would have been just another breakup. Anyway, we've stayed in touch. He's married now but, because he stayed here in Anchorage, we get together for lunch now and then.

"As far as your case is concerned, just know that I called him and asked him to help. I explained your circumstances and some of the background, the problems everywhere with the fish cops, and so on. I won't tell you his name or what he does. Just know that he's involved in high-up state police business. He told me he would do what he could."

Mill suddenly understands why the FBI had been given access to the Alaska State Patrol's inner workings.

"Jim Lowell," Mill blurts out. "ASP Colonel Jim Lowell is your old lover, isn't he?"

Charli laughs delightedly, "Why, yes he is, darlin' Mill. How did you ever figure that out? I thought I was being remarkably discrete, particularly for me."

Mill knows she, too, should not say too much, "Well I can only say I heard that he went from reluctant to very cooperative overnight. And it turns out that his change of heart is thanks to you, you wonderful God-lover, darlin' Charli!"

Charli responds, "You're most welcome, dear one. Just an unrelated thought, but do you know you have the ability to turn nuance into fact, to make intuitive but logical leaps. It's a rare thing, a sign of an excellent mind. I think you'd make a great research scientist or investigator, maybe a detective or something. I know you're happy being a fish person, but just a thought…."

Mill thinks of Manny Suemez. Could she be like him?

No, the idea of Mill as an old-West sheriff is crazy.

She smiles at the thought of wearing a badge and toting a gun. Nice of Charli to think of such a thing, but no.

The two women talk warmly for a few more minutes and then hang up.

Mill spends a few minutes stretched out on her bed, aching a little for Charli's embrace. What a wonderful lover, now much more a friend, Charli Jenkins had become. Mill hopes she always would be.

Mill picks up the phone again and punches in Mitch's number. She is surprised when he answers on the first ring,

"Meacham…good. I needed to talk to you." Mitch's voice is brusque but not impersonal.

Mendenhall clears his throat, "Damn air in this building. Best fresh air in the world outside and nothing but stale pollution in here. I never get rid of the frog in my throat. So, apologies to you as I gurgle and choke in your ear. Look, here's why I called. The FBI has pretty well concluded their investigation. The AUSA has the initial findings. We're having a case meeting later this week or early next."

He clears his throat again, "You don't have to be a part of that meeting. But I need your consent to use the facts in your case as a part of the charging documents, that is, if the AUSA decides to charge anyone. I just need to know going in if you're planning to settle with the fish cops or whether you're going to continue to contest them."

"If you're going to settle, we'll just drop your business and proceed along somewhat different lines. But if you're staying in, that will materially improve our case. Interference with a federal employee. Attempted extortion under color of the law. And so on. So, what is your intention, Meacham?"

Mill's answer is an easy one, "Kick those bastards' asses, Mitch. As far as I'm concerned, charge them with everything you can. You definitely have my consent to use my case in your charging thingy."

Mendenhall laughs, "Good, Mill. Many thanks. Look, I need to call the AUSA with your answer. We'll be in touch."

"Wait, Mitch," Mill says quickly, "Just for me to know, but what are you guys thinking about charging the fish cops with? I don't really know anything about the law but…"

228

Mendenhall's voice comes back to her clearly, "Well, that's up to the AUSA. But although we might use several laws to charge different people, the one that seems to apply best is the 'Racketeer Influenced and Corrupt Organizations Act' or 'RICO.' That's the same law we feds use to take down organized crime. One of many choices…and I don't know yet. Got to go. Thanks again."

Mill hangs up the phone. RICO? Fish-cop mobsters? Well, who-da thought anything like that could happen?

Chapter 46 – Folly on Denali

Towering so high, Mt. McKinley is one of the last objects in Alaska to lose August daylight. Below, shadows are beginning to lengthen, unseen by the racers still struggling upwards under bright sunshine.

Bonet and Skinner suck and hold each breath, lungs and hearts straining to gather oxygen. They keep going.

Lift…kick…step. Lift…kick…step.

Roped up with Ben, and occasionally on belay, they move up the West Buttress like determined zombies.

Enoch and Melissa have ranged slowly ahead of the two racers and reached 18,000 feet. They stand fifty or so feet to each side of the cache site, recording the racers' struggle, and ready to record Bonet and Skinner reaching the location and digging out supplies.

Ben is trailing the two racers by a few yards, climbing in the trail the racers' boots cut through the snow.

17,900 feet.

The racers move into a leveler spot and go off the rope. Reggie breaks trail past a tall rocky spike towering two or three hundred feet above them. He uses the knobby rock surface to steady and pull himself along and upwards—fast technique that will bring them more quickly to the turn-around point.

Marie does the same, followed by Ben.

Pulling as strongly as they can, the group bunches up.

They ready themselves for the last hundred-yard-or-so dash to reach the cache.

Reggie pulls himself to the edge of the towering outcrop. He smiles and waves for Enoch's cameras.

Suddenly and without warning, tons of snow and ice break free from the face of the rocky spike. The load crashes down and smashes the racers and Gibbons under its weight.

Snow and mist cyclone for a moment before blowing away in McKinley's sharp wind.

When the air clears, only Bonet's hands can be seen protruding from under the lumpy drift.

Gibbons and Skinner are completely buried.

Horrified, Enoch and Melissa launch themselves down the snowy slope and quickly reach the drift. They toss cameras into their packs except for one which Enoch hastily mounts on a portable tripod. He sticks that in the snow, aims the camera at the snow heap, and immediately forgets about it.

Hurrying to the spot most likely to hold the climbers, Enoch takes out a small folding shovel. He brought the shovel up the mountain to dig out support-team caches or, if needed, carve them snow caves for emergency shelter.

The other Green Group shovel lies buried with Bonet. Now both shovels are needed to rescue the buried climbers before they suffocate.

Avalanche snow often sets like concrete, moved or dug easily to begin with, then firming up and almost impossible to shovel later. The change has something to do with how friction warms the snow as it moves and the way the snow mass refreezes after coming to rest.

Enoch realizes that this avalanche dropped essentially straight down the rock face, so maybe it didn't develop much friction-heat. He is hopeful that it won't solidify too quickly.

He and Melissa might have a few extra, precious minutes to save Reggie, Marie, and Ben.

Enoch points to Bonet with his shovel and tells Melissa, "Get going…on Regg. Hurry. We need his shovel."

Then he climbs onto the heap above Marie and Ben and starts to dig furiously.

Seeing Bonet's arms struggling to clear snow from his head, Melissa drops to her knees next to him, "Reggie…it's me, Melissa. Hold still, dear. I'll get your…face clear."

Scooping and pushing with her gloved hands, she quickly clears the man's face, then his shoulders and pack.

She gasps, "Keep working…get free. I'm taking…the shovel…to help Enoch with…the others." She pulls the shovel from his pack and runs to where Enoch is at work on the drift.

Under the snow's heavy weight, Bonet wiggles and makes swimming motions with his arms, gripping and elbowing the snow to move ahead. He had little air before Melissa cleared his face, but now, gasping and straining, he makes steady progress out of the icy vise around his hips and legs.

Once out, he gets to his knees, and then turns and sits down, played out.

Melissa and Enoch dig frantically in the ten feet or so of the drift directly behind Reggie. Enoch works skillfully, building a tunnel of sorts. Melissa follows suit, driving down more slowly because of her shorter arms.

They have to reach the buried pair before any air available to them runs out.

There is a little air in the snow itself. And mountaineers are trained to throw their arms up around their faces to create an air pocket before an avalanche hits.

The tech folks hope that Marie and Ben had enough warning before being slammed.

The tech team makes the snow fly….

––––––––––––––––––––––––//––––––––––––––––––––––––

Unnngh! Unnngh! Unnngh!

Joe Schmoker looks sharply at his computer screen. An alarm screeches out of its tiny speakers. Over and over, a red dot expands out across the screen, signaling an emergency.

Joe looks at a pop-up display. Three Emergency Position-Indicating Radio Beacons or EPIRBs have been triggered on McKinley.

Damn.

EPIRBs are like fire shelters. It's never good news when they deploy.

Schmoker pounds several keys and reaches a more detailed screen. EPIRBS for Bonet, Skinner, and Gibbons have gone active at 17,900 feet due to impact-acceleration.

All triangulate to the same place. He checks quickly. They're at a location not accessible by aircraft. Any rescue landings will have to be lower down the West Buttress and rescue or recovery carried out from there.

He starts to call the green-racer sat phone then realizes that it's with Gibbons, the agency rep for this stage. He hesitates and then finishes punching in the numbers anyway.

The phone rings a dozen times; his call goes to a "no one available…try again later" recording. He has no way of knowing if the phone is in the clear enough to get the satellite signal. But at least he didn't get a "not in range" recording.

He dials the Denali Search and Rescue unit. Time to saddle up with SAR....

_____ // _____

Melissa and Enoch dig as fast as they can. The snow is hardening up. Snow chunks still come out of the tunnels, but slower and slower.

The diggers can't tell if they're close to Ben or Marie. But they keep driving downwards into the drift...four feet...five feet.

Marie hears the sat phone's faint ring. The noise seems to come from a spot to her left a couple of feet. She angles her tunnel that way.

Enoch suddenly gives a joyous high-altitude wheeze. Six feet down, he has reached Skinner's legs. He pinches her thigh firmly and yells, "Almost there, Marie."

She tenses her leg muscles in response.

"Thank God," Enoch breathes, puffing frosty breath. He drives the shovel laterally now, digging over Marie's pack towards her head.

A foot in, Enoch discovers a large chunk of ice resting on top of Marie's pack. Enoch prays that the pack served to blunt the force of the ice as it fell. He figures it's a good sign that she could tense her leg muscles when he touched her.

Enoch cuts around the ice chunk, man-handles it off her, and lifts it up the tunnel. As he struggles to push it out, Bonet's gloved hands come into view. Reggie grabs the basketball-sized chunk, lifts it clear, and rolls it away.

"Enoch," he pants, "Want me to take over?"

Enoch shakes his head, "Almost there...."

And indeed, a few moments later, Enoch tenderly clears Marie's head and helps her pull her arms free. Then he helps her crawfish backwards in the little tunnel and climb out.

Reggie lifts Marie carefully into the sunshine.

Reggie and Marie embrace. Cold lips touch. Reggie helps her sit, wraps both of them in a space blanket, and holds his shaking partner closely.

Enoch goes to Melissa's tunnel and looks down past his partner's head. He sees Ben Gibbons' snowy face, eyes closed...no sign of life.

Enoch's mind goes blank. Like most rescue-trained people, Enoch only wants to bring lost or hurt people home safely, alive.

He stares, almost paralyzed by uncertainty. "Is Ben…dead?" he gasps to Melissa.

Melissa croaks a reply, "He's got…a pulse. Help me get him…out of here. Widen…the dig."

Enoch begins to make the snow fly again.

A helo drops Joe Schmoker and the Park Service SAR team off at 15,500 feet.

The helo pilot uses a dangerous technique allowed only for emergencies like this one. He hovers the aircraft, resting one skid on a rock ledge, and lets the passengers off to huddle below the churning blades until he can lift up and away. A slight miscalculation by the pilot or sudden wind gust and the maneuver kills all aboard.

They make it.

The team adjusts their gear and gets ready to climb. Joe's satellite phone rings. "Yeah," he gasps in the thin air, "What?"

Enoch's breathless voice comes through clearly, "This is Enoch Saarinen, videographer with…the Green Group." He pauses to take a breath, "We have a man down… unconscious, unresponsive. Ben Gibbons…the ranger. Rock fall got him. Racers okay…shaken up. They're at…the high cache…getting food and water. We got Gibbons…to the surface…wrapped him in…space blanket. Melissa's in it…with him…for warmth. We await…your instructions."

Joe takes a shuddering breath. Damn! Man down but, thank God, not dead. So, it will be a rescue, not a recovery.

"Okay, Enoch," he gasps, "I'm here at fifteen-five with SAR…on our way up…to your location. Got your… EPIRB signals…there in an hour…or less. But need to know what…the racers want to do…evac…or race."

Enoch already knows that answer, "Race."

At 10 p.m., Mill leaves her room to find the drink machine on her floor. When she gets there, she finds one of those little sticky-note signs that says "Out of order. You owe me $1.00. Room 422."

Not a good sign.

So Mill runs up to the fifth floor and locates the drink machine there. She puts in her money and a bottle drops with a solid thunk.

As Mill leaves the little alcove that holds the drink and ice machines, she looks down the hall and sees Tilly backing out of a room, talking to someone within. Tilly looks uncharacteristically disheveled-- hair askew, blouse partly out of her skirt, and carrying her shoes.

A hand reaches out and pulls Tilly back to doorway. A face emerges gives Tilly a long kiss. Art Childs!

Tilly puts her hand lightly on the back of his neck and presses her mouth more tightly on his. They end their kiss. Mill hears their murmured voices but nothing she can understand.

Then Tilly turns towards Mill and walks casually in her direction, a slight frown on her face.

Suddenly shy and embarrassed, Mill ducks back into the alcove. She slips behind the drink machine. Peeking around its bulk, she watches Tilly's elegant profile go by. A moment later, she hears the bell-and-door sound of the elevator.

Mill relaxes. Irritation sets in.

So this was Tilly's "Geo-Challenge meeting!"

Well clearly, the only geography Tilly had been navigating tonight was Art's!

But wasn't Tilly a lesbian?

It had seemed so at Charli's party. And what about Mill's reaction to Tilly's touch...the empathy between them. Was it just friendship or something else?

Should she confront Tilly about skipping their drink for a tryst with Art? Based on what?

Mill shakes her head, "Too much for me to figure out. If there's ever going to be something between Tilly and me, she'll have to make the next move. It's too confusing for this country girl."

236

Chapter 47 - Haines Junction

Mill sits in one of the fancy semi-trailers the Geo-Challenge producers have converted to office and storage space. In ten minutes or so, the agency reps will travel to the jump-off point for the Alsek River Run. It's about a half-hour ride by highway into Canada's Kluane National Park, followed by a bumpy drive down a long gravel road to the launch point.

Mill enjoyed the road trip from Denali National Park in the U.S. to Haines Junction in the Yukon immensely. From what she saw, Canada's Kluane National Park is breathtakingly beautiful, like the Teton Mountains Mill's so familiar with, only much grander.

On the ride down from Fairbanks, she gaped at one magnificent peak after another stretching along the huge, green, glacially fed Kluane Lake.

After travelling through such magnificent country, Mill is more than ready to start the Alsek River Run, two hundred miles or so to the sea.

In Mill's mind, the river run should be quite a bit easier than the Arctic trek. After all, they will be going downriver in little boats, travelling with the river flow, not up and down…up and down…laboring against gravity and mountain terrain ready to sprain or break body parts.

She checks her gear again. Waterproof bags filled with her personal stuff, sleeping bag and tent, a couple days' food, and her water-filter pump. She counts her three sets of polypropylene long underwear, quick to dry, warm when wet, and smell like a skunk after a few days wear.

Mill spends the most time looking over the specialized anorak she will wear in the kayak, the skirt and its closure string that will keep water from flooding in, the tight Velcro closures at the wrists.

Everything's top quality and the same Green Group color she has worn for a couple of weeks, down to her double-ended paddle, her slim, foam flotation vest, her tough-looking helmet and spray cover, and her gloves.

She had not thought about it before today, but the whole outfit strikes her now as looking a lot like a Girl Scout get-up. She snorts, "Some Girl Scout."

Considering her private life, the thought is more than absurd.

Art smiles at her, "Amusing yourself, Meacham? You ready to go?"

Mill looks up at his kind face, wondering about his relationships with Tilly but afraid to ask, "Sure am, Art. Able, rested, and ready to serve!"

The agency reps all laugh, Cal somewhat grimly. Cal has a lot less kayak experience then his two companions, enough to handle the assignment but not without an internal qualm or two.

"Mill," Cal asks, "Have you ever run this river before?"

Mill answers honestly, "No, I haven't, not a clue how to do it really. But I've read a lot about it and I talked to a couple of sea-kayakers I know in Cordova who ran it several years ago. I heard from them pretty much what Art was asking the director about in Denali, only more detail. They said it was quite decent. There's some cool white-water in the upper parts...then pretty tame lower down. I guess it gets really wide in spots, particularly after the Tatshenshini River joins the Alsek way lower down. And it's all glacially fed so it's really turbid, grey silty water. You can't see your hand two inches under the surface."

She pauses, then voices a concern of her own, "Considering that the racers are going to push hard, we'll probably get a half-day of interesting water and some lakes, then everything broadens out, gets braided, like the lower Kongakut was towards the bay. The kayakers I talked to really got jammed up several times on sand bars and shallows. And then they got separated for almost a day when one of them went down a fast channel and the other got hung up."

Mill shakes her head, "The faster one figured out pretty quickly what had happened and landed. He climbed one of the little dunes and watched for his buddy who then went right past him, out of sight in another channel. No landmarks out in the middle of the Alsek, just up-river, down-river, side channels. Got kind of weird for them. They could talk to each other on their radios but couldn't see each other."

"After leapfrogging each other a couple of times, they finally hooked back up using their radios. They both spotted a big log sticking up from a dune and met there. For the rest of the trip, they never went down separate channels again unless they could see each other the whole way. Made it back just fine, but learned a lesson."

She looks at her two companions earnestly, "I know what the director told us about the pylons. That's cool. But if our racers and techies get separated by more than five miles, how are you guys planning to get back together?"

238

Art nods, "Yeah, I had the same issue, Mill. What my tech guys and I finally figured out is that we'll just truck on down to the next cache and wait there. We may have to really bust our hump to get there before the racers, but that's what we'll have to do or get stuck out there on the river to look like idiots coming in by ourselves."

He smiles wanly, "Guess that wouldn't be much different than a lot of things in my life…." They all laugh.

A horn honks outside the trailer. The agency reps grab their gear and walk out into the sunshine of the still-green, late-summer environment of Haines Junction.

Mill grins at the funny, mushroom-looking sculpture at the tee-junction of the main roads. The thing is decorated with a moose, trees, and mountains—quite wacky and nice.

Three kayaks rest in cradles on the Suburban's roof--Mill's light green, Art's light blue, and Cal's light brown. They walk to the Suburban, put their gear in the back, and climb in.

Just as the Suburban leaves the parking lot, Mill's cell rings.

It's Manny Suemez, "Mill, I just got a call from Cordova, a guy you know, Chick Sorensen. He couldn't reach you, so he called me. He's pretty upset. Corporal Craven and his side-kick heard what you're doing…found out where you are."

Manny's voice is getting scratchier as the SUV drives away from the only cell tower within a hundred miles. The signal starts to break up, "They…come...finish line…arrest. Media…there."

Manny's voice fades out altogether…lost in the vast Yukon.

So Toad Craven's coming to the Alsek, maybe to arrest her in front of the media.

Damn!

What should she do now?

One answer.

Race.

Chapter 48 - Blue Sky

7,000 feet above Mill and the hurtling Suburban, a Beechcraft 99 lines up on a skydiver jump zone laid out near the start of the Alsek River Run. Inside, the racers sit calmly, holding hands.

Melissa sits across from them, fiddling with her recording gear and checking her parachute. The more experienced sky-diver techie, Melissa will jump with the racers, leaving the Beech first and covering Reggie and Marie in the air.

Enoch is on the ground readying his equipment for shots of the two racers diving towards a big red circle-x laid out across a grassy quarter-acre near him.

If one of the racers lands within the circle, the team gets a five minute head-start on the Alsek stage. If both land within the circle, they get a twenty-minute bonus.

Bonet and Skinner have vowed to hit the circle...together, if possible. As Reggie said before boarding the Beech, "Enoch, our Alsek gift to you, a fabulous action shot!"

From the co-pilot's seat, the jump master yells back over his shoulder, "Two minutes to drop. I'll give you a warning...then count down my fingers...five...four...three...two...one. When I show you my fist, you jump. Count to ten between jumpers in case someone has a problem."

The jump master looks out the cockpit window. He consults a GPS on his lap and then talks by radio to the race controllers on the ground.

He turns back towards the three jumpers, "Okay...ready. On my signal."

Melissa steps to the open door, adjusts her camera-helmet and goggles, pulls down her visor and looks at the jump master. He brings his hand into the cabin. She starts the camera and sees the red "record" light flash on the inside of her visor.

The jump master counts down his fingers...three...two...one... fist. Go!

Melissa throws herself into the clear sky. She drops, easily clears the plane's tail, and dives, arched and beautiful, a video angel on a mission.

In a few moments, Melissa rolls back-down and spreads her arms and legs against the upwind to create a stable platform for her helmet-cam. She locks the cross-hairs etched in her helmet visor on the door to the Beech.

Bonet jumps clear and, ten seconds later, the smaller figure of Skinner leaves the plane.

They lock their arms against their sides and fly straight down for Melissa. In a few seconds they reach her, brake, and perform some aerial acrobatics for the camera, their yells mostly lost in the screaming upwind.

They do a couple of flips and, holding hands, do some flat spins. Finally, they release each other and line up for chute deployment and landing.

This is the serious part of their jump, aiming for the big red circle-x, the time bonus, and pride. They came in second on the Arctic trek and first on McKinley.

Now they want the Alsek win, to take the Geo-Challenge, and claim sports immortality.

2,000 feet to chute-open.

The racers drop down, in formation, side-by-side and fifty feet apart, locked on the landing site.

Melissa wants to stay out of Enoch's shots from below. So, she gets a few last shots of the racers dropping below her, turns off the camera, and pulls her ripcord.

Her big rectangular parachute opens with a thump and a jerk. She grabs the control handles and gently wheels away to the north where a Jeep waits to take her to the Alsek launch site.

Enoch sees Melissa's light purple chute open and peacefully float away. This signal means that the racers must be getting close.

He peers upwards and catches sight of Bonet and Skinner. He has to get this right; there will be no do-over's.

Enoch locks the camera on them and focuses the telephoto lens. He magnifies them until he has them tightly framed. Light-green jumpsuits flap and twist in the slipstream…helmets gleam in the sunlight.

Their narrowed, rigid postures make them look like raptors stooped on prey, hurtling down, intent on destruction. He slowly pans the camera and adjusts the telephoto as they swiftly drop closer.

The racers make a slight, synchronized turn. Now they're headed straight at Enoch.

He no longer has to pan the camera, just keep the racers in focus. The telephoto lens makes them seem right on top of him…an uncanny feeling.

Enoch sees the bigger figure of Bonet pull his ripcord and jerk out of the picture. Marie pulls a moment later and she, too, jerks out of view. Enoch rapidly refocuses the telephoto to take in both racers, now spread widely apart.

The two parachuting figures wheel and turn, coming closer, lining up on the target.

Marie comes in first, dropping gently into the slight breeze, closing on the circle-x.

Reggie flies a hundred feet behind her and fifty feet above.

Marie adjusts her trajectory once…twice.

Reggie follows.

Now Marie is a hundred feet up…fifty…twenty…. She touches down, rolls, and stands exactly on the center-cross of the x.

Reggie lands a moment later twenty or so feet behind her, well inside the circle. As he rises from his roll, a gust of wind tugs his chute and drags him running for several steps. He and Marie battle the chute down.

Reggie raises his arms in victory for the camera. They have a twenty-minute time bonus.

Time to hit the kayaks.

Chapter 49 - No Surrender

Hard Rock Gruber checks the AR15 he got from a gun-runner several years ago. He pulls back the charging handle and loads a round.

"Watch this," he says to Casey, and fires an automatic burst across the Alsek. The rifle fire peppers the surface, twenty slugs sending separate spouts several feet in the air.

Summerland grimaces at the ripping noise. He had served with Canadian troops in Afghanistan right after the Taliban were ousted. The sounds of automatic rifle fire still haunt his sleep.

"B-but, Hard Rock," he stammers, "Why the rifle? You're not going to shoot anyone are you? I mean, a whole bunch of people are going to be here over the next few days with helicopters and boats. A gun doesn't make any sense."

"Where's your head, Case?" Gruber asks, "I'm not shooting anybody, just creating a distraction. I've got a plan, nothing you should know about, nothing around the mine here. I'll take care of everything myself, eh? You take care of the mine."

He tucks the AR15 into the crook of his left arm and puts his free hand on Casey's shoulder.

He feels muscles trembling there. Casey sure can't be trusted on this mission. It's Hard Rock's job alone.

The race may delay the next shipment for a day or two, but no one will come snooping around Alsek Blue Billions. Hard Rock will make sure of that.

Chapter 50 - Run River Run

The green racers are twenty miles downriver from where the Alsek begins at the confluence of the Dezadeash and Kaskawulsh Rivers. Lowell Lake is coming up soon.

Mill's paddle chops the Class III whitewater that surrounds her. She swings the bow of her kayak wide to the right, misses a small boulder, then swings left into a chute…down…down…foam and spray, then out clear into a flat patch.

She measures the next hundred feet of the Alsek's rapids with her eyes, then spins the kayak and backs it into an eddy. Time for Mill to hold here while the others catch up.

They had wanted her to go first in the upper reaches of the Alsek to check out any environmental-protection issues before the others came through and to stay out of camera shots. The river was too narrow for anything else.

Mill checks her gear quickly and tightens her spray mask over her nose and mouth. The mask has a tendency to slide down. That last bit of rapids had thrown foam and water in her mouth, lots of it.

No more of that. It's too hard to stay focused on the rapids while coughing up a water-filled lung.

She is ready. As soon as Melissa or Enoch show, she will spin her kayak back out into the rushing river and hit the next patch of white water.

My God, what fun! Hard to believe she is here, now, and doing this. She quickly scans the nearby river banks and then looks above to the hills. There, trees toss in the strong winds coming upriver from the Alaska coast into British Columbia where she now hovers.

No sign of humans.

She sees a dark brown flash in the alder brush along the river bank. Mink? Fisher?

Fast moving little critter no matter what it was. Not a bear thankfully.

A couple of little brown birds bob and flirt their wings, feet gripping twigs tightly against the wind. "Hold on, little guys," she thinks, "Or you're in for a wild ride like mine."

Enoch's light green kayak shoots into the flat water in front of Mill. He spins his kayak, backs it out of the flow much as Mill had, and aims his camera upstream.

With a warning yell, Mill paddles past him and sends her kayak into the next wild patch of rocks, waves, and foam.

Three miles downriver, Mill hits a long, calm stretch of clear water. As she enters it, she sees a black-bear sow with three cubs fishing along the river's edge. One of the cubs is cinnamon-colored and the other two are black with white chest patches. As mom fishes, the cubs tumble and play along the bank, waiting for breakfast.

Mill looks over the side of her kayak. She sees several fish lying quietly in long rows along the bottom.

Her fish biologist training tells her they are silver salmon on their way to the Alsek's upper tributaries to spawn. Big fish, full of protein. Their presence here explains the fishing bears.

The sow splashes into the gravely shallows and grabs a mature fish in her teeth. She carries it flipping back to the bank and chomps its guts out. Chewing a few morsels, she swipes the still-wiggling fish up onto the bank. The three cubs run to it and begin fighting over the carcass. Mock-battle growls fill the air.

Mill paddles gently towards the bank opposite the bears. She tries not to make any splashes, to keep quiet and avoid startling the sow.

Mill pats the small can of bear spray in the front pocket of her anorak for comfort. Each of the kayakers has one. She knows she can evade and outdistance the sow in the kayak, or spray her if she must, but she sees no point in creating chaos for the little family.

Mill's precautions work. The bears pay her no notice as she floats past them. A hundred more feet down the river, Mill hears a small splash behind her.

She realizes she has been so focused on the bears that she has forgotten about her companions. "How's that for concentration?" she asks herself, "Get me killed sometime."

She carefully swings her kayak perpendicular to the river, prow towards the far bank, and looks back upriver. She is amazed to see the rest of the EMM team and the racers drifting downriver, bear watching, as she had done.

Out in front of the racers, Enoch shoots first the bears, then the racers, and then, when distance and angle allow him to cover both, human and bears together.

Dramatic shots.

Melissa has her little parabolic mike out, too, capturing bear sounds.

Reggie and Marie simply seem to have forgotten about the race and stare raptly at the bears, drifting side-by-side down the Alsek.

As she watches her friends upstream, Mill's kayak clears a large willow patch along the bank behind her.

Suddenly, Mill hears a loud splash behind her. Snapping her head around, she sees that a bear has jumped into the shallows directly at her, maybe fifty feet away.

Fear and adrenaline stab her. She grips her paddle and frantically drives her kayak downstream, eyes on the bear.

The big bear swims out a few feet, then turns and heads back to shore. Just a false charge, thank God. She must have startled the bear by coming out suddenly and silently from around the willow cover.

She gets her breathing under control.

She turns her kayak to face the animal, a large boar. He looks odd.

Mill wonders if there's something has discolored his fur or caused him to lose large patches of it. She lifts her binoculars out of her anorak pocket and focuses on him.

She sees what locals call a "glacier bear" or "blue bear." She has never seen this color phase before and thinks, ""Blue he's not. At least not this one. Grey for sure, mottled with black. Looks like the coloring on an Australian shepherd dog."

The boar looks her over, too, snapping his jaws as a warning. Then he notices the other kayaks—too much for him. Ears back, he gives a couple of fearful woofs, turns, leaps upslope, and races into the brushy fringe.

Mill turns her kayak downstream and digs in. The racers are coming at her again, fast. Bear break is over. Lake Lowell with its fantastic bergs is next.

———————————————————// ———————————————————

At late-day, the Green Group reaches the confluence of the Alsek and Bates rivers…one big and one small flow merging in a chaos of choppy waves and whirlpools. The group whoops over wave crests and digs hard to break through the whirlpools.

A helicopter makes a high pass over the racers. Thinking that the helo probably contains a Geo-Challenge film crew, the racers wave and shake paddles over their heads. The pilot circles them high and low, close in, then far.

Mill sees no markings on the little white chopper. She gets irritated when the blade wash stirs up spray and silt-water to fling her way.

The helo finally climbs and whack-whacks its way upriver, giving the Green Group back to sounds of the coastal wind and the rumbling, grumbling river.

They're almost seventy miles down the Alsek now. Here, the faster upper river has changed to a broad, braided flow filled with mud flats, low dunes, tree roots, snags, brownish grassy patches, and gravel bars. Mill recognizes this part of the river from what the kayakers had told her--oddly, the most difficult part.

The lower Alsek offers one advantage over the upper. Now Mill can use side channels to run parallel to Enoch and the racers. She just has to avoid the shallows, getting separated, or being stuck in the wildly slippery mudflats.

On this wider, slower portion of the Alsek, the racers work to keep the fast pace they had enjoyed upriver. They dig their paddles in hard and straight, clearly experienced at driving kayaks at top speed.

But they'll not be able to sustain their previous ten-mile-an-hour pace in the twisty Alsek labyrinth that surrounds them. They've been fortunate so far that often-present, powerful headwinds haven't confronted them here.

To keep up with the surging racers, Mill starts her "long-and-strong" paddling…reaching…pulling. She feels her upper body strain.

Heat builds under her anorak. She thrusts forward, pacing the racers. Okay for now.

A few miles later, Mill spots an eagles' nest high in a cottonwood tree, the white puffball of the resident female's head turned in their direction. She paddles ahead quickly to reach Enoch at the lead. She points to the nest.

Turning her kayak, she gestures to the racers to take a route more to the center of the river, away from the nesting eagles. They swing southerly into a new channel and forge ahead.

Mill checks her etrex. Twenty miles to Turnback Canyon and the Tweedsmuir Glacier portage. Soon they will leave British Columbia and enter Alaska again. After portaging, they'll push to the finish near Alsek Lake.

As if they had read her mind, the racers drive their paddles in even harder. If they can portage across Tweedsmuir by daylight or dusk today, they'll be in a great position to run hard at first light.

It's too dangerous to run the lower Alsek in the dark even with headlamps and GPSes. Blind channels, snags, and sweepers could divert or even kill them.

But even partial light in the morning will be enough to spot the hazards in time to miss them or to portage around them.

Chapter 51 - Gun Ship

Hard Rock waves at the five kayakers dressed in light green. He spots black letters spelling "Great Land Geo-Challenge" on the sides of their kayaks.

Definitely a race team.

Four pretty much in a row.

One flanking them to the south.

Gruber needs to know how far the next bunch is behind this first group. Gotta be at least a half hour for his plan to work…to divert attention from the area around Alsek Blue Billions.

He smiles grimly and pulls back on the collective. The little chopper lifts quickly and points east, upriver.

He looks over to the second seat to his right. The AR15 rests there with an ammo box full of preloaded 20-round clips, a field chair, and his lunch.

He plans to make life interesting for these green racers…these hot-dogs, these first-ones-in-line.

Chapter 52 – Back Turns at Turnback

The green racers are less than a mile from Turnback Canyon. The Tweedsmuir Glacier towers above them to the north, its cold air pouring over them. Only the heat generated by paddling keeps the Green Group warm now.

Ignoring Tweedsmuir's cold exhale, Mill ponders the upcoming take-out and portage. The Turnback take-out is on the north side of the river on the edge of the glacier's terminal moraine, a mountainous pile of boulders, cobbles, and gravel. Her etrex clearly shows the take-out as a flashing red dot.

The Green Group also has caches there to open and off-load…caches that contain food, fuel, batteries, and other supplies.

The racers want to portage the kayaks by sliding them over the Tweedsmuir full of gear and supplies. It's a question of getting the weight and sheer bulkiness right so no one strains backs or joints or loses irreplaceable items into a crevasse or a deep glacial run-off. To keep the race fair, the racers have to handle their own kayaks and gear-load alone, separate from the support team.

Enoch heads the little flotilla towards the north bank. A large helo flies by, wearing a banner that displays the Geo-Challenge logo. It hovers for a few minutes well above them, obviously recording them, then turns hard and flies upriver to visit the next group of racers.

Free of that distraction, Mill turns her attention back to the rapidly approaching take-out point. The river is starting to move faster here. The river banks are closing in. Rocky outcrops along the banks are rising into tall canyon walls visible ahead.

She and Enoch sweep around a small gravel bar and see an orange pylon with green, blue, and brown flagging fluttering at the top, clearly the take-out.

Above it on the moraine perches the little white helicopter that videoed them earlier. At river's edge, a small male figure sits in a camp chair.

Mill figures the person has a tripod and camera set up, ready to record the racers' landing, but she is too far away to be sure.

She swings downstream a little to get out of the camera angle. As she pulls clear, the rest of the Green Group rounds the bar and paddles hard for the take-out. Once they see him, they wave to the fellow on the beach.

They get to within a hundred feet of the river bank. Suddenly, the guy jumps to his feet with a military-looking rifle in his hands and fires a long burst of automatic gunfire.

Bullets zip and whine over their heads.

Shell casings rattle into a loose mesh bag clamped to the rifle.

Marie cries out in panic.

Everyone starts to backwater.

Hard Rock calmly strips the clip out of his empty rifle, drops it, and snaps in another one. He volleys bullets upstream of the green kayakers, kicking up a mane of water and blocking any move in that direction.

Hard Rock reloads and fires another clip. He cuts the stream of bullets close to them again.

The maniac's gunfire drives the Green Group downriver. They have to get out of range. The next burst could easily cut their kayaks to shreds and kill them all.

They turn and start to paddle. Kayaks crunch together, almost tipping.

Wobbling, they straighten out and paddle hard, another clip of bullets chasing them.

The firing stops.

In less than a quarter mile, the ever-faster river current grips them firmly.

They are headed into Turnback Canyon…into six miles of high-water Hell.

Chapter 53 - Mayday...Mayday

Hard Rock watches the green-clad kayakers disappear towards Turnback Canyon.

Very satisfying.

He folds his camp chair. Slinging the chair, a thermos, and his rifle over his shoulder, he picks up three empty clips and the ammo container.

Hefting the load, he trudges up to his little helicopter, strips off the tape covering the helo's identification, steps inside, starts the engine, and spools up the rotor.

Lifting off, Hard Rock points the nose towards Canada.

Back home for this bird. Out of sight, out of mind.

No connection to Alsek Blue Billions or Hard Rock.

Tomorrow, he will charter a helo to fly back and drop him off a mile or so from the mine.

Ten miles east of Turnback Canyon, Gruber picks up his radio mike, "Mayday...Mayday...Mayday...this is November 2-6-5-4 Bravo...repeat November 2-6-5-4 Bravo...Mayday...Mayday...Mayday."

Hard Rock had copied this tail number off a small plane flying by Alsek Blue Billions a few days ago.

His little helicopter is Canadian registry with tail number C-NBTA. He sure didn't want to call his correct tail number out on the airwaves.

But no eyes can see his radio transmission and his helo's transceiver-locator is turned off.

A voice blares loudly in Hard Rock's earphones, "This the U.S. Coast Guard responding to a Mayday. All other parties on this channel stop transmission. 5-4 Bravo what is the nature of your emergency. I say again, 5-4-Bravo what is the nature of your emergency?"

The voice waits for Hard Rock to answer.

Hard Rock keys his mike, "Coast Guard, this is 5-4 Bravo, I just saw five kayakers run into Turnback Canyon on the Alsek. It's off limits, too dangerous. I think there's some kind of race going on, but they shouldn't be in there. I saw one of them crash into rocks and disappear. They need help. That's all. 5-4 Bravo out."

"5-4 Bravo, when did this happen?"

Silence.

"I repeat, 5-4 Bravo, when did this happen?"

No answer, just static.

The ensign in charge of Coast Guard emergency response in Juneau, Alaska, turns to the specialist working for her, "Notify Sea King 9-8. They're going out in five. Destination west end of Turnback Canyon on the Alsek."

She picks up her phone and calls the watch officer, "I read in the *Juneau Empire* a couple of days ago that some reality show is filming a race up on the Alsek. Get in touch with them and let them know they may have some of their people in trouble in Turnback Canyon, five of them. And tell them air rescue lifts off in five. ETA Turnback in fifty minutes."

At the Coast Guard's Sitka airbase out on the Alaska coast, a crew runs to a giant Sikorsky HSS-2 Sea King helicopter. As they have so many times before, the crew races through the checklist.

A few minutes later the helo's huge rotor assembly begins to turn. A minute later, the twin-turbine engines are warm and all avionics are green.

A moment later, they lift off, beating their "plus five" by a full minute.

No time to waste when wild water once again puts human lives in danger.

————————————————//————————————————

A few days earlier, the Geo-Challenge producers had brought a large barge outfitted as a floating hotel into Dry Bay to serve as race headquarters, control room, media center, helicopter pad, and party central.

Because the race results will be kept secret until the show's last episode, the international media are present to interview the producers on subjects like how they organized the race and, of course, to interview the racers and scrounge intimate details, with everything embargoed for later release. All this will hype the show both before and during its eight-week run months from now.

Tilly Corcoran and Joe Schmoker occupy a little hole-in-the-wall office at water line. From here, Tilly can handle any media questions about the federal permit process and other government kinds of things. Joe can cover the incident command system, his role with the federal agency reps, and so on.

But, of course, the media aren't interested in such mundane subjects. Neither Tilly nor Joe is surprised or hurt.

258

Leave the limelight to the stars. They press their noses to paper grindstones.

Joe's sitting at his desk when, as before, his computer begins screeching an alarm, Unnnngh, unnngh, unnngh!"

Joe changes screens, "Tilly we have five EPIRB alarms. Saarinen, Bonet, Skinner, Bagley, and Meacham—the Green Group. EPIRB signal says they're in the water, in trouble."

Tilly jumps up from her desk and moves quickly to his side, "Where…where are they?"

Joe answers tersely, "Hard to tell from this signal, but we'll know soon. Tilly, please go get someone from the Geo-Challenge down here."

Tilly rounds his desk and runs for the door.

Before she can get there, the producer's staff assistant almost collides with her, running in.

He stammers, "Joe, our safety guy has some Eper-thing alarms and we had a call from the Coast Guard. They got a Mayday from an airplane flying over the Alsek. The pilot saw our Green Group go into Turnback Canyon…."

Chapter 54 - Fight to the Death

Mill bobs away from her companions' tangle of kayaks and paddles. For the third time, gunfire rips the river close to Mill, sending spray over her head.

She points the bow of her little craft downriver and paddles like crazy. She hears the rifle chatter again, more faintly than before, and glances back to see if everyone's okay.

Sure enough, everyone's charging down the Alsek behind her as fast as they can paddle.

In a few minutes, she figures she has gone beyond rifle range…at least out of the little bastard's sight.

Now she sees mist rising several stories in the air ahead and hears the roar of rapids and falls. She glances to each side of the river, praying for a landing spot. But, since they left the landing, the canyon walls have grown closer and higher.

There's no place to land.

Only one way is open to her now, down Turnback Canyon.

She tries to remember the short write-up she read about Dr. Walt Blackadar's pioneering trip through the canyon in the 70's. His message had been that you can't paddle in the canyon's impossible chaos. You just hold on, steer as you can, and hope for a clear route. Other experts had gone through since. They urged future kayakers to scout the water before entering the canyon. It was the only way to survive, they said.

Mill won't be scouting anything today. No, she will just have to hold on, steer, and hope….

Now the wild water's pulsing roar pounds against her ears. It beats against her chest, forcing puffs of air out of her mouth.

She sees the arching curve of a waterfall's top to her right, who knew how high.

She looks left and sees a steep boil of impossible boulders and spray.

Mill swings right, pulls the chin strap on her helmet tighter, lifts her spray mask higher on her nose, and grips her paddle tightly.

It will be the waterfall.

She hits the curling top water dead center, arches clear of the stream, and drops…fast…faster…keel just touching spray, airborne, water-falling.

She has less than a second to tilt her bow slightly down and pray for enough momentum to reach the leading edge of the standing wave that surely lies below the falls.

The broken second passes.

The kayak slams hard, missing the wave's edge by a yard. Mill loses her paddle, and then bounces up and almost over backwards, air driven from her lungs.

Instantly, the waterfall's outwash spins her around the fast-moving eddy-pool towards the falls. If she lets herself get pulled under it, she will die under the tons of water falling from above.

Stunned, trying to catch her breath, she scrambles to retrieve her paddle. She pulls on the safety cord that secures it to the kayak…quickly, quickly.

Now she grips the paddle and digs hard away from the roaring falls. Before she can go far, pelting spray volleys down on her. She's too close, undertow sucking her in.

Facing death, Mill pulls so hard that dark spots fill her vision. Finally, she gains a little…now more. A few more huge pulls and she breaks free.

With a dozen hard strokes, Mill crests the waterfall's standing wave and shoots forward into a steep, boulder-strewn maelstrom. Spray, foam, and pounding waves instantly engulf her.

She crests another large wave so fast that she grabs air under her kayak again.

She slams rock and spins.

Slams and spins again.

She can't maneuver, can't think, just moves instinctively.

Five minutes pass, then ten.

Suddenly the force of a large cross-wave rips the paddle from her hands. And the next moment she hits a rock and rolls…once…twice.

Underwater upside-down, she hears the sound of rocks and boulders grinding, tumbling down the steep canyon floor beneath her.

Cold…cold…cold assaults her face, then her ears.

Somehow a flailing hand finds her paddle's safety line. She hauls it in and tries an Eskimo roll, misses it and tries again.

Her head clears the water for a moment and she sucks blessed air through her spray mask. Again the kayak smacks a rock and spins her so it points backwards.

She thrusts with the paddle, touches rock. She thrusts again and forces the kayak upright.

Blessed air again.

Then a sharp granite point breaches the kayak's tough polypropylene hull. As the boat spins with the current, the rocky knife rips a large hole in the hull.

The kayak settles rapidly, threatening to pull her under with it.

Mill feels water rush in around her legs. She rips her anorak skirt loose and rolls clumsily out of the kayak into the rushing river, buoyed by her floatation vest.

The relentless current sweeps Mill away from the drowned kayak.

As she plunges forward, Mill remembers to aim her feet downstream and to guide herself with her hands-- no swimming, she just lets the current take her.

Over and over, she spins through chutes and troughs and rolls belly-down over standing waves, then swings her feet back downstream again.

Pointed downstream this way, her feet slam into rocks. Even numb from the cold, she feels the bruising impacts through her thin river shoes.

After endless smacks, she turns her feet upriver to get some relief.

Just as she does, the thrusting current slams her lower back against a shallow stony shelf. Flipping heels over head, her helmet hits the shelf, splitting the Styrofoam core. It holds together only because of its tough plastic surface.

Stunned and tumbling in the current, Mill zips by a sharp outcrop. The rough stone rips through her tough anorak and scrapes flesh off her arm.

She raises her arm and sees blood.

Her spray mask dangles below her chin. She takes a big wave in the face and chokes on the water flooding her throat and lungs.

As she coughs, a wave throws her airborne.

She lands with a bruising jolt on top of a rock ledge, suddenly, oddly, at rest.

The river roars around her. Sound thunders and echoes off the canyon walls.

Mill discovers the smashed helmet when she grabs at the stabbing pains in her back and head.

She is suddenly dizzy, her hearing dim.

She rips off her spray mask and vomits grey river water into the Alsek. Miserably sick, she rests for a moment, a few inches of water rushing around her, surrounded by mind-numbing chaos.

After a few moments, she rouses. How far has she come? She searches the now-empty pocket in her anorak--no GPS, no binoculars, no bear spray. All her other gear, including the sat phone, went down with the kayak.

She climbs to her knees and looks at the fantastic river that boils around her.

Can she force herself back into this?

She has to.

Mill is suddenly struck by a savage truth. She can't stay here, can't go back, and can't wait for help that might never come, never see her buried in white water.

Moreover, and most important, she can battle this river all she wants, but she now knows will not survive the Alsek River Run.

With a sob, she thinks of her mostly wonderful life...of Wild Girl's rage and dark despair...of Charli's light touch.

She remembers the warm, healing water of Cottonwood Creek where she had bathed after her rape so many years ago.

She lets go of pain...sends God a prayer for her friends' safety...closes her eyes...makes peace with Turnback Canyon...with its strength, her weakness...the sureness of her death.

Finally accepting fate, Mill rolls off the ledge and lets the river take her. The swoopy, bumpy, banging ride begins again.

Mill keeps her eyes closed and waits for death.

Ten minutes later, Mill slides feet-first over a long standing wave, feels rough rock brush her pants, and then simply bobs.

She opens her eyes and sees a broad channel around her, grey waters hurrying along.

A few boulders, no white water, no spray.

Turnback Canyon has set her free...alive.

Chapter 55 - Rescue and Recovery

Joe Schmoker fumes with impatience. He has no way of reaching the lower end of Turnback Canyon.

Daylight is almost gone and the Geo-Challenge helo is at the upper end of the Alsek. It has turned back to help with the search, but it won't come all the way to Dry Bay to pick him up.

So, all Joe can do is fume and pace around his desk.

As Joe fumes, Tilly stares out of the barge-hotel's rain-streaked porthole, seeing nothing, numb with anxiety.

When she was ten, her adored older brother and a car full of family friends had been killed in a train accident near San Diego. Ever since, the death of anyone or anything close to her, grandmother or goldfish, causes her to detach, get quiet, crawl inside.

The radio on Joe's desk crackles. A clipped voice speaks clearly. "Geo-Challenge base…Geo-Challenge base, this is Coast Guard Juneau."

There's a pause, then the radio operator on the barge replies, "Yes, Juneau, this is Geo-Challenge base."

"Geo-Challenge, standby…I'm going to connect you to Sea King 9-8."

The radio crackles for several agonizing seconds then, "Go ahead, 9-8, we have Geo-Challenge base on this frequency. What do you see, 9-8?"

Tilly and Joe hear a much more distant voice, one battered by the loud thumping of the helicopter, "Juneau, we have rescue swimmers in the water and three live, repeat three rescued in the ship. Two no sign."

The speaker pauses, "Hold on, Juneau, swimmers report recovering one more…repeat, recovering one more with severe injuries. Missing one."

Joe can't stand it. He has to know who's been recovered and in what condition. He reaches for the radio.

But before he can break protocol and speak to 9-8 directly, the cool Geo-Challenge voice cuts in, "9-8, what's the condition of the rescued parties and their names, please?"

"Oh, sorry, Geo-Challenge. Three are aboard with no major injuries. Names…stand by…Bonet, Skinner, and Meacham. Standby, basket coming on board…and Bagley, according to Bonet…"

"Bagley's hurt, head and arm injuries. EMT's working on her. EMT says ten more and then we go bingo to Juneau trauma. Can't wait any longer or might lose Bagley."

At the sound of the rescued-ones' names, Tilly puts her head down on her desk and sobs. The numbness has left her, replaced by a desperate, bottomless sorrow.

Joe walks two steps to her side and puts his hand on her shoulder; grateful tears show in his eyes, too.

"Roger and thank you, Sea King 9-8. We appreciate your information. We will send our helo to your location to look for our fifth kayaker, Enoch Saarinen. We...."

The voice of 9-8 breaks in, "Geo-Challenge, this is 9-8, we have located your fifth kayaker. Standby, confirming...."

"Yes, Geo-Challenge, I regret to inform you that he didn't survive. Rescue swimmer reports broken neck and clavicle, other injuries."

"Juneau base, this is Sea King 9-8. We will recover fifth kayaker, and then depart Alsek for Juneau trauma. Rescue 9-8 clear."

Tilly lets out a long wail. Her tears drip down her nose to the desktop. Joe kneels beside her, puts his arm around her, and snugs her close.

————————————//————————————

Mill floats along for only a few minutes when she hears the deep thumping of a large helicopter. Then a huge, staggeringly bright searchlight finds her in the water.

The giant chopper hovers seemingly just above her head for only a few moments before a person in a wet suit drops into the water beside her.

Mill points up at the helo that seems so close, "C-can't I j-just climb in?"

But her words are lost in the spray and thunder of the helicopter's downdraft.

The swimmer gently hauls Mill close and yells her ear, "Are you hurt?"

Mill shakes her head, "No."

A long, shallow basket touches the water next to them, "Can you climb into this?"

Mill answers, "Yes" and nods her head.

266

But when it comes to Mill actually climbing in, it takes both of them to get her into the basket. The swimmer quickly straps her in and signals up to the winch operator standing in the chopper's door. Mill is treated to a short whirling trip up and into the helicopter's interior.

Immediately, an EMT swaddles her in blankets and begins to check her for injuries. Looking at her forearm, the EMT quickly cuts away her anorak sleeve and the long underwear beneath, and applies a tight bandage to her wound. He removes her battered helmet, checks her head, and flashes a light in her eyes.

Nodding reassuringly to her, he straps her into a seat, and goes back to the rescue-landing area.

The next basket comes in through the open door. Bonet moves weakly to climb out, almost immobilized by hypothermia.

The crew gently unstraps him and helps him up. He seems untouched.

Mill feels gratitude wash over her…one of her racers is safe.

Now warm, she gets sleepy. She lets her head loll, chin falling on her chest.

She misses seeing Skinner come through the door, a blue-lipped smile on her face, hand reaching for Bonet.

Then Melissa, limp and bloody.

And finally Enoch's body, quickly covered by the compassionate helicopter crew.

Mill only wakes up when paramedics unstrap her to take her to the ambulance in Juneau.

The Geo-Challenge helicopter waits at the Juneau airport the next day as Mill and the racers arrive.

They had been held overnight at the hospital for head-injury observation and to make sure mild hypothermia effects had worn off. After being chased by the Copper River bear, Mill knows that for the next day or two she will probably grow quickly sleepy and be weaker than normal. She would manage.

Melissa Bagley had been life-flighted to Seattle a few minutes after Sea King 9-8 had dropped them at the airport. Alaska Airlines had cleared a row of seats for Melissa's small body and given up another seat across the aisle for an experienced ER nurse practitioner.

This morning's report from Harborview Hospital is that Melissa is stable and improving.

Mill and the two racers board the Geo-Challenge helo. Tom Burrows sits next to the pilot, "Hey, Green Group, welcome home. I am certainly relieved that you guys came through safely."

Looking at his weary, lined face, Mill believes Tom is completely sincere. She has renewed respect for Mr. Gorgeous, his lined face not so gorgeous now, sagging under grief's weight.

Tom looks at the two racers, "Reggie and Marie, I can't tell you how glad I am to have you back alive."

He smiles grimly in sympathy, "The other teams have finished. We're almost ready to declare a winner."

Bonet and Skinner look shocked, horrified. Burrows shakes his head regretfully, "Too bad you disqualified yourselves by trying to run Turnback. I mean I can understand the desire to win, but the race rules...."

His voice gets drowned out by cries of protest from Mill and the two racers, "Like Hell, we were forced in there by gunfire...by some guy."

After the survivors had told their story about being confronted by a gunman to the Coast Guard crew, an ASP investigator had met them at the hospital and took their statements.

Either the word hasn't reached Burrows or he is testing their truthfulness. "Wait, wait," he protests, "Mill, you have no stake in whether these guys finish or not, so give me the story."

Mill thinks for a moment, sorting out her memories of the last peaceful mile above Turnback and what happened next. She decides to pitch this story much as Burrows had done in Fairbanks, aiming for a no-hitter.

"Tom," she says, "get ready for a story, one that will make a Hollywood legend out of the Great Land Geo-Challenge and increase your viewing audience ten times."

Pausing for effect, Mill begins, "Well, we were digging hard, trying to get to the take-out before dark...."

_____//_____

Mill and the green racers sit outside a small conference room where the producers are meeting to decide their fate.

268

Mill reads the race rules for the tenth time. "Damn," she thinks, mind running in circles, "These people could give legalese lessons to the government."

She turns to Reggie, "The race rules for the Alsek River Run are clear, 'anyone entering Turnback Canyon will be disqualified.' But there's this other rule that covers the whole race, one for 'uncontrollable conditions outside the scope.'"

She shakes her head, "Some lawyer wrote that I bet. Anyway, as I read it, let's say you racer types got caught up in a natural catastrophe of such magnitude that you can't finish. Then the producers can stop the race clock, move you to another location, and restart the clock. That location has to be equally far away from the finish."

Marie says vehemently, "That definitely describes that shitty little bastard with the gun. He was a natural catastrophe alright, the little coward, shooting at us with an automatic rifle. All we had to defend ourselves were our paddles...."

Reggie takes her hand, "Look, Marie, bad shit happened. Enoch and Melissa...."

He chokes back tightness in his throat, "But if the little prick had wanted to kill us, we'd be dead. He kinda herded us into Turnback. Law enforcement's workin' on that, tryin' to find him. But now, now we need to refocus on the race. I know this is hard, but let's let Mill finish, okay?"

Marie's extreme mental toughness takes charge, "Go ahead, Mill. So, do we fit this 'catastrophe' rule?"

Mill looks thoughtful, "Of course it's up to the producers, but I think so. For example, if a landslide blocked a river and formed a lake, it would create an obstacle not displayed on your GPSes and radically change the race course. If you then found it impossible to reach the finish line because of the lake, you could call in and ask for relocation. So, I think our situation fits this 'uncontrollable conditions' rule pretty well."

Marie says, "I get it. Okay, in our case it's maybe even clearer than a landslide. The gunman forced us into the Canyon. He's the 'uncontrollable condition.' The producers have the time the EPIRBs went off, so they knew when the time should be stopped. They also have sworn statements from us that a gunman forced us into Turnback Canyon from the take-out. And law enforcement found an empty clip at the take-out, wet but not rusty. So they know where to start the race again."

Reggie smiles grimly, "Now all we have to wonder is if they actually believe us and are willing to bear the expense of letting us finish the race."

Twenty minutes later, Tom Burrows comes out of the meeting room.

His face is serious, almost grim.

Three hearts sink.

He points at Bonet and Skinner, "One word for you two, Race!"

Chapter 55 – Race Redux

Mill, Reggie, and Marie wait by the Geo-Challenge helicopter on the barge top deck.

To keep everything fair, the producers require that they be dropped at the Turnback take-out at the same time of day that the gunman forced them down-canyon. Then, just as before, they'll have to decide whether to camp for the night at the take-out or attempt an evening-into-night portage across Tweedsmuir Glacier.

Reggie and Marie haven't made a decision about the glacier-haul because a significant part of the choice depends on the weather. Trying to portage in the dark, especially with rain or snow, or worse, fog, could be very hazardous. So the two racers hope for relatively clear conditions like those that they had two nights before.

After the decision by the producers, the three had a day of rest. No one bothered them except for medical staff and a grief counselor flown in from Juneau.

Mill wonders if one day's rest has been enough for Marie who had been significantly hypothermic two days before and deeply frightened by the gunman.

Marie had been even more pained by Enoch's death because it followed so closely on the heels of Ben Gibbon's serious injury on McKinley. Ben had just come out of a coma at Fairbanks General Hospital and might take months to recover.

But Marie and the Geo-Challenge doctor declared Marie ready to race. So here they are on the helo pad waiting for a replacement tech team.

"Mill!" A familiar voice calls her name. She looks up.

Manny Suemez walks towards her across the pad, "Manny! What are you doing here?"

Manny smiles his wonderful bright grin, which quickly vanishes into his "sheriff" face. From his expression, Mill realizes he is here on business, serious business.

He waves her towards the corner of the helipad, "Walk with me, Mill, okay?"

They walk to the edge of the helipad and gaze out over the vast, foam-dappled expanse of Dry Bay and the misty wall of the Yakutat forelands beyond.

Mill points east to Turnback, "Manny, my trip through the canyon was pretty hairy."

Manny speaks with sympathy in his voice, "So, how're you doin', Mill? First the bear thing on the Copper and now this gunman on the Alsek. You really okay to keep on with this race thing?"

Mill rotates her neck to work out some stiffness and nods, "Yeah, I think so, Manny. I'm still bruised and stiff but I'd like to see the race through, you know, do my job…like you said."

Manny laughs a little ruefully, "Mill, doin' your job can include calling for backup. Know what I mean?"

She replies, "Yeah, I get you. I could let go of this now, have them get another agency person in here, maybe ask Art or Cal to take my place, and turn the whole thing over to them. But I said I would do this, and I gotta keep my word."

"Yes", he replies, "I know."

His voice deepens with emotion, "Mill, I know you may not be interested, now or ever, but I think you'd make a fine law enforcement officer. You've got the guts, smarts, honor, and field skills. You're even a little lucky, all of what you need to be a LEO."

He looks her in the eyes, "I know I'm springing this on you while you're waiting to go out and do your race job. I just thought I would say it when I had the chance. I might not see you in person again for awhile. So, no need for an answer or anything today. Just think about it, okay?"

Mill blushes at Manny's praise then looks thoughtful. She looks down at her feet, anxious and embarrassed, "Another person I know recently told me I might make a good cop, too. But, Manny, what if I…I…I've messed up? You know…uh…legally and all."

Manny snorts, "I checked. You've got no record, Mill, clear as sunshine. Unless you're talking about this fish-cop thing?"

Mill clears her throat, "Uh, well there's that, but there's more, too. But I think that it's now kinda in the past, you know what I mean? I don't know. Some things happened to me over the past couple of months…on this trip…especially in the Canyon. I'm still sorting everything out. But I feel like I should be making some changes, clean up some stuff…fix some things."

She surprises herself and hugs the lean man tightly. Then she stands on her tiptoes and speaks quietly near his ear, "I really appreciate you asking me. I will definitely think about it. I'm just not sure…a lot's happened and everything."

272

She releases him.

Mill suddenly feels an impulse to blurt out all her secrets. To avoid that, she changes the subject, "What about the fish cops? I got your call but the signal was breaking up. All I heard was that they might be coming here or something."

Manny smiles grimly, "Yeah, we heard from Chick Sorensen that they were planning to give you a surprise party here…bust you in front of media, all that. I made a quick call to Colonel Lowell at ASP headquarters. He checked and called me back. He said that Corporal Craven and his sidekick denied that they were coming here."

"An hour later Chick calls again and tells me that, because Lowell hadn't ordered them not to come, they're gonna do it whether he wants them to or not…won't tell Lowell in advance, just go. That's when I saddled up and came down here."

Mill looks puzzled, "But Manny, why are you even in Alaska? I thought you were back in Albuquerque."

He smiles, "The FBI asked me to come up and sit in on their case assessment about the fish cops. I'd gathered a lot of the initial interviews, ones that the FBI had decided not to do again so they could keep their investigation as low-profile as possible."

Mill gives him a challenging look, "Well? Are they going to charge Toad and his buddies with anything?"

Manny puts up his hands in mock surrender, "Mill, don't shoot your posse. I'm really not sure. I left Anchorage to come down here before any decisions were made. Could be something big. Could be nothing. It's a fed-state thing. If anything is gonna happen, the USA in Anchorage first has to clear everything through Washington, DC. Who knows how long that will take?"

Mill suddenly realizes that Manny is here to back her up, no matter what the Department of Justice decides.

He may not be able to stop the fish cops if they come for her, but he will do what he can.

She grows warm with grateful embarrassment, "Manny…thanks…really, thanks." Her voice trails off as the lump in her throat starts to rise.

"It's okay, *chica*," he says softly, "Just part of the job."

She punches him lightly on the arm, "No, it's not, Special Agent Suemez. You're just here to see the fireworks and join the party when my racers win this God-awful race!"

She puts her hands on her hips in mock indignation, "And what kind of use of public money is that?" They both laugh.

At that moment, two tough-looking guys walk onto the helipad. Manny catches sight of them over Mill's shoulder. He takes her arm, moves her slightly to one side, and readies a hand to reach for his gun.

The two men ignore them and walk towards the helicopter. Manny relaxes but watches the men closely.

Behind the men, Tom Burrows runs up the access ladder. Seeing Mill with Manny at the edge of the helipad, he motions to her and yells, "Come on, Meacham, haul ass. Time to go. These two guys are your new tech team."

Manny releases her arm, "Get goin', *chica*. Just do your job. Let me do mine. I'll see you when you get back."

Mill had wanted to talk to him about the gunman, if anything had been found out about him, why he might have forced them down Turnback Canyon, and why he thought Enoch's life was worth losing...what could be so important.

But that would have to wait.

Mill turns and trots towards the helo.

Time for the Green Group to get back on the Alsek.

274

Chapter 56 - Tweedsmuir and Go

The Geo-Challenge helo drops them off where Hard Rock's smaller chopper squatted previously, on top of the terminal moraine, high above the take-out.

The race clock starts as it lifts off.

The two racers and the support team quickly move down to the kayaks and the pile of gear the helo crew dropped off earlier.

Reggie and Marie have two light green kayaks, the only ones salvaged from the crushing run down Turnback in good enough condition to use for the rest of the trip.

Mill and the tech guys get some battered yellow ones that the Geo-Challenge producers rented from an outfitter in Haines, Alaska.

Mill looks at her banana boat closely. The tough yellow hide shows some cuts and abrasions but the kayak is solid and serviceable. She quickly gets her waterproof bags of personal gear, food, and supplies loaded.

At least it's a cheerful color, she thinks, as she stares briefly down the canyon towards the waterfall and white water that almost killed her. She looks up and sees that the tech guys have loaded their stuff, too.

Reggie motions the three support-team members over, "Okay, look, Marie and I have decided to portage now and camp on the other side of the canyon."

He points up at Tweedsmuir. The glacier is shrouded in rain and gloomy fog with hints of sleet or snow in the clouds. "We think that the cross-glacier route is too dangerous with this weather. The GPSes won't be able to warn us about crevasses. And there may be ice ridges we can't see to go around and can't climb without axes or, for that matter, with the kayaks in tow."

"So, we want to portage over this terminal moraine…it's shorter by maybe two miles than the glacier route…but it's lots rougher. We won't be able to slide the boats nearly as easily as we could have over ice. Probably can't carry them very well either because of the broken surface. And some places there are sure to be streams and rivers of run-off from the glacier, hopefully shallow but slick.

"We'll be walkin' on smooth rock, cobbles, and maybe ice all the way. Anybody see any problems I haven't mentioned with taking the moraine route?"

Reggie looks around the faces.

"Your call, Mr. Bonet," one of the tech guys says.

Mill and the other techie nod.

Marie speaks up, "Okay, we'll trek the moraine. But before we start, I want to spend a couple of minutes talking about Enoch Saarinen, our videographer, the guy who died two days ago running this race with us. I don't care if it costs us the race, I just feel like we ought to take a minute or two to remember him…things he did for us…how he mattered to us. And a little while to think or pray about Melissa Bagley who's lying in a Seattle hospital because some nut job with a gun put us down that Hellhole called Turnback Canyon."

"Everybody okay with taking a minute or two to do this?"

Mill and Reggie say, "Okay" almost simultaneously.

Both are used to the way Marie's strong character comes through in a crisis.

The two techies just shrug. They would do whatever the racers wanted.

It was the racers' Geo-Challenge to win or lose, not the techies. And they had not known Enoch or Melissa.

Marie looks upwards and speaks to the air, "Enoch, I am so sorry you died trying to tape a reality show to make us famous or something. This race seems so trivial, such a small thing to waste your life on. I know that it was your job and you loved it, so that brings me some peace. But I also miss you and wish I'd known you better. Wherever you are, wherever your spirit is, I want you to know we are going to finish this so that your work and our work will be done. I know I will see you somewhere down winding trails to wild places, my friend Enoch."

"And Melissa, I reach out to you now and say 'heal.' You and I will be friends, forever. I look forward to more rivers run and mountains climbed with you, my sister."

At this point, Marie sobs and can't continue speaking.

Reggie and Mill close around her, hugging her and whispering consoling words.

She cries for a long time and the two cry with her. Finally their tears end and, for now at least, there's nothing left to grieve.

Marie steps free of their circling arms.

She points westward, out along the rough, debris-piled moraine, "Let's race."

_____//_____

Hours later, Mill drags her weary butt over yet another pile of cobbles and small boulders. Then she turns to haul on the line connected to the two kayaks she tows behind her. The normally vivid yellow of the little boats shows pale in the light of her headlamp.

Mill partnered with the sound guy, Simon. They've tied their kayaks together and are out in front of the rest of Green Group.

One pulls the string of two kayaks forward. The other guides and pulls them from the up-slope side. The side-hauler keeps the little boats from sliding down, out of control, and making huge nuisances out of themselves.

Mill and Simon switch off positions every ten minutes or so to prevent muscle cramps.

At the rear of the line, Marie and Reggie are following a similar haul-and-guide routine. The video guy is well out in front of them with his own kayak in tow just behind his heels, a line tied to each end twisted into a clumsy harness around his upper body.

Simon's mikes pick up sounds of rushing glacier-melt water, the kayaks' hollow banging, and the Green Group's panting curses and encouragements.

Four miles and a little more so far. Mill glances down at her etrex. In the last ten minutes, the little direction arrow pointing the way to their camp site has shifted from west to south. They are past the west end of chaos canyon.

A moment later, Reggie sees the same thing and shouts, "This way."

The Green Group begins the bumpy, sliding trip down the moraine to the Alsek River bank. The gravel bench above the river will be their bed tonight.

They will be back on the river at first-light.

Working by headlamp the next morning, Mill rolls up her tent and sleeping bag and puts them in waterproof bags with rest of her gear. She checks her kayak, helmet, and river clothing. Everything's ready.

She walks to where Reggie and Marie are heating water to make coffee and rehydrate freeze-dried meals. Their little spirit stove hisses and pops.

"Mill, you rest okay last night?" Marie asks.

"Yes, I pretty well croaked after the death march over the moraine," Mill smiles, then instantly regrets the use of the words "croaked" and "death."

But Marie ignores her words and replies ruefully, "Yeah, tell me about it. I'm so stiff this morning; I could barely get out of the tent. I literally had to wiggle out on my belly. Reggie got our gear packed while I started boiling water. I'll shake it out on the river, I guess."

They chat a little more.

Mill gets her first cup of coffee and her bag of powdered, chunky eggs-'n'-who-knows-what breakfast. At this point Mill doesn't care what's in the mix as long as it's full of warm calories.

She walks down to riverside with the hot bag and a cup of coffee, and sits, facing east, her back to a boulder.

She turns off her headlamp, sips, munches, and waits for her first glimpse of the light that will put them back on the Alsek.

Chapter 57 - Tatshenshini Junction

The Green Group passes the mouth of the Tatshenshini River, a broad, braided river almost the size of the Alsek. Past this junction, the Alsek is simply huge. Swift channels, shallows, and separate waterways sprawl all across the wide river bottom.

Mill peers out under low clouds and fog patches drifting over the surface. The river seems miles wide.

No way to stand up in a kayak to look ahead, so Bonet and Skinner get caught every now and then by little waterways that end in gravel or silty mud. Sometimes they push through with their paddles; other times they get out and haul.

Reggie's language turns quite colorful after a few slips and smacks into the incredibly slippery mud.

Mill figures the editing guys will have a good time bleeping him out.

Mill checks her *e*trex. The direction arrow is spinning slowly around and the map behind the arrow has vanished.

Marie is closest to her. Mill yells and points to her GPS. Marie looks at hers and yells to Reggie, "Look at your GPS."

She holds up the little unit. He checks his. His curses get louder.

The race controllers have struck again.

The GPSes are dead.

For now at least, the Green Group has no idea exactly where they are on the Alsek or, for that matter, where to find their finish-poles downriver.

Reggie stops cursing and paddles close to Marie. Mill drifts closer and hears him tell Marie, "The last check I made on the distance to the finish line, it was about twenty-three miles. We were about a mile above the mouth of the Tatshenshini at that point. We're maybe a mile below now, so twenty or twenty-one miles to go. That fit with what you know?"

Marie nods, "Yeah, and the last pylon I saw was about three miles above the Tat, so we should see another in a mile or so. That'd mean four more pylons, counting the one ahead, and then we should be somewhere near the finish. Make sense?"

Bonet grimaces, "Sure. Makes sense. But I'm not sure we're going to see every pylon in this fog. So, let's stop-watch our time. I figure we're averaging six to eight miles an hour, what with pulling hard and getting caught by shallows every now and then. So, we should be somewhere close to a pylon every half hour to forty-five minutes. Rough estimate but at least we can start looking around extra sharp whenever the time is up."

Marie thinks for a moment, "Okay, sounds good to me. I say whoever's trailing can keep time and whoever's got the lead keeps a close eye out for the pylons. That okay?"

Reggie nods, "Let's do it."

With that, the two racers turn downriver and drive their kayaks hard into the stream.

The weather is intensely bad…low ceiling…fog. An hour has gone by since they reached the second pylon but no third pylon has appeared in the swirling mist. Ignoring the missing pylon and the weather, the racers keep up the pace.

Mill knows that, with this weather, the Green Group could easily miss the next pylon. If they do, they will probably wind up in ice-choked Alsek Lake, well past the finish-line poles.

From there, they would probably be too tired to fight their way back up the river, even if they could figure out the way.

She keeps up the pace, fingers crossed for the racers.

Suddenly Reggie yells, "Over there."

Mill peers in the direction Reggie points his paddle. On the south side of the river, a little upriver from their location, stand two dimly seen, candy-striped poles.

Squinting at the mist-shrouded poles, Mill realizes that if it hadn't been for Bonet's keen vision and a small clearish pocket in the fog, they would have paddled right past them.

There are three sets of poles down here, one for each team. In the fog, Mill can't see whether the poles have green flagging on top or not.

She backwaters.

The racers pull hard across her bow, and then fight upstream against the Alsek's current, their efforts aided a trifle by a slight upriver wind from the coast.

Now they racers approach the river's edge. After a struggle through shoaling water, the racers can paddle no further.

They jump out of their kayaks. She watches the two tough tri-athletes wade through the last of the mud and climb over driftwood to the gravel bank. They rush up the slope.

Reggie turns back towards Mill and shouts, "Green!"

She watches Skinner and Bonet separate and run to the poles.

They press the buttons.

Race over!

Mill paddles forward wearily to congratulate her friends.

Chapter 58 - Dry Bay Day

On shore, Mill waits while the videographer does several takes of Reggie and Marie running up the river bank and over to the poles. He also gets close-ups of them congratulating each other. After that, Simon, the sound tech, starts doing stand-up interviews with the pair.

Mill can see that her friends won't be free for awhile. She figures that the Geo-Challenge producers will be sending a power boat for them since the helo is certainly socked in. She may have to wait for some private time with the racers back at the barge-hotel in Dry Bay. So, she walks back up slope to stay well out of video range.

Mill sits on some driftwood for a few minutes watching the happy racers and then realizes she has to pee.

She thinks to herself, "Amazing that I'd have any water left in me after sweating a million gallons since sunrise."

She works her way into the rock maze beyond the shore, drops her clothes, and squats.

After a few moments, she realizes that she can see a lug-soled boot print in the rain-dimpled, wind-blown silt and sand. And beyond that one is another, rapidly disappearing under the rain's patter-drop.

The members of Green Group are all wearing river shoes with very little tread, not boots with lug soles.

"Hmmm," she thinks, "Pretty fresh tracks. I wonder if some of the Geo-Challenge people are running around here. If so, why wouldn't they show themselves…help out? Maybe they don't know we're here. Could be campers, I guess. Won't they be surprised at our being here?"

She stands up, fixes her clothes, turns, and follows the tracks away from the beach…fifty feet…a hundred.

The tracks run out about the time she hears a faint noise, some sort of hum and a low, echoing rumble.

Could the Geo-Challenge folks have a shelter out here or something? Or maybe the Park Service has a cabin or work center here that doesn't show on the GPSes.

Following the sound, Mill walks around a large, up-thrust, pile of boulders. There she sees a big camouflage tarp hanging over a rock face, a little light spilling out around the edges, low sounds coming from within.

"What the Hell is this doing here," she wonders, "Looks like a mine, but this is a National Park, no drilling or mining allowed. And then, why wouldn't it show on the maps? Could this be some kind of secret military installation? How weird."

Curious, she edges over, slips behind the tarp, cranes her neck around a rocky corner, and peers in. Before her eyes, a long, well-lit tunnel choked with stacked barrels stretches downward.

Two men are walking rapidly her way, one tall and slender and one small, stocky. The smaller one is waving his hands excitedly and speaking loudly.

She begins to catch a few of his echoing words, "…I tell you…they're out there…should have…poles. Damn…kill the bastards." The speaker slaps the holster on his hip.

The bigger man says, "No, Hard Rock…people…alone."

They move towards her quickly. She doesn't like the looks of this pair at all, particularly the little guy. She squints down the tunnel into the harsh light washing over the men.

"My God," she thinks to herself, "The one with the holster looks like the little bastard who shot at us. I have to warn the others. Now!"

She turns and runs, heading directly back to the two poles. She gets about fifty yards when she hears a shout behind her, then a loud pistol shot. They must have seen her tracks in the wet sand…caught sight of her running.

Suddenly Mill's feet have wings. She never knew what that expression meant before. But the sound of the shot makes her tired body leap ahead and drive hard for the river bank.

Rounding the last boulder, she yells to her companions, "Run, run! Guy with a gun! Get in the kayaks. *Guy with a gun!*"

But then she slows. A solid-looking, flat-bottomed boat rests on a nearby gravel bar, marked with the Great Land Geo-Challenge logo.

And, here's a bigger surprise, Manny Suemez trots her way, his hand reaching for his gun.

He moves past her, stops, pulls the automatic, and raises it.

Hard Rock Gruber rounds the last boulder, a protesting Casey Summerland on his heels. Before him Manny stands in combat stance, trigger finger extended along his Glock's slide.

His dead-or-alive eyes are fixed on the two men.

They skid to a stop in front of him.

Manny yells, "Police. Drop your weapons. Get on your knees. Put your hands behind your backs! Do it now!"

The miners' faces go white.

Casey puts up his hands and drops to his knees.

Manny sees no weapon on him but can't tell what he might have hidden behind his back.

The other guy has a revolver in his hand. That guy gets Manny's full attention.

Hard Rock stands for a moment, .44 by his side. "Last time before I shoot," Manny yells, sliding his finger onto the trigger, "Drop your weapon…."

Hard Rock looks at the tall guy in front of him, his body taut, crouched in a two-handed shooter's stance. Gruber sees the black "o" of the Glock's muzzle, the guy's dead-level eyes.

Live or die, this is the end of Hard Rock's dream.

Alsek Blue Billions, everything he has worked for his whole life, lost, over…steam-boated.

Only jail lies ahead.

Hard Rock Gruber will never mine again. One last gamble is all he has left.

Hard Rock raises his .44.

Suemez' shot takes him center-chest. Gruber whips violently backwards and spin-twists to the ground… dead, suicide by cop.

An hour later, fully loaded, the boat leaves for Dry Bay. A crewman waits at the shooting site with Gruber's body for ASP investigators to arrive.

Mill sits by Manny inside the cabin. He explains why he had been at the finish line, "Because the helo couldn't fly, the producers stationed this boat upriver of Alsek Lake, waitin' to pick up your gang when you reached the finish. That's why it took only a few minutes to get to you."

He shakes his head, "After being bored out of my skull at the Geo-Challenge barge, I figured I'd come along for the ride. And the finish line certainly wasn't what I expected but it wasn't boring either, anything but."

He tells her, "I'm always numb after this kind of thing. Not so much the shooting…that's bad. I only ever had to shoot somebody twice before. No, for me it's the confrontation, havin' to draw my piece. It's so much adrenaline from not knowin' what the *pendejo* will do. That's the tough part. And then wonderin' if it could have been any other way, you know, to not have to shoot."

Back at the barge, Mill cleans up a little.

Then she joins Manny in a small conference room, waiting to board the Geo-Challenge helo for a flight to Juneau. Although still on duty until he gets home, Manny is technically on administrative leave until the shooting gets cleared by the Forest Service's Washington Office Law Enforcement Director and Alaska's Public Safety Director.

ASP will take both of their statements about the shooting in Juneau.

Except for filing Geo-Challenge reports, Mill's job is over.

A hot shower and reunion with the racers awaits her at Juneau's Breakwater Hotel.

She sighs with the thought of clean sheets and then shudders again at the memory of Gruber's body slamming into the Alsek River bank, his blood draining into the soil.

Manny and Mill get up and pour fresh cups of coffee. Above them, they hear the sound of a helicopter landing. A moment later, a security guard walks in and says to Manny, "The flight you've been waiting for has arrived."

Manny smiles tightly and says to Mill, "I'll check it out to make sure it's our ride. You stay here for a minute. Enjoy your coffee."

He puts down his cup, moves to the door, and goes out. She sits and sips, watching patches of sunlight and small fishing boats move over Dry Bay's choppy surface.

Ten minutes later, Manny walks back in to the room, smiling pleasantly. He motions to her, "Let's go, our helicopter's waiting." The two walk up the open-air stairway to the helipad.

At the top of the stairs, Mill is surprised to see the insignia of the Alaska State Police on the helo's side.

"What the Hell," she thinks, "Why is ASP here and not up at the mine? Wouldn't they fly there directly?"

Then an awful thought strikes her, "Is this Toad coming to get me?"

Panicking, she looks sharply at Manny. Had he set her up?

But no, she sees his big, wonderful smile, "Look in the back seat, *chica*. Who do you see?"

286

She peers through the Perspex bubble. There, sitting uncomfortably on tight handcuffs, are Toad Craven and his best fish-cop buddy, holsters empty, hats off, glowering at Manny and Mill.

"Busted 'em for about forty things," Manny says happily, "I got a call this morning from the AUSA to pick these birds up. He faxed the warrants right after he called. And Toad's pilot says he'll be happy to fly us back to Juneau as a professional courtesy, seeing as how these guys have to go into federal lockup there pending bail or trial. Seems the pilot doesn't like 'em much either."

"Since some of the charges include racketeering and wire fraud, I suspect they won't make bail, so they'll be enjoying Uncle Sammy's hospitality for quite awhile."

Mill can't help flipping the two off and then blowing them each a kiss before she puts on her flight suit and helmet for the trip to Juneau.

As she climbs into the aircraft, she turns to Manny, "I think the answer to your question from a few days ago is 'yes.' I'd like to try law enforcement. I have…uh…some things to make up for, to get straightened out."

Manny pats her arm, "We all do, *chica*, we all do. Okay, I'll be in touch." Once they're seated, he tries to say more but the sound of the helo's engine spooling up drowns out his words.

The Breakwater Hotel overlooks Juneau's busy Aurora Harbor. Mill sits in the Breakwater's homey bar, looking out on the boats and water. Her boulder-bruised feet are up on another chair, high and dry.

Mill sips her second pint of Alaskan Amber, the best alt-style beer she has ever tasted. Pint three will be an Alaskan Smoked Porter, one of the weirdest beers she has ever heard of.

She says a little tipsily to the empty chair next to her, "I mean how do you light a beer and keep it burning long enough to smoke it?" She giggles at her silliness.

She feels a tap on her shoulder. It's Tilly, her face smiling…radiant.

"Mill, dear, the answer is 'you smoke beer the same way you smoke salmon, set fire to one end and suck hard on the other.'"

Both women laugh and Tilly says briskly, "I'm so glad I found you here. May I join you? I'd like that drink now."

In answer, Mill drops her feet too quickly to the floor and winces at the impact. Then she stands and motions to the bartender, "Another Amber, please."

Tilly sits down next to Mill and faces her. Before the beer arrives, Tilly's composure crumbles.

She wrings her hands in her lap and shoots quick glances at Mill's face, "Mill, I know this sounds crazy but hear me out. I've wanted to be with you since Charli's party. You know, to be close to you. But I couldn't tell if you were interested in girls…uh, me…or anything. And I was so busy with the Geo-Challenge. But now with Ben and Melissa hurt and Enoch dead. Crazy Gruber almost killed you…*you*. Well, I just couldn't *not* say this to you if you know what I mean."

Tilly stops for a moment. She sighs deeply, "Mill, I'm saying I want a life with you. I don't know. We just really met sort of, but somehow there's something between us. Do you feel it, too, maybe a little? I want something I haven't had before, something with you. I can't even describe it, I guess, but I want it, a real, true life…together."

Mill studies Tilly' elegant face, sorts through her torrent of words. She reflects on her memory of Tilly with Art Childs at Denali Lodge, her confusion about Tilly's behavior there. No matter now, here….

After all, Mill's love life has been nothing if not chaos before. Why not Tilly's, too? It's something the two of them can sort out later if they ever need to.

Sometimes, secrets should remain secrets.

Mill realizes that Tilly is offering her love, stability, acceptance…even happiness.

She thinks about the brown bear, Drag, Turnback Canyon…her Anchorage life.

She shudders at how close she had come to having her secrets revealed…to dying.

She remembers Charli's warmth and tender touch, loving her without drugs or drink.

Running the race with her team—surviving, thriving.

A life with Tilly might be the safe, warm home-place her heart had sought for so many years. She looks searchingly into Tilly's deep blue eyes, "Yes, Tilly, I feel it too, a lot. Something good, solid. Okay, I want the same thing, to try anyway. Let's start something good together and see how it works out."

Tilly takes Mill's hand and holds it in both of hers.

The two women just sit.

They look out the window and admire the boats bobbing at anchor in Aurora Harbor, masts and cabins framed against the far, rocky breakwater and, further away across Gastineau Channel, the high, dark bulk of Douglas Island.

Somewhere beyond the island's deep blue shadows, the sun is setting. That end to this day lights the grey-blue sky above the island with pink and orange, a gorgeous sight.

Mill murmurs, "Time to race."

She squeezes Tilly's hand and smiles.

END

Epilogue

Ten months later.

Marie Skinner and Reggie Bonet carefully kick-step up the last hundred feet to the summit of Mt. McKinley. Standing on the rocky knob that is North America's highest point, and braced against one another to blunt the east wind's hammering force, the pair gaze around the horizon. Taking turns, they pass an oxygen bottle back and forth between them and savor the metallic taste as if it were champagne.

A bank of clouds obscures everything to the east. Clear air and the vast, wild landscape stretch out before them to the west.

Reggie suddenly bends down and kisses Skinner on her well-balmed lips. She chuckles, making a wheezy thin-air sound.

Reggie stands upright again and asks Marie, "Ready?"

She nods.

Reggie turns and Marie opens his pack. She removes a small wooden box.

Turning her back to the whistling wind, she opens it.

Enoch Saarinen's ashes leap up from the box, dance before Marie, and then whirl high, gone in an instant into the vast Alaskan sky.

Marie yells to the hastening, pale, whirling wraith, "I told you…I would see you…down the winding trail, Enoch. And here we are…where you wanted to come…but never had the chance. God bless you, my friend, Enoch…enjoy your freedom."

The pair stands for a few minutes more. Marie kisses Reggie. Then they turn towards their descent, a not-so-difficult technical climb back to 15,000 feet where they plan to spend the night.

The Great Land Geo-Challenge producers had wanted to film their climb with Enoch's ashes.

But the winners of the greatest race ever would have none of it.

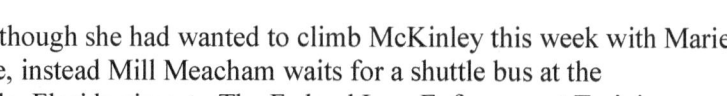

Although she had wanted to climb McKinley this week with Marie and Reggie, instead Mill Meacham waits for a shuttle bus at the Jacksonville, Florida airport. The Federal Law Enforcement Training Center or FLETC, as acronym-crazed bureaucrats like to call it, runs a bus from JAX to the Center in nearby Georgia on a regular basis.

Mill had just missed the last shuttle and has about an hour wait before the next. Thankfully, she can cower inside the little JAX transportation center and hide from the cottony blob of exhaust, humidity, and heat outside.

She opens her cell phone and turns it on. It shows several messages, including one from her Dad, W.A. She shudders a little, thinking of the fights they'd had over her going into law enforcement.

When she first told him, he was speechless, something she had rarely experienced before. And when he found his voice, he used it to curse.

When the curses wound down, he called her choice, "The stupidest thing she'd done since she kicked the fuckin' gas can into the campfire," a youthful mistake that cost them their tents and sleeping bags on a cold Utah night.

How rude of him to remind her of that.

W.A. had been clear, "Forest Service Law Enforcement is fulla lazy men and dyke women. I won't have you volunteering for that no-account crew."

"No, no, no, you won't!" he yelled before slamming down the phone.

But Mill stood her ground, arguing that she could become a LEO with his support or without it.

And as a Legacy leader, wouldn't W.A. look better using her choice to his advantage? He could make the claim that he was sending her into law enforcement to broaden her career. He could hint to the other Legacies that her presence inside the organization would give him insider information...control.

After a long battle of words, W.A. relented.

Grumbling and complaining, he said, "Damn, Milly, now I know what that bear felt like when you was a-ridin' him. 'Either give in, Dad, or drown,' that's your motto. Okay, look, I'll let you go off on this Keystone-cop caper of yours, but only for a few years. Then, it's back to real work, okay?"

Sensing victory, Mill smiled into the phone, "Well, let's talk about that after I've made it through the training and actually get a job, okay?"

"Sure, sure," W.A. replied, wondering if he could somehow use his contacts to get her washed out. No, that wouldn't work; his reputation would suffer if that happened.

And so, their truce began.

292

Even with the truce in place, Mill's heart beats apprehensively as she connects to her Dad's cell.

"This is Meacham," he bellows into the phone.

Holding the phone a few inches from her ear, Mill says evenly, "It's Milly, Dad."

W.A.'s voice booms, "Look, I know you're just startin' your training but I got your first assignment lined up. You know, after you get done with that field-trainee thing they do. Anyway, it's on the Siuslaw, the Mapleton District, out there in western Oregon, near Corvallis. Should be real neat. Seashore. Mountains. Good people. You can thank me later." Click.

Mill stares at her silent phone.

"Well, damn," she thinks, "Nice to know Dad is still trying to run my life. Some things never change."

She closes the phone, her normal frown much deeper. Siuslaw? Nice enough place, but it wouldn't have been her first pick. She had been hoping for somewhere in the Rockies.

Then a thought strikes her and her frown lifts. Mill's wonderful four-note laugh bursts out and puts smiles on the other traveler's faces.

She opens her cell again and calls Tilly Corcoran in Fairbanks, "Tilly, good news, I know where my first assignment will be after FLETC...."

Now, if it could be arranged, wouldn't Tilly moving in with her out in Oregon just frost her Dad's ass?

"Dyke women" indeed.

A few months before Mill had arrived in Jacksonville, Toad Craven and seven of his Game and Fish Enforcement colleagues were either sent to jail or forced to resign their commissions.

Toad got 16 years in the federal penitentiary at Chico, CA. where his froggy ass resides today.

Over six months, the FBI and USA finished their work investigating corruption outside the ASP organization. As a result, two state magistrates and several defense attorneys lost their jobs or licenses.

Colonel Lowell got credit for cleaning up the fish-cop mess and beginning the process of healing relationships with rural Alaskans.

Alaska is better for it all, all around.

Thinking and Talking About this Book

Principal Characters

Armando "Manny" Suemez - a tough, experienced Forest Service Special Agent in a powerful position and Mill Meacham's law-enforcement mentor

Charli Jenkins – a successful Anchorage real estate agent who becomes Mill Meacham's lover and nurturing supporter

Drag Carlson – a human predator who stalks Mill Meacham and teaches her what it means to be prey

Enoch Saarinen – a talented, experienced outdoor videographer who works with Mill on a Geo-Challenge support team; Melissa Bagley's partner

Hard Rock Gruber – an unscrupulous miner who drives Mill and the Green Group into deadly Turnback Canyon during the Geo-Challenge

Joe "Smoky Joe" Schmoker – a senior wildland firefighter who assists Mill and her agency-representative counterparts during the race

Marie Skinner – a highly trained, pragmatic tri-athlete who partners with Reggie Bonet on the Great Land Geo-Challenge

Chick Sorensen – an Eyak native who lives in Cordova, Alaska and who is fond of Mill Meacham; he helps her on the job and in her struggles with unethical Alaska Game and Fish Enforcement Officers

Matilda "Tilly" Corcoran - Mill's colleague who becomes her friend and lover

Melissa Bagley – a talented, experienced outdoor sound technician who works with Mill on a Geo-Challenge support team; Enoch Saarinen's partner

Millicent "Mill" Meacham - a dependent, endearing, and self-reliant young woman with a painful background; she is a fifth-generation Forest Service employee with a promising career as a fisheries biologist

Mitch Mendenhall – an attorney working for the Forest Service in Juneau, Alaska

Wolfgang Amadeus "W.A." Meacham - Mill's father, a tough narcissist with huge Forest Service career ambitions

Race Controllers – a shadowy group who make racers' lives difficult during the Geo-Challenge

Reggie Bonet - a highly trained, passionate tri-athlete who partners with Marie Skinner on the Great Land Geo-Challenge

"Dill" Dillard – Mill's assistant, a Forest Service fisheries technician with extensive experience in wild Alaska

Thaddeus "Toad" Craven – an unscrupulous Game and Fish Enforcement Officer who wrongly targets and harasses Mill Meacham and Dill Dillard

Tom "Mr. Gorgeous" Burrows – the executive producer for the Great Land Geo-Challenge

Questions about the Characters

Who did you identify with most? Which characters changed, grew, or developed? Which remained the same? Why?

Which characters held secrets? How did secrecy affect their lives? Make them vulnerable? Help them grow?

Did any of the characters represent "good" or "evil" in a pure sense? Why?

Which characters cared most about the environment? How did they show this caring? Was their expression of caring constructive or destructive?

Plot

A Deep Blue Abyss has a basic plot that 1) explores the effects of Mill Meacham's self-destructive behaviors on her life and how she eventually confronts and resolves her problems, and 2) describes an epic race across Alaska and how competition, greed, and performance affect the outcome.

Who wins? Who loses? Why? How does teamwork figure into the plot?

Sub-plots and themes

A Deep Blue Abyss has several sub-plots and themes: 1) Mill's relationships with her lovers from Wyoming to Charli to Tilly, 2) Mill's professional competence in wild Alaska, 3) Mill's struggle and development first with the Copper River brown bear, then Drag Carlson, then the race and Turnback Canyon, 4) the Great Land Geo-Challenge and how it's developed, managed, and run, 5) how the race pits the racers and support teams against nature, one another, and the race controllers, 6) secrets and addition, 7) relationships between state and federal agencies, and 8) how Mill's career aspirations change from fish biologist to law enforcement officer as a result of her experiences.

Who is in love? With whom? What kind of love? How do the love relationships work out?

Who wants to control nature? Control other people? How does that desire for control affect relationships and outcomes?

Do sex and sexual relationships mirror other aspects of characters and how they support, control, or dominate others? How does anonymous sex work for Mill in the beginning? How is that lifestyle connected to her addiction, symbolized by Wild Girl Hunting? How do drugs and alcohol enable Wild Girl to hunt? Why would she carry a dagger concealed in her panties? Is it just for self-defense or does it reflect her potential for rage and violence against others? How does her addiction and rage relate to her abandonment at age seven by her mother, neglectful parenting by W.A., and later rape? How does her rage and potential for violence change as she adventures through wild Alaska?

Trust, or the lack of trust, plays a major role in Mill's life. At the start of the book, she can't trust herself to have normal social and sexual relationships. Does this change? How are any changes in Mill's trust relationship with herself reflected in how she perceives threats and support from other people? Agencies? Nature?

How about the idea that how one person treats others reflects how they treat nature? What does it mean when a character like Hard Rock Gruber treats both people and natural resources as objects to be used to further his fortunes? Contrast that approach to how Mill and the Geo-Challenge producers treat nature.

What is Hard Rock's addiction? How does the idea of "winning a jackpot" fit with how he behaves? How does "jackpot thinking" color natural resource issues in the U.S. and worldwide? Could Gruber have been successful as a legitimate miner?

How does the Alaska fish cops' treatment of Mill and Dill reflect how agencies might deal with one another? Even in the face of important reasons to work together, can trust and commitment develop between agencies with hidden agendas, false intentions, and aggressive territorialism? Can mission-overlap make relations between agencies easier or harder? Contrast the state versus federal tensions with the cooperative relationships among the federal agencies that make the Geo-Challenge possible.

What crimes are committed? By whom? How are the criminals punished or how do they escape punishment?

How do bears figure in the story? A brown bear attacks Mill on the Copper, a Tolkat grizzly forages near the racers on the Brooks-Romanzof Trek, and the Green Group watches black bears fishing along the Alsek. How do bears represent wild Alaska in this story? In real life?

The Bible gives us the idea that people's eyes are windows into their souls. This idea supposes we can perceive someone's emotions, intentions, and hurts through their eyes. Mill looks into her own eyes several times in *A Deep Blue Abyss*. Does she gain knowledge from this inward look? How does her eye-perception change over time?

In a horrifying dream, eyes peer up at Mill from glacier ice. Tilly's eyes are a deep blue. Does eye color relate to the book title? Glacier crevasses? Lakes?

Rivers also play a big role in *Deep Blue Abyss,* including the Copper, Kongakut, and Alsek rivers. How is Mill's experience of each river different? Similar? How do the rivers play a role in changing her life? Does what happens on the rivers compare to the flows and currents in Mill's personal life?

Crisis

At a certain point in *Deep Blue Abyss,* Mill's life changes significantly, perhaps irrevocably. Is it after she is attacked by Drag and defeats him? After she survives Turnback Canyon's whitewater? Or is it after she accepts both Manny Suemez' and Tilly Corcoran's offers of a changed life? How did race experiences shape and change Mill? Are these changes similar to species' adaptation and survival in nature or a matter of choice and free will?

Satiric Elements

Satire uses mockery to reveal and denounce vice or folly. *A Deep Blue Abyss* has satiric touches including names, behaviors, and concepts. First names and nicknames such as "Millicent" and "Mill," "Tilly," "Dill," "Chick," "Gruber," and "Toad" have both direct and implied meanings. Some, like "Millicent," evoke ideas ("innocent") and may speak to

298

feelings or an emotional state. Others, like "Mill," speak to behavior or character traits like persistence or tenacity. "Gruber" as "grub-er" or "Toad" as "slimy, warty creature" refer to behavior or personality.

How does the nickname "Tilly" fit with Tilly's behavior? The name has a certain cute, casual charm to it. Does the charm disguise anything? What?

What about the rest of the names on the list like "Chick" and "Toad?"

Last names also contain satiric elements. These include: "Meacham" (me), "Craven" (cowardly), "Burrows" (tunnels in), and the racer-partners, "Skinner" (skin) and "Bonet" (bone). First and last names like "Toad Craven" combine to enhance satiric impact.

How do the names on this list reflect the behavior of the characters or the character of the individuals? How do they emphasize conflicts or influences over outcomes?

The Forest Service has a strong culture with many admirable characteristics. Straight talk, hard work, bravery, and strong personal relationships are among them. *A Deep Blue Abyss* introduces the idea that some elements of the Forest Service culture are less desirable. These less-desirable traits are reflected in the satiric presentation of a "Green Creed," a credo developed and forced on others by agency aristocrats, the "Legacies."

What effects on morale and performance might grow out of an aristocratic culture in which favoritism, privilege, and advancement are the birth right of a few people? Does the presence of an aristocracy affect who can be promoted? Rewarded? What role might employees and retirees play in promoting or defending such an aristocracy?

How would the existence of unstated public policy such as the Green Creed affect agency performance? Relationships? While it could reinforce tradition, how would the Green Creed help define the agency's future? Help it react to changing times, relationships, and leadership?

Humor

A Deep Blue Abyss describes some pranks, jokes, and teasing. These include pranks such as Dill presenting Mill with a bear's-ear cupcake and, on a grander scale, the race controllers changing critical information in the racers' GPSes.

How does such basic and often transparent humor support the plot? Does it reflect culture? Teamwork? How does it disguise conflicts or secrets? Does it bring people together or separate them? Build trust or defeat it?

Word Play

The novel contains occasional word play in the form of chapter titles, unusual word mixtures, people's names (for example, "Toad Craven"), and the use of certain punctuation such as the ellipse (…).

How does word play contribute to the story? To our understanding of the characters? To their approach to life or other people? For example, puns are inherently competitive and intellectual. Colorful figures of speech reveal a lot about a character's approach to others and may serve to disguise their true feelings. How do those ideas fit with certain characters?

Thanks for reading!

Look for more about Mill's life and

experiences, next in Oregon!

<u>A Deep Green War</u>

The Second Mill Meacham Story

A Carson A. Pierce Novel

Now available!

www.ingramcontent.com/pod-product-compliance
Lightning Source LLC
Chambersburg PA
CBHW051411170626

46809CB00006B/2114